Callistus of Rome

JILL FRANCIS HUDSON

Best wishes,

Jill F. Hudson

Copyright © 2023 Jill Francis Hudson

This edition published by
Glannoventa Publishing, Drigg, Cumbria.

All rights reserved.

ISBN:979-8388087645

In memory of Callistus I;
slave, convict, pope and martyr.

Cover illustration: *Pope Callistus I*,
detail from a mosaic in the Basilica of Santa Maria
in Trastevere, Rome, where Callistus' remains are preserved.

Callistus of Rome

Part One:
Callistus and Marcia

Part Two:
Callistus Alone

Part Three:
Callistus and Mamaea

Part One:
Callistus and Marcia

CHAPTER ONE: CALLISTUS

Scarcely a streak of dawn brightened the eastern sky as the boy slipped silently out of his master's house. From force of habit he paused on the threshold to check that he wasn't being followed.

Away in the distance he could hear the yelling of tradesmen and the rumble of ox-carts as they headed out of the forum after making their morning deliveries. But here among the slumbering mansions of the rich, the streets were deserted and the motionless air smelled of jasmine rather than rotting fish, leather-tanning and sewage.

Usually he would walk to the Assembly with his master and a handful of fellow slaves, but this morning they had gone on without him. He'd been late getting up and was half asleep even now. But he dared not risk staying at home lest the housekeeper catch him idling.

So he headed out alone, picking his way unerringly past pilaster and portico though it was still too dark to see them. For he had walked this route almost every week since the first time the master had deemed him old enough to understand where they were going and why.

When he arrived at his destination the meeting had already begun. He exchanged the secret sign with the watcher on the door and crossed the lamp-lit hallway to join the silent throng gathered in the mansion's vast courtyard. It was hundreds, even a thousand strong these days, and had spawned other groups like itself which met elsewhere in the City and beyond its walls. But the mother congregation gathered here in the house of Piso and Valeria was by far the largest.

Torches burned in brackets mounted on the pillars surrounding the courtyard and on the podium at the far end, from which the meeting was being conducted. But the crowd was far too dense for the boy to push through and join his master now, though he knew exactly where the members of his household would be standing. So he lingered a while with some other latecomers in the shadows, until he spotted the back of his best friend's head not much more than a spear-length nearer to the podium than he was himself.

He hadn't recognized his friend at first, because he still wasn't used to the sight of Hippolytus' stiff black hair cropped so closely. Nor was he yet accustomed to seeing the youth's angular, rather awkward, frame draped in the formal white toga of a Roman citizen, which at fourteen Hippolytus had only recently begun to wear. His own hair was still artlessly shaggy; slaves did not come of age or have expensive haircuts. But the increased disparity in the two boys' appearance had done nothing to weaken their friendship, forged half their lifetimes ago. Now the slave-boy wormed his way forward through the tightly packed throng until they were standing side by side.

'Looking more like your father every day,' the slave-boy whispered with a grin. But in reply Hippolytus grunted only his name, Callistus, and grasped him briefly by the wrist without taking his eyes from the podium. The service itself had not yet got under way, but the bishop Eleutherius was reading out a letter sent to Rome from some other congregation in a faraway city, and Hippolytus was engrossed.

Callistus did his best to listen too. He gleaned that the letter had come from Irenaeus, Bishop of Lugdunum in Gaul. Irenaeus was reminding his Christian brothers and sisters of the essence of their faith: that the Word of Almighty God had been made flesh so that the power of evil over humanity might be destroyed. A true Christian no longer had need of the Law of Moses to keep him in line, because he had no more desire for earthly things. He was storing up treasure in heaven.

No doubt the venerable scholar was going over this familiar ground for a reason, but Callistus' attention had drifted long before he found out what it was. It was all very well for the high-born Hippolytus to rise with the birds on a Sunday morning and concentrate on following tortuous metaphysical arguments at a time when most of his patrician friends would still be tucking into their breakfasts. Hippolytus didn't have to get up hours before sunrise all the rest of the week to dance attendance on a demanding master.

If only these meetings didn't have to start so early! But the practice had begun when believers really did have to gather in secret, and besides, many of them were dirt-poor day-labourers or artisans who could ill afford the luxury of keeping the Lord's Day holy in the way Jews kept the Sabbath. At least Callistus' master didn't make his Christian slaves work on a Sunday, and members of his household who were Jewish as well as Christian had Saturdays free too. But Callistus was no more Jewish than an Athenian black pudding. His mother had been Greek and he'd never been told who his father was. He had been born into slavery, and slaves no more had fathers than they had expensive haircuts.

So instead of listening to the rest of Irenaeus' epistle, Callistus found himself studying its audience. Now that it was getting lighter he spotted his master almost straight away: Marcus Aurelius Carpophorus, freedman of the late emperor whose names he had assumed along with his liberty. Banker, financier and financial adviser to the great and the good, he was standing with a cluster of prosperous Jewish Christians who had made their fortunes in much the same sort of way as he had himself. They owned ships or traded in jewels or purple dye, and most of them had made use of Carpophorus' services at one time or another. Carpophorus was a big man with big eyebrows, a big voice and a big banker's paunch, the girth of which was only accentuated by the wide linen sash he wore around it. He had big aspirations to match, never missing an opportunity to make his money work as hard as he did. But rubbing shoulders with these affluent Jewish entrepreneurs were Gentiles of every age and class: patricians, potters and poultrymen, muleteers and mat-weavers, women and children, slave and free.

In fact the whole gathering was absurdly, gloriously diverse, unlike any other sort of gathering Callistus could have imagined – and he'd been told often enough that his imagination was far too active for his own good. Rome was full of societies – burial clubs, masons' guilds, musicians' unions and so on – but none was like the Church. Callistus never ceased to wonder at the spectacle created by all these unlikely people with their different clothing and customs, united only by their common desire to do the will of God.

Not that they always lived up to their own high standards, let alone their Creator's, and there could still be some ferocious disagreements. The Church of Rome, like the City itself, attracted fortune-seekers from the furthest flung regions of the empire; some of those from the eastern provinces did not even celebrate Easter on the same day as everyone else. And there were dozens of different ideas about what it really meant to say that Jesus was God's Son. Callistus knew very well that these differences could – and did – sometimes blow up into fiery altercations, the smoke from which could take a long time to disperse. But mostly the arguments went straight over Callistus' head.

Hippolytus, however, liked nothing more than getting to grips with a complicated scholarly dispute. Senators' sons had plenty of time for reading, and this one had already carved out for himself quite a reputation for precocious learning and eloquence. Sometimes Callistus wondered quite why Hippolytus bothered to talk to *him* any more at all. A rather nasty boy who didn't like either of them had once suggested that it was a twisted kind of Christian pride on Hippolytus' part, to strut about boasting that he, for all his wealth and privilege, had a humble slave for a friend. Callistus hoped this wasn't true.

Suddenly, as he went on gazing about him and the daylight went on getting stronger, Callistus noticed a young woman he couldn't recall having seen at Assembly before. He didn't as a rule find girls interesting, but there was something about this one that put the glamour of her companions into the shade. Obviously rich as royalty, she was with a party of women he knew belonged to the imperial court, all of whom shimmered like goddesses in their silken robes and sparkling jewels, and there was a fat elderly eunuch with a bald head fussing about her.

But it wasn't her silks or her jewels that fascinated Callistus, nor the swathes of shining hair piled precariously on top of her head, nor even her figure, which any sculptor might have been happy to use as a model for Helen of Troy. It was more the haunted gravity of her painted face as she strove to follow the drift of the bishop's reading. For she was listening as intently as Hippolytus, yet the more she heard the sadder she looked, and Callistus found himself marvelling that someone like her could possibly be sad about anything.

So it took him by surprise when all at once the reading of Irenaeus' letter was over and the service had begun. A lilting responsive chant rose up into the cool morning air; Callistus joined in – at least, his voice did, but his eyes and mind were still on the girl from the palace, for she seemed distracted now, too, and like him she was only half singing. The readings from Scripture passed Callistus by altogether, and when it was time for the prayers he could no more close his eyes than his mouth. For now the girl was again fully involved, head and hands tilted upward, and suddenly all the misery and tension in her features had evaporated. The hint of a smile graced her lips and her eyelids fluttered as though she were dreaming, and Callistus had never witnessed such rapture in all his life.

Hippolytus was praying as well, though it seemed to cost him a lot more effort. As for Callistus himself, he had never really tried. What he thought of as the religious side of Christianity had never particularly appealed to him. He had always been much more impressed by the Christians' behaviour than their beliefs, and in particular by their regard for widows and orphans and anyone else in need. In the Roman Church slaves and even women held office; the Order of Widows was respected by everyone and its leaders were as highly esteemed as the elders and deacons. To join them – or the Consecrated Virgins, their spinster sisters – a woman had renounce marriage and child-bearing altogether. A place where a childless woman or a slave could command respect had always seemed to Callistus to be the next best thing to heaven on earth. So when Carpophorus had invited any of his slaves who wished it to be baptized, Callistus had agreed straight away – and not only so he wouldn't have to work on Sundays.

Then out of the blue, as he went on staring and his mind went on drifting, the young woman chanced to open her eyes, and briefly they met his. He tried to look away; she smiled, and he smiled too; then once again her eyes were closed in prayer. All this was over in less than the time it had taken Hippolytus to grunt Callistus' name, but Callistus would never forget the moment as long as he lived.

Now the unbaptized and the penitents were preparing to leave the meeting before the sharing of the bread and wine began. They were escorted by two of the elders, Victor and Urbanus, and by two of the widows, one of whom was Hermione, head of their order. Victor was dark, with intensely brown eyes, strong features and a warrior's bearing, for he hailed from the province of Africa. Urbanus was as tall and refined-looking as his name suggested, and, for a man who held the rank of elder, very young.

Hermione was tall, too, for a woman, but her face was almost invisible, being heavily shrouded by her veil. By no means all the women wore veils when attending Assembly, though those who regularly prayed or prophesied aloud tended to do so. As for the folk who were being escorted away, you could easily tell the penitents from the unbaptized because the penitents had to wear sackcloth over their everyday clothing, and a smudge of ash on their foreheads. You couldn't help wondering what sins they were guilty of, though it couldn't be anything as dreadful as apostasy, murder, adultery or fraud committed after baptism, for which there could be no absolution from the Church at all. These were sins such as God alone could remit.

Then to Callistus' surprise and dismay, he saw the young woman from the palace and her eunuch join the procession of those who were departing. Since clearly they weren't penitents, this must mean that they were unbaptized – catechumens, as these were known. To think that a novice in the faith could experience such close communion with the Divine as that girl had done! It was beyond Callistus' comprehension.

The rite of the Eucharist itself was still a mystery which no one but a fully-fledged Christian was permitted to witness. So secretive had its weekly celebration once been that many pagans had concluded from rumours that the Followers of the Way were cannibals, literally consuming the flesh and drinking the blood of a fresh victim every Sunday. It *was* a mystery, Callistus thought, how bread and wine could become the flesh and blood of Christ himself. And it *could* still be risky to be known as a Christian. The previous emperor Marcus Aurelius had considered the Christians a threat to state security because they would not sacrifice to Roman gods or to the emperor's statue. His son and successor Commodus, admittedly, did not seem so concerned. In fact Commodus didn't seem to be concerned about very much at all, beyond living a life of luxury and staging spectacular games so the common people would love him. The Senate had no love for him whatsoever; there had been several bungled attempts on his life. So far he had foiled them all, though he kept more and more out of the public eye and left the real business of running the empire to a succession of disreputable favourites. But at least he left the Church alone too – or had done so far.

It was only during the interval in the service while the catechumens and penitents were leaving that Hippolytus at last condescended to take notice of Callistus. Once the girl from the palace was out of sight, Callistus turned to find Hippolytus looking at him askance; Callistus gave him a crooked smile and a shrug, then pretended to be deeply interested in watching the bishop prepare to receive the bread and wine for consecration. Two young acolytes, a boy and a girl, were carrying the elements up to the podium whilst others brought forward the weekly offerings made for the poor. A woman near the front had broken into song and her neighbours were joining in, some singing the tune and others weaving counter-melodies around it. Then the song died away as some of the elders and widows seated on the podium with the bishop rose to assist him with the ritual. Callistus was pleased to see that one of those on duty this week was Zephyrinus, who had a soft spot for him and Hippolytus and knew them well. Despite being at least twice as old as both of them put together Zephyrinus was one of those people you could approach with any problem and he would do his best to help you. He wasn't quite so good at explaining the finer points of Christian theology, but he was fond of reminding people that Jesus had welcomed little children unto him and commended the simple faith of those who were like them.

Now the bishop and elders were laying their hands on the bread and blessing the bowl of wine to consecrate them to God, and these began to be shared out among the congregation. It was Hippolytus who passed the plate and cup to Callistus, and Callistus still thought there was something very wonderful about a slave being served in this way by a senator's son.

Then the final hymn began, during which some folk started to leave whilst others moved towards the podium seeking prayer or counsel. Gradually the press of the multitude lessened, and here and there conversations were struck up until more people were talking than singing, affording welcome privacy for those to whom the leaders were offering ministry. It was not uncommon for some of the suppliants to weep or cry out or even fall as though in a swoon when the ministers' hands were laid upon them, and afterwards to claim that they had received the healing or deliverance they needed. Today some unfortunate woman was sobbing and wailing so pitifully that Callistus didn't register at first that Hippolytus was tugging on the sleeve of his tunic, enthusing about the contents of the letter from Irenaeus..

'What a mind that man has, Callistus! What a way with words! Perhaps when I have completed my schooling here in Rome I shall ask my parents to send me to Gaul to study with him... Callistus? What has got into you today? I swear you weren't even listening to the prayers. Is something the matter? Are you ill? Has Carpophorus been cruel to you?'

'No. There's nothing the matter. I'm perfectly well.'

'You're a perfect dreamer, more like. I never knew anyone whose mind was so often in a different place from his body. But today... it was those women from the palace, wasn't it? *I* saw you staring as they left before communion.'

'No, Hippos. Not those *women*. Just one of them.'

'Just one? That's even worse! *Which* one, for pity's sake?'

Callistus' expression grew dreamier than ever as he strove to describe her. 'The prettiest one of course. The one with the shiniest hair and the loveliest smile – '

'That gives me a *great* deal to go on, I'm sure,' said Hippolytus, folding his arms and rolling his eyes.

'Very well, if you must know.' Irritation at last burst Callistus' bubble; Hippolytus could be like a hound at a hunt once he got his teeth into something. 'She was the one the others were sucking up to, even though she was younger than most of them – maybe nineteen or twenty? But she had more jewels. And a fat old eunuch fawning over her.'

Now Hippolytus could not have looked more shocked if Callistus had suddenly sprouted horns from the top of his head. He said, 'Heaven preserve us, that was Marcia, the emperor's mistress! He dotes on her even more shamelessly than he used to worship his own sister Lucilla – until he had her executed for trying to kill him. Certainly he thinks more of Marcia than he does of his wife, or those horrid naked little boys he has crawling around on his lap all the time. You must stop thinking about her at once, Callistus. She's a whore.'

'How can you say that? You don't know the first thing about her!' Callistus snapped back, surprising even himself with the strength of his own reaction. 'She may not have *chosen* to live with Commodus. And she wouldn't have been at our meeting if she didn't want to live a virtuous Christian life.'

'A virtuous Christian life? Have you lost your wits completely? She isn't living any sort of Christian life; she shouldn't even have *been* here, polluting the body of Christ with her noxious presence. No matter how long she comes for instruction, she can *never* be baptized or be a proper Christian at all. She can only hope and pray that God will show her mercy on the Day of Judgement; no woman living in sin like her can be a member of the Church whether it's her choice to live like a harlot or not.'

'She looked so sad when I first noticed her,' said Callistus wistfully. 'But so happy once she was praying. And part way through the prayers she looked at *me*. She smiled at me. I know she did.'

'Everyone looks at you, Callistus. They can't help it, since you look like Adonis himself! But deceive you not, she would never waste a moment's thought on a silly slave still wet behind the ears, pretty face or no, when she is the mistress of an emperor who fancies himself as being as handsome and strong as Hercules, and who rules over half the world.'

'I thought that kind of thing wasn't meant to matter any more. Didn't Saint Paul say there is neither slave nor free in the Church, neither Jew nor Greek? Even some of our elders are slaves. And *we* are good friends, Hippos, aren't we?'

'In the Kingdom of God these things might not matter. But we live in the Empire of Commodus too, and try telling that to *him*. Or to Marcia's parents – assuming she has any – or whoever else it was who made sure she came to the emperor's attention. I'm disappointed in you, Callistus. I thought you had more sense. In fact I'm *angry*.' And he turned his back on Callistus to prove it, pulling his white citizen's toga tightly about him.

Callistus was bewildered, unable to fathom why either of them should be treating this trifling incident so seriously. It was true that he had a pretty face; everyone had said so, ever since he had been a tiny child. This was why he had been called Callistus in the first place. 'Kallistos' meant 'most beautiful' in Greek, and it was Carpophorus' wife who had given him the nickname, because his mother had been her slave. He could no longer remember the name his mother herself had given him, and neither could anyone else. She had died in one of the plagues that ravaged Rome in the latter years of Marcus Aurelius. He was always being told he was lucky that his master's household was Christian. A pagan owner would have sold a beauty like him to a pimp.

But he didn't enjoy falling out with Hippolytus. It upset him; yet somehow it upset him even more to hear his friend maligning the character of a woman he didn't even know. Hippolytus could be almost scary when he got up on his high moral horse like this; it wasn't the first time Callistus had feared being trampled under its hooves. Hippolytus' name meant 'unleasher of horses' after all.

When the kindly Zephyrinus waddled over to them a little

later on, the two friends still weren't speaking.

'Now now, my proud young princes,' he said, for he liked to remind every boy in the Church that he was joint heir with Christ of the Kingdom of God, and the timidest girl that she was a princess as privileged as Cleopatra. 'Why so bad-tempered on this beautiful morning? The sun's already shining, and the sky hasn't fallen on your heads.'

'It's nothing,' Callistus muttered, but Hippolytus rounded on him, hissing, 'Nothing? Zephyrinus, Callistus has developed a passion for a harlot! How can any one of us claim to be a disciple of Christ if he chases after vanity like a puppy chasing shadows? Surely we shall all be swept away on the rising tide of immorality if we don't take a stand against it here and now, while our feet are still planted on solid ground! How can we hold out hope to the world if we are no better than the pagans, and just as confused and compromised as they are? We shouldn't be admitting whores like Marcia into the Church even as catechumens; what sort of reputation will we get? Did the apostles, and the martyrs who followed in their footsteps, die in vain?'

Zephyrinus' smile-crinkled eyes went wide as libation-bowls; he said, 'Whoa, Hippolytus, I did not think that your expensive training in rhetoric was meant to be squandered in spiteful squabbling with your nearest and dearest. Surely it is the scope of our compassion which is meant to distinguish us from the heathen, our acceptance of those damaged sinners in whom we recognize God's tainted image, just as we see it in ourselves. It was certainly compassion which distinguished Jesus from those Pharisees who opposed him. *They* had enough high standards for everyone else in Judea put together.'

Now it was Hippolytus' turn to mutter something under his breath, while Callistus said forlornly, 'Poor Lady Marcia. Is it true that she can never be baptized?'

'Marcia the emperor's mistress? No, it's not true at all,' Zephyrinus reassured him with a pat on the shoulder. 'She could be baptized just like anyone else, if she could only get away from Commodus. She could never marry, of course – the Church could not condone her joining herself to yet another man – but she could take a vow of chastity and become a Consecrated Virgin to prove she had put her past behind her. Sin committed *before* baptism can *always* be forgiven, even sin as serious as hers.'

Hippolytus said, 'But it will already have ruined her character, won't it? Not to mention her... Don't look at me like that, Zephyrinus. You know exactly what I mean. How can she possibly become a Consecrated Virgin? Baptism won't bring back her maidenhead.'

'Baptism washes the whole of *anyone*'s past away,' Zephyrinus reminded him, and quoted from the Hebrew scriptures: '"Though your sins be as scarlet, they shall be white as snow."' And taking hold of both boys' hands, he joined them together between his own. At that moment Carpophorus appeared, to rebuke Callistus for being so slow in getting up, and to tell him it was time to go home.

But Callistus was used to being scolded, and let his master's harsh words pass him by. Nor did he pay any attention to his fellow slaves' banter as they made their way back to the house. He was too busy recalling Marcia's face and smile, and picturing her robed in white for her baptism and wedding after he, her champion and bridegroom Callistus the Most Beautiful, had heroically snatched her from Commodus' grasp.

In the real world they could no more marry one another and live happily ever after than a scullery-maid could become Queen of Egypt. But even a slave can dream.

CHAPTER TWO: MARCIA

'My lady, your bath is ready,' the handmaid said again, with a nervous bob of the head. Outside it was nearly dark, and Marcia was preparing for bed, not yet knowing whether she would sleep alone or with Commodus. In the glow of the lamplight her room looked especially opulent. Shadows accentuated the sumptuous folds in the curtains, the golden threads woven into the tapestries glittered as the little flames flickered, and the leopard-skin rugs on the floor seemed poised to spring into life. Letting her shift glide from her shoulders into the girl's waiting arms, Marcia slid naiad-like into the sunken pool which had been installed for her in the bedroom. The water was hot as a thermal spring and rose petals drifted on its surface.

Basking in the steaming water with her hair floating around her, she allowed the cares of the day to drift away with the petals, though she knew they would return all too swiftly. Meanwhile other handmaids were fussing with her night-clothes, and the eunuch Hyacinthus whom Commodus had appointed to watch over her dozed in his chair by a window. The slave-girls thought him a doddering old relic but Marcia was sure that he loved her in his way, just as she had grown to love him, and he called her 'my lady' just as the girls did, as if he were her servant and not her keeper.

If only the emperor would give her more warning on the nights he decided to summon her! Marcia shared Commodus' bed more frequently than anyone else – certainly far more frequently than his poor, terrified, childless little wife – but was never told when this was going to happen. As for Bruttia Crispina, vapid as she was aristocratic, she had been made to marry Commodus at the tender age of fourteen, when Commodus had been no more than sixteen himself. And he had tried very hard to ignore her ever since, despite his avowed determination to beget an heir. The Senate still professed to believe that each head of state should be appointed on his own merits, but this was about as likely to happen nowadays as the Circus Maximus was to be turned into a flower garden.

It was strange, though, Marcia mused as she admired her neatly painted toenails peeping out above the water, that Commodus had not yet succeeded in getting a son on any one of his many mistresses. Perhaps this was why he liked to lie with little boys instead? No one was going to look askance at him when *their* bellies failed to swell. Perhaps he would fancy a boy for his bed tonight, and she could look forward to a decent night's sleep instead of being forced to pander to His Excellency's ever more preposterous whims.

For Commodus was never the same man twice. Sometimes he would flatter her outrageously and shower her with extravagant gifts; she had more bangles and baubles than twenty women would ever need, along with her own personal box at the Games. Yet just as often he would lash out at her with his tongue or even a fist as though she were an ill-trained mule. On other nights again he would feel like indulging his passion for mythology and dress up as Hercules in a lion-skin, obliging Marcia to impersonate the Queen of the Amazons whose girdle Hercules had captured as the ninth of his twelve legendary labours.

This might have been funny if it hadn't so often ended in tears. Rome's all-powerful master would chase her about the imperial bedroom waving a huge wooden club in one hand and attempting to tear off her clothing with the other, and she would have to let him catch her at exactly the right moment or his prodigious anger would be unleashed. Once he had even struck her with the club so hard that she had passed out altogether, and come round to find him prostrate with remorse. According to legend Hercules had been like this too: consumed with fury at one moment and conscience-stricken the next. As a very small boy Commodus was said to have flown into a rage and demanded that his bath-keeper be flung into the furnace because the water in his tub had been too cold. Someone had thrown a fleece in the furnace instead so the stench of its burning would convince the screaming child that the deed had been done. By the time he learned the truth Commodus' tantrum had abated and he was overjoyed to discover that his devoted servant was still alive after all.

Recalling this disturbing story made Marcia realize that her own bath was fast cooling down. She sent two of the slave-girls for more hot water, which prompted old Hyacinthus to pretend to have been wide awake all along and offer to fetch her a towel. But Marcia was reluctant to get out of the water or let anyone dry her off until she knew whether she was meant to be dressing for sleep or for seduction. It was getting increasingly unlikely now that His Excellency would summon her, for some of the lamps would soon need refilling, and outside her window it was almost pitch dark. But you never quite knew with Commodus.

All this uncertainty and the stress to which it led had been the goad which had first driven Marcia to seek out the Christians. She had heard not only of their beliefs about the afterlife but also of the respect which women and even slaves enjoyed among them, and had been desperate to inject a little hope and meaning into her own sorry existence. And sometimes when she prayed with other believers around her, she *could* feel pure and clean and happy, just for a few short moments.

Though a free-born daughter of Rome, Marcia hadn't become Commodus' plaything for the fun of it. She had her step-father to thank for that, a shameless social climber intent on achieving maximal personal gain and glory in return for minimal effort. He had arranged their meeting through her mother, a freedwoman of Lucius Verus who had briefly been co-emperor with Marcus Aurelius. Marcia smiled faintly as a fleeting memory of her mother's touch took her by surprise. When she'd been a child her mother had bathed her every night, and hugged her as she wrapped the towel around her back. It felt like a very long time ago.

Not that Commodus was the first illustrious personage on whom her step-father had foisted her. At seventeen she'd been forced to seduce the senator Marcus Ummidius Quadratus Annianus, Marcus' nephew and Commodus' cousin, whose regular mistress she had then become. An undemanding bedfellow, Quadratus had nevertheless been so much older than Marcia that she had sought refuge in the arms of his body-slave Eclectus, the first and only man she had ever loved. A feisty young Egyptian with long hair black as bitumen, fire in his eyes and a fighter's spirit which no birch-rod could beat out of him... even now she could not picture Eclectus without aching to feel his arms around her once again.

Not that she had ever slept with him. Her step-father would have strangled them both with his own bare hands.

But now the senator himself was dead, which still made Marcia feel horribly guilty. She had no idea what had become of Eclectus.

Naturally her step-father would have preferred it if she could have married a senator rather than merely seducing one, but he'd been only too aware that this could never happen. In fact Marcia doubted if it would even have been worth while. The Senate no longer possessed the power or prestige it had once enjoyed. The emperor, his household, and the Praetorian Guard held all the cards these days. A woman could probably gain more from marrying an imperial freedman than a senator.

But undoubtedly the most enviable position which any Roman woman could hope to attain in the modern world, Marcia knew, was the one which she herself held already. Of course no woman who envied Marcia could possibly know what her life – or her lover – was really like. Marcia knew slaves who had more freedom.

Thinking now about the Christians she knew who were slaves, she couldn't help but remember the face of the slave-boy she'd caught sight of at Assembly this morning and then again at the love-feast just a few hours ago. She always had to leave the so-called Agape early, after the meal but before the singing; Hyacinthus was under strict instructions from Commodus not to let Marcia be away from the palace after dark. Otherwise she might have sought an excuse to speak to the lad in person, if only because he reminded her so disconcertingly of Eclectus. With his dusky complexion and all that rampant hair hanging to his shoulders he was quite the most beautiful youth she had seen in a very long time, yet he'd looked so care-worn – until he noticed her! Marcia smiled again, slid down even further in the water and even giggled in a rueful sort of way to think how worshipfully he'd been staring at her. It was nice to know, after all, that she could still turn heads – and especially such pretty ones. She dreaded the day when her trials would begin to take their toll on her face.

This latest thought made her rise and prepare at last to get out of the bath before her skin got too pink and puckered. She accepted the towel from Hyacinthus and draped it about her shoulders in a token gesture towards modesty as she emerged from the water. Her eunuch and handmaids saw her naked day in and day out; it was all part of having slaves to attend you whether you liked it or not, and there were many worse things to worry about.

The swirling mosaics on the floor were cold underfoot

after the water, so it was with a brief tingle of relief that she stepped onto the leopard-skin rug by the table where her mirror and cosmetics were kept. She propped up the mirror on its little silver stand and checked herself for wrinkles and stray grey hairs. So far there had been none, but the day must come, and sometimes she was sure she looked more hollow-cheeked and haunted than she ought to have done at her age. But then, she had plenty of things to haunt her, including Quadratus' ghost.

At least she wasn't pregnant – though whether this was in answer to her prayers or because of the herbs she used, or because there really was something wrong with Commodus' seed, she couldn't be sure. But the last thing she wanted was *his* child growing within her, even though it might be a future emperor of Rome. In a moment of panic she pressed her hands to her still-naked belly and was reassured to find it flat and taut as ever.

No one could really understand how the late great Marcus Aurelius had managed to beget a son such as Commodus. He'd provided the boy with the trustiest of Stoic philosophers as tutors, yet Commodus was cruel, conceited, and conspicuously lacking in self-control. Perhaps he'd been *too* strictly brought up, denied any sort of luxury, let alone those which an emperor's son might expect to enjoy. Or perhaps the rumours were true that Commodus was actually the son of a gladiator with whom his mother Faustina had supposedly had an affair. Whatever the reason, the death of Marcus Aurelius had marked the end of an eighty-year golden age of confident and capable emperors, including Trajan and Hadrian who had won great victories and built great monuments which might stand for thousands of years. Now it seemed that the empire was falling back into the sort of madness it had known under Nero, when no one was safe from the emperor's caprice. At least Commodus didn't use Christians as torches in his garden – well, not yet.

As Marcia went on gazing in the mirror, Hyacinthus came

shuffling hopefully up behind her. So she let him brush out her damp brown hair, which he loved to do, and did better than any of her handmaids.

'How lovely you look this evening, my lady; surely you don't need a mirror to tell you?' he enthused as he often did. 'You look perfectly ready to please His Excellency even with your hair undone and no paint on your face, should he desire your company tonight.'

'Oh Hyacinthus, how I hope he won't,' she responded with rather too much feeling. But then, she seldom made much attempt to guard her feelings from Hyacinthus. It was all too easy to forget that he worked for Commodus and not for her.

'You don't mean to say that you would rather sleep alone, my lady?' Hyacinthus exclaimed. 'His Excellency is so *very* handsome.' And he sounded so wistful that Marcia tutted at him under her breath.

Not that she could complain, in all honesty, about what the emperor looked like. He was still in his twenties, and his hair was so bright and fair that many people thought he sprinkled it with gold-dust. His muscles were well developed from sparring and wrestling with his training partner, Narcissus, a comely young athlete who was obliged to spend most of his days with Commodus just as Marcia had to yield him her nights. Commodus would even invite gladiators to the palace and practise fencing with them; Marcia had frequently been required to applaud his performances, and it had to be said that he did acquit himself rather well. But it was also true that he was starting to run to fat about the midriff from his rich diet and all the wine he drank, and his facial features, though fine and noble by nature, were often twisted in disdain.

It was Perennis his erstwhile favourite, lately Commander of the Praetorian Guard, who had encouraged Commodus in dissolute living. For the more Commodus drank, the less he interfered when Perennis appropriated imperial prerogatives for himself. After Perennis' spectacular demise he had been replaced in Commodus' good books by the greedy and unscrupulous Phrygian freedman who had engineered it, the mere mention of whose name – Cleander – was enough to send shivers down Marcia's spine. In theory Cleander was merely Commodus' chamberlain, but in practice he sold political offices and military commissions to the highest bidder. He hated Marcia with a passion because he knew that Commodus was besotted with her, and he resented the influence she must wield. Marcia herself doubted that she had any real influence over Commodus at all, and knew she would have less than none if he ever learned the full story of her past.

'Come, my lady, let me play the lyre for you, or fetch you something to eat,' Hyacinthus suggested, noting her despondency. She smiled at his anxious reflection caught behind hers in the mirror.

'Hyacinthus,' she said, 'Only one thing could really make me happy, and that would be to leave this prison of a palace for ever, and have real Christian friends instead of those empty-headed girls from court who go with me to Assembly just to show off their jewels.' Then seeing Hyacinthus' reflected face fall like a scolded schoolboy's she spun around on her seat and gave him an unexpected hug which made him blush all down his beardless cheeks. 'Don't worry, you old fusspot, I would take you with me! The Church would look after us both; I could have all my sins forgiven – and they are many, Hyacinthus, you couldn't imagine – and be baptized, and so could you. If *all* my dreams could come true, I would marry a lovely Christian man and bear his children, and bring them up to honour God and their own bodies and never give them to anyone except in love...' But then her voice trailed away, because she would *never* be able to marry a Christian. No woman with a past like hers could ever be properly married in the eyes of the Church.

There were in fact members of the Assembly who had

secretly offered to smuggle her away from the palace, including an imperial freedman called Clemens who worked there himself. The Order of Widows had promised to help her too, should she choose to make her escape. Her many transgressions could all be washed away in baptism provided that she was prepared to do penance, especially since the way she'd been living had been forced upon her.

But she would still have to take a vow of chastity and become a Consecrated Virgin – a Bride of Christ, as it were – for the rest of her life. She would be like one of the Widows, yet without ever having been widowed, without ever having known the joy of giving herself in love to a man who had bound himself only to her. Marcia thought it might be quite easy to take a vow of chastity if you had already been happily married for years, probably with children and grandchildren to boot. Then it might be very nice to pass your time taking food to the poor, and visiting believers in prison, and praying for those in need. But *now*... it wasn't merely Christian fellowship that Marcia longed for, if she was honest with herself, but love such as she had known so briefly with Eclectus. And if she did take the Christians up on their offer, how could she be sure that they would have the wherewithal to protect her from Commodus and Cleander?

Nor was unchastity the worst of the sins for which she needed absolution.

'Wouldn't you *like* to be baptized, Hyacinthus?' she asked him, seeing that he still looked glum. 'You *do* believe, don't you? I know you only went along to meetings of the Assembly to look after me to start off with, but you say all the prayers and sing all the hymns and you're a good person, too, kind and affectionate. You're everything a baptized Christian should be.'

'I'm sure I don't know, my lady.' Hyacinthus began brushing her hair with renewed vigour, so that Marcia couldn't help smiling, then laughing out loud.

'Poor Hyacinthus, you never had a choice about anything,

did you?' she said. 'We have much in common, you and I. But among the Christians even eunuchs get to make their own choices. No wonder the faith is spreading so fast – don't you know there are growing assemblies in every province of the empire now, and even beyond its borders? And *thousands* of Christians here in Rome.'

This was no exaggeration. Between the mother Church and its daughters in the suburbs Marcia knew that there were probably more Christians than there were initiates into any of the multifarious cults to which the City's inhabitants would turn when they couldn't find solace in Roman state religion. It wasn't really surprising when you recalled that both Peter and Paul, giants among Christ's early followers, had preached and been martyred here. And no self-respecting Roman citizen seriously believed in Jupiter or Juno, Mars or Venus and the like any more, though on state occasions they had to pretend to.

So it wasn't only slaves, women and the poor who were converted nowadays. Some of the greatest minds in paganism were embracing the Christian faith, following in the footsteps of the famous philosopher Justin Martyr who had become a Christian some fifty years before. They would write books and letters encouraging other pagans to look into Christianity too, just as Bishop Irenaeus in Gaul had written a letter of exhortation to the Church in Rome.

'Wasn't Irenaeus' letter inspiring?' Marcia demanded of Hyacinthus now. 'Didn't it make you want to tell *everyone* that their sins can be forgiven and that they can start afresh as though they'd been born as babies all over again?' And when Hyacinthus looked less than convinced, Marcia hugged him a second time and said, 'Dear Hyacinthus, you are so sweet and kind, I swear you don't need to be forgiven for *anything*. Whereas I...' She let her arms fall to her sides and wandered to the window, where she stood and looked out across the courtyard in the moonlight towards the part of the palace where the emperor had his private rooms.

For she really did have much more to atone for than her unchastity with Commodus, though she had never confessed the full truth about the conspiracy to another living soul. There had been no need to, because anyone who could have known of her guilt was now dead.

Suddenly the chief of her handmaids touched Marcia gently but urgently on the elbow saying, 'My lady, he's here now!' and Marcia realized with a start that the poor girl must have been trying to attract her attention for quite some time.

'Here? Who is here?' she responded vaguely, only to have the slave-girl tug again at her elbow and hiss, 'The emperor, my lady! He's here now, in the hallway.'

'But he *never* comes here; what does he want? Is he angry? Is he drunk?'

'N-no, my lady. At least, I don't think so. I don't know what's wrong with him. Perhaps he is ill.'

Before the maid could explain any further, Commodus himself staggered through into Marcia's bedroom. His flaxen curls were unkempt, his purple robe was sliding off his shoulders, and his face was awash with tears.

'Marcia, thank the gods. Embrace me, my darling. Love me…' he stammered, lurching towards her before collapsing, with her pinned beneath him, onto her bed. He *was* drunk; she could smell the wine on his breath as he wept into her neck. But usually it made him amorous or violent, whilst this evening it had rendered him helpless as an orphaned puppy. With Marcia struggling for breath under his weight, the emperor of Rome began whimpering pathetically about how everyone who should have loved him had deserted or betrayed him. His own father had loathed him because he had not lived up to his exacting standards; his sister had tried to kill him; the twin brother who ought to have been his companion for life had died when they were infants; his wife must surely despise him, else by now she would have given him a son. The people cheered and shouted for him at the Games, yet was all this an act, or even a mockery?

'But *you* love me, don't you, Marcia?' he finished up, lifting his head at last and gazing at her with bloodshot eyes. '*You* would never forsake me, or do anything to hurt me? You know you're all I have left...' Then abandoning himself once more to self-pity he buried his head afresh in Marcia's bosom, his whole body shaking as he wept.

Meanwhile Marcia lay rigid as a washboard beneath him, paralysed by terror and guilt. She told herself there was no reason why she *should* feel guilty. Commodus was a bully, a tyrant, and never once in all this outpouring of emotion – or indeed, ever – had he said that *he* loved *her*.

Yet not for the first time she felt her heart go out to him in his hour of need and loneliness. Perhaps it was the mother in her rather than the lover which had been awakened, but either way she found her arms going around him of their own accord, and her lips seeking to cover his own so that the tide of his words might be stemmed and he need humiliate himself no further.

And as her body reached out to his, so his own responded: she felt him hard and desperate against her, and his lips clamped upon hers as though to suck the very air from her lungs. Then he was inside her, thrusting and pumping until she feared he would burst her bones asunder. But her own passion was rising at the same time as her fear, along with the guilt and the pity and the longing, until the whole heady mix brought them both to climax together. Then as he moaned and went limp and again became a dead weight upon her, sated and oblivious of all that troubled him, it was Marcia's turn to weep, because whenever this happened she was left feeling so wicked and confused.

For she knew that she *had* chosen to live in sin with him, on some level, and was that so very wrong? Yet she had also chosen once upon a time to make an attempt on his life, and if he ever found out about *that,* it would be the end of the road for both of them.

CHAPTER THREE: CALLISTUS

The afternoon was already half gone when Callistus realized that he was too hungry to think. Seated in the small yet exquisitely decorated chamber which his master used as an office, he was poring over multiple columns of figures which it was his job to balance up. But they were swaying like charmed snakes in front of his eyes.

Everything about Carpophorus' house was elegant and expensive, including its location in Piscina Publica. The name was unassuming enough, 'public pool'; apparently there had once been an enormous cistern there, but that was long gone. Today there were only grandiose mansions, many of which belonged to the businessmen – both Jews and Gentiles – whose investments Carpophorus handled. Less prosperous Jews lived cheek by jowl in a scruffy quarter across the river – Trans Tiberim – a teeming cultural melting pot where many poverty-stricken Gentiles lived too. Right now Callistus would happily have exchanged places with any one of them.

'Not finished yet, egg-head?' a fellow slave taunted him, poking his head around the office door and waving a half-eaten crust of bread in Callistus' face. 'What's taking you so long? We've eaten your lunch for you. Seemed a shame to let good food go to waste.'

Callistus gave a wordless grunt in reply, being well used to his companions' jibes. He knew they begrudged him his sedentary life, since most of theirs were spent stoking the fires for the under-floor heating or cleaning out blocked-up drains. But it amused him that they should think him clever, when alongside Hippolytus he felt like a halfwit. Still, he knew his letters, and had a facility with numbers which even Carpophorus had to acknowledge.

Not that being one of Carpophorus' favourites amounted to very much. The master never praised a slave to his face. The only kind of recognition Callistus was accustomed to getting came from overhearing comments like, 'Why can't you follow a simple instruction the way Callistus can?' or 'Callistus would never do anything so stupid.' But Carpophorus wasn't a bad master, all things considered. He didn't beat his slaves unless they deserved it, and he didn't beat Callistus at all. For Callistus had learnt how to handle him, when to be ubiquitous and when to make himself scarce.

Carpophorus *was* rather full of his own importance, though, which was particularly unbecoming in a Christian. He prided himself on being a freedman of the late lamented Marcus Aurelius, and on having found favour in the great man's eyes in spite of being both a Christian by persuasion and a son of Abraham according to the flesh. He ascribed his achievement to his incisive business acumen and to knowing how and when to keep his big mouth shut. But Marcus Aurelius had always preferred Jewish Christians to Gentile ones. Converts from paganism he had distrusted far more, because they were always trying to lead other perfectly decent Roman citizens astray.

Certainly Carpophorus was scrupulous in observing the full Law of Moses – aside from his willingness to lend at interest – and there weren't many followers of the Way who could say that. After the Fall of Jerusalem to the Romans and a failed revolt sixty years later, the Church as a whole had begun to look more and more Gentile. Many Jerusalem Christians had finished up in Rome, which was all to the good for Carpophorus, to whom the Diaspora meant lots of clients needing loans and advances as they sought to expand their commercial operations, but not so good for Callistus who had to balance their accounts.

And today he simply could not get his figures to add up. Raking both hands through his hair, he cursed once again the cumbersome system of Roman numerals he had to work with, which made doing any sort of calculation so difficult. Carpophorus was constantly banging on about how much simpler the Hebrew system was, and how the Indians reputedly had a better one still. But when in Rome one *had* to do as the Romans did.

Moreover Callistus was well aware that juggling with numbers in a warm dry office *was* much less unpleasant than pretty well any other situation in which a young household slave might find himself. It certainly beat being put up for sale in the market, having your buttocks slapped by fat ugly women or your mouth forced open like a horse's muzzle while some pimp with bad breath inspected your teeth.

In fact his master had been entrusting Callistus with significantly greater responsibility than he was used to in these past few months. As well as keeping the accounts, he had been assigned small pots of money to invest on his own initiative by way of practice. Carpophorus had so much of it, he could afford to lose a little to Callistus' mistakes. But so far Callistus hadn't made mistakes. He had earned his master a tidy profit, and himself more than the occasional grunt of approbation.

Just then the office door swung open once again. Callistus braced himself for more baiting, but it was Carpophorus himself who sailed in, his podgy bejewelled fingers laced over his big banker's belly as though its girth in itself were a legitimate source of pride. With a quizzical arching of one prodigious eyebrow he asked without needing words the same question which the crust-waving slave had asked already. But before Callistus could respond Carpophorus waved a glittering hand and said, 'No matter, you can leave your sums until later. There's another challenge I need you to rise to in the meantime. The fact is that I am constantly being prevailed upon to accept more work than I can manage, so you are going to have to take some more of it off my hands.'

'Yes, master. Of course, master. I should be glad to share some of your burden,' Callistus assured him, with perhaps a little too much enthusiasm.

Carpophorus' eyebrow went up further; he gave an inscrutable harrumph and closed the hinged wooden tablet at which Callistus had been staring, with such a decisive snap that he almost took the tip off Callistus' nose. 'Come,' he said brusquely, and wheeling about with remarkable speed for his size he headed out into the atrium without troubling himself to check that Callistus was following. He was.

The principal reception room of Carpophorus' residence was lofty and spacious, its floor a maze of spiralling mosaics, its walls a riot of frescoes, and its star-spangled ceiling supported by pink marble pillars graceful enough to have held up the sky itself. Carpophorus could brook no idolatrous depictions of gods or men in the artwork he commissioned, so all of it was based on elaborate patterns which might have had their origins in flowers or foliage a very long time ago. But in the centre of the room was a very Roman impluvium – a pool of water with a rectangular hole the same size and shape in the ceiling above it – and sitting squarely beside it was the largest wooden chest Callistus had ever seen.

'This,' said Carpophorus, approaching the chest and throwing open the lid to reveal its contents, 'constitutes the savings of all the members of the Order of Widows, and the orphans for whom they are responsible, in the Church of Rome. Individually their fortunes are paltry. All collected together they amount to a considerable sum, as you can see.'

Callistus certainly could. The chest was full to the brim with silver coins.

'Up until now the elders of the Church have been looking after these funds and ensuring that the depositors have had access to them when required. But now the depositors are too many and the funds so substantial that they have recognized the need to entrust the whole enterprise to a professional. That, Callistus, is where we come in. All this money must be counted, the names of its depositors entered onto our records, and then the whole lot must be stored safely in our strongroom until such time as it can be invested wisely. Meanwhile someone will have to be on hand to deal with fresh deposits and requests for withdrawals as they arise. But I must leave the City on business in two days' time, so I have no choice but to hand over responsibility for all of this to you.' Then, when Callistus did nothing but stare agog at the treasure displayed before him, Carpophorus barked, 'Callistus? Why are you standing there with your mouth hanging open like the jaws of Molech?'

'I – I am honoured, master, that's all. That you think I could do it.'

'Well I don't exactly have anyone else to call upon who could do it any better, now do I? I'm not like the emperor with a host of fleet-footed freedmen with fancy qualifications to run around after him, and beggars cannot be choosers, boy, you know that as well as I do. I haven't been training you up solely for my own amusement. But you needn't start flapping like an old hen; I'll be back here to help you in no time at all. I shall expect you to put the money to work, mind, and earn its depositors a reasonable return; it is doing no good sitting in this chest.' Picking up the staff he was wont to take with him when walking abroad, Carpophorus thrust it down into the chest and stirred it around as proof that there was nothing but coins right down to the bottom. 'You know the parable of the talents, Callistus, now don't you? The wise servants resolved to put their master's money to good use, while the one who buried it in the ground got a clip around the ear, if I remember rightly.'

Callistus nodded, deeming it impolitic to mention Hippolytus' exposition of the parable, in which he claimed that Jesus hadn't really intended to say anything about financial investments whatsoever. After all, Jesus had had no desire to be rich, and many Christians, Jewish or otherwise, disapproved of lending at interest altogether.

'Good.' Carpophorus withdrew his staff from the chest and tapped it smartly on the open lid. 'You can start by checking the value of this hoard against the figure we've been given by the elders. Once it has been counted and stored and the depositors' names recorded in our ledgers – in triplicate, of course – you can look into investing it in some suitable project so that we can pay the good folk to whom it belongs a respectable dividend. Now get it out of my atrium before burglars break in and go off with it. Oh – and here is a seal-ring you can use for stamping documents. I shall honour any contract you sign with it as though I had signed it myself.' Then tucking the staff beneath his arm Carpophorus swept away, leaving Callistus to gawp after him, clutching the ring in his fist lest he drop it into the pool in his astonishment.

The strongroom was at the back of the house, as far from the street as it was possible to get. It had double-thick walls and a wooden door so heavy it had to be opened with special levers. The door was further secured by a whole gamut of complicated iron locks, and guarded by a pair of immense armed slaves twenty four hours a day. Inside it was pitch black and had its own peculiar smell, for there were no windows and the only ventilation came from three tiny holes drilled above the door-locks, through which you could look to make sure that anyone working at the cramped little desk by lamplight hadn't expired there and been forgotten. Callistus sent for the guards who worked the night shift to be woken and made to carry the chest to its place of safety. There was no one else available who could have lifted it.

And there Callistus sat and worked late into the evening, though there was no knowing how late it was except from the level of oil left in the lamp. He even forgot his hunger – he still hadn't eaten since early morning – because at the same time as counting the money his mind was racing with excitement. If I'm now to be handling investments, he was thinking, Carpophorus must surely intend to reward me, and not merely with more responsibility. Perhaps he will let me keep some of my profits for myself, so that one day I can buy my freedom? Maybe he will even *give* me my freedom if I pledge to go on working for him, and he'll pay me a wage as well. Or maybe – and as this thought came to his mind he left off counting altogether – maybe Carpophorus means to make me his partner one day and leave the whole of his fortune to me? After all, he has neither sons nor daughters to inherit it, and the wife of his youth who gave me my nickname has been dead so many years, surely he cannot be planning to acquire another one now?

So seductive was this fantasy that Callistus even laid down his stylus and tablet and sat for a while with his chin in his hands, staring not into the gloom of the strongroom but into the rosy light of a fairytale future in which he would be invited to rich men's banquets and introduced to famous poets and playwrights and courted by aspiring politicians in need of funds for their campaigns. Then Marcia would see that he was very much more than a pretty face, and her parents would be only too eager to encourage their friendship. Finally he could offer Commodus a huge sum of money to release her from his harem and allow her to marry the man of her dreams...

For Marcia and Callistus had seen one another almost every week since their first encounter at the Assembly. He had always looked forward to Sundays; now he craved them as a drunkard craves his cups. Not that he had ever once spoken to Marcia in all that time. He could only gaze from a distance imbibing her gentle beauty, tracking her graceful movements, marvelling at her rapture when she prayed.

But she *had* noticed him, there could be no question of that. She would smile at him whenever she looked his way, and her expression gave no indication whatever that she resented his staring. In fact once or twice he had caught *her* gazing at *him,* and those were the moments when he dared to believe that even though he was still only sixteen years old and she must be twenty at least, there were grounds for hope. After all, it wasn't as if men hadn't married women older than themselves before now. And even though the odds were stacked so heavily against him, it was true that Carpophorus was starting to see him as very much more than a petty clerk fit only for adding up columns of numbers and balancing accounts.

Then he recalled both Hippolytus and Zephyrinus explaining to him that Marcia could never get married to anyone, at least not in the eyes of God or his Church. Nor was Commodus likely to part with her, however much money he was offered, when he was already master of half the world.

Still, someone might surely accept payment to *kidnap* Marcia..? Then she and Callistus could run off and hide somewhere far, far away where neither of them would ever be recognized, and they could pretend to be two different people altogether…

'Callistus? Don't you want any supper, now, either?' A shrill female voice brought him back from his dreamworld with a jolt. Naomi the master's housekeeper was shouting and banging on the great wooden door as though she thought he might be dead. Callistus sighed, closing the lid of the chest on his unfinished task and on his fantasies. There was certainly no chance of any of his grand ambitions coming to fruition if he died of starvation.

Two days later Carpophorus packed his bags and boarded a carriage to Neapolis, where a company he financed was building some new apartments. The master would take off like this at regular intervals to check on his clients' ventures and his household would run itself quite efficiently during his absence – or rather, Naomi would run it, and woe betide anyone who didn't toe her line. Naomi wasn't a Christian, but she was Jewish like Carpophorus and a slave like those she ordered around, though you wouldn't have known it from the airs she gave herself. She had allegedly been offered her freedom more than once, and there were many who heartily wished she'd taken it; though she kept the Sabbath as scrupulously as she kept her kosher kitchen, she made it her personal business to see that none of the Gentile slaves did. Hippolytus had assured Callistus that according to the Hebrew scriptures *all* of a Jewish master's slaves were entitled to rest on the Sabbath. But Callistus wasn't going to try telling that to Naomi.

A few days after Carpophorus' departure, an acquaintance of his turned up at the house wanting to see him. On being informed that the master was away, he demanded to see someone reliable from his office, so Naomi sent for Callistus. She evidently knew the man already, but Callistus had no recollection of ever having seen him before.

'Shadrach ben Abner at your service,' the visitor said with a dapper little bow which rendered Callistus speechless, for no one had ever bowed to him in all his life. And although his name was much more Jewish than Carpophorus', Shadrach was dressed as a Roman citizen, in toga and sandals; his face was clean-shaven and his greying hair cropped close. 'Now you must be Callistus, his young apprentice? *Yes,*' he said firmly, when Callistus seemed about to ask him how he knew. 'Carpophorus has spoken of you often; he holds you in *mighty* high regard. But what a pity he isn't here. I have a very exciting business opportunity to put his way.'

Taken aback by the second-hand compliment, Callistus still couldn't summon a response. But then he heard his tongue replying of its own accord, 'I don't suppose he'll be away for very long. He normally returns from trips like this in no more than a week.'

'A week! Well that is just too bad, because the opportunity won't last as long as that. Others will certainly have carved up the available cake by then, and there will be nothing left for poor Carpophorus, even though this is exactly the kind of project which particularly appeals to him when making new investments. Still, it can't be helped. If he isn't here, he isn't here. Goodbye, Callistus; it has been my pleasure to meet you. I'll be on my way.'

So saying, he bowed again and made as if to leave, but Callistus said, 'No, sir, do please wait; it may be that your visit has not been in vain after all.' And when Shadrach paused in the doorway with an inquisitive little smile on his lips, Callistus added hurriedly, 'As it happens, there is a sum of money awaiting investment, and my master has granted me authority to handle the matter myself.'

'Well well,' Shadrach responded. 'How very fortuitous. The Lord does indeed move in mysterious ways. May I sit down?'

'Yes; of course. I'm sorry.' Callistus scolded himself for being so socially inept, but this wasn't the kind of thing he'd been trained for at all.

'The fact is – and I shall come straight to the point with you, Callistus, for I can see that you are not a man for wasting time on pointless pleasantries – I have many important contacts just as your master does, except that my business is in developing property rather than in finance. Now one of the men I deal with is the emperor's chamberlain Cleander who, as you will certainly know, is a highly enterprising and public-spirited businessman in his own right. He is minded to build a complex of apartments to house some of Rome's neediest and most deserving poor, and an ideal plot of land near the Tiber has just come up for sale. Obviously we want to acquire it before it is sold to someone else, but neither he nor I can marshal sufficient funds overnight. I was thinking that if Carpophorus heard of our plight – and the plight of the unfortunate families we are eager to help – he would leap at the chance of stumping up some of the cash we require in return for a share of the profits – which would be considerable – once the property is occupied and the rent money starts to come in. If you cannot help me I may be able to find what I am looking for elsewhere, but Carpophorus will never forgive himself for having been out of town at exactly the wrong moment.'

'Cleander. Yes, of course I know of him.' It was true; there was no one who hadn't heard of Cleander, but although he was undeniably famous and influential, he was hardly famous for philanthropy. Then again, he *had* provided housing for many of Rome's poor who would otherwise have been homeless; surely it wasn't impossible that his name had been unfairly blackened by his political rivals?

'You see, Callistus,' Shadrach had resumed when Callistus was paying attention again, 'there are two ways in which your master could choose to invest in our project. He could elect to be paid back in full and with interest once our initial costs have been recovered, or he could become a partner in our company and receive a percentage of the rent money every year in perpetuity. Either way he cannot lose.'

'Your proposal does sound very attractive, sir.' Callistus bit his lip, only too aware of how nervous and gullible he must sound. Then Shadrach smiled warmly and patted him on the shoulder.

'Young Callistus, I do apologize. I can see that this matter is much weightier than the responsibilities you are used to bearing, and it would be shamelessly unprincipled of me to take advantage of your lack of experience. Let me make things easier for you. We could draw up between us the simplest of contracts, whereby I guarantee to pay back a minimum of double what you invest, a year from today, regardless of how successful our enterprise is proving to be. I am being unusually generous because I can see that in the future you will become as shrewd and well-respected a banker as your master already is, and because I should like to do a favour for the apprentice of one of my oldest friends. What do you say? Shall we draw up our contract here and now?'

'I'm – not sure.' Callistus was desperately trying to evaluate all the implications which the making of such an agreement might have. 'What if some of the people who have entrusted their money to Carpophorus want it back before the year is up?'

'A fair question, young man, and indicative of your commendable perspicacity. But this need not pose us any problem. We shall write it into our contract from the outset that you may withdraw any part of your investment at any time – with the proviso of course that in those circumstances the amount which you withdraw will earn no dividend. Now what is your decision, my friend? Shall we get this transaction sewn up?'

Callistus did think briefly of refusing outright and sending Shadrach on his way. Then he remembered the parable of the talents, and the way Carpophorus had stirred up the coins in the chest with his staff and kept saying how they were doing no one any good sitting there. So he nodded his head, not trusting himself to speak, and Shadrach announced, 'Splendid! You are a wise and capable servant indeed. Carpophorus will be proud of you I'm sure.' And he set to work straight away writing out two copies of the contract for them both to sign, asking Callistus to fill in the amount he was intending to invest. When it was done he handed both copies to Callistus for him to read through and check against each other, which he did with meticulous thoroughness and furrowed brow. Then Shadrach stamped each document with his seal-ring and invited Callistus to do the same. Callistus hesitated only a moment before stamping down his mark, and the deal was done.

But he began to have misgivings as soon as Shadrach had departed with the intention of sending slaves to collect Carpophorus' chest and its contents later in the day. For if Shadrach and Carpophorus were really such good friends, shouldn't Shadrach have known that Carpophorus was going away? And how could it be that Callistus had never set eyes on the fellow before?

Then again, Naomi had certainly known him. And it seemed that Shadrach for his part knew quite a lot about Callistus. In the end Callistus decided that he was getting himself worked up over nothing; rather, he should be congratulating himself on having acted so incisively.

All the same, when Carpophorus returned from his travels not many days later, Callistus found himself curiously reluctant to tell his master what he had done. But Carpophorus would enter the strongroom soon enough and see for himself that the chest was missing; it was undoubtedly in Callistus' interests to prepare him for the shock. So he heaved an inward sigh of relief when Carpophorus barked in response to his confession, 'Shadrach? Shadrach ben Abner, you say? Oh yes, I know him. I have lent him money, too, on occasions, though I shouldn't go so far as to call him a friend. Well, what's done is done; who can say whether you have been prudent or reckless? Time will tell, boy, time will tell. That's often the way of things in the world of business. Succeed, and they will call you bold and inventive; fail, and the world and his wife will be able to tell you exactly where you went wrong.' But then the weight sank back onto Callistus' shoulders as Carpophorus appended, 'Mind you, I'm much less happy about Cleander's part in all this. The day *he* does anything which is truly for the public good will be the day I walk on water. But never mind that now. Come, Callistus; you can help me deal with the correspondence which has been piling up since I left.'

Two days after this, Carpophorus sent Callistus on an errand to the imperial palace. The emperor himself had money invested with Carpophorus, as did several members of his household including one Clemens, a freedman who worked in the office of the emperor's steward. Clemens' deposit had earned him a dividend; Callistus was to ask him whether he wanted the payment in coin or reinvested for a second term.

Clemens turned out to be bearded and sprightly, younger perhaps than the beard made him look. He received Callistus as politely as he would have done the master himself, and beamed, 'So you are Callistus! I've been hearing remarkable things about you. You must be as sharp as a barber's razor if you've managed to impress old Carpophorus.' Again Callistus was taken aback, and the more so when, as he was leaving, Clemens gave him the believers' sacred sign: a thumb and one fingertip pressed together against the bent thumb-knuckle of the other hand to mimic the shape of a fish. Callistus made the sign back, recalling as he did so that he had in fact seen Clemens at the Assembly. When the master had first started taking him along, the Church had still been small enough for all the members to know each other's names as well as faces; nowadays you couldn't always be sure if you had seen someone there or not. It wasn't so surprising that Clemens should remember seeing *him;* as Hippolytus had told him many times, Callistus' face wasn't the sort you forgot in a hurry.

Retracing his steps along the corridors of power, Callistus was savouring the sweetness of what Clemens had said to him and looking once again into the future of his dreams rather than where he was going. So he walked straight into a portly palace eunuch who was puffing his way along with a huge pile of scrolls in his arms. The scrolls scattered everywhere and the eunuch threw up his hands squeaking, 'Oh! Oh my word!' while forlornly watching his burden roll away as though he really couldn't imagine how he was going to bend down far enough over his belly to do anything about it. Blurting out apologies, Callistus dropped to his knees and retrieved everything; when he stood up to hand it all over and shook back the hair which had fallen in his face, he saw to his astonishment that the eunuch was now smiling broadly, and *he* was making the secret sign too. Then Callistus realized with a gasp that this was not just any palace eunuch, but Marcia's.

'Oh sir, I'm so sorry.' Callistus began to apologize all over again, but the eunuch said, 'No, no, young man, the fault was mine. I was carrying far too much at once. Perhaps you can help me, as I am not going far, and my mistress will be *so* pleased to see you. She's been very out of sorts today; she doesn't get many visits from fellow Christians, you see.'

Unable to believe his good fortune, Callistus took back the greater part of the eunuch's load and followed him without another word, his heart flapping like a trapped bird's wings against the bars of his ribcage. When they arrived at Marcia's apartment the eunuch ushered Callistus straight inside. Anyone else might have marvelled at the splendour of his new surroundings but Callistus saw none of it, looking only for the woman around whom all his happiest fantasies revolved.

There was nothing happy about Marcia when at last his eyes found her. She was languishing on a couch by a window looking as glamorous as ever, but hedged about by scrolls she wasn't reading and food she wasn't eating. When the eunuch coughed discreetly and said he had brought her a visitor, she merely waved one hand in dismissal. Then she saw who it was.

'My little friend from the Assembly!' she exclaimed, and Callistus could have sworn that beneath her face-paint she was blushing, as was he. 'Come closer,' she urged him. 'Don't be shy. I'm a Christian just like you.' And she held out both her hands in welcome.

But Callistus could no more take hold of them than he could get any kind of grip on himself. For he had never before heard her speak, and in his infatuation her voice sounded sweeter than the calling of the doves in Carpophorus' garden. Then she laughed and added, 'There's really nothing to be afraid of just because I am Commodus' mistress. I'm a woman like any other.'

This only made things worse, for it wasn't Marcia's social status which was tying Callistus' tongue in knots and binding his arms to his sides. How could he help but notice the milky smoothness of her neck below her dangling earrings, or stop his eyes tracing its line as it led them downward to her gently swelling breasts, which the sheer silk garment she was wearing did precious little to conceal? How could he not see the tendrils of soft brown hair which had escaped being bound up with the rest of it on top of her head, or her delicate hands with their shapely varnished nails; how could he not smell the intoxicating scent of her perfume or wilt beneath the warmth of her gaze? He had never in his life stood so close to a young woman who wasn't a slave or the wife of a butcher or a tanner or a muleteer, whose hands weren't red and raw from scrubbing doorsteps and scouring pans, and who didn't stink of dead meat or urine or worse.

'Oh Callistus – that *is* your name, isn't it? – how can we be friends if you won't even speak to me?' she demanded at last, and his mind began doing cartwheels all over again because she *did* somehow know his name. 'I have so few real friends. I'm so tired of flighty girls who want to be seen with me just so *they* will get noticed, and fawning men who flatter me to win the emperor's favour. But you always look so sweet and innocent, as though there isn't a breath of deceit in your whole body! If only you would sit beside me and talk to me a little while before you have to go; then you could forget just for now that you're a slave, and I could forget that I'm Commodus' mistress and no more free than you are.'

With that she swept away the scrolls which were littering her couch, and moved some bowls of fruit onto a table. Then she patted the cushion beside her, and Callistus sat down.

But even though he still couldn't think of a single word to say to her, it didn't seem to matter. For Marcia talked on and on, as though she really hadn't had anyone else to talk to in weeks, about how lonely she was and how eagerly she looked forward to Sundays when she could go and listen to the bishop's teaching, and sing, and pray, and briefly believe there could be more to life than clothes and cosmetics, baths and banquets, empty chatter and malicious gossip. Meanwhile Callistus was lurching inwardly from fervent hope to silent despair and back again; surely she wouldn't be sharing these private thoughts with him if she didn't feel the same about him as he did about her? But no, she couldn't possibly, or she would be as tongue-tied as he was; either that, or she would have said it was *him* she looked forward to seeing on a Sunday... Or maybe it *was*, and she just didn't dare to admit it, or even realize the truth for herself?

Or maybe she despised him altogether, and secretly she was mocking him, and when he had gone she and her handmaids would be splitting their sides laughing at his expense.

When her words had come full circle and she started talking for the third time at least about how lonely she was at the palace, Callistus decided that the moment had come for him to say something at last about how *he* felt, too, and how if she was really so unhappy where she was, he would find a way of helping her escape.

'Lady Marcia, you don't have to stay here!' he babbled when she paused for breath. 'I know people from the Assembly who could rescue you and hide you from Commodus. I could go and talk to them for you. I could...'

But suddenly Marcia's eyes went very wide; she was shaking her head and holding up her hands to bid him be quiet, when a matter of moments ago she had been begging him to speak. Then she said, 'Callistus, I think you should go now. Your master will be wondering where you have got to' – and when Callistus tried to protest – 'No, I mean it. You must go. Hyacinthus? Would you show this young gentleman to the door?'

And so the eunuch showed him out with even less ceremony than he had shown him in, leaving Callistus to stand outside in the passageway asking himself in bewilderment whether this had been the best day of his life or the worst.

CHAPTER FOUR: MARCIA

Marcia sat by the open window with her chin in her hands on the sill. It was her favourite place to spend a quiet afternoon; it looked out across well-kept rose beds, where she could watch the palace gardeners at work and envy them their ordered outdoor lives.

But today she was staring at nothing, because it hurt too much to do anything else. Her ribs were still sore, and underneath her clothing the skin which should have been smooth and white as fresh milk was still a lumpen tapestry of purple blotches. At least she didn't have great black eyes any more, but they were red-rimmed from crying and she couldn't bear the thought of having face-paint anywhere near them. Looking out of the window seemed to bring them some relief, and feeling the breeze on her face helped too.

Unexpectedly she was roused from her sorry vigil by Hyacinthus, who came scuttling in from the hallway saying, 'My lady? The freedman Clemens is at the door, with a letter addressed to you.'

'Clemens? Well show him in, Hyacinthus. Don't leave him standing on the doorstep.'

'My lady, he says that he cannot come in just now, but he

won't give the letter to me. It seems that you must go to him.'

'Very well.' Wincing, Marcia rose and made her way slowly to the door. Clemens was standing there smiling – they knew each other well – but she could tell that he was shocked at the sight of her.

'A letter from your aunt, my lady,' he announced, clearing his throat, and pressed a little tablet into her hands. 'She told me I was to give it to no one but you.' Then he bowed smartly and was gone.

Intrigued in spite of everything, Marcia took the tablet back to her window. She had several aunts, but none who made a habit of writing her letters, and certainly not the sort of letter which couldn't perfectly well be entrusted to one of her handmaids or to Hyacinthus.

But when she examined the tablet more closely and recognized the seal, she saw it wasn't from any of her real aunts at all. It had come from Hermione, Head of the Order of Widows. Many of the younger Christians called her aunt, because she was exactly what everyone's ideal aunt should be: caring and capable, witty and wise, but not one to stand any nonsense.

'My dearest niece,' the letter began. 'You cannot imagine how delighted I am that you have decided to take pity on your poor old aunt and are coming to visit me very soon. Do not worry about making arrangements; everything has been taken care of. I look forward eagerly to seeing you – not long to wait now, my sweetest! Look after yourself and be of good cheer. Your ever-loving aunt H.'

It was just as well that Marcia was already sitting down. For she knew full well what the letter was really saying, and why its message had been couched in such gushing generalities.

'My lady, have you received bad news?' Hyacinthus enquired, shuffling closer and looking sideways at the little tablet. 'You have turned uncommonly pale.'

'No,' she replied automatically, and then, 'I mean, yes…

just leave me alone for a while, would you, Hyacinthus? I need some time by myself.'

Looking predictably hurt, Hyacinthus bowed himself out of her presence. Marcia shooed her handmaids away after him, and suddenly oblivious of her aches and pains got up again and began to walk in circles round the room. Have I done the right thing? she asked herself with each revolution. I have fantasized for so many months about getting away from this place, yet changed my mind a hundred times. No wonder I got so jumpy when Carpophorus' slave-boy started talking that way in front of Hyacinthus. The whole thing is so fraught with danger; perhaps I ought never to have asked Clemens to tell Hermione that I am ready, vow of chastity and all, or agreed to let her set everything in motion at last. Yet how could I have done otherwise, after this?

Things had come to a head after another failed attempt on the emperor's life. A deserter from the army known only as Maternus had plotted to assassinate Commodus during a festival to honour the Great Mother Goddess to whom he was devoted. Since then Commodus had been seeing plots and betrayals everywhere; he scarcely left the palace – every corridor of which was now crawling with Praetorians – or carried out any imperial duties at all. This meant that he was spending more time than usual with Marcia, during which he'd had several fits of what could only be described as madness, culminating in the most recent when he had set upon her in a foaming frenzy with his club. When his own guards had finally dragged him away from her he was stricken with remorse more extreme than his fury, howling as though *he* were the one who had been beaten well-nigh senseless, and babbling about Greek mythology, claiming that Hera – the Roman Juno, Hercules' implacable enemy – had driven him insane. Marcia knew the story to which he referred: Juno had goaded Hercules into a blind rage in which he had murdered his own wife and children. It was to atone for this atrocity that Hercules had undertaken his famous twelve labours.

To atone for his own latest explosion, Commodus had smothered Marcia with a senator's fortune in precious stones and silks from the east. But she already had more jewellery and clothes than she knew what to do with, and it was plain to her that this state of affairs could not go on any longer. With all his gladiatorial training Commodus was strong as a bear, and for many days Marcia had been confined to her chambers, at first too damaged to be seen in public and then too wretched to want to be.

But in the meantime Commodus had taken to visiting her every evening with a spray of flowers from the garden, or a single rose, and he had looked so lonely and lost that she had been unable to keep herself from folding him in her arms and saying she forgave him and even that she loved him. For at times like those she *did* love him, though certainly more as a mother than as a mistress, which was rather how she felt about little Callistus too. Deep down Marcia knew that what she really needed was the one thing which could never happen: to marry and have children of her own. Her only hope of sanctuary lay with the Church, but to take it she must take her vow of chastity as well.

Though the arrangements had now been put in place, for her own protection Marcia had not been told what they were. It was two days later when Clemens fetched up on her doorstep a second time and informed her that the litter had arrived to convey her to her aunt's residence for lunch, and was she ready? Swallowing hard, Marcia stuffed a few of her favourite possessions into a bag and nodded her head.

'*Where* are we going for lunch, my lady?' asked Hyacinthus; she thrust Hermione's letter under his nose without speaking. Then with a last fleeting look at the luxury she was leaving behind, it was time to go.

Marcia had no idea where Hermione lived. The litter-bearers were men she did not recognize, dressed as slaves of a wealthy household, but they could have been deacons in disguise for all that she knew. The litter could only carry a single passenger, so Hyacinthus was obliged to trot alongside it, constantly out of breath, but there was no way that he would have allowed her to leave him behind. Nor would she have wanted to.

But the litter never reached Hermione's house. As Marcia peeped out from between its curtains she saw that the streets through which they passed were growing narrower and darker. Instead of elegant mansions there were ramshackle tenements with barefoot children grubbing in the hallways and harlots plying their trade quite openly from the doorsteps. The Suburra, thought Marcia with creeping dread, the poorest and ugliest and seamiest district in the whole of the City.

Just as she was beginning to wonder whether her litter had been sent by Hermione at all, it lurched to a standstill and toppled drunkenly onto the ground, tipping Marcia unceremoniously into the road. There was mayhem on all sides as the litter-bearers sought to fight off the thugs who had attacked them; Marcia's hands flew to her mouth as she watched Hyacinthus roll senseless into the gutter. One by one the litter-bearers collapsed in their turn, then just as she decided to make a run for it all by herself, an arm as hard and strong as Commodus' locked around her waist and yanked her upwards until her feet left the ground. Though she kicked and beat on the arm with clenched fists she might as well have been a mouse caught by an eagle. When she had no more fight left in her, a blindfold was wrapped around her eyes and a gag shoved in her mouth, and with hands tied together she was dumped in the back of what must have been some sort of wagon, for she felt it judder and move off, and heard the clopping hooves of whatever animals were pulling it.

Not even with Commodus had she known such terror. She could not begin to think who had kidnapped her or where they were taking her, or what they meant to do with her when they got there. Without doubt Hyacinthus was dead; poor, sweet Hyacinthus, who had been more of a kindly uncle to her than a guard, and who had cared much more about her welfare than those of her own flesh and blood had ever done. And what of Hermione's servants or friends who had been carrying her litter? The inhabitants of the district through which they had been passing looked like the sort who wouldn't think twice about slitting someone's throat to steal the very clothes from his back.

All too soon the wagon ground to a halt. Suddenly there was someone beside her, stripping off her blindfold and untying her hands. Before the gag was removed from her mouth, the person – who might have been a woman, it was hard to be sure, for the wagon had a thick leather awning which blocked out the sun – held up a warning hand and hissed in the uncouth Latin of the streets, 'Don't make a sound, if you know what's good for you. Get down and walk like nothing is wrong. No fuss, mind, unless you want this.' And the hand which had been held up in front of her was swiped like a blade across Marcia's throat.

Abruptly the wagon's awning was thrown back and there were arms reaching up to pull her out. *Don't hurt me! Commodus will pay handsomely for my return!* she was longing to say, but mindful of the threat she did not. Nevertheless, perhaps someone had already told the thugs that she was not to be injured, because the hands that took hold of her were firm but not brutal and she wasn't threatened again. Finally with each of her elbows forcibly linked with her captors', she was marched into the nearest building.

It seemed to be a private dwelling, though it was too dark and smoky to tell for certain, and she had never in her life set foot in a place which reeked so revoltingly of stale garlic and unwashed flesh. Once inside she began to blurt out what she had been too afraid to say before: 'Whatever you want, please don't hurt me. I belong to Commodus. He'll pay whatever you ask him to have me back unharmed.'

'Oh, we know very well who you are,' said a voice from behind her; the words in themselves were alarming, yet she was confused to hear something more like humour in the voice than menace. Then someone else said, 'Surely you don't want to go back to *him*, after all the trouble we've taken to get you away?' And to her amazement a hulking great savage with one eye and most of his nose missing made the sign of the fish with his sausage-thick fingers as he leered toothlessly into her face.

'You mean… all that was…'

'Staged?' came the voice from behind her once again; then its owner moved to stand where she could see him, revealing him to be one of the Church's orphans grown into the prime of manhood. 'Yes, and convincingly done, don't you think, though I say it myself? But by far the safest way to snatch you from Commodus' clutches without Cleander's finger being pointed straight at the Christians.'

'The safest?' repeated Marcia in dismay. 'But Hyacinthus…'

'Oh, your eunuch will make a full recovery; our lads know what they are doing. And at least when he's found he won't be punished for neglecting his duty.'

'No. No, I don't suppose he will…' Marcia's voice trailed off as the smell and squalor of her surroundings began to turn her stomach. But the Orphan smiled at her brightly and said, 'Don't worry, my lady. You won't be staying here. The folks who have offered to take you in will be coming to collect you soon enough. In the meantime we need to get rid of Marcia the emperor's mistress and replace her with Melissa the stonemason's sister.'

At once from an unlit corner emerged half a dozen members of the widows' order, equipped like handmaids with the trappings of a lady's toilette. But what a strange and inverted kind of toilette it turned out to be. The widows swapped Marcia's gown for a rough-spun tunic which made her itch all over as though she had fallen in a bed of nettles. Then they exchanged her slippers for coarse thonged sandals which made her feet look as flat and wide as a duck's. They scrubbed the varnish from her fingernails and toenails and filed them flat as spatulas; they brushed out her ringlets, cut a fringe into the front of her hair – which poked outwards at once with a will of its own – and tied up the rest in a workaday twist at the back of her neck. They whipped the rings from her ears and fingers and the necklace from her throat, and would have stripped the paint from her face just as briskly, had they needed to. Then they finished everything off by rubbing dust and chalk into her skin, and when their work was complete they brought her a cracked bronze mirror so she could pay homage to their handiwork. Marcia took one look at her gruesome reflection and burst into tears.

Thus when her new family arrived to claim her, her ugliness was compounded by bloodshot eyes and blotched red cheeks, which were further marred by damp lines scored through the dust.

None of this seemed to worry the rough and ready young couple who were to be her hosts, nor their brood of noisy children. The man was called Corvus, the Latin for crow – whether for his bright sharp eyes or his prominent beak, Marcia could not be sure. His wife Junia was as plain as Marcia felt, but her smile was as fresh and winsome as Callistus'. They couldn't afford a slave, which was why they had agreed to take in Marcia – or rather, Melissa – to look after their children and perhaps even teach them their letters; they had high hopes for their lively offspring and wanted them able to read the scriptures for themselves. The Church would pay the family for Melissa's keep, so long as she also helped the widows at the Assembly on Sundays who taught the children of the baptized while their parents were receiving the sacraments. A woman who could read and write with ease might be regarded with suspicion by the regular man in the street, but among Christians of every class she was treasure in human form.

Much to her own surprise, Marcia felt settled at Corvus and Junia's almost from the outset. They did not live in an apartment block but in a very much older sort of dwelling, a cottage crammed shoulder to shoulder with others just like it in a whole street of masons and sculptors in stone. The front room of the cottage was its workshop where Corvus and his brother Caelus earned their bread together hammering and chiselling, crafting capitals for columns and balustrades for the balconies and rooftops of the rich. Caelus and his wife Cottia – who was as shrill as he was silent – lived in the cottage too; they had no children of their own, which was perhaps just as well, for the place was crowded enough as it was.

Nevertheless Marcia was given a cramped little room all to herself, scarcely bigger than a cupboard but with no handmaids and no Hyacinthus to scrutinize her every move. Of course it meant she had to get used to washing in stone cold water she had fetched for herself until she could face going to the public baths. She had to dress herself and brush her own hair and clean her own room, and Junia even began to teach her how to cook without burning her fingers. But she still felt freer than she ever had at the palace, because for the first time in very many years she was mistress of her own body; there was no Commodus or Quadratus to send for her on a whim or descend upon her uninvited at any hour of the day or night.

And Corvus and Junia were so generous with the little they had; their faith was firm and uncomplicated, as was their love for one another. Their children were mostly manageable too, once they got used to their strange new nurse-cum-tutor, and they adored her stories of life at the imperial court. They crowed with delight when she told them that palace guests got to eat jellyfish and roast parrot and dormice stuffed with nuts, and that sometimes when a pie-crust was cut, live birds would fly out and flap squawking all over the dining room.

Had it not been for Hyacinthus, Marcia might even have been happy. She remembered with shame her rash promise that if ever she left the palace she would take him with her. But in the event she hadn't had the choice, and he could never have coped with the life she was living now.

On the first Sunday of her stay, the whole family attended Assembly together. Marcia was introduced to everyone as Corvus' and Caelus' sister who had come in from the country to help their wives around the house, and even those among the widows and orphans who knew perfectly well who she was were scrupulous in calling her Melissa. No one who hadn't been involved in her abduction showed the remotest sign of recognizing her, but it was only when she glimpsed Callistus from a distance and he didn't look twice that she dared to believe her disguise was perfect.

In the evening Caelus and Cottia took Marcia to the Agape feast while Corvus and Junia stayed at home with the children, and Marcia found herself sitting close enough to Callistus for her to have reached out and taken his hand. Once during the meal her eyes caught his; for a moment he seemed confused, but then he just looked away.

Still, Marcia was much too excited to think about Callistus now. She had never been allowed to stay to the end of the Agape before, and felt like a little girl at her best friend's party. Once the food had been finished and the dishes cleared away, lamps were brought in and it was time for the singing, which might last for a very long time. For the weekly love-feast of the Church was meant to be a foretaste of the banquet which Christ's followers would one day share with him in heaven.

Marcia felt to be in heaven already, as one by one men, women and even a few of the children got up to sing for their fellow believers. Some sang psalms or other songs based on the scriptures; some of these being songs they had composed themselves, or even invented on the spot. Marcia listened in awe as a singer and a boy with a lyre got up to improvise together; she marvelled that they could know their God and one another well enough to create such ravishing sounds from nothing. Some of the Christians seemed to know God in a way that she still couldn't fathom, and to hear his voice in their heads as clearly as a child might pick out its father's voice in a crowd. She did feel a wonderful peace sometimes when praying, but it did not last.

Suddenly, as she listened entranced, Marcia became aware that Callistus was looking at her again. She dared to catch his eye, and it was asking the question which she knew he must surely ask sooner or later. She smiled and thought: he knows. But she put one finger to her lips and he understood.

After the singing was over and the banqueters had moved off to talk amongst themselves, she found Callistus waiting in the shadows. Swiftly she steered him outside.

'Lady Marcia! It *is* you,' he whispered as they stood face to face in a corner of the moonlit courtyard, and she was surprised and touched to see tears in his huge dark eyes. 'But how did you escape? Where are you staying?'

She did not answer his questions directly, instead asking others of her own. 'Callistus, how did you know? And why should only you have guessed, and no one else?'

'I knew when we were listening to the music,' he confessed. 'It made me think of the first time I saw you. When everyone was praying, and…' Then he checked himself and looked at the ground, and his hair half covered his face as he murmured, 'Lady Marcia, I have been so worried. When you didn't come to Assembly for two weeks running, and then rumours were going round that you'd been attacked in the street! I didn't know who to ask…'

'Oh Callistus, you silly boy, fretting yourself over me! But you really mustn't call me Lady Marcia any more. My name is Melissa; I'm the sister of Corvus and Caelus the masons now. And you mustn't breathe a word about this to anyone else, especially not to your friend Hippolytus. Do you promise to keep my secret?'

'I promise,' Callistus said, but all of a sudden he seemed somehow put out, as though she'd been tactless enough to remind him that he was a slave whilst she was free. 'I must go now,' he told her. 'My master will be waiting.' And she was left there standing alone in the moonlight, puzzled as to whether she had said something wrong or not.

The following Sunday a smiling Hermione gave Marcia permission to begin preparing for baptism. The rite would take place at Pentecost, which was only a month or so away; she need not wait any longer, Hermione said, since she'd been attending Assembly and absorbing the Church's teachings for so many months already. She would take her vow of chastity as soon as she arose from the baptistery, in the presence of the whole congregation, and until then she must do penance to prove her repentance sincere. Not that she must make a show of her fasting, or wear sackcloth, or be otherwise humiliated in public. People might start to ask awkward questions.

So for a while instead of teaching the children she went back to went back to school herself, attending classes with the regular catechumens, who were told that Melissa had begun her studies elsewhere before moving to live in the City.

Whatever it was that she shouldn't have said to Callistus, he must have decided to forgive her, for somehow they contrived to meet for a few brief moments after Assembly every week. He never gave her true name away, though he did admit rather coyly that he'd had to pretend to be upset when Hippolytus informed him with some relish that the emperor's concubine who had once turned his head had been kidnapped and never seen again. 'Yet there has never been any demand for ransom,' Hippolytus had remarked rather pointedly. 'Don't you find that peculiar?' Callistus had had no idea what to say, so had simply shrugged his shoulders and kept his mouth shut.

'But Hippos says the emperor has Cleander looking everywhere for you,' Callistus told Marcia now. 'He's offered a senator's fortune for your safe return.'

'Cleander won't be in any hurry to find me,' she answered with a shudder. 'He would rather see me dead than back with Commodus.' But this disturbing conversation served to remind her all too keenly how important it was that she never be found at all.

Marcia was well aware that her friendship with Callistus in itself helped make her disguise more convincing: a slave-boy was much more likely to be befriended by a peasant girl from the backwoods than by the emperor's former mistress. But deep down she knew this wasn't her only reason for continuing to see him. With Callistus she did not need to pretend to be something she was not, even though he called her Melissa even in private now, so that he wouldn't forget when it mattered. And he was simply so young, so perfectly childlike and innocent, she didn't need to worry that any sort of inappropriate feelings might develop between them.

All the same, she couldn't help wondering why *he* should want to waste time on *her*. Why should a handsome lad who was cuter than Cupid himself want to fritter away his few free moments with a plain children's tutor so much older than he was, when he could have charmed any pretty little maid he fancied? There was no shortage of doe-eyed servant girls of Callistus' own age among the believers who would have welcomed his advances, and the Christians weren't averse to boys and girls befriending one another so long as the relationship was chaste. Trust and self-control were more the Church's style than strict segregation of the sexes.

Yet she did find it uncommonly easy to talk to Callistus, and he to her, once he got past his initial shyness. Scarcely any subject was taboo, and it was just so refreshing, so healing, to be able to share with another human being the anger she had felt towards her mother and step-father for the way they had used her, and the guilt she still suffered for having felt this way about them for so long, and for having eventually rebelled against everything they'd expected her to do.

The one thing she did not tell Callistus anything about was the conspiracy she'd been involved in to take Commodus' life. She had resolved never, ever, to tell anyone of that.

She did try to tell him how hard it had been to live with His Excellency day by day. She told him how Commodus would venerate her like a goddess at one moment and beat her like a mangy dog the next. When she tried to tell him what the nights were like too, and Callistus for once looked as though he wished he were somewhere else, she put it down to endearing naïveté on his part where such delicate topics were concerned. Then he shocked her by asking outright, 'Weren't you afraid he would get you with child?'

'Yes. Yes, I was,' she confessed without stopping to think. 'But I knew what to do to prevent it.'

Callistus' eyes went wide as saucers, for everyone knew that it was harlots who had learnt how to stave off pregnancy with herbs.

'Well, would *you* want to bring a child into the world with a father like Commodus?' she retorted, suddenly defensive. 'Surely God would understand why I did it, since I wasn't thinking of myself. Don't you think he would forgive me, Callistus? After all, we are told to forgive one another seven times over, or seventy times seven if need be.'

'Are we? Seventy times seven?' Callistus repeated. 'I never heard of that before. Who told us to do that?'

'It's what Jesus himself told us,' Marcia assured him. 'His disciples asked him how often we should forgive one another, and he said seventy times seven to show that we should never stop. Surely Hippolytus must have taught you that?'

'Hippos doesn't really talk about forgiveness much at all,' said Callistus after a moment, as though he were only reaching this conclusion as the words came out of his mouth.

Then Marcia said wistfully, 'Sometimes I do grieve because I'll never be able to have children of my own, though. I'm sure you already know that I must take a vow of chastity on the day of my baptism. It's a condition of my receiving absolution… Callistus, what is the matter?' she finished up abruptly, for she had realized that he was no longer looking at her, but past her, as though at something very far away.

'Nothing.' He blinked and shook his head, but looked downward now rather than having to meet her questioning gaze. 'I'm sorry, Melissa.'

On an impulse she reached out to pat his hand in reassurance, but the instant her fingertips touched his skin, it was as though a bolt of lightning had gone right through him, and he withdrew his hand more rapidly than a lizard will dart into the undergrowth if you poke it with a stick. Mortified, Marcia withdrew her hand as well, as it dawned on her that maybe he was regularly slapped or beaten or worse and therefore could not abide being touched in any way at all.

Yet somehow his reaction hadn't been quite like that of other misused slaves she had encountered. And although she couldn't be certain, there seemed to have been tears once more in his faraway eyes. What could his strange reaction have meant?

So she said, 'No, it is I who should be sorry; I wasn't thinking. But something has upset you. Has your master been treating you cruelly?'

'No. Not at all.' Callistus shook his head again, then quite unexpectedly he smiled, his dark mood gone like a passing cloud. 'In fact he treats me better these days than he ever has, and gives me proper grown-up responsibilities. I shouldn't be telling you, but he's put me in charge of all the savings of the Order of Widows, and let me invest the money myself.'

It wasn't hard for Marcia to see why he *was* telling her these things, for his head was no longer bowed and his shoulders seemed to have broadened even as he'd been speaking. But *why* he should want her to think him so grown-up she wasn't sure, especially since she had told him more than once that it was only because he *wasn't,* that she was happy for them to be friends. So she said, 'That's a serious undertaking. How did you know where to start?'

'I probably wouldn't have, if a friend of my master's hadn't come to the house and offered to invest it for me in a project of Cleander's.'

Cleander's! Heaven preserve us! Marcia thought but did not say, for now it was she who felt as though a thunderbolt had struck her. With dread in the pit of her stomach she asked only, 'Aren't you terribly young to be taking on something like this?'

All at once Callistus' smile was gone, along with his visible surge of confidence. In fact he could not have looked more devastated if she had spat in his face. When he had mastered himself sufficiently to respond, the words came pouring out of him in a torrent.

'Well, aren't *you* too young to be taking on a vow of chastity? Is it *your* fault you had to let that monster Commodus have his way with you? What about unending forgiveness, what about seventy times seven? What about the woman taken in adultery, whom Jesus refused to condemn? Oh yes, Marcia – Melissa – I know *that* story well enough. Did he say anything to *her* about taking a vow of chastity?'

'He did tell her to go away and not sin again, so that's probably what he meant,' said Marcia, doing her best to speak softly to calm him down, though her own heart was racing and her throat was dry. 'Callistus, I really can't see why you are getting so upset about this. It has nothing to do with you at all.'

He swallowed hard before saying stiffly, 'No. No, I don't suppose it has.' Then standing up very suddenly with his hands clenched into fists he said, 'Goodbye, Melissa. Perhaps I shall see you next week.' And once again he rushed away to lose himself in the milling throng, leaving her to wonder what on earth she could have said or done this time to offend him so badly.

As the weeks leading up to her baptism flew by, she found herself growing increasingly yet unaccountably nervous. It wasn't the ceremony itself that worried her – it wasn't as if she was frightened of water, or even of being the centre of attention. Nor was she nervous about speaking her vows in front of a large crowd of people. Perhaps it was just that after baptism there could be no going back; from then on she would be a real Christian and everyone would know it, and she would have to face whatever trials and tribulations life threw at her, and whatever persecutions the authorities might dream up, as a child of God.

Whatever the reason, when the day of Pentecost came she woke up feeling sick and feverish and almost told Corvus and Junia that she was ill and could not go to Assembly at all. But the children were so excited at the prospect of seeing their nurse and teacher step down into the baptismal pool with the bishop and come out reborn – and dripping wet from head to foot – that she could not bear to disappoint them, and forced herself to get ready. For the baptism itself she would wear a plain white robe, then change into dry clothes afterwards to make her vow and then receive the body and blood of Christ for the very first time.

As soon as Corvus and his family entered the hallway of Piso and Valeria's house Callistus rushed forward to greet them. Hippolytus was with him, but his greeting was rather less effusive.

'Melissa, wait,' Callistus entreated her, and when she stopped and let the others go on ahead of her he pressed something into the palm of her hand. She looked, and it was a tiny fish carved out of olive-wood, a symbol of the faith she had adopted.

'I carved it myself,' he said, reddening as she examined the untutored yet painstaking handiwork. 'Will you wear it when you go down into the water?'

'Of course.' Marcia's face lit up; the fish had a cord through its tail, and straight away she slipped it over her head and around her neck, which would once have been encircled with precious stones but was now quite unadorned.

'There, doesn't that look pretty?' Callistus enquired of Hippolytus, who gave a grudging sort of shrug before evidently deciding that he probably ought to show a little more enthusiasm since this woman was about to dedicate her life publicly to Christ. So he said, 'I must admit it does, Callistus. Melissa is certainly a much finer example of Christian womanhood than that whore of the emperor's you used to be obsessed with.'

Callistus cringed visibly; Marcia didn't know whether to be offended or amused, but in the end succeeded in not reacting at all, for life with Commodus had taught her to mask her feelings as skilfully as any actor. She did not doubt that Hippolytus was clever with books, but with people he was clueless as well as being prudish and priggish into the bargain.

While the three of them were still standing there together, old Zephyrinus came beetling over to join them; he always reminded Marcia all too poignantly of Hyacinthus. To her astonishment he too had a small gift to present to her: a miniature papyrus scroll onto which he had copied the Lord's Prayer. 'Now remember, my little princess,' he said as he folded her hands around it, 'Your baptism will do you no good at all unless you commit your life into God's hands just as I am placing this scroll into yours. You must be sure to pray and to read the scriptures every day. Oh, and don't be surprised if the next week of your life is one of the hardest you've ever had. The Evil One resents it fiercely every time someone makes a stand for the Lord Jesus. That's why you're feeling so dreadful.'

How had he known? Marcia stared at him in amazement. But Zephyrinus merely winked at her conspiratorially and hurried away.

The first part of the service went by with her scarcely hearing a word that was being spoken. She sang the hymns and prayed the prayers, but could not have told anyone afterwards what they had been about. Then the Liturgy of the Word was over; the baptismal candidates were ushered forward and led by the bishop and elders from the courtyard into the atrium, which had a pool in the middle like the atrium of any other rich Roman's house except that a flight of stone steps led down into the water. The families and close friends of the candidates crowded into the atrium after them, followed by as many of the congregation as could pack themselves in.

In spite of her nervousness beforehand, as Marcia watched the first few candidates being baptized and heard their responses to the bishop's questions, she could scarcely wait for her own turn to come. Indeed she felt almost drunk with excitement as Zephyrinus himself led her down the steps into the pool to take her place between him and the bishop, Eleutherius, where she stood with her arms folded across her chest ready for the two men to plunge her fully under the water.

'Do you believe in God, the Father Almighty?' Eleutherius asked her, and when she responded boldly, 'I believe,' she was swiftly and expertly tipped over backwards and brought back up with water streaming down her face.

'Do you believe in his Son Jesus Christ, who was born of the Virgin Mary by the power of the Holy Spirit, who was crucified for us under Pontius Pilate, dead and buried, and who rose again and ascended to heaven in glory?'

'I believe,' Marcia declared and was at once tipped backwards a second time, to come up smiling, laughing almost, as the water ran down her face and shoulders and she felt as though her sins were truly being washed away along with it.

'Do you believe in the Holy Spirit, in the Holy Church of Christ, and the life of the world to come?' came the third and final question; when Marcia cried, 'I believe!' and was plunged into the water yet again, she found that she was weeping and laughing at the same time. Her tears mingled with the baptismal water, and she could barely stand upright as from every side she was bombarded with applause and shouts of welcome into the communion of Christ. Dizzy with relief and exhilaration she was led from the pool into the arms of Hermione, who wrapped a towel around her shoulders and kissed her.

As soon as the final candidate had been baptized and everyone had put on dry clothes, Marcia would have to stand before the congregation to take her vow of chastity. But she was so elated that this no longer seemed like any sort of sacrifice. Her feet scarcely touched the ground as she was escorted through the cheering crowd back to the courtyard and onto the podium to stand with the bishop and elders and widows' leaders. She barely even heard the questions which were put to her, or her own voice answering, 'Yes,' 'I will,' and 'With all my heart.' She was thinking only: I have given up a sordid and meaningless life which counted for nothing, in return for a salvation which will last for ever; how could I possibly have taken so long in deciding to do it? So she did not perceive Callistus' agony as he turned his back on the whole proceedings and fought his way out of the meeting and into the street, too blinded by his own tears to believe for a moment that Marcia could really be happy.

She was still walking on air after the Agape feast that evening, though it hadn't escaped her notice that Callistus hadn't been there. While marvelling as ever at the singers and instrumentalists who sang and prayed as though God were their closest friend, she had almost begun to believe that one day soon she might be like them.

But by the time she retired to bed, her high hopes had already hit the ground. For while she was on the way back to her room with a jar of water for washing, she overheard Caelus and Cottia in the next room talking and laughing at Commodus' expense. She had never heard Caelus so forthcoming.

'No, it's true,' Corvus' usually taciturn brother was repeating with relish, much to his wife's delight. 'I had it from Clemens himself; he knows everything that happens at the palace. The emperor had a dream in which he fought in the arena as a gladiator, trouncing one famous opponent after another. Now he wants to do it for real. He wants to fight in the Flavian Amphitheatre – the Colosseum, as some have called it.'

Cottia let out a peal of laughter; then Junia's voice cut in quietly, 'Only little boys who know no better dream of being gladiators.' Her comment was clearly meant as a warning to her brother-in-law that he had said enough.

'Little boys and madmen.' This came from Corvus, who sounded even less amused than Junia, but Caelus forged on.

'That's just it, brother; my point exactly. Our empire is being run by a first-rate idiot with feathers for brains. He'll finish up burning down half of Rome like Nero did, just so he can build another arena even bigger than the one we've got already and call it the Commodisseum or something equally ridiculous. He'll be put out of his misery soon enough, no doubt, if he does take to the sand. But the dignity of the principate will go down with him and Rome will never be the same again.'

All four of them fell silent after that, but when Marcia lay down for the night their words were still jangling in her head. And an insinuating voice was repeating in the background: *it's your fault, Marcia, that Commodus' madness is getting worse. You were the only person to whom he could turn, and you too have forsaken him. wouldn't care if he did die in the arena, now that you are gone.*

And if he does die, what will happen to Rome? Commodus has no son. Will the Senate be permitted to choose the best man to be head of state in his place, as in days of old before the empire became so decadent? No it won't; it will be Cleander who inherits the emperor's mantle. Is that what you want to see happen? With Cleander in charge there will be cruelty and corruption everywhere, and what few tarnished slivers remain of Marcus Aurelius' Golden Age will be swept out to sea with the Tiber. All that the best emperors built up will collapse in ruins; the barbarians on our frontiers and the plagues and the chaos which Marcus Aurelius held at bay will overwhelm us, and all because you failed to give Commodus the support he needed to stand tall in his great father's shoes.

Thus Marcia's day which had begun in trepidation and culminated in rapture ended with her crying herself to sleep. Zephyrinus' counsel and warning were forgotten; she could think only of Commodus reaching out for her like a frightened child whining, 'Marcia! Embrace me. Love me… before exhaustion overcame her.

CHAPTER FIVE: CALLISTUS

Callistus sat in Carpophorus' office drumming his fingers on the table as he waited for Shadrach to arrive for their meeting. It was a year to the day since their contract had been drawn up, and now they had arranged to meet so that Callistus' deposit could be repaid, along with the same amount again in interest as Shadrach had promised. Then Callistus could decide whether to invest all or some of it with him afresh or put it to work elsewhere. He could even add more to the sum if he chose, for over the course of the past twelve months the widows and orphans had saved and brought him more money, and now he had quite a substantial hoard of coins stashed away in the master's strongroom.

Callistus had grown too in the year which had passed. When he looked in the mirror these days he thought he saw a man rather than a boy, though he was still as slim as a reed, with considerably more hair on his head than on his chin, and he still turned the heads of older men as well as maidens whenever he walked down the street. But he wondered, not entirely without vanity, whether Shadrach would recognize him now that he was so much taller and his voice was almost as deep as Carpophorus'.

He hadn't seen Shadrach since their first encounter, but the businessman had sent him messages now and again to confirm that the plot of land he coveted had been acquired and the tenement built. Lately the first batch of tenants had moved in and were starting to pay him rent.

While he waited, Callistus' mind was drifting as usual. For wherever he chose to direct his thoughts, he would end up dreaming of Marcia. Today he was remembering how beautiful she had looked at her baptism in her simple white robe, with his little wooden fish around her neck. He didn't think she looked any less lovely than she used to, now that she wore no other jewellery and kept her hair pulled back in a no-nonsense bunch like Naomi's. It had well nigh broken his heart to hear her take her vow of chastity; not until that moment had he realized that he'd never fully given up the foolish notion of being able to marry her himself. But he had come to uneasy terms with it now, and at least it meant that the two of them could continue to be friends. Although in his less selfish moments Callistus was profoundly sorry that Marcia would never be a wife or a mother, he knew it would have torn him apart if he had seen her on another man's arm.

Just then the office door opened and Callistus looked up, expecting to see Naomi or one of the other slaves ushering Shadrach into his presence. But it was the master, returned from a morning in the forum; he cocked an eyebrow at Callistus and said, 'No Shadrach yet? I thought you were expecting him after breakfast?'

'So I was, master. But he still isn't here.'

'Evidently not, my boy, evidently not. And now it is way past noon. Well, I am going to take the weight off my feet for a while. Wake me if you need me. Though I must say the sun has gone to my head a little this morning; I may not get up until supper time. Don't you forget to eat lunch again, mind, Callistus. We don't want you fading away.'

But Callistus wasn't hungry. There were butterflies stirring in his stomach and he was starting to feel as though he too had had too much sun even though he hadn't been outside. He got up and began to pace about the office, then sat down again, fiddling with the signet ring his master had given him, which seemed to have become rather loose. Then he decided to work on some accounts to pass the time, but couldn't concentrate and kept making stupid mistakes.

As the afternoon wore on and still Shadrach did not appear, Callistus began to be seriously concerned. He could have had some sort of accident, or been taken ill; but surely he would have sent a messenger to say so? It was only a matter of days since their meeting had been arranged – through intermediaries, it had to be said – but there had been no suggestion that Shadrach might have difficulty keeping the appointment in person.

When it was almost time for the slaves to have their evening meal, Callistus wondered whether he should go and tell Carpophorus that Shadrach had failed to turn up. But for some reason he was loath to do so; he told himself it was merely because the master hadn't been feeling very well and he didn't want to trouble him. When Naomi came to say it was time to eat, he sent her away, saying he didn't feel well either.

Eventually, when it began to get dark and he could no longer see the figures in front of him, Callistus made up his mind that the best thing to do was call at Shadrach's house the next day on his way back from the palace, for he would be going there first thing on his master's account to see the freedman Clemens. So with a heavy sigh he closed up the office and went to bed via the kitchens, where he picked up a loaf of bread and a lump of cheese to keep starvation at bay, though he still wasn't hungry and feared they might make him sick.

The following morning Callistus rose early; he had slept little in any case and was glad not to have to lie there tossing and turning any longer. Studiously avoiding Carpophorus he went to see Clemens as arranged, and began to feel a little better when the freedman told him again how highly Carpophorus was wont to speak of him whenever an opportunity presented itself.

'Melissa the stonemason's sister seems quite taken with you too,' added Clemens with a wink, sending Callistus on his way with a spring in his step and a song in his heart, confident now that he would find Shadrach with no difficulty and everything would be all right; his failure to put in an appearance yesterday would turn out to be the result of a simple misunderstanding.

Callistus had never been to Shadrach's house, but he had an address for him from which he had reliably received a reply whenever he sent a letter. It was in the Trans Tiberim district – not exactly a very salubrious place for a self-respecting property developer to live, Callistus reflected as he made his way there now, but perhaps it was merely an office which Shadrach had there rather than his principal place of residence? No doubt it was expedient for him to maintain some kind of presence in the part of the City where the largest concentration of Jews was to be found, even though presumably he wouldn't want to live there himself.

As he crossed the bridge over the river, leaving the imperial palace and the great Circus Maximus behind him, Callistus decided that he for one wouldn't want to spend a moment longer in Trans Tiberim than he absolutely had to. The proud stone bridge itself was infested with beggars who called out to him as he passed by, and even clawed at the hem of his tunic with their skeletal fingers. On the opposite bank grim tenement blocks rose up like the walls of Hades, their rows of shutterless windows reminding Callistus of the eye-sockets of crucified men which the crows have left empty and black. But as he drew nearer he saw they weren't empty at all. Over the sills of many leaned gaggles of mat-haired children shouting down to their playmates below. Others were festooned with drying clothes which flapped against the walls and must have ended up just as dirty as they'd been before they were washed. Spent old harlots advertised their services from grimy doorways; some of them called out to Callistus as he went past: 'Hey, pretty boy, over here! Come learn a lesson from Lady Love! Twenty years in the trade,' or 'A special rate for you, Adonis, just for today! Don't miss out on your chance, now.' He shuddered and walked a little faster, uncomfortably reminded once again that there were many worse things to be than a slave in the house of Carpophorus. Legally these people were no man's property, yet they could scarcely be described as free.

The deeper he penetrated into the labyrinth that was Trans Tiberim the more oppressive its atmosphere became. He was glad to be young and strong, and carrying nothing of value on his person. Not that he would have known how to defend himself effectively if he were attacked, but at least his age and robust appearance made it less likely that he would be.

It took him quite some time to find the streets where most of the Jewish people lived, but he knew when he had found them because instead of harlots in the doorways there were mezuzot sprouting from the frames, and everything was cleaner and more tidily maintained. The children stared but did not shout out at each other or at him, and he did not feel quite so much under threat.

But when he began to ask around and show people the address which Shadrach had given him, he met only with stares as blank as the children's, until eventually a severe-looking rabbi with a huge black beard told him, 'That's not a Jewish street at all. You'd best seek him out among the Gentiles, young man. That old weasel wouldn't want his own people watching his every move, oh no. You wouldn't catch him living round here.' For which small mercy the rabbi seemed to be profoundly grateful.

So reluctantly Callistus went back to searching the dirty downtrodden alleyways where his quest had begun. The towering tenements shut out the sunlight almost completely; piles of refuse stank sickly-sweet on every corner, with rats scurrying freely between them. Callistus began to feel sick again himself as he realized that this was no doubt the kind of housing which his own generous investment had gone into providing. So much for helping the needy; this was more like throwing them into prison.

At long last he found the establishment he was looking for. It was a ground-floor apartment in as shoddy and rickety a building as Callistus had ever set eyes on. He could only be thankful that he didn't have to take his life in his hands by going up the stairs. But there was no way of telling whether it was an office or a dwelling after all, because there was no one there, and you couldn't see in through the windows because they had all been boarded up. The place had evidently been shut up for good, though not very long ago, by the look of things, for no one had yet daubed graffiti over the window boards and there was no rubbish piled up against the door.

As soon as they caught sight of Callistus Shadrach's neighbours must have deliberately made themselves scarce, for the street was as empty and quiet as a ransacked tomb. But Callistus was growing desperate, and had no intention of returning home until he had found out where Shadrach had gone. So he started banging on nearby doors, no longer caring very much whether the residents were prostitutes, pimps or cutthroats.

'Oh yes, that's Shadrach's place all right,' he was told by those few who eventually confessed to knowing him. 'But we haven't seen him for days.'

'The Jew?' said one old man, spitting as he spoke. 'I reckon he's scarpered off back to his poxy Promised Land, and good riddance to him too. Tried to charge my son rent on a room he'd already thrown him out of. He's a crook with a serpent for a mother. You want to keep out of his way, like most of his own people have the good sense to do.'

Frantic with frustration, Callistus was forced to accept that he would find out nothing further from the inhabitants of Trans Tiberim. Still, he could not risk facing Carpophorus with things as they were, so he decided to try some of his master's own neighbours, the wealthy Jews and Jewish Christians of Piscina Publica. Surely some of *them* must have had dealings with Shadrach and would offer what assistance they could, for Carpophorus' sake?

Yet none of them did, though some seemed sympathetic, assuring Callistus that Shadrach could not have gone very far and that he would probably return in a day or two's time; he usually did. At his wits' end Callistus finally questioned Naomi, but she only narrowed her eyes at him and demanded to know *why* he needed to find Shadrach so very urgently, finishing up by hissing at him, 'I don't believe I would tell you where he was even if I knew. You look ready to murder him, Callistus. I can't think what has got into you.'

As for Callistus, he could scarcely think at all. His head was spinning, and his heart was beating so hard by now that he couldn't hear anything else. He could not go to Carpophorus; he dared not. Marcia had been right all along; he *had* been much too young to shoulder the kind of responsibility his master had laid upon him. If only he could confide in *her*, ask *her* what he ought to do next. Marcia was so much older and wiser than he was, surely she would know...

But Corvus and Junia's house was a long way from Carpophorus', and in the Suburra, a part of town even rougher than Trans Tiberim; it was suicide for a stranger to wander its streets alone. Nor did Callistus want Marcia mixed up in his misfortunes. Besides, he doubted he would even reach the place without collapsing in a gutter. He had barely eaten or slept for over twenty four hours, and his legs felt as wobbly as a newborn foal's.

Hippolytus, on the other hand, lived in aristocratic magnificence on the Esquiline hill, and although he was only a month or two older than Callistus he was surely very much wiser. Yes, he was the son of a senator and Callistus had never called on him at home before, but his parents were Christians as he was; surely they would not turn their son's best friend away in his hour of need?

So Callistus summoned what remained of his strength and courage, and went to the house of Hippolytus.

Though the senator's mansion was certainly imposing, this in itself wasn't enough to intimidate someone who was required to run regular errands to the imperial palace. But the slave who came to the door curled his lip and pretended not to know who Callistus was, then ordered him to wait in the kitchens rather than the atrium while he went to find out whether the young master would agree to receive him. By the time someone else came to fetch him into the atrium after all, Callistus was beside himself. There was still no sign of Hippolytus and Callistus was not invited to sit down.

At last the great panelled door at the far end of the atrium swung open and Hippolytus entered in haste, his sandals clapping on the hard mosaic floor. He had come from his family's private bathhouse; his hair, freshly clipped, was still wet and his toga thrown on awry, yet he looked – and his perfume smelled – so utterly, horribly, patrician that it was all Callistus could do not to turn round and bolt into the street.

'Callistus? What are you *doing* here?' Hippolytus demanded, as though Callistus had profaned some sacred ritual by his unclean presence.

'Hippos, please, you have to help me. I am in the most terrible trouble.'

'Trouble? What kind of trouble?' Hippolytus' eyes had darkened, and he still hadn't asked Callistus to sit down. 'What have you done?'

'Nothing; you don't understand.' Callistus glanced around quickly to check there was no one else within earshot, suddenly not knowing where to begin. 'You see, I lent some money to a man, and he hasn't paid me back…'

But once he got started, the whole sorry tale came pouring out from beginning to end. He had never before told Hippolytus anything about the work he did for Carpophorus because he had been warned time and again that such things were confidential. Now he no longer cared a jot who else was listening. But when he came to the end of his story and Hippolytus hadn't uttered another word, Callistus forgot that the senator's son was supposed to be his friend and fellow Christian, and fell on his knees at his feet.

'So – you lent the widows' and orphans' savings to a man you didn't know?' Hippolytus commented eventually, when the torrent of Callistus' words had dried up and the weight of his bowed head was pressing the thongs of Hippolytus' sandals into his flesh. 'I can't believe you did something so stupid. Whatever were you thinking of?'

'He said he was the master's friend!' Callistus dared to look up at him, only now aware that he had hold of Hippolytus' ankles.

'And was he?'

'Yes! I mean, no… I mean… Naomi our housekeeper knew who he was. And it was Carpophorus he'd come to see; he didn't know he wasn't there – '

'On the contrary, Callistus, I should think he knew very well, and that he also knew you had money to invest. That's why he came when he did, so he could hoodwink you when your master wasn't around to stop him. He's gone off with every penny of that fortune, you mark my words, and you'll never see him again. He'll be living in luxury by now in some far-flung province where no one knows him from Adam. Don't you remember that our Lord warned us to be as shrewd as serpents as well as innocent as doves when dealing with those who do not share our faith?'

By this time Callistus was weeping into Hippolytus' feet as shamelessly as the woman who bathed the feet of Jesus with her tears. 'But what can I do?' he wailed, gripping Hippolytus' ankles even harder.

'Do? There's nothing you *can* do, apart from run away like Shadrach has done, or confess everything to Carpophorus.'

'Run away? But where would I go? Surely someone from the Church could help me. You could approach the elders on my behalf – '

'Someone from *Church?* Are you mad as well as stupid? Hordes of its most vulnerable members are now destitute thanks to you. You have cheated them of what little they had; you'll be excommunicated for fraud! Don't you know it's a deadly sin in the bishop's eyes?'

'But I haven't committed fraud! *I* haven't stolen the money. Zephyrinus, he would understand – '

'I'm sure he would; he always sympathizes with the feckless. But what do you expect him to do? Yes, I know he's nice. But he has hardly any money, even less influence and no brains.'

'Then at least let me stay here, Hippos, just for today while I try to think. I can't go back home now; Carpophorus will tear me limb from limb once he finds out what's happened.'

'Callistus, you *have* gone mad, I swear it. It's illegal to harbour a runaway slave. Are you seriously asking me to break the law, when as Christians we are duty bound to uphold it? Confess the truth to Carpophorus; it's your only hope.'

'No, believe me it is not. I'd be better off slitting my wrists – or stowing away on the first ship out of Portus. But you needn't worry about getting yourself into trouble on my account. Whatever happens, I won't ask for your help again.' With that, Callistus scrambled to his feet and bolted from the house, only wishing he had done so a good deal sooner.

He didn't return to his master's house. Nor did he go to the harbour. Instead he went back to the Tiber and found a scrubby patch of grass by the bridge where he could sit and be alone with his fears and his misery and his mixed-up thoughts. He could not believe that his life had fallen apart so quickly. The day before yesterday he'd been his master's favourite servant, with every chance of gaining his freedom one day and running a successful business of his own, as so many freedmen in Rome already did. Now he had lost everything. The fortune entrusted to him was gone, spelling financial ruin for hundreds of others. His master's respect for him would be lost along with it once he learned what had happened, and so would the trust and affection of the whole Roman Church, Marcia's – Melissa's – included. Chancing to glance down at his trembling hands he saw that his master's signet ring was gone too; in all his chasing around it must have fallen off and he hadn't even noticed.

Yet somehow worse than any of this was what had happened at Hippolytus' house. He and Hippolytus had known each other for half their lives. They had grown up together in the Church, singing the hymns and chanting the prayers together side by side, bringing smiles to the faces of all who saw and heard them because the friendship between a slave and a senator's son was such a clear demonstration of the Gospel of Christ. But now Callistus wondered if Hippolytus had ever truly been his friend at all.

As he sat and watched the Tiber's sluggish waters slide past him, he knew he should have been praying. He knew that a real Christian would cast himself upon the mercy of God when in straits as dire as these. But Callistus didn't feel like a real Christian, especially not now. If he had let down everyone he knew, then surely he had let God down most of all.

No, he decided, it would be foolish as well as presumptuous of him to expect God to do anything for him. It had been a mistake to go to Hippolytus for help and it would be a bigger one still to wait for any kind of help from heaven. *No* one really cared about the fate of a common slave, whatever Bishop Eleutherius or plausible old Zephyrinus might say to the contrary. Callistus had only ever had himself to rely on, and in this respect at least nothing had changed.

Thus it was that as the Tiber flowed on by, Callistus' tears dried up and his face and resolve began to harden even as his thoughts straightened out. *He* knew that his life had fallen apart, but so far no one else did apart from Hippolytus. For all that Carpophorus knew, Callistus might have met successfully with Shadrach by now and got everything cleared up. There was no reason for Callistus not to call at the house, collect his belongings – such as they were – then take the money he had stashed in the strongroom and *buy* his passage on the ship of his choice; there would be no need for him to stow away. By the time Carpophorus learned the truth Callistus would be long gone, and though a runaway slave might legally be tortured or even put to death, they would have to find him first.

With his plan in place Callistus stood up, brushed the grass from his tunic and imagined his worries floating away with the Tiber down to the sea.

Walking back to his master's house, he even began to be excited about where he might go. His mother had been Greek, so if he could find a ship bound for Greece he would go there; he might even find members of the family he had never known. Or perhaps he would go to Alexandria in Egypt where men of every nationality under the sun lived cheek by jowl and no one would notice him at all. Here he could change his name and pretend to be somebody else altogether, and hire himself out as a scribe or a keeper of accounts and become so rich and successful that no one would guess he had ever been anybody's slave. Perhaps one day far in the future it might even be safe for him to return to Rome and confess who he really was to Marcia – Melissa – alone. The two of them might go on being friends, *both* with assumed names and invented identities.

In the event Callistus did not have to lie to Carpophorus about where he had spent the morning or whether he had managed to meet up with Shadrach. For when he got back to the house early in the afternoon the master was out on business. No one questioned him when he went to his room to pack up the few things he owned; as the master's favourite he hadn't had to share sleeping space with his fellow slaves for many months. No one turned a hair when he opened the strongroom and gathered up as many of the coins he'd amassed as he could reasonably carry. He did feel a pang of guilt as he took them, but compared with the fortune he had lost already he decided that it scarcely mattered. He thought it was a pity that he didn't have anything to remind him of Marcia the way she had his little wooden fish, but since he couldn't help but see her face whenever he closed his eyes this didn't matter so very much either. Just before he left, he changed into travelling clothes, tied the coins in a purse to his belt… and ran straight into Naomi.

'And where do you think you're going, young man?' she demanded. With her hands on her hips she effectively blocked the passageway in which she had planted herself.

Callistus had his answer already worked out. 'I'm to meet up with the master in the forum; we are going to view Shadrach's latest building project together. Now if you'll let me pass I may avoid missing him and getting both you *and* me into trouble.' So saying, he strode forward, leaving Naomi little choice but to move aside. She didn't look entirely convinced, but these days Callistus' standing with the master had grown to be as high as hers, and formidable as she was she dared not incur Carpophorus' wrath.

Callistus didn't rightly know how far it was from Rome to Portus, but he knew men much older and slower than himself who had walked there in a day, so he reckoned on getting there well before nightfall. He also knew that if he took the most direct route through Trans Tiberim and chose the right gateway in the city walls the road would lead him straight there so there was no danger of getting lost on the way.

But he had never stepped outside the walls of Rome in all his life. So it was with a curious mixture of fear, guilt and intoxication that he left the sordid alleyways of Trans Tiberim behind him and passed through the great Porta Portuensis with its double archway out into the big wide world beyond. The sun was shining and he was really beginning to believe that everything might turn out for the best after all.

He had no clear picture in his mind of what the world outside the City might look like, but he might have imagined a patchwork of fields and forests, and maybe villas and little farmsteads here and there with cows and sheep cropping the grass. Instead there were just more houses to begin with, mostly mean and mouldering affairs more like sheds thrown up by peasants who had likely migrated to Rome to seek their fortunes but been unable to pay the rents required to live there. Lining the roadside itself were tombs, many like small houses themselves, and some of those which were more neglected than others looked to have acquired living occupants as well as dead ones. Callistus shuddered, reminded once again that many slaves were better off than some of the free.

Further on the tombs and shanties were replaced by the homesteads of market gardeners who grew fruit and vegetables to feed the City's insatiable hunger, and then by larger farms. But although the houses were fewer and farther between out here, the road itself was still surprisingly busy with wagons and pedestrians and the scanty grass to either side had been reduced to dust by the trampling of the many animals which had been ridden or driven over it to protect their hooves from the road's hard surface.

To begin with Callistus feared that every person he passed would be staring at him in suspicion. But he realized very quickly that few of them were paying him any attention whatever, and that those who did look twice were noticing him only for the same reason that so many others had noticed him before. There was no way that anyone could tell him for a runaway slave just by looking, or for any kind of slave at all, and one in four of *them* was likely to be a slave in any case.

Of course if a slave had a history of running away, it was a different matter. Callistus shuddered again as he recalled that a recaptured runaway – if he were allowed to live – could be made to wear an iron ring around his neck indefinitely or even have 'fug' (for 'fugitive') branded on his forehead.

When he had been walking for a good few hours, an affable-looking man driving a smart horse-drawn carriage pulled up alongside him and offered him a ride. 'I'm going through to Portus to collect my master from the harbour, if that's where you're headed,' the fellow told him cheerily. 'Don't worry, there's no charge. I'd be glad of the company.'

Deciding it would be churlish and look suspicious to do otherwise, Callistus accepted the driver's offer and climbed up beside him. Besides, he had never ridden on a carriage before and the chance was too good to miss. As the vineyards and olive groves rolled on by, Callistus put his fertile imagination to work making up a story about who he was and where he was going, but he didn't need to use it because his companion talked incessantly the whole way along. Though their progress was scarcely swift, they still reached Portus in half the time it would have taken Callistus to walk there, and there was plenty of daylight left when he bade his garrulous companion goodbye, surprised to find how stiff he was from all the rocking and jolting.

By now it was early evening, but Portus was still noisy with the shouts of fishermen returning with their catch and sailors loading or unloading their cargoes along the wharves. Once upon a time their ships would have docked at Ostia, Rome's old port at the mouth of the Tiber, but Ostia had long been unable to cope with the volume of sea-traffic generated by Rome's ever-growing need for imported grain and her craving for exotic luxuries.

Still, Callistus couldn't afford to waste time enjoying the bustling atmosphere or savouring the seaside smells of salt and fresh fish, unfamiliar and thrilling as they were. He combed the wharves, going from ship to ship in search of a vessel on the point of departure for Athens or Alexandria. But he couldn't find one going anywhere at all before the morning, and inevitably his excitement began to be diluted once more by foreboding. Every hour he lost meant one more in which Carpophorus might catch up with him, for certainly by this time the master would have realized that his apprentice was absent without leave. He might also have discovered that there was money missing from the strongroom. It was probable that Callistus' fellow slaves were already out searching the streets of Piscina Publica and hammering on the doors of anyone and everyone with whom he might have taken refuge. As soon as it became clear that they weren't going to turn him up, Carpophorus would have little choice but to hire a gang of professionals to run the fugitive to ground.

At long last Callistus found a ship bound for the Athenian port of Piraeus, though like all the rest it was not due to leave until morning. But its grizzled bear of a captain was happy enough to let Callistus spend the night on board once he had relieved him of much of the weight around his waist. The ship's cargo consisted of strangely shaped wooden containers, the like of which Callistus had never seen; when he asked what was inside them the captain roared with laughter and said, 'Oh, we don't put nothing inside them. It's the barrels as brings in the money all by theirselves.' Apparently the Gauls had become expert in making oaken containers watertight, and they were rapidly becoming all the rage among the vine-growers of Italy and Greece because unlike amphorae they did not break when they banged against one another in a rough sea. The larger ones were easily big enough for a man to hide inside, so Callistus took advantage of the fact and curled himself up where Carpophorus' hirelings would never think to look even if they traced him to the harbour. In spite of being cramped as a caterpillar in a chrysalis he fell asleep almost at once.

The ship set sail at first light. Callistus crawled out of his barrel to find that the ropes had already been untied and the sail was being unfurled; the rowers were heaving on their oars and the smell of salt in the air was somehow like the scent of freedom itself. Once they pulled away from the shore Callistus decided it must be safe for him to stand in the stern and watch his old life of servitude slipping away behind him.

He couldn't have been more wrong. For while he was happily watching the ship's wake spreading out across the harbour like the tail of a great white peacock, he heard raised voices carrying over the water and saw a small boat being furiously rowed out after them.

'That's him! Thief! Runaway! Don't let him escape!' someone was yelling; to Callistus' dismay he saw that it was Carpophorus himself, standing up in the boat and waving his arms about with such urgency that the little craft was pitching and tossing alarmingly as though intent on plunging its entire crew overboard. Callistus was desperately wishing it would, but instead had to listen to Carpophorus shouting at his own vessel's captain, 'Stop! Wait! I'll pay you his weight in silver! Bring him back; hand him over! He's my slave!'

The mention of silver grabbed the captain's attention straight away. He started yelling at his own crewmen just as frantically, 'Stop rowing! Lower the sail! Get that boy and fetch him to me!'

But Callistus wasn't going to wait to be got or fetched, and there was no longer any point in trying to hide. He did the only thing he could do: he leaped overboard and swam for his life.

He knew very well that he wouldn't be able to outswim his master's boat over any distance, small and unstable though it was. But they were still so close to the wharf there was at least an outside chance that he might get back there while Carpophorus was attempting to change course. He had no choice but to undo his belt and rid himself of the rest of his money before it dragged him down with it; he tore off his cloak as well, and once it was gone he thrashed and kicked for all he was worth towards the shore he had been so eager to leave.

Yet even as he began to make some headway he knew it was hopeless. Though he had swum a few strokes in the plunge pool at the public baths he had never in his life swum in the sea, and the salt water stung his eyes and got in his mouth and made him want to throw up. More bitter still was the knowledge that Hippolytus had almost certainly betrayed him, probably repeating their conversation verbatim to Carpophorus in the firm belief that he was doing the right thing.

And soon it wasn't only Carpophorus' boat that was bearing down on him. From the other side he caught a watery glimpse of another one very like it headed his way, no doubt the landing-craft which the big ship would use in places where there was no harbour suitable for it to dock.

Caught between the two of them, there was nowhere left for him to go. So when strong arms reached down to hoist him from the waves like a fish on a line, Callistus was forced to accept that his short-lived bid for freedom had failed.

CHAPTER SIX: MARCIA

'Alpha, beta, gamma, delta,' chanted the older children dutifully, as Marcia sat teaching them their letters in the cramped little room behind Corvus' workshop. If they were to read the Gospels and the writings of the apostle Paul for themselves they would have to master Greek as well as Latin.

But today it was the teacher's mind which wasn't fully focussed on the lesson. Marcia was toying with the olive-wood fish around her neck, wondering why Callistus hadn't been at the Assembly or the Agape on Sunday. It was unheard-of these days for him to miss either; was he ill? Was he being punished for something and not allowed to leave the house? She supposed she should have asked Hippolytus; surely he would know. But Marcia was always disinclined to speak to Hippolytus when Callistus wasn't there, because he was never less than prickly and often downright rude. She wasn't sure if it was jealousy of her friendship with *his* friend that made him so objectionable, or simply a fear of talking to women. Either way, Marcia hadn't relished the prospect of provoking his anger whilst in all probability embarrassing him into the bargain.

She was surprised how much she had missed her little

friend, though. It wasn't that they ever spent very long in each other's company, but somehow they would always manage to snatch a few moments after the morning meeting at least to chat about the week which had passed, before Carpophorus or one of his other servants appeared to tell Callistus it was time to go home. This week Carpophorus and the rest of his household had been at Piso and Valeria's as usual, but without Callistus.

'Lambda, mu, nu, pi – ' Suddenly her pupils' chanting was cut short, and Marcia herself was startled from her reverie as there came a loud and insistent banging on the door – not the door from their schoolroom through to the workshop, but the workshop's door onto the street. Marcia froze with one finger pressed to her lips, but the children needed no warning to keep them quiet. They all stared round-eyed in the direction from which the noise had come, as it started again louder still and a harsh male voice shouted, 'Open up in the name of the emperor.' There was a scuffling and the sound of Corvus' and Caelus' voices, hoarse and anxious. Then the door must have opened, because the banging stopped and Marcia could hear someone entering the workshop. He was not alone.

Still motioning them to be silent, Marcia gathered the children into her arms, wincing as one of them let his wax tablet slip through his fingers. Thankfully the floor was made of beaten earth, not stone, and the tablet made no sound when it landed. But now the harsh voice was shouting again, from much closer quarters, and Marcia began to think it was a voice she had heard before.

'You are the stonemason known as Corvus? You are under arrest.'

Marcia didn't hear Corvus say anything in reply, but Caelus his brother was objecting, 'Arrest? What for? There must be some mistake.'

'No mistake. Seize him, centurion. You men: search the house.'

At this Junia could be heard protesting as well, making

Marcia wince once again; she hadn't realized that Corvus' wife was in the workshop too. 'Search the house?' Junia echoed in terror. 'Why? What do you want from us?'

'Keep out of this, woman, if you still have the sense you were born with.'

'No, please! Just tell us what you want, and we can get it...'

Whatever she said after that was drowned in loud guffaws, and a moment later Junia was screaming.

Noticing that one of the little girls was now weeping copious silent tears, Marcia clasped her cowering pupils against her in an agony of indecision. Surely it must be *her* that the men were searching for, and if she simply gave herself up, the rest of the family need not be harmed?

But supposing it wasn't? Then she would have blown her disguise for nothing, and got Corvus and Junia into even more trouble than they were in already. She would also have been responsible for leading a company of uncouth soldiers straight to the place where the children were gathered.

All at once the decision was taken out of her hands. The door through to the workshop burst open and a broad brutish figure stood on the threshold, his bulk almost blotting out the light that should have come spilling through. It was Cleander himself who stood there. The half-familiar voice had been his.

'That's her,' he announced in smug self-satisfaction. 'The emperor's missing whore, no less. Well well, you little hussy. His Excellency *will* be pleased when we get you back home.'

'I beg your pardon?' Corvus spoke up at last, though Marcia still couldn't see him for Cleander's bulk. 'That is my sister, Melissa. Anyone will tell you – '

'Really? I wonder if your woman agrees.' Cleander made some gesture at one of his soldiers, and Junia started screaming again. Marcia could take no more.

'It's true, Cleander,' she said. 'I *am* the woman you have been searching for. But these are not the people who kidnapped me. They rescued me. I owe them my life, and if you harm them Commodus will see to it that yours is no longer worth living.'

When she had finished, no one else spoke or moved. So Marcia gave the forlorn huddle of children a final squeeze around the shoulders and walked away from them towards Commodus' henchman. Cleander was sufficiently taken aback to let her march right past him into the workshop. Here not only Corvus but his brother too were each restrained between a pair of soldiers of the Praetorian Guard. Junia crouched stricken on the ground, her dress torn open and her breasts exposed and bleeding.

Even now Corvus had not given up. 'Marcia,' he said – and it was the first time he had ever used her real name – 'You are a free woman. You don't have to go with them.'

'I do,' she told him. 'I knew it before they even came here. Commodus needs me.'

Corvus opened his mouth to protest again, but something about the set of Marcia's face made him close it. The more he said, the more likely he was to lead Cleander to suspect that the Christians might have something to do with all this, a factor of which the brute might still be unaware. But Junia was crying again, and begging, 'Melissa – Marcia – don't leave us! You're part of our family now. We love you.'

Marcia turned to face Cleander and looked him straight in the eye. She said, 'Let these innocent people go free. Swear to me in the emperor's name that they will not be harmed further and I shall come with you without complaint.'

Cleander hesitated only a moment. Then he whirled around with astonishing speed for a man of his size, and punched Corvus and then Caelus squarely in the face with full force, growling, 'Perhaps you will think twice before you go offending His Imperial Excellency again.' As the brothers sagged in their captors' arms Cleander turned back to Marcia with a leer and said, '*Now* I swear.' The soldiers loosed their prisoners instantly, depositing them one on top of the other on the ground.

Outside the workshop a palace litter was waiting, such an

incongruous sight in the depths of the Suburra that a crowd had gathered about it. Two of Cleander's Praetorians made as if to manhandle Marcia inside, but she shook them away and got in of her own volition with all the dignity she could muster, much to the awe of the spectators. It was hard to know what had impressed them most: the litter, the Praetorians in their gleaming armour, or Melissa the stonemason's sister being borne away in grandeur by four German slaves from the palace as flaxen-haired and smartly dressed as they were identical.

As long as she had been on public view Marcia had maintained her gravitas. Once the curtains of the litter had been closed around her she gave up the struggle. Between sobs she found herself praying over and over again in her head: oh dear Lord Jesus, *please* don't let Corvus or Junia or their household be subjected to further suffering on my account. And please don't let Commodus find out it was the Christians who took me away from the palace.

Meanwhile she couldn't help but wonder who it was who had betrayed her, or whether she might simply have been recognized at the market-place or in the street. Could some member of the Church who knew the truth have given her away by mistake, or conceivably even on purpose? She was confident that Callistus would never have done such a thing, but Hippolytus… could *he* have worked out who she was?

As soon as the suspicion had formed itself in her mind she pushed it aside. There was no place in the Christian faith for vengeance, betrayal or deception, and whatever else Hippolytus was or was not, he was surely a true believer.

Then again, hadn't she herself been deceiving the Church all along about her very identity? Nor had she ever confessed before any of its members her involvement in the plot to kill Commodus. Perhaps it was she who had never been a real Christian at all.

Certainly she wouldn't be able to remain one any longer. For before the sun came up tomorrow morning she would without a doubt have broken her vow of chastity. To commit such an appalling sin after baptism would render her excommunicate for ever.

On their arrival back at the palace Marcia expected to be taken before Commodus straight away. However, Cleander appraised her appearance with disdain and said, 'Do you really think he will want to see you looking and smelling like the wife of a sausage-seller? Make yourself presentable, woman. His Excellency will be informed of your safe return and you will be summoned when he is disposed to receive you.' Thereupon she was escorted back to the chambers she had left with such mixed feelings all those months ago. As the door opened and she looked once again upon the opulence of her palatial prison, it felt as if she had left it only yesterday, and her heart was as heavy as a millstone in her breast.

But then an incredulous voice pitched somewhere between a man's and a boy's was exclaiming, 'My lady? Lady Marcia? Oh, may every god in the heavens be praised!' and suddenly there was dear old Hyacinthus falling to his knees before her, clasping her hands and pressing his forehead against them. At first sight he looked none the worse for the ordeal to which she had subjected him, until she realized how much thinner he was than she remembered; perhaps it was just as well that he'd had plenty of surplus weight to lose. But when she opened her mouth to say how glad she was to see him, her voice failed her. So she merely held him tight against her and surveyed her surroundings with freshly falling tears.

Presently her handmaids appeared as well, and set gamely about undoing all the work which the widows had done to turn Marcia into Melissa. Now she didn't know whether to cry or laugh as the tangles were teased from her hair and the dust of the masons' workshop sloughed from her skin and scrubbed from her fingernails. Not that very much could be done about her nails' shape or shortness; with all the fetching and carrying and general housework Marcia had been doing of late she had scarcely needed to file them down to keep them looking like a peasant-woman's, or to rub the backs of her hands with pumice to roughen the skin. Though she wouldn't be fetching her own water from the public fountain or scouring cooking pots again any time soon, when the thought occurred to her it brought Marcia an unexpected rush of regret rather than relief.

Once the grime was gone, it was time for her hair and wrists and most intimate places to be anointed with His Excellency's favourite scent, and for her neck, arms, ankles and ears to be hung with the most flamboyant of the many jewels he had lavished upon her. But when one of her handmaids made off with Callistus' little wooden fish to discard it along with everything else which had belonged to Melissa, Marcia snatched it back with such ferocity that the girl squealed in alarm. Naturally Marcia would not wear it here in the palace, but she insisted on stowing it in one of the caskets reserved for her most precious things.

The slave-girls' handiwork had scarcely been completed when the imperial summons came. Marcia was escorted directly to Commodus' private chambers where so often she had been tormented, beaten, chased with a club or a whip, and almost as often worshipped like the goddess Venus herself. Now she closed her eyes as she tried to guess which of the many Commodi would be receiving her today.

But as she waited, sick with apprehension in his vestibule with her handmaids clustered behind her, she heard nothing from the emperor at all, neither reprimand nor curse nor greeting. Daring to open her eyes at last she found herself looking straight into those of a Commodus she had seen so rarely that she had almost ceased to believe in his existence.

For he stood there sober but smiling, dressed in the simplest of plain white tunics, his celebrated golden hair shining and his eyes alight. Like Hyacinthus he had shed surplus weight during her absence, and as he held out his arms towards her it was like being beckoned by a young Apollo in human flesh. In spite of everything her heart went out to him as it so often had, and without waiting any longer for him to speak she ran to him and they embraced one another like village sweethearts reunited after fickle fortune has wrenched them apart. As Marcia laid her head upon Commodus' shoulder he ordered her slave-girls and his own attendants to leave, then began smothering her perfumed hair with his kisses, murmuring as he did so, 'My beautiful Marcia, make me believe I'm not dreaming. I love you; I love you so much. I thought I would never see you again. I thought you were dead.'

'Oh my lord, you are not dreaming,' she said, but could barely get the words out of her mouth because Commodus had never before said that he loved her. It had only ever been, '*You* love *me*, don't you, Marcia?' or at best, 'I need you. Only you can make me happy.' Now her heart felt so light and yet so full, she could have believed it might tear itself free of its traces and burst right out of her body. To vent her euphoria she sought the emperor's lips with her own and kissed him with a hunger and a passion she had never experienced even for Eclectus. And if Commodus had swept her off her feet and flung her upon his bed with no further ceremony she would not merely have broken her vow of chastity with him quite willingly, but would have taken unbridled delight in its destruction, not caring that he had a wife and countless other concubines and catamites with whom he would doubtless have been cavorting all the time she had been away.

But he didn't sweep her onto his bed or impose himself upon her at all. Instead he fixed her with limpid eyes and whispered with disarming vulnerability, 'Oh Marcia, you didn't ever want to leave me, did you? You only left me because wicked men took you away.' Instantly the bubble of her happiness burst, reality rushed upon her like a surge of dirty water from a drain, and the deception and pretence began all over again.

'No, my lord,' she lied to him. 'You know I would never choose to leave you. Wicked men did kidnap me and ill-treat me, but good people found and rescued me and restored me to health, and thanks to them I am safe and we are together once more as we were always meant to be.'

Now at last he did sweep her up, not hungrily but tenderly, and as if she were a fragile doll he laid her with painstaking care upon the bed where in the past he had ravaged her like a common whore. Then he made love to her so gently, so considerately, that she wept and wept, and he took her tears for joy and her passivity for unconditional surrender.

Later, when he had spent himself inside her and lay with his head cradled in her arms, he said, 'Marcia, my darling, weep no more, for you shall be Empress of Rome.' And smiling blissfully, he fell fast asleep with his lips nuzzling her breast.

So innocent he looked as he lay there, she thought, and so beautiful – almost as innocent and beautiful as Callistus. Yet this was Commodus, who had had innumerable men and women put to death on the flimsiest of pretexts, on the faintest whiff of a rumour that they had been plotting to bring him down. So now he was minded to exalt *her* to imperial status too, but how could he do that when his wife Bruttia Crispina was Augusta already?

No, Marcia resolved, I will not even think about how he might be intending to accomplish it.

But what was there to think about instead? About Callistus, who hadn't been at Assembly on Sunday, and whom she would likely never see again? About Corvus and Junia, who had taken her into the bosom of their own family, and been cruelly beaten for their pains? About Clemens or Hermione, or the Orphan who had put their bold plans into action, or the many other good people whose names she did not even know, and yet who had risked their lives to snatch her from the clutches of an evil tyrant to whom she had now crawled back of her own free will?

No, there was nothing to be gained from thinking about these people either. The best thing she could do instead,

Marcia decided, was concentrate on retaining Commodus' love, on giving him the support he needed to build his sense of self-worth so that he would no longer need to torment or torture others or have them condemned for crimes they had never committed, just to make himself feel powerful and secure. Perhaps, just perhaps, she might be capable of curbing his worst excesses, and instead of relying vainly on Jesus' sacrifice to save her, she might atone for her own past crimes against Commodus by doing in future what was best for him and best for Rome as well.

But as Marcia sat with the sleeping tyrant's head held to her breast she vowed that she would never, ever forget the kindness of the Christians who had done their utmost to help her. If she did gain some influence over her imperial lover's actions, she would ensure that never again would the Church be persecuted as it had been under Nero or Domitian, or even sporadically in the time of Marcus Aurelius. Moreover she would do all that she could to secure the release of those Christians who even now languished in Rome's prisons as a result of the malicious accusations of individuals who hated them. Then it might even be conceivable that on the Day of Judgement God would pardon her after all and welcome her into his big high heaven. And if he did not, at least when the fires of hell consumed her, she would perish with the consolation that she had done a few good deeds in her worthless and otherwise wasted life.

CHAPTER SEVEN: CALLISTUS

'Push, you vermin. Push!' The curses of the foreman stung the slaves' ears as harshly as his whip lashed out across their backs, which were already bruised and bleeding.

Not that you could rightly see the sorry state they were in. It was much too dark to see anything at all most of the time except for the vague shape of the poor wretch in front of you as he grunted and sweated and struggled to dredge up some extra strength from the well of his misery. Round and round and round the men trudged like two-legged mules. But few muleteers would treat their beasts as brutally as a slave could expect to be treated once he'd been consigned to the treadmill.

The warehouse they worked in belonged to the state, and the slaves were a pitiful rabble of delinquents and runaways obliged to power the great grinding mill-wheel until they dropped, unless their masters saw fit to reclaim them. Each man's feet were chained to the shackles of the man in front of him, and he was also chained to his own spoke of the wheel, which ground away day after day making flour for the recipients of the corn dole, lifeline of the urban poor. As long as they were able to keep working, their masters were paid for their labour, but not enough to induce a master to hire out his slave to the treadmill for profit. The slaves were there to be punished, and it was their foreman's exquisite vocation to make sure that they didn't forget it.

Callistus had long since lost track of how many months he'd been there. He hadn't been sent to the treadmill right away after Carpophorus had had him hauled out of the sea like a speared squid. For a week or more he'd been imprisoned in the master's strongroom while Carpophorus sought some way of covering up the fiasco which threatened to heap disgrace on his own head. Finally he had chosen to give it out that Callistus had wilfully embezzled the funds for which he'd been made responsible because he was a dyed-in-the-wool deceiver who for years had duped his master into trusting him. Hence Callistus had been sentenced to the hell-hole in which he now found himself.

Not that 'sentenced' was quite the right word. There hadn't been any sort of trial. Callistus had been under no illusions; he was Carpophorus' property to be disposed of as he willed. And whilst Christian masters were actively discouraged from treating their slaves too roughly, there would undoubtedly be plenty of sympathy for the well-respected banker who had been so heinously taken for a ride – especially among those who had lost their savings.

Some folk would even be saying that Callistus should be kept where he was until he had earned Carpophorus enough money to pay everyone back. But Callistus knew full well that he wouldn't manage that in a lifetime – especially since life expectancy for a slave at the treadmill was notoriously short. On top of the gruelling labour and the whippings, there was the toxic, dust-laden atmosphere which gave you an incessant cough and made your eyes so red and swollen that they would neither shut nor fully open. So even when you were permitted a few hours' rest each night on a heap of rotting straw, it was almost impossible to sleep. You were much more likely to fall asleep on your feet as they tramped round all day one after the other, or over the bowl of sticky porridge you were given in the evening, which was made from murky water and the flour you'd been grinding yourself. Then there was the heat, often so stifling that it was better to go naked than wear the bristly tunic you'd been issued with.

But at least I am suffering for my own stupidity, Callistus had reminded himself time and again as he trudged; those poor people whose money I lost had done nothing to deserve the poverty they must now be facing on my account.

And he *was* suffering, badly, in body and in mind. Physically he was failing fast. Though he now had muscles where he was sure he'd had none before, they were more like tautened ropes under his skin than fleshy bulk. His back troubled him constantly, alternately smarting and aching so abominably that he could no longer stand up straight. His ankles were chafed raw from the iron rings which rubbed against them with every step. There were gruesome calluses on his hands and feet. His face was puffed up like a boxer's and he could hardly see even when the door was opened and a brief shaft of light spilled in. One side of his head had been shaven, like that of all his fellows, meaning that if they somehow contrived to escape it would be only too obvious where they had come from. So now half his head was bald whilst the other was covered with a dust-caked, louse-infested thatch. At least so far he hadn't been branded with the shameful syllable 'fug' in the middle of his forehead, unlike the man slogging round in front of him, who had tried to escape more than once. But if Callistus had been able to see well enough to glimpse his reflection in the cup of water they gave him in a morning, he certainly wouldn't have recognized the face looking back at him. Callistus, the Most Beautiful… even his nickname was nothing to him now but a sick joke.

As for his mind, this was more of a mess than his body. He was constantly tormented by a guilt which he dared not ask God to take away. Carpophorus had been at pains to impress upon him while he'd still been locked in the strongroom at home that Eleutherius the bishop had already declared him excommunicate for larceny and fraud.

'But I *haven't* committed fraud! I'm not a thief!' Callistus had shouted back through the air-holes in the door – all to no avail, because Carpophorus had retorted, 'No? Then what happened to the money deposited with you *after* you "lost" the fortune you had to start off with? Wasn't that still in this strongroom before you absconded? Because it's not there now, is it?' And Callistus had swallowed very hard, for indeed it was not. Most of it was at the bottom of Portus' harbour.

'Perhaps a few weeks on the treadmill will help you remember where it is, then,' Carpophorus had suggested as he dragged Callistus out of his temporary prison by the ear. 'And who knows, you might remember where you stashed the elders' chest as well, if you're kept there long enough. Don't forget to tell the mill master when you do, that's all, and I *may* come and release you. But don't expect Eleutherius to welcome you back with open arms. Fraud is a deadly sin in his book; there can be no absolution from the Church for that.'

One thing only had kept Callistus going as he ground his youth away in this dark deadly workplace: the gift he had for losing himself in his daydreams. He would pretend that he was working to win Marcia's hand in marriage, and he would picture her safe and happy in Corvus' and Junia's cottage taking care of their children and attending Assembly with them on Sundays. During the first few weeks of his punishment he had trained himself to count off the days so that he would know exactly when the Lord's Day was, and then he would spend it imagining that Marcia was missing him in the same way as he was missing her.

But he'd long since lost the capacity for counting. His once agile brain, which in the past had juggled with columns of figures as readily as it had conjured up dreams, felt as callused and misshapen as his body. Only the smiling picture of Marcia remained, and even that was growing fainter by the hour.

Suddenly Callistus tripped and fell over something large

and heavy bumping along in front of him. Dully he grasped that the fug-branded man he'd been following had collapsed at the wheel, which was now dragging him with it. The foreman's whip cracked out over the poor fellow's back and chanced to catch Callistus a glancing blow in the face. So he didn't notice at first that the door to their hell-hole had banged open and an order had been given for the milling to cease. The mill master had entered with a visitor in tow.

Sagging on his spoke, Callistus reminded himself to relish the respite for as long as it lasted. Then he heard the visitor's voice, and of its own accord his head jerked up. When he succeeded in blinking enough blood and pus from his eyes to see anything at all, he found himself face to face with Carpophorus.

Not that Carpophorus would have known Callistus from any of his workmates had the foreman not taken the trouble to point him out. Then after master and slave had stared at each other for some while with little more comprehension than a pair of punch-drunk brawlers in a tavern, Carpophorus' great eyebrows met momentarily above the bridge of his nose and a faint flicker passed across his features, though whether this twitch was a sign of pity, guilt or merely shock, it was too fleeting to tell. Finally he turned and nodded curtly to the mill master, who ordered the foreman to have Callistus released.

Afraid he must be asleep and dreaming on his feet, Callistus lolled in a daze as his shackles were removed and a spare tunic was pulled on over his head. Then he was dragged into the mill master's office behind Carpophorus, where the latter was promptly paid in coin for the work his slave had done. When the amount had been checked Callistus was led outside to be taken home.

Some derelict part of his brain had recovered itself enough to wonder vaguely why all this should be happening now, but then he was so dazzled by the midday sun as it blazed upon him that a wave of nausea knocked him to the ground. The next he knew, he was lying on a pile of rugs in a corner of

Carpophorus' kitchen where he'd been deposited like a mauled kitten found in the street. Once he'd groaned loudly enough to convince the kitchen slaves that he wasn't dead, he was stripped again and thrown in a tub of cold water to be scrubbed of his filth and fleas. Then the last of his hair was pared away, leaving him bald as Marcia's eunuch. But even this brisk and offhand treatment felt so much better than the treadmill that he wept with relief, scooping handfuls of the scummy bath water into his eyes.

Carpophorus strode in while he was still languishing stark naked, and bent over him officiously to see how he was scrubbing up. He almost jumped out of his skin when Callistus seized hold of both his hands and began kissing them and pressing them against his wet cheeks while an unintelligible stream of gratitude poured from lips as parched and cracked as his throat was.

'Well it wasn't my choice to release you, you may be sure of that,' Carpophorus barked back at him. 'Now get yourself dressed and report to me in my office an hour from now.' And with that he beat a hasty retreat.

Not his choice? Who else's could it have been? But the questions would scarcely form themselves coherently even in Callistus' mind. More asleep than awake he was hauled from the bath-tub and bundled into a fresh tunic and sandals, plain and meanly fashioned, but to Callistus they felt luxurious as Coan silk and calfskin. He was given food as well – barley-bread and hard cheese – but a state banquet thrown in his honour couldn't have been more welcome. Not to his stomach, however; so many months had gone past without its having to digest solid food that Callistus was violently sick and had to be washed and dressed and fed all over again. Then somehow he managed to stagger to Carpophorus' office, where the master took one look at him and said grudgingly, 'I think you had better be seated.'

Then while Callistus strove manfully to keep his head up and his food down, Carpophorus condescended to explain to him why he had been released. It certainly wasn't pity or any sense of justice which had led him to have his renegade slave brought home. Rather, pressure had been put on him by the elders of the Church to pay back the lost fortune himself since he was the one to whom they had entrusted it, and reluctantly Carpophorus had done so.

'But I fail to see why *I* should be paying for your gross misconduct any more than the paupers you bankrupted should have to,' he thundered, wagging a finger under Callistus' nose. 'And it would take me a century to recoup my losses from the pittance you've been earning me at the treadmill. Since your ordeal doesn't appear to have refreshed your memory as to where the treasure is buried, perhaps we shall have to conclude that you lent it to Shadrach after all. So now you must hunt him down and make *him* pay it back. You have one month, from today. Succeed, and it may be that I shall find you a place in my household once again – probably emptying buckets of night-soil. Fail, and you'll return to the treadmill until you die in harness, and long may you rot! Dismissed.'

Callistus was quite unable to respond. It took him all his time to push himself upright and feel his way back to the little room which had once been his refuge, because he knew that he wouldn't be capable of achieving anything at all until he'd had some rest. But when he got there he found that his quarters had been taken over by someone else so he had no choice but to stagger on to the place where the lowlier slaves were all billeted together. Here he collapsed in an unoccupied corner and slept the sleep of the dead.

When he awoke he had no idea what time or even what day it was, but finding himself quite alone he assumed that his fellow slaves must be going about their chores. He himself had one assignment only: to find Shadrach and call him to account, though there was no reason why this should be any more feasible now than it had been in the first place, except that this time round he would have rather longer to accomplish it. But the search couldn't begin until he'd regained some strength in his legs and the capacity to think without his mind fogging up like a mirror in a bathhouse.

So for the next few days he did little but eat and sleep, much to the annoyance of his comrades who clearly thought he should be doing the same work as the rest of them. Naomi must have thought so too; she glared at him with open hostility every time she was required to fill his food bowl. Callistus merely bowed his head to her in gratitude, since he was planning to start his search for Shadrach by interrogating *her*, once he felt up to talking to anyone.

Gradually the weals on his back stopped oozing and his raw red ankles stopped hurting, and the skin of his hands and feet grew softer as he rubbed them with grease he begged from the cooks when Naomi wasn't looking. Black stubble began to grow back on his head and the swelling round his eyes went down, so that when his vision cleared enough for him to make out his own reflection in the impluvium it was considerably less hideous than it would have been a week before. Eventually he decided that the time had come for him to embark upon his quest, since his life was going to depend on it.

Quizzing Naomi got him nowhere. She folded her arms and informed him that Shadrach had been the master's acquaintance, not hers; how would *she* know where he was? So putting on a cap to hide his stubble – it was becoming increasingly common for Jewish men to wear these all the time, and Carpophorus had several – he went directly to Shadrach's house in Trans Tiberim.

Here all was exactly as it had been on his previous visit, except that now there *was* graffiti daubed across the shutters: nasty anti-Jewish graffiti, since Shadrach's place was in a Gentile part of town. Callistus made Trans Tiberim's Jewish quarter his second port of call, but here too the outcome was the same as before. No one had seen Shadrach ben Abner, and no one had any idea where he was. Next he called upon as many clients of Carpophorus as he could turn up, Jewish and Gentile, Christian and pagan, in every part of the City. Many were surprisingly sympathetic. But none gave him even the faintest lead to follow, until when Callistus had all but abandoned hope a Jewish dealer in salves and ointments whom he recognized as a catechumen from the Assembly said to him, 'I'm sorry, my friend, I really do wish I could help you. But I know of someone who might. Tobias ben Joseph, the apothecary, is Shadrach's cousin. If *anyone* knows where he is, it'll be Tobias.'

Thanking the dealer profusely, Callistus headed straight for the apothecary's premises back in Trans Tiberim. He knew Tobias by sight, having been sent to buy things from him more than once, and he realized on reflection that Tobias and Shadrach did look quite alike.

But Tobias' servants strenuously denied that their master was at home; and even if he had been, they said, he wouldn't want to talk to anyone about Shadrach. Frustrated and despairing, Callistus dragged himself back to Carpophorus' house and curled himself up in his corner, falling into a fitful sleep.

The next day turned out to be a Sunday. When Callistus awoke, most of the other slaves were readying themselves to accompany their master to Assembly, but nothing was said about Callistus going with them. As an excommunicate he wasn't barred from the first part of the service, though few of those permanently excluded from the second part ever went. It didn't seem to have occurred to anyone that Callistus might want to.

But Callistus was thinking: maybe, just maybe, there might be an acquaintance of Shadrach's there to whom I haven't yet spoken, who might know *something*, and be ashamed to lie to me in front of his fellow believers? And even if everyone else *does* snub me, surely at least Hippolytus must be sorry he betrayed me, and think I have been punished enough? And Marcia... even though she reckoned me hopelessly naïve to trust Shadrach when I didn't know him – as indeed I was – surely she of all people won't drive me away?

So he went to Carpophorus and asked if he might join the party going to Assembly. Carpophorus gawped as though he'd been hit on the head by a slingstone, and agreed.

As soon as they crossed the threshold of Piso and Valeria's home Callistus began to wish he hadn't come. Many of the people he recognized looked right through him as though they didn't know who he was – which perhaps they did not. Of those who plainly did, the majority turned hurriedly away, especially when Carpophorus fixed them with his most irascible glare.

Once the service had begun, Callistus took to scouring the teeming throng for a glimpse of either Marcia or Hippolytus, but for a long time could not locate either. At length he spotted Hippolytus and even managed to catch his eye, but Hippolytus' expression was as forbidding as Carpophorus'; was it possible that even *he* didn't know who Callistus was? Of Marcia there was still no sign, though he did see Corvus and Junia and their children, all in their customary good spirits. Might this mean that there was nothing unusual in her not being with them? This disconcerting thought caused a horrible griping to start deep down in Callistus' stomach. As a result, when the time came for him to leave with the catechumens and penitents he was frankly relieved, and sat down in an alcove all by himself feeling shivery and sick to await the end of the service.

To his surprise the dealer in salves approached him almost at once and asked him if he was all right. When Callistus shook his head the man sat down beside him and said, 'Don't be despondent, Callistus. Our Lord will help you with your quest if justice is on your side. Be of good cheer, and put your trust in him.' Not rightly knowing what to say to this, Callistus just nodded and smiled weakly, so the man got up again and went on his way. Callistus closed his eyes and wrapped his arms more tightly around his belly.

As he sat there and shivered, he tried to think more about Hippolytus and less about Marcia. At least Hippolytus was here; if Callistus could intercept him before he left, he could perhaps have another go at explaining that he might be a fool but he wasn't a criminal. Perhaps he could even reassure himself that it hadn't been Hippolytus who had given him away to Carpophorus in the first place. He decided to begin by apologizing to his old friend for assuming the worst of him all this time.

So when the service was over and Hippolytus duly appeared, Callistus got up and planted himself in his path, but it became immediately obvious that Hippolytus hadn't the faintest idea who he was.

'Hippos, it's me. Callistus!' exclaimed Callistus in exasperation, presuming to take hold of his old friend by the forearm. But Hippolytus started as though he'd been touched by a leper, and shook Callistus away, attempting to push past him as he did so.

'Please Hippos, wait. I only wanted to say I was sorry – '

'Sorry?' At length Hippolytus condescended to engage with Callistus but was in no mood for conciliation. '*Sorry*, you thieving hypocrite? It's no use your apologizing to *me*, is it? It's not me you have ruined. What about the poor wretches whose savings you embezzled? What about Carpophorus whose trust you betrayed? What about the elders, the Church, what about Christ himself whose name you have blackened, whose reputation you have dragged through the mud – '

'I didn't embezzle anything! I *told* you what happened! *I'm* the one who was cheated!'

'Really? Then why did you try to commit suicide by jumping into the sea as soon as justice caught up with you? I think everything you told me was a pack of lies. You *hid* the money, and the mind boggles where it is now.'

'But that's not how it was! I wasn't trying to kill myself!'

'No? Then why didn't you wait to stand trial and prove your innocence?'

'Slaves don't *get* trials, Hippos. They get *tortured*.'

'As well they might, because most of them are liars just like you are! Besides, you had already admitted your guilt by absconding in the first place.'

'That's not why I ran away, and you know it. We've been friends half our lives; how could you *think* like this of me? You *must* know me better than that!'

All the time they had been arguing, their voices had been getting louder and the pitch rising higher; by now a ring of astonished faces surrounded them. Slave and patrician became aware of this in the same moment; Hippolytus dropped his voice to a whisper and said, 'I thought I knew you, Callistus, but I was wrong. You're not my friend, not any more; I should have realized. In Christ there may be neither slave nor free when it comes to rights and responsibilities. But you're a slave to the core, just as your mongrel parents were before you. You're a liar with no conscience, a dog concerned only to preserve its mangy hide.' Whereupon Hippolytus turned his back on Callistus quite literally, his pristine white toga whirling round after him. Then he stalked away through the crowd, which parted hastily to let him through.

Callistus, left in the centre of the ring with so many eyes boring into him, sank down on his haunches with his arms held over his head, too wretched even to weep. For a long time no one went near him. Then he felt a steadying arm go round his back, and looked up into the crinkled face of Zephyrinus.

'Come,' the unassuming elder said softly, yet that single syllable seemed to encapsulate all the compassion in the world. Slowly he helped Callistus to his feet and led him away in search of a place where prying eyes would not follow them; the look in Zephyrinus' own eyes defied anyone to interfere. And the fact that these no longer saw as clearly as they once had offered him welcome protection from any disapproving glances.

'Don't be afraid, little prince,' he said, when he had found a bench in a secluded spot in the courtyard garden where they could sit down side by side. 'God knows your heart much better than Hippolytus does. And even if you *had* stolen all that money on purpose he would forgive you.'

But Callistus only laughed a bitter laugh and retorted, 'Then why won't his people?'

'My poor boy, if only it were all so simple.' Zephyrinus gave a sigh which came from a deep, deep place down inside him. 'But you should know that the belief that there can be but a single remission for life's most grievous sins, and none at all for such that are committed after baptism, is not found in our holy scriptures. It comes from a book called The Shepherd of Hermas, which does not carry the authority of any apostle.'

Callistus was taken aback. This was so unlike anything he might have expected Zephyrinus to say just then that he found himself asking, less bitterly now, 'Then why does the Church follow its teachings?'

'Because of the terrible persecutions which our fathers endured in days gone by. Because men and women who claimed to be Christians were rushing to sacrifice to the emperor to avoid being thrown to the lions, and then expecting to be forgiven and reinstated as soon as the danger was past, when others had gone to their deaths for what they believed. How could those who had lost their nearest and dearest to martyrdom be expected to welcome back apostates as though nothing had changed? And what would prevent a shameless adulterer compromising one woman after another and "repenting" after each misdeed, if absolution were so easy to come by?'

'But no true Christian would behave like that.'

'No, indeed he would not. But not everyone who attends the Assembly *is* a true Christian, Callistus. It is because of unscrupulous wolves who roam among the sheep that the doctrine of deadly sins has developed. The Church does not presume to claim that God himself will never forgive you, but our bishop Eleutherius does not believe that *he* – or any other human being – has the right to pardon you on the Almighty's behalf.'

'I don't understand. Didn't Jesus tell his disciples that what they bound on earth would be bound in heaven? Hippolytus told me that once. But instead it's *sin* that binds us! Even someone who tells a rude joke or contradicts an elder must go around dressed in sackcloth with ash on his forehead and be told off in public by the bishop before he can be restored to communion. It seems all wrong.'

Zephyrinus sighed again and patted Callistus on the arm. 'Even our Lord Jesus himself told the woman taken in adultery to "Go and sin no more." We don't know what he would have said if he'd met her afterwards and found out that she'd gone on sleeping with other men as if their conversation had made no difference to her at all. The Church is meant to be changing lives, not condoning the sort of wrongdoing which leads only to despair. I just wish I knew better how we are supposed to go about it. Jesus told Nicodemus that he must be born again, yet so few in the Church today seem to be living regenerate lives.'

For some while Callistus said nothing in response to this, even though Zephyrinus had stopped speaking and briefly looked almost as despondent as Callistus felt. Then Callistus ventured in a whisper, 'But how does someone *get* reborn? How do you know if you *are*?'

Zephyrinus rallied visibly, finding himself on firmer ground. 'To be reborn is to surrender yourself without reservation to God the Father, to ask his Son to be your Saviour and his Holy Spirit to come and dwell within you. This is what baptism is meant to be about. It's as though your old self is washed away along with all your sins, and you rise from the water a wholly new person. Only *you* know whether you have surrendered your life to God and let him light the flame of his love within you. Only you and God know if that flame is growing brighter each day and burning away the residue of your old pre-Christian self. Only you know if God dwells in your innermost being.'

Once more Callistus fell silent. He was pretty sure that none of what Zephyrinus had been talking about had ever happened to him, but when Zephyrinus touched his arm again gently and asked him what he was thinking, he said, 'I don't know, Zephyrinus. I don't think I understand anything. All I can remember is Ma... Melissa telling me that Jesus said we should forgive one another seventy times seven... Zephyrinus, where *is* Melissa? Why isn't she here?'

Zephyrinus said resignedly, 'You mean Marcia, I suppose.'

Callistus stared. 'You knew?'

'Everyone knows now, because she has gone back to him.'

'Gone back to whom?'

'To Commodus. The emperor. That's why she's not here.'

'No. No, I don't believe it.' In all the time they had been talking, Callistus had forgotten how ill he'd been feeling when he had walked out of the Assembly meeting with the catechumens and penitents. Now he went hot and cold all over, and shook Zephyrinus' hand away from his arm as a man with a fever will toss off a blanket. 'Commodus is a monster,' he insisted. 'He used to beat her. She was frightened to death of him. She took a vow – '

'All of which may be true, but it doesn't alter the fact that she is his mistress once again, fully restored to his favour.' Zephyrinus shifted his position on their hard stone seat. 'Melissa disappeared from our meetings at exactly the same time as the kidnapped imperial concubine Marcia was declared to have been found, and all kinds of entertainments and special Games were staged as a result. At that point Hermione, Corvus and Junia felt it right to tell the Church the truth. All three of them were heartbroken, but assured us that it had been her own choice to return to her former life. I doubt that Commodus would have welcomed her back so readily had it *not* been, but she appeared with him in public at the Games even though he is married to another woman;

Marcia was decked out like an empress while Bruttia Crispina was nowhere to be seen. Moreover Marcia's step-father has been given a priesthood, so it seems that Commodus is falling over backwards to please her now that they are back together. I'm sorry, Callistus, but it seems that Marcia is not the person that *either* of us thought she was. And now she is excommunicate just like you.'

Now they both fell silent for what seemed like a very long time. Then Callistus said in a small, choked voice, 'If you want to know what I'm thinking *now*, I'm thinking that no merciful God could send a defenceless woman back to live with a monster, however it came about. Nor would he exclude anyone as good-hearted as Marcia from his presence. Either God is not merciful, or there *is* no God.'

Zephyrinus opened his mouth to reply, but no words came out of it. Instead he put an arm around Callistus' shoulders, which Callistus was now too far past caring to be bothered to push away. Then as they sat there in desolate if companionable silence, they were startled to be approached by Hippolytus, who stopped dead in his tracks when he saw them. Making no attempt to disguise his disgust, Hippolytus bolted without saying a word.

'I should go too,' Callistus said, feeling suddenly sicker than ever. 'I don't want to get you into trouble as well.'

'You need not concern yourself on my account,' Zephyrinus reassured him, but withdrew his arm all the same. 'I am much too old to worry about getting into trouble any more.' And his eyes said: it's obvious that you have troubles enough for both of us already.

'It's all right. The service must have been over for ages by now; Carpophorus will be looking for me. That's if he hasn't gone home without me.' Callistus got up, though his head was swimming and everything around him was a blur. 'Don't worry, Zephyrinus,' he said, as the elder seemed about to say something else. 'I won't be coming to Assembly any more. I won't embarrass you again.' And he stumbled away, hoping only that his master would find him before he passed out altogether.

To his intense relief this wish at least was granted. But he must have looked as sick as he felt, because rather than letting him tag along behind the rest of the party, Carpophorus had two of the other slaves steer him home with their elbows through his.

Callistus fell at once upon his pallet and pulled a blanket over his head. It felt as heavy as all the sin and suffering of the world, and he was sure he would never be able to stand up again. He didn't even want to. He wanted nothing more than to lie there in darkness and solitude until he died. He wished he *had* died, when he had jumped into the sea in Portus' harbour, just as Hippolytus believed he'd been intending to do all along.

But even if he refused all requests to get up or see anyone or even to eat, Callistus knew that ultimately the master wouldn't allow him to lie there on his floor and starve himself to death. For not only would this be of no avail in recovering the lost money, but it would deprive Carpophorus permanently of another valuable asset. A slave who could read and count and balance books was worth a pretty penny in good condition, and Carpophorus would have to dig deep into his own pockets once again to purchase, house and train a replacement capable of taking on the kind of role he had evidently intended for Callistus. No; if Callistus did not find Shadrach and the money, he would certainly be sent to the slave-market long before he died of hunger. He was another man's property, and didn't even have the right to take his own life.

He might be able to take a knife from the kitchens, though, and slit his wrists before anyone could stop him. Or he might even manage to acquire poison from somewhere, which would enable him to lie down and die after all, very much sooner than waiting until he starved. Shadrach's cousin, Tobias ben Joseph... he was an apothecary! There was something grimly ironic about this thought, which unexpectedly mitigated Callistus' despair.

Suddenly, while he was reflecting upon it, a fresh idea occurred to him. The synagogue! If Tobias was a Jew but not a Christian, then surely he would be at synagogue on the coming Sabbath? If Callistus went *there* and confronted him, surely Tobias would have no choice but to speak to him? Then even if he would not divulge the whereabouts of his cousin, he might at least be prevailed upon to sell Callistus some of his wares...

Finding this gruesome chain of thought oddly reassuring, Callistus fell promptly into a deep and dreamless sleep, from which he did not fully awaken for several days. Afterwards he was told that he'd had a serious bout of fever, brought on no doubt by the exertions, worries and shocks with which he'd been contending since his release from the treadmill when he had been so weak and worn down to begin with.

At least it meant that the Sabbath came around more swiftly for him than it might have done otherwise. When Saturday morning arrived, he got up at the crack of dawn feeling clearer in the head than he had felt for many months, and prepared to present himself at the synagogue.

Not that this was as straightforward as he'd supposed it might be; he had learnt from Naomi that there was more than one synagogue in Trans Tiberim alone. But the largest congregation met in a building just around the corner from Tobias' shop, so he would just have to bank on this being the one which Tobias attended.

He made sure he was there well before the service was due to begin. It was obvious to Callistus that he had found the right building because even from the outside its appearance was distinctive; on account of official dispensation to practise their religion without interference, the Jews did not need to be particularly secretive about where they met. The synagogue was set back from the street, and there was a monumental gateway with four marble pillars at the entrance to its grounds, with a well to draw water for ritual washing.

Though Callistus had taken the precaution of wearing a prayer-cap and shawl to walk through the Jewish Quarter this Sabbath morning, he could not risk loitering visibly outside a synagogue of which everyone would know he was not a member, so he hid himself just inside the gateway behind the wall which adjoined it, where there were some scrubby bushes ideal for seeing without being seen.

He was in no doubt that he would recognize Tobias as soon as he saw him. But as the men started to arrive – there were few women with them – none remotely resembled the one he was looking for. At least none of those passing saw him; they were too intent upon their conversations, apart from the more pious among them who were lost in their own holy thoughts. As more and more of them passed by and went into the synagogue building, Callistus began to feel the butterflies stirring once more in his stomach, and a thin film of sweat dewed his brow.

After a while the stream of congregants became a trickle, and at length dried up altogether. Still there had been no sign of the apothecary. Watching a steward looking about for stragglers before shutting the door, Callistus held his breath and froze still as a statue lest any movement on his part attract the man's attention. But he couldn't do anything to stop his heart sinking like a stone as he watched the fellow disappear inside and the door begin closing behind him.

Suddenly two men came bustling through the gateway from the street, and they quickened their pace still more as they saw that they were in danger of being too late. One of them was Tobias the apothecary, and the other was his cousin, Shadrach ben Abner himself.

Momentarily Callistus was too stunned to react. He'd been led to believe that Shadrach had been disowned by the Jewish community entirely, as well he deserved to be. But such a golden opportunity to confront him was not to be wasted. Gathering the remnants of his courage, Callistus burst from his hiding place and ran ahead of the startled cousins, positioning himself squarely between them and the door for which they were aiming.

'Shadrach!' he called out in the most authoritative voice he could muster. 'You *have* to speak to me. You have been avoiding me ever since you missed our meeting.'

But Shadrach evidently felt no such compulsion. 'How dare you address me in this manner? Get out of my way at once!' he ordered him, thrusting him bodily to one side as he did so. 'I will see you tomorrow; surely even an ignorant puppy like you knows that no son of Abraham can do business on the Sabbath.'

'No, you'll see me now!' Callistus persisted, once more blocking Shadrach's path to the door. 'I have searched the whole City to find you. I shan't let you out of my sight until I get justice!'

'It is sacrilege to pollute the Lord's house with worldly trifles on his holy day!' Tobias muscled in to lend weight to his cousin's cause. 'You are a common slave! Be gone, before we have you flogged!'

'No, I shall *not* be gone!' Callistus shouted back, compounding his impropriety by seizing both men by their forearms and hanging on for grim death despite their strenuous efforts to swat him away. By now their altercation had been heard inside the building, and the door flew open again as several burly members of the synagogue staff issued forth to find out why their preparations for the morning service had been interrupted. Two of them succeeded in freeing Shadrach and Tobias from Callistus' grasp; they took hold of him firmly but not brutally, doing their best to calm him down and prevail upon him to leave quietly without causing further offence.

But Callistus was in no mood to be calmed down, and was way beyond caring who he offended. Yelling, 'This man Shadrach is a thief! It's *he* who is polluting your synagogue with his wickedness! He stole my money! He tried to ruin my master too, who is as much a son of Abraham as any of you! He robbed innocent widows and orphans of every penny they owned!' he writhed and kicked and lashed out with his fists until his two captors could no longer restrain him. Two more hastened to their assistance, and soon all four of them had hold of him, one to each limb.

By now most of the rest of the congregation was outside again as well, all talking and gesticulating once their initial shock at the spectacle had been overcome. Some were asking who Callistus was, whilst others were maintaining that it did not matter; whoever he was, he should be flogged. Then someone – it might have been Tobias – shouted out, 'I know exactly who he is. He's Carpophorus' slave, a Christian. He is trying to disrupt a legitimate licensed meeting to make converts for his illegal cult. Take him to the City Prefect. This is a capital offence.'

'No!' Callistus screamed, lashing out more wildly than ever. He wouldn't have cared remotely any more about being condemned to death on the spot, if it had meant that he would be beheaded or stabbed through the heart with a sword. But as a slave he would be tortured for the sheer hell of it until he confessed to whatever anyone accused him of. After that he would likely be crucified or thrown to wild animals in Commodus' arena, where Marcia would probably witness them tearing him to shreds. She might even enjoy it.

So he was ranting and raving half out of his senses by the time he was dragged before Fuscianus the City Prefect, who would no doubt start by forcing him to sacrifice to the emperor's statue. Thus apostasy would be added to the sorry list of crimes of which Callistus was already reckoned to be guilty.

CHAPTER EIGHT: MARCIA

The early morning sun poured in through Marcia's window as she ate her breakfast alone. It was a light breakfast, just bread and a few olives, though she knew she could have requested anything that took her fancy – oysters, quails' eggs, peacocks' tongues – and it would have been brought to her hotfoot on a silver platter. Outside, the palace gardens were alive with birdsong, and bright water raced along artificial rills or danced skywards in sparkling fountains. Indoors Marcia's handmaids were busy setting out the utensils and cosmetics they would need later to arrange her hair and paint her face. She could look forward to having the rest of the morning to herself, but in the afternoons she would invariably receive a deluge of visitors – most of whom would be coming to ask her to secure some boon for them from the emperor – so she always had to look her best. While the handmaids worked, Hyacinthus pottered about watering plants and arranging flowers, and attempting to distract the smallest and most recent addition to Marcia's entourage, a small boy known as Ursulus.

This wasn't the child's real name. It meant 'Little Bear' and was a pet name given him by Commodus on account of his dimpled chubbiness and shock of rust-red hair. Commodus doted on him and spoiled him outrageously. He still had no children of his own.

If only Commodus would act more like a father towards him... it was true that the boy was being brought up with every possible privilege. But no father Marcia knew would show affection for his son in the sort of way Commodus showed his. Nor would any right-thinking father have his son run around naked all the time except for jangling clusters of great golden bangles and anklets.

Just now, Ursulus was doing his best to climb onto Marcia's lap while she was eating. He loved her, as all children seemed to, and it was impossible for her not to love him back, because she missed Corvus and Junia's children so keenly. It was such a relief to hear on a regular basis from Clemens that her adoptive family was still safe, and the children happy, and that so far Cleander seemed to have kept his promise to leave them be. Also Marcia liked to think that she could be a positive and normalizing influence in Ursulus' sickeningly twisted little life.

Yet she could not help but see the face of the child's real father reflected in those innocent features. For notwithstanding the mop of rich russet hair he must have got from his mother – whoever she had been – Ursulus' father was Cleander himself: erstwhile Phrygian slave, erstwhile royal chamberlain, now supreme commander of the Praetorian Guard.

Cleander's official title was 'Bearer of the Dagger', a position created by Commodus uniquely for him, by virtue of which he outranked both of the commanders already in post. Praetorian commanders had historically been appointed in pairs, like the consuls, lest too much power become concentrated in the hands of a single man. Inevitably one wound up dominating the other. But Cleander had succeeded in destroying two of these pre-eminent commanders in succession: a certain Atilius Albutianus, and before him the infamous Perennis who had once been the apple of the emperor's eye much as Cleander was now.

So it was scarcely surprising that Cleander had little time to spare for his dimple-cheeked son. He was much too busy selling military commissions, seats in the Senate and even consulships to the highest bidder, to fill his own coffers and keep Commodus in the eye-watering luxury which he reckoned his due.

Marcia at last got Ursulus settled in her lap in such a way that she could contrive to finish her breakfast. He lolled there sucking his thumb like a baby - though she guessed he was going on four years old - and fixed her unwaveringly with his big brown eyes. At once she found herself dreaming, as she so often did, that she was a simple married woman like Junia, and that the little boy was hers. Yet even though her vow of chastity had been shattered, she still couldn't bring herself to contemplate carrying a child for Commodus. Oh, he had been kindness and generosity incarnate since Cleander had brought her back to him, and it was true that any child they had together was likely to be as beautiful as Apollo or Venus. But she would not bring a new life into the world to have it ruined like Ursulus'.

Then, as she sat smiling wistfully into Ursulus' upturned face, a messenger came from the emperor to say that Marcia must dress immediately and formally and present herself before him. She was required to be in attendance at court this morning while Commodus delivered judgement in a most disturbing case.

Marcia was baffled, and at once deeply suspicious. Commodus scarcely ever dispensed justice himself, though in theory any one of his subjects might request his intervention in a legal dispute, and any Roman citizen condemned to death had the right to appeal to him in person. As for Commodus summoning *her* to be present... she could not begin to imagine what all this was about.

Easing the reluctant Ursulus out of her lap she submitted

herself to her handmaids' ministrations. Deftly they piled up her hair, coloured her eyelids, cheeks and lips in the way His Excellency liked them, swathed her in the robes he'd most recently given her and loaded her with his jewellery. Meanwhile Ursulus was whining and getting under foot and pleading, 'Take me with you, Auntie Marcia. I want to see Uncle Commodus too.' In the end she agreed, for Ursulus was the one person Commodus never got angry with. And with any luck, if the emperor had fallen prey to some dark and dangerous mood, the boy's antics might put him in a better humour.

Commodus' messenger had waited patiently to escort them into the imperial presence. But they were not taken to the aula regia, the emperor's audience hall in the public part of the palace, or to any court room, or even to one of the many reception rooms in which His Excellency was wont to entertain his visitors. Instead they were led to his most private apartment, where they found him sitting incongruously on a curule chair. This was a glorified cross-legged stool, of the kind which magistrates had traditionally occupied when presiding over trials. Beside it was another exactly the same, and with an exaggerated sweep of his arm Commodus indicated that Marcia herself should be seated upon it.

She did as she was bidden, all the time striving to fathom his mood while keeping her eyes averted. For the bizarre situation in which she now found herself was even more irregular than Commodus' escorting her to the Games, which had also happened on a number of occasions since her return to the palace. But Ursulus ran to the emperor without reservation, gurgling in delight as Commodus swung him up onto his knee and fondled him, tickling and nuzzling his chubby pink flesh in intimate play.

Then Commodus turned his attention back to Marcia, exclaiming in a gush of emotion that she looked lovelier than a goddess and was unquestionably a woman without peer on earth or in heaven. 'And it is especially appropriate that you have brought this delightful little boy with you today, my darling,' he finished up as she acknowledged his compliments with a forced smile. 'For my point will be made all the more exquisitely when in due course I am constrained to say in the presence of this court something which no emperor of Rome should *ever* have to admit to another living soul.'

Marcia inclined her head and contrived to keep smiling. So far the court to which he referred consisted of no one but the emperor, his manservants, herself and Ursulus.

Soon after this, however, with a great banging of doors and barking of commands, Cleander the Bearer of the Dagger strode in, huger and more loathsome than ever in his brazen military finery. But he was not alone, Slight as a wood-sprite in his shadow walked Bruttia Crispina, the emperor's wife – the Augusta – who could not have looked more terrified.

Marcia's breath caught in her throat as she realized that it was Crispina herself who awaited the emperor's judgement. When Commodus signed to Cleander that the Augusta was to be brought forward, Cleander obliged so zealously that she fell sideways to her knees at her husband's feet. Ursulus' eyes went very wide; from his vantage point on the emperor's lap he was staring at his father in horrified fascination, though he had made no attempt to call out or approach him.

Commodus did not bid his wife rise, but said while regarding her distastefully, 'You see, my dear Marcia, I wanted you to understand fully why it was that I missed you so dreadfully when you were taken from me, and why I love you so passionately now. It is because this woman who was meant to be my empress has made me so unhappy.' Here Commodus struck an embarrassingly tragic pose before continuing, 'Throughout our marriage she has done nothing but disappoint me, never loving me as I needed or deserved, and never giving me a son. For it should be my own little boy playing here in my lap, not that of another man! And now to cap it all, Marcia my darling, she has been found guilty of adultery. She has betrayed me – cuckolded me! – me, not only her rightful lord and husband, but master of half the world, and with a baseborn peasant not worthy of washing my feet.'

Of course the hypocrisy of this outburst was lost on none of those present except Ursulus. Least of all was it lost on Bruttia Crispina, who had ventured to raise her head and was now gazing through a tangle of unkempt hair not at Commodus but at Marcia, with a smouldering mixture of misery, envy, hatred and disbelief. Nor was Marcia under any illusions about the inviolability of her own position. It could so easily have been *her* cowering there on the receiving end of Commodus' wrath. 'Well?' demanded Commodus, 'Have you nothing to say?' And Marcia started in astonishment upon realizing that these words too were directed not at Crispina but at her.

'I, my lord?' she faltered. 'But what would you have me say? Surely it is for the noble Augusta to speak, to be given a chance to defend herself against this most grievous of accusations.'

'*Defend* herself? We are not here to *try* her but to *sentence* her, my dearest, for she has confessed to her crime already. Haven't you, you despicable whore?'

At this, Crispina broke down in a torrent of tears, nodding her head and clutching at her hair with white-knuckled hands. Marcia had no idea whether she was guilty as charged or not; and even if she was, who could have blamed her? But it was more than likely that she was not.

Commodus, however, looking down his nose at his wife more scornfully than ever, went back to addressing his comments to Marcia. 'I thought you might like to impress upon her how wicked she is, that is all,' he explained loftily, 'since I understand that your new friends the Christians view adultery with the same uncompromising severity as did the most pious and strait-laced of our Roman ancestors such as Cato the Censor or Augustus the first and noblest of our emperors.'

Marcia froze. Cold sweat had broken out on her brow and

it was all she could do to steady her hands, which she had so far kept modestly folded in her lap, let alone speak. What was Commodus implying? Of course he must know that she favoured the Christians; for months she had been championing their rights exactly as she had resolved to. But could he know more? She became acutely conscious that Cleander was staring right at her; had *he* been learning more about her too? His cruelty was as legendary as his corruption, and his hatred for her was deepening by the day.

But whatever was she to say? According to the teachings of the Church a man's adulterous relationships were no less sinful than a woman's – certainly *not* a view shared by the pagan moralists of old – and Commodus had lain with any number of men, women and children since marrying Bruttia Crispina. In the end Marcia looked straight into Commodus' eyes and said, 'My lord, I do not understand how anyone could wish to hurt you, when you desire one thing only of those to whom you are close, namely that they love you from the depths of their hearts.'

Thankfully Commodus seemed to find this response profoundly satisfactory. Having smiled at her beatifically he turned back to Crispina and declared, 'Since you have confessed to the crime of adultery with your own tainted lips, I should be perfectly justified in having you strangled on the spot. But lest it ever be said that the Emperor Commodus is not merciful, I shall content myself with the customary punishment for adultery prescribed by my ancestors. I hereby divorce you, and banish you in perpetuity to the island of Capri. Now be gone from my sight before I change my mind.'

Cleander promptly dragged the sobbing woman to her feet and led her away.

Marcia bowed her head once again and tried not to register her relief at Cleander's departure. Privately she was wondering how long Crispina would be allowed to live on Capri before someone was sent from the palace to have her put quietly out of her misery. And she was reflecting that nothing had been said regarding the punishment or even the identity of Crispina's partner in crime. Overtly she waited in demure silence for Commodus to give her leave to return to her apartment.

But Commodus had something very different in mind. Leaning towards her and stretching out one hand, he laid it gently but firmly over both of Marcia's, which were still clamped together in her lap, and said, 'Now, my darling, it will be for *you* to give me the son and heir I need.'

'My lord?' Marcia whispered, venturing to look again into his face. He was gazing at her in apparent rapture, his pupils so dilated that his eyes seemed black as caves.

'What is the matter, dearest Marcia?' he asked her with a disarming smile; his grip on her hands grew tighter. 'You cannot mean to say you don't *want* to be Empress of Rome?'

'I beg your pardon, my lord, but for that to happen, or for me to provide you with a legitimate heir, you and I would have to be married.'

'Married?' Instantly his pupils shrank and his grip on her hands became tight enough to hurt. 'Oh no, Marcia dear. I shall never again be married, for marriage has brought me nothing but anguish. But *any* son of mine will be recognized as my heir, if that is what I choose to make him.' Then he pushed Ursulus out of the way and moved to kneel on the floor in front of her like a slave before his owner, with his splendid purple robes pooling about him. Winding both of his arms round Marcia's neck he murmured, 'Come, my darling. Let us make an heir for our glorious empire here and now.' And he sought her lips with his own, while the arms he had wrapped around her shifted their position so he could begin to undo the pins that fastened her garments with a skill born of regular practice.

Marcia stammered, 'Now, my lord? Here? But your official duties... it's the middle of the morning... what about Ursulus? Aren't you forgetting *him?*'

'Ursulus?' repeated Commodus between kisses. 'He needs

to learn how babies are made soon enough. Not to mention what being a man is all about.' Somehow contriving to shed his own outer garments without allowing Marcia to escape, clad only in the meagrest of tunics he sought to straddle her right there where she sat on her curule chair.

Marcia did her best to stave him off but knew from long experience that it was futile. Crowing, 'How it excites me when you fight me, my Amazon queen!' His Excellency toppled her backwards from the stool and pinned her down beneath him on the hard mosaic floor.

By the time it was over, her dazzling dress was ruined, and pearls, emeralds and sapphires from her necklaces and bracelets were rolling away under the furniture because their delicate golden chains had snagged and broken. There were gashes on her breasts where Commodus' hands had clawed them, and blood dripped from one of her ears where his teeth had torn an earring from its lobe. Her whole body from the waist downwards hurt so badly that she could find neither the strength nor the will to extricate herself from His Excellency's embrace even though he had fallen noisily asleep on top of her, Hercules exhausted by his labours. She simply lay numbly underneath him, until two of his manservants saw fit to haul their master off to put him to bed.

At first she was still unable to move. Eventually, having pushed herself up on to hands and knees, Marcia began to crawl without thinking towards the door by which she and Ursulus had been escorted into the imperial presence. But before she could reach it Commodus had revived enough in his retreating servants' arms to call out after her, '*Now* who's forgetting little Ursulus? You surely can't leave without *him!*' And he was still laughing at this pathetic apology for wit as the servants dumped him on his bed and left him to sleep off his heroic exertions.

For a long time after that, Marcia crouched on the floor without attempting to crawl any further. The wreckage of her elaborate coiffure hung down in front of her eyes, a mass of tangles just like Crispina's. Then she felt a timid but insistent pulling on the remnants of her dress, and looked up through her hair to see Ursulus staring round-eyed at her naked breasts. Bursting into tears all over again, she hugged him so tightly that he couldn't even squirm.

Somehow she found herself presently back in her own apartment, with Hyacinthus and her handmaids doing what they could to repair the damage the emperor had done. Someone must have carried her there and put her in her bath just as they'd carried off Commodus, for she was sure she couldn't have got there by herself. None of the servants spoke as they sponged away the blood; none passed any comment as they teased the tangles from her hair or massaged perfumed oils into her punctured skin. Nor did she say anything to them; she felt too filthy to want to speak to anyone ever again.

Yet in the afternoon her stream of visitors would flow as it always did, and Marcia knew that she would open her doors to let it pour in, because many of the poor wretches who came to her with their requests and grievances had suffered crueller things at Commodus' hands even than she had. She would not allow the emperor's latest bout of brutality to stand in the way of her helping them, any more than she had done up to now.

At least his seed was no more likely to have taken root in her womb than it ever had. But she hated to think what Ursulus must have learnt from his lesson about the making of babies and what it meant to be a man.

When her visitors started to arrive and Hyacinthus took charge of admitting them as usual, none of them could have guessed what had happened to Marcia in the morning. After all, it was hardly the first time that the emperor had forced himself upon her, though he had seldom done so in front of servants, and never in front of a child. But she had learnt over the weeks and months that it helped, a little, at times like these to focus her attention on solving other people's problems and on appreciating the gifts which many of her petitioners brought her in their anxiety to have her give ear to their pleas.

Not that everyone came with complaints about the emperor's conduct. Some merely had requests to which they hoped his mistress might be sympathetic. Today there was a master musician who wanted to recommend the services of his company to the imperial court, and the leader of a troupe of acrobats who wished to secure an engagement at one of Commodus' famous banquets. More difficult to deal with was the owner of a brothel who was demanding the return of a batch of slave-boys Commodus had 'borrowed', and more surprising was the arrival of a group of senators who had swallowed their pride sufficiently to protest to her about the increasingly exorbitant taxes they were being required to pay into the imperial treasury. These taxes were becoming so heavy that some senatorial families would soon be unable to meet the financial criteria necessary to remain members of their class.

At least there was no one wanting her to procure him a magistracy or a military commission. Most people had realized that Cleander was the one to approach for those.

'My lady, you will soon be as rich as the emperor yourself,' Hyacinthus observed as they snatched a break in their punishing schedule and he gazed enviously at the day's accumulating gifts. There were Greek amphorae, a collection of ivory statuettes from India or somewhere even further to the east, furs and leopard-skins and gold and silver vessels. More touching in Marcia's eyes were the humble presents of the poor: a simple earthenware pot lovingly painted with coloured flowers, and a sparrow whittled from olive-wood which suddenly and poignantly reminded her of Callistus' fish. When she had first come back from Corvus and Junia's she had taken it from its casket very often and wound its cord around her fingers or stroked it so obsessively that its surface had been polished to a dark sheen. Lately somehow she had lost track of it and no longer knew where it was.

But she knew that Hyacinthus loved anything that sparkled, so in a moment of welling emotion Marcia seized upon a heavy gold chain that was lying on top of the pile of treasures and draped it around his neck. 'Then *you* shall be rich *too*, Hyacinthus,' she declared. 'For truly I do not know how I should manage without you.'

His round podgy face blushed bright as an apricot and he gushed in return, 'Oh, my lady, you are as bounteous as Ceres the Mother of Harvests herself!' Then he lowered his voice and said with a little more circumspection, 'I cannot help but wonder sometimes, my lady, whether you are not in fact Empress of Rome already.'

Marcia tried to smile wryly in response to this but could only manage a shudder. It was true that she was very much better at manipulating Commodus than Bruttia Crispina had ever been, and she was becoming more successful by the day at winning for her suppliants what they wanted from him. Furthermore, at the present rate of progress she would soon be sufficiently rich to lift many of them permanently out of their poverty.

If only all of this did not have to come at the price of her self-respect... And if only the leadership of the Roman Church were as grateful to her for her efforts as Hyacinthus was for his necklace. By now she had rescued scores if not hundreds of Roman Christians from random persecution and injustice, yet never so much as a word of gratitude came back from the bishop, let alone the remotest suggestion that she might ever be restored to communion. So much for seventy times seven. Commodus himself seemed to know more about forgiveness than Eleutherius did.

The first of her petitioners to be admitted when proceedings resumed was typical of many: a Christian widow with no gift to bring but her tears. As she threw herself at Marcia's feet, it came to Marcia that she knew the woman's face already; more often than not the Christians who sought her aid were people she recognized only too well. Not that they ever gave any indication of recognizing her.

'Oh Your Majesty,' the suppliant blurted, drawing from

Marcia the wry smile which had previously eluded her. 'Please, please persuade the emperor to let my sister go free! She's been thrown into prison for stealing, but she never stole a crumb in all her life; her neighbours told lies against her because she's a Christian. She's a widow, just like me; she and I worked together weaving cloth to sell at market. Now I cannot make enough money on my own to feed our children, and the Church can't help us because Callistus robbed us all.'

Callistus? How strange, Marcia thought, that someone called Callistus should be partly to blame for this widow's predicament, when she had only been thinking about *her* Callistus that very afternoon. Distractedly she gave her some silver coins and said she would do her best to have her sister released; when the woman had gone on her way, Marcia said to Hyacinthus, 'She must have meant a different Callistus, of course. The Callistus we knew would never have swatted a fly, let alone taken anyone's money. Mind you, he must be doing pretty well enough for himself these days as Carpophorus' right-hand man, don't you think?'

'What? Oh yes, yes, my lady, certainly he must. That widow must have been talking about someone else entirely,' Hyacinthus agreed, and Marcia sighed, for he had clearly been far too busy admiring his new necklace to pay attention to what she had been saying.

But when the stream of suppliants had at last dried up and Marcia's handmaids were already setting out her evening meal, Hyacinthus announced that there was someone else at her door. Before she had even given permission for the visitor to be admitted, he had entered of his own accord, and it was Cleander.

He was no longer wearing his armour, but might as well have been. Clearing her throat Marcia managed to say, 'I'm sorry, Cleander. Your son is no longer here. I sent him back to his nursery.'

'Oh, it's not the Little Bear I came to see.'

'So – to what do I owe this unexpected pleasure?' Marcia

kept her voice steady, but did not invite Cleander to be seated. He sat down nonetheless.

'I am here with your best interests at heart, Lady Marcia,' he assured her, noticing some cherries in a nearby bowl and taking the whole bunch in his great broad hand. Popping one of them nonchalantly into his mouth he said, 'I considered it my duty to bring you a timely warning, that is all. I should hate to see you come to any harm through my hesitation in speaking to you frankly.'

'A warning? Of what, in particular?'

'Well, my lady, you must be all too aware of what can happen to a woman who hurts the tender feelings of our emperor, especially when she has been very dear to him in the past.'

'Poor Bruttia Crispina. I'm sure if she had been able to bear his children, she would never have been led astray by another man...'

'Oh, I do not refer merely to Crispina, my lady. Surely you remember Commodus' beloved sister Lucilla, who swore her undying devotion to him many times, yet was later found guilty of plotting against him.' Cleander plucked a second cherry from the bunch, rolled it thoughtfully between his fingers, then unexpectedly leaned forward and dropped his voice to a whisper as though he wished to conspire with Marcia himself. 'You see,' he continued, 'I have long suspected that not all those who plotted with Lucilla were brought to justice. Wouldn't it be horribly dangerous for all concerned if some of those criminals who wanted to see her brother dead were found still to be at large?' Then he crushed the cherry in the palm of his hand so that the juice ran out between his fingers and said, 'Good day to you, my lady. Do think upon my advice, which was offered with the kindest of intentions.' And tossing the remaining cherries back in their bowl, he left.

Though her handmaids continued to set out her supper once he had gone, Marcia felt too sick even to watch. She had

Hyacinthus help her to bed, and lay there rigid, fully clothed, with her face still painted and hair still bound.

Did Cleander *know* she had been involved in Lucilla's conspiracy? How could he, since there was no one still alive who could have told him? And even if he had dreamt up a connection between Commodus' late sister and his latest mistress all by himself, if he should sow seeds of suspicion in Commodus' mind, it would mean the end of everything.

For Marcia was well aware that Commodus didn't need evidence that she had once tried to kill him, for *him* to resolve to kill *her*. He needed only to suspect that she did not love him unreservedly, unstintingly, with every fibre of her being. More than any other treasure an emperor could covet, Commodus wanted to be loved. Yet he had no better idea about how to gain or nurture the affection of those closest to him than he knew how to win the hearts of his subjects at large. He understood only presents and force.

Yet neither Commodus nor Marcia exercised the real power in Rome any more, and she was acutely aware of that too. It was Cleander now who wielded the imperial sceptre. Rome was ruled by a Phrygian, a foreigner born a slave. Cleander was more powerful than the Senate, the consuls, the Praetorians, the emperor and his mistress put together..

Rolling over onto her side, Marcia drew her knees up to her chest and hugged them. Her head was pounding and her body ached, not merely below the waist but everywhere, as though she had been in a battle. How she hated everything about the way her life had turned out; how she wished she had never come back to the palace.

But it was too late now to undo what had been done, and besides, she still didn't see how she could have made any other choice.

CHAPTER NINE: CALLISTUS

Callistus put down his pickaxe and scraped the sweat from his brow with the back of one hand. By the feeble glow of his lamp, stashed nearby in a fissure of the rock, he could just make out the silhouette of the man working ahead of him, and was fleetingly taken back to his months at the treadmill. But this place was worse. The seam of ore they were mining was scarcely any easier to see than each other, and it was harder to breathe down here than it had been at the mill. The air, such as it was, was fouller and more stagnant than a Tiber smog because they had penetrated way beyond the last of the ventilation shafts.

Callistus was failing fast. He was permanently exhausted and had begun to suffer from chronic pains in his chest and a persistent cough. If he had cared any longer about the future he might have been afraid. The man who had worked behind him until last week had been carted off to the burial pit not long after starting with the same pains and same cough.

But there were plenty of other ways to die down here, any one of which was likely to kill you before the coughing did. You could be swept away and drowned when water surged through the tunnels after heavy rain, or when water already pent up in lakes underground broke through into the mine workings. When fires had to be set against rock too hard to dig out you could be overcome by smoke or crushed by the rock as it exploded, or even burnt to death where you stood if you didn't move fast enough. And it was hard to do anything very quickly when you and your workmates were chained together at the neck, hacking away in almost total darkness, and you were fed on nothing but gruel. To drink, all you got was the worst kind of posca: a revolting mixture of water and stale vinegary wine with which the slaves were woken up in the morning and then kept drugged into submission until their shift was ended.

How long must he have been here? Callistus had long since lost track, but it had certainly been more than a year, because the mines had gone from dry to wet to dry again. You couldn't tell the time of year from how warm you were, any more than you could discern the length of the days from what little you could see around you. If you were working near the surface it was always cool and draughty, but if you were far underground it could be so hot that most of the miners worked all but naked regardless of the season.

The ore they were extracting with their axes and fires contained both silver and lead, for each of which the Romans seemed to have an insatiable greed. It wasn't hard to see why. The silver they needed for coinage, and for families like Hippolytus' to eat their breakfast from; the lead they used to make pipes for ever more ambitious schemes to carry water from the countryside into their teeming cities. The population of Rome itself had been growing for centuries as more and more small farmers were forced off the land to wind up trapped in Rome's slums. In spite of his head for figures Callistus had never had any real idea how many people lived in the City these days. Although censuses were taken by the authorities from time to time no one believed they were accurate. But it was certainly more than a million.

What Callistus did know was that he had been among the

first men to work in the mines of Sardinia as a convict and slave of the state. Until recently these death-traps had been worked by free men, but the wages they demanded to do it had risen too high. After all, who would volunteer to stare death in the face on a daily basis when he could drift idly round Rome living on handouts and enjoying gratuitous entertainments laid on by the likes of Cleander?

But every one of the criminals who had arrived in Sardinia along with Callistus had been dead within weeks. Now and again it occurred to him to wonder why he alone had survived, and he could only conclude that the time he had put in on the treadmill had left him better prepared for this hell-hole than most. Certainly his survival owed nothing to the dreaminess which had served him so well in the years he had worked for Carpophorus. Back then his daydreams had been a precious source of hope, but not any more. He couldn't even picture Marcia's face with any clarity, and wasn't sure he would want to, since these days it would be all painted up like a strumpet's and probably as hard as the rock he was hewing. For now she was Commodus' woman once again, and this time by choice.

There was only one way to survive in the long term, however, if fate had marked you out for the mines. This was to have yourself transferred to surface operations: smelting the ore, perhaps, or supervising windlasses, or tending to the animals which were kept for turning wheels or carrying buckets when there weren't enough men to do it instead. But surface jobs were for the favoured few, and Callistus wasn't one of them.

As he hefted his axe once again and went back to hacking at the seam in front of him, Callistus heard the unlikely sound of singing echoing eerily down the tunnel. It was a song he knew: a Christian hymn. There was a sizeable Christian contingent down here, and those whose lungs weren't yet clogged with dust would sing as they worked, to keep up their spirits and perhaps lift those of the men who worked with them.

But Callistus didn't sing. Singing only brought on the coughing; and besides, he hadn't been sent to the mines for being a Christian. He'd been sent for causing an affray, and there *had* been a trial, of sorts, this time, or at least a hearing, before the Prefect Publius Seius Fuscianus, the magistrate responsible for enforcing law and order in the City of Rome. This Fuscianus had been a childhood friend of Marcus Aurelius; he was a distinguished senator and former consul to boot. But in spite of his judge's eminence and experience, Callistus knew he had stood no chance of acquittal. The most eloquent members of Shadrach's synagogue had given evidence against him, accusing him of deliberately disrupting a licensed act of worship with the aim of fomenting civil unrest. He'd been inspired, they claimed, by his pernicious Christian beliefs; but then Carpophorus had turned up right on cue and testified that Callistus was no kind of Christian at all, merely a common embezzler and a thief.

What could have prompted his old master to say such a thing? Callistus had asked himself this question over and over again on the boat to Sardinia, crouching where he'd been thrown – bound and gagged – into the hold with his fellow convicts, all naked and slippery with sweat like a catch of human fish. It was conceivable that Carpophorus had been concerned to protect the Church's reputation. But more likely he had realized that if Callistus were sentenced to death or to the mines, he himself would lose all claim to him and would not be paid a clipped denarius in compensation for the loss of what had once been a valuable asset. And it was far more likely that someone *would* get this sort of sentence if he were found to be a Christian and not just an all-round bad lot.

In the end Callistus had been condemned to the mines in any case, probably because there was such a crying need for men to work them. Nothing had been said about his being a Christian when the sentence was read out, and he hadn't been made to sacrifice to the emperor. Now officially a slave of the state – just about the worst thing it was possible to be – Callistus had been flogged and then put on the next slave-ship to Sardinia, a ferocious rugged island swept by seemingly continuous winds: bitterly damp and cold ones in the winter and furnace-hot in the summer.

Not that Callistus ever got to feel any kind of wind on his face any more. He had barely seen the light of day since his arrival on the island; like most of his comrades he worked and ate, and usually slept, underground. At least in the tunnel he was hacking at today he could just about stand upright. Sometimes you had to kneel or even lie down, with the full weight of the mountain right above your head, reminding you all too forcefully that you could be squashed flatter than a lump of unleavened bread at any moment if the tunnel collapsed, as they frequently did.

Right now Callistus was not unduly concerned about the mass of rock above his head or the likelihood of his being crushed without warning like a beetle in a winepress. He wished only that the confounded singing down the passageway would stop. He didn't want to remember that he had ever been a Christian, because too many memories surged up inside him when he did. Neither were the Christians themselves especially keen to acknowledge that he had once been one of them. There were a few who had clearly recognized him when he'd first arrived from Rome, and even tried to exchange with him the secret sign – not that there was much point in being secretive about it where they were now. But the most outspoken of the rest maintained that it was scoundrels like Callistus who brought the Church into disrepute and stirred up the kind of persecution which had cost so many brethren their lives.

It was odd, Callistus thought on those rare days when he still had the capacity to think straight at all, that there seemed to be two breeds of Christian even down here in the bowels of the earth. There were those who prided themselves on being better men than others – condemned criminals though they were — and those who had a weird kind of light burning within them which made them different without their even trying. Whenever he became aware of it, Callistus was painfully reminded of the conversation he'd had with Zephyrinus about being born again and having a sort of candle-flame ignited inside your soul. It baffled Callistus that any of them still clung to their futile faith in Christ, when Christ had so clearly abandoned them. When they chanced to be billeted together, some would even try to pray with one another and share a sorry kind of communion with their stale bread and posca.

Abruptly the singing stopped in mid strain, and Callistus felt a distinctive pulling on his neck ring: three sharp tugs, a pause, and then three more. This was the signal for the end of the shift, and he passed it on to the next man just as the one behind had passed it on to him. Soon the men at the far end of the tunnel came feeling their way towards him, and as they approached he began to move along in front of them. There was no space for one man to get past another; they all had to hobble in single file, staying close enough together to avoid chafing their necks on their iron collars. Each man would carry his own axe and lamp, whilst the ore they had mined would be hauled to the surface separately in great buckets and cages.

It turned out that tonight Callistus and his fellows were going to the surface as well, for once they had emerged from their tunnel they were directed to scale the ladders which led upward through shafts drilled down into the mountainside. Temporarily their chains were detached, though not the iron rings to which they had been fixed; once one of those was clamped around your neck you would almost certainly be wearing it when you died. They would have buried you in it, too, if it hadn't been worth too much to waste on a corpse.

It took Callistus — and therefore all those men behind him as well — twice as long as it should have done to reach the top of the shaft, because half way up he had a coughing fit and it was all he could do to keep hold of the ladder. When at last they got to the surface it was already as dark as it had been in the tunnels, and the slaves' spirits sank still further as their hopes of a rare glimpse of daylight were dashed. At least on the few occasions they emerged from their subterranean prison they were permitted to wash, albeit in cold grey water which got grimier and grittier the further you were down the line. Then they were herded together into one of the shacks which served as barracks, where their tools were taken away lest they attempt to dig their way to freedom during the night. Here they were mercifully left unchained, for the single door was locked, barred and guarded; none of the miners was going anywhere until morning.

Before they lay down the men had to queue for their evening rations, but by now Callistus was coughing so badly that he dropped his bowl and his gruel spilled out on the floor. As he was stooping to salvage what he could, a quiet young man only lately arrived from Rome knelt alongside him to help.

'You worked for Carpophorus the money-lender, didn't you,' the young man said under his breath while spooning some of his own food into Callistus' bowl on top of the little they had managed to rescue.

'Yes,' Callistus grunted when the coughing had stopped, though Carpophorus would scarcely have appreciated this starkly unflattering description of his business activities.

'So you're good with numbers and accounts? You can read pretty well, and add up?'

'Could once.' Glancing down into his bowl Callistus nodded a gruff acknowledgement of the fellow's generosity. Acts of kindness were few and far between among the miners.

'Then speak to the foreman directly. They're looking for help in the office; the old accountant was cooking the books. Might be your only chance to get out of here before...' He shied away from saying before what, but it was all too obvious. Then as he shambled off to eat what remained of his own gruel, the young man gave Callistus the Christians' secret sign, leaving Callistus to stare after him, too taken aback to have returned the gesture even had he wanted to.

As soon as he had finished eating, Callistus staggered to his feet and went to seek out the supervisor of his shift. This man was a hard-bitten Sicilian, a slave like the rest of them, though full of his own importance and much fonder of his whip than he was of words. Because he got double the ration of his charges he was still eating when Callistus found him. Callistus loitered nearby, waiting for him to finish before venturing to speak, but the foreman barked out at him, 'Well, lad, what is it you want? Or are you going to stand there gawping like a ruddy goldfish all night?'

'Sir... I was told they are looking for someone to work in the office, with numbers. I can do that. I was trained for it.' Even as he was speaking, a voice inside his head was telling him there was no way he'd be able to do it any more.

'You?' the foreman snorted, but he put down his bowl all the same, and regarded Callistus long and hard while masticating noisily like a fat old bull. Then without another word he re-attached Callistus' neck-chain and dragged him to the door of the barracks, on which he proceeded to hammer until it was opened by the guards outside. They probably assumed someone was dead.

Callistus was duly taken to the squat stone building which contained the mine manager's quarters and office. The manager was one of the few free men the mine employed; a Roman citizen of no particular distinction, he wore a toga all the time so that no one could doubt his gentility. When the foreman shunted Callistus into his presence he was hunched over on his couch attempting to read from a dog-eared scroll by candle-light. As soon as he learned that Callistus could read he shoved the scroll into his hands and said, 'Then read to me from this, boy. Confounded thing keeps rolling up on me. Can't find anyone in this place who can read more than three words in a row without getting his tongue tied in knots.'

Callistus wasn't at all sure that he would get more than three words out before coughing his guts up. But as soon as he had the scroll in his hands it was as though a great wave of energy broke over him, and he felt suddenly and gloriously human for the first time in months. For the scroll contained not columns of figures but poetry, and even more astonishingly, it was poetry which Callistus recognized. It came from the Aeneid, the epic masterpiece of Publius Vergilius Maro – Virgil – one of the few pagan authors whose works Christian children were given to study. Hippolytus had read this very passage to Callistus many years ago, when they had still been friends and Hippolytus had still deemed it fitting to cast before a slave selected pearls of the wisdom which his senatorial education was showering upon him.

So he read aloud from it now with increasing confidence, even remembering how the rhythm of the metre should be expressed to bring out the beauty of each meticulously chosen syllable. After a mere half dozen lines the mine manager's eyes were all but starting from his head, and he was content to let Callistus read on and on until eventually the scroll and its reader's surge of strength came to an end at exactly the same moment and Callistus was overcome by such a fit of coughing that the mine manager sent his own body-slave to fetch him a cup of water.

When he had recovered he was given some columns of figures to add up and calculations to do after all. He struggled with these rather more than with the poetry, for the coughing had left him badly shaken up and his head felt to be full of the ghastly green mist that pervaded the tunnels where he worked. Nonetheless it struck him as just as well that the records of his trial would say he'd been sent down for causing an affray, and not for fraud.

'Well,' said the manager, once Callistus' tasks had been completed to his satisfaction, 'I guess you will do for now, in the absence of anyone better qualified. Of course, once they do send someone from Rome you will have to return to your previous duties.' Then as Callistus' 'thank you' was consumed by yet another bout of coughing, he shot him a sideways look meaning: if you last that long.

After this Callistus was taken by the manager's body-slave to be cleaned up and fed, and he was given a threadbare rug to sleep on in the corner of the office where he would be working from now on. All of which he would have relished like a kiss from the Virgin Mary herself if he hadn't felt so horribly ill. It would be only too ironic, he reflected as he huddled there coughing himself to sleep, if he were to have been rescued from the jaws of hell only to die doing sums at a desk.

Part of him didn't really care; part of him would have been quite content to expire in the night and be tossed on the slag heap, flea-ridden rug and all. But the survivor inside him was already fighting back, saying: don't give up yet, Callistus. It can't be just luck which has kept you alive until now.

Zephyrinus would have said: you *know* it's not luck.

In the morning he was awakened even earlier than usual. Apparently the provincial governor was going to be visiting the mine at short notice the following day and all of its bureaucracy would have to be in order, which currently it certainly wasn't. The governor hadn't said why he was coming, but presumably it was to carry out some kind of inspection. What other motive could he have?

Accordingly Callistus was given a hunk of bread and put to work straight away going through the inventory of supplies, tools and provisions, and the records of how much silver and lead had lately been shipped to Rome. The prisoners' names were listed alongside the pickaxes, hammers and chisels they used, though considerably more men than tools were marked down as 'lost'. When he collapsed onto his rug again that evening he was almost as exhausted as he would have been after a day below ground, and his cough was getting worse.

The governor arrived midway through the following morning, accompanied by an appropriate entourage of horsemen, foot-soldiers and slaves. He swept into the office resplendent in a pristine magistrate's toga which made the mine manager's look distinctly down-at-heel. With his close-cropped silver hair and clean-shaven face he might have been a god from Olympus cast down into the world of mortals as he observed his shabby surroundings with consummate disdain. The mine manager bowed and scraped and offered to provide him with an escort to show him around the installation, but the governor waved his hand and said, 'I know perfectly well what a mine looks like, Petronius. I'm not here to check up on you. I'm here because an emissary of the First Lady has come from Rome with a letter demanding the liberation of some of the convicts who were sentenced to work for you.'

'Liberation?' repeated the manager, as though he had never heard the word before and certainly wouldn't have known how to use it. Meanwhile Callistus, struggling to stand at attention in the corner, was thinking that he had never heard the manager's *name* used before, or the peculiar title 'First Lady'. The usual title for the emperor's wife was Augusta – Empress – and that was Bruttia Crispina. He couldn't begin to imagine why the famously mousy Crispina should suddenly be taking an interest in freeing convicts from the mines.

But when the aforementioned emissary was shown in, it was Marcia's eunuch Hyacinthus.

Callistus knew him at once, though unsurprisingly Hyacinthus showed no sign of ever having seen Callistus before in his life. The eunuch came bustling forward and thrust a wooden tablet into Petronius' hands. 'Well?' the governor demanded, after Petronius had taken the tablet to the window and studied it for some while without making a comment. 'Do you have these men here or don't you?'

Petronius grunted and passed the tablet to Callistus. 'Here,' he said. 'Compare these names with the ones on your list.'

Callistus began to do as he was bidden, finding most of the names quite quickly, though some belonged to men who had died. While he was hunting down the rest, Petronius enquired of Hyacinthus if he might be told why these particular men were to be freed. But Callistus had already worked it out. They were Christians.

Naturally his own name was not among them. But listening to Petronius issuing orders for the fortunate men to be found and brought to the surface, Callistus, whose pulse was racing like a boxer's before a bout, made up his mind that he must stake everything on getting Hyacinthus to acknowledge him for who he was and take him back to Rome with the others. This was his one big chance, for surely if Hyacinthus knew him for Marcia's friend he wouldn't leave him to die?

So Callistus tossed tablet and lists to one side and fell on his knees at the astonished eunuch's feet. 'Hyacinthus? It's me, Callistus, Lady Marcia's friend from the Church. I helped you carry your scrolls to her chambers when you dropped them, don't you remember? And I made her that little wooden fish. I'm a Christian too; we gave each other the secret sign.'

'Goodness me!' exclaimed Hyacinthus, whose hands Callistus was now bathing in kisses. 'I do believe you *are* Callistus, though your name isn't on my list, and the Lady Marcia wrote the names on it herself after consulting with the Church's elders.'

'That's because she doesn't know I'm here! The elders must have missed my name out by mistake. *You* know I'm a Christian, don't you? And you know that Marcia would want me freed if she knew where I was.'

'Indeed I do,' Hyacinthus agreed. 'She talks about you often, even after all this time.'

'She does?' Callistus whispered, and suddenly he was weeping and coughing and grovelling so pitifully that Hyacinthus turned to Petronius and then to the governor and said, 'This boy must be freed as well.'

'Impossible,' retorted the governor, who had snatched up the documents Callistus had tossed away. 'It says here that he was condemned for causing an affray. I don't have the authority to release him even if I wanted to.'

'You won't be held accountable. I shall take responsibility for the decision myself,' Hyacinthus assured him pompously, to Callistus' amazement, for he wouldn't have thought Hyacinthus had it in him to speak with such conviction. The change in Marcia's circumstances must have changed Hyacinthus as well. He continued, 'In fact, if you *don't* release him, Lady Marcia will have the emperor replace you as governor before your next batch of prisoners arrives. I guarantee it.'

'Very well.' The governor shrugged his shoulders and turned to Petronius, who was looking distinctly disgruntled. 'Free the boy too. It's of no consequence.' Which of course was a lie however you looked at it, though Callistus was far too ecstatic to look at it from anyone's viewpoint but his own. For not only would he be free of the threat of being sent back down underground, but he would be free full stop, because any man reprieved by imperial decree from a sentence of slavery to the state became a freedman of the emperor. From now on he would be Lucius Commodus Callistus, a Roman citizen in his own right. He was far too excited to notice that although he was certainly to be released, his name had not been added to Hyacinthus' list.

Presently the other Christians were brought into the office one by one in the order in which they had been found and scrubbed up. Some were weeping like Callistus, whilst others seemed too far gone even to understand what was happening and simply stood with shoulders bowed and faces blank, awaiting whatever fate had in store for them. One of the first to arrive was the young man to whom Callistus owed so much; his tear-stained face broke into a smile as soon as he saw that Callistus too had been granted his freedom. A few of the man's companions looked at Callistus askance, but none was uncharitable enough to denounce him as excommunicate even if they knew that he was.

Once their number was complete they were taken to the smithy to have their neck-rings removed. After this Hyacinthus' ship would carry them back to Rome, where they would receive official manumission at the palace and be given a handout to help them embark on their new lives as freedmen and 'clients' of the emperor.

The homeward voyage seemed to Callistus a more wonderful experience than anything his imagination could have conjured up. The sun shone, the winds were kind, and the pardoned men were free to stroll on deck, sleep, sing or pray as the fancy took them. Most of them *did* want to pray, to offer up thanks for their miraculous deliverance and for the honour in which they would henceforth be held. For no one enjoyed higher prestige among the Christians of Rome than 'confessors': those who had been condemned to suffer and die for their faith but had somehow lived to tell the tale.

For the most part Callistus kept out of their way. Once his eyes had got used to the brightness he spent much of his time gazing out to sea, entranced by the surging of the swell and the sparkling of the wave crests in the sunshine. Leaning over the bulwark he could cough and spit the dust from his lungs and the oppression from his spirit with impunity, and dream to his heart's content about what it would be like to see Marcia again. Of course she would no longer be the girl he had known, but at least if she was going out of her way to help Christians she couldn't have become the hard-bitten harridan he'd feared her reunion with Commodus must have made her.

Callistus wasn't the only passenger to make himself scarce during the spontaneous acts of worship which broke out on board. The faith of many had taken a battering, and there were some who were still too sick in body or in mind to want to mix with anyone at all. But on the second day of their voyage the quiet young man who had saved Callistus' life sidled up to him, stood by the bulwark beside him and said, 'Peace be with you, my friend. My name is Marcus Pollius. Of course I understand if you don't want to pray with the rest of us, but you would be truly welcome if you did.'

'No, you *don't* understand,' Callistus replied, still looking out to sea. 'I'm not a Christian any more. Bishop Eleutherius banned me from communion.'

'But Eleutherius is bishop no longer. He died before I left Rome, and Victor the African elder was elected in his place. He's a man after Christ's own heart, even if he does look more like a Numidian warrior than a clergyman. And even though he has to steer a perilous course between pardoning mass murderers, as some of the other elders would have him do, and indulging those for whom stealing one barley-cake after baptism would be enough to condemn a man to everlasting torment.'

Callistus gave a humourless laugh which sounded more contemptuous than he had meant it to. 'Victor may have been decent enough as an elder but he won't re-admit me to communion. He can't. I have committed a deadly sin for which *no* man can forgive me.'

'But God himself has saved you from the mines, Callistus. If I know Victor, that will be all the evidence he needs to grant you a pardon.'

'Then has he granted Marcia a pardon too? Her sins were never as terrible as mine, and look how providence has exalted *her!* She never stole anyone's money or made anyone into a pauper. And she has done more for the Church than any of its bishops. It's *you* who saved me from the mines, Marcus, for which I thank you from the bottom of my heart.'

At this Marcus sighed and laid a brotherly hand on Callistus' arm. 'It isn't what we do for God or for anyone else that saves us, but what Christ did for us upon the cross,' he said, sounding far too much like Zephyrinus for Callistus' comfort. But then Callistus succumbed to yet another bout of coughing, and their conversation was over.

By the time they were back in Rome awaiting their manumission Callistus had expected to feel a good deal healthier, yet found that he did not. It was summer, and the sultry city air smelled little fresher than the air in the mines. Swarms of mosquitoes rose from the marshes and brought with them the summer fever which had seen off many folk much fitter than Callistus. So he was coughing, sweating and shivering by turns as he sat with his fellows in a palace anteroom waiting for the Gracious Lady to whom they owed their deliverance to pronounce them free. He was painfully torn between his eagerness to look once more upon her face and his horror of her seeing him like this.

But they didn't get to see her at all. Instead an anonymous palace steward breezed in, armed with the appropriate documents and an overblown sense of his own dignity. One by one the Christians' names were called out, and each man stepped forward to the steward's table to receive his manumission certificate and a small sum of money to help him on his way, though the steward looked rather as though he begrudged them every denarius. When everyone else had gone, Callistus still sat on his bench coughing forlornly like the last boy left behind when children pick teams for a game.

As the steward peered at him in myopic surprise, Hyacinthus took it upon himself to launch into an explanation of who Callistus was and what he was doing there. But the more he explained, the more the steward peered, and the more his surprise deepened into distaste. Eventually he cut Hyacinthus short with a rap of his knuckles on the table and said, 'It seems to me that you have overstepped your authority enough already, eunuch. You would be well advised to hold your tongue before I report you to Cleander and he has *that* cut off as well.'

At this Hyacinthus turned pale as porridge and said no more. Then the steward looked down his nose at Callistus and said, 'Get out. If I ever set eyes on *you* again I shall have you arrested as a runaway. Be grateful, both of you, that I have decided to overlook this irregularity for the sake of His Excellency's magnanimous consort, who, like me, is inclined to be more generous than wise.'

Callistus attempted to do as he was told but found that he couldn't stand up. Accordingly two slaves were directed to take hold of him under the armpits and eject him from the palace forthwith.

Once outside he knew he *had* to get up; had he been found lying in the gutter anywhere on the Palatine Hill he would likely have been arrested all over again or carried away with the refuse. But sick and destitute, neither any man's slave nor officially free, where was he to go? He supposed he should think himself lucky that the steward had been too lazy to arrange for his passage straight back to Sardinia.

For two days Callistus lived on the streets, or rather in the forum, where there was always waste food to be scavenged when the stallholders were looking the other way. No one gave him anything out of charity, and even his fellow beggars shunned him. He obviously wasn't blind or crippled and therefore had no right in their opinion to expect any sort of alms from anyone. And all the time he was getting sicker and weaker, until eventually he keeled over by a public fountain he'd been trying to climb into for a drink. When he next knew what was happening, someone was dribbling water into his mouth, and it was Marcus Pollius.

'Brother Callistus!' Marcus was saying over and over again as he struggled to hold Callistus' head off the ground and pat his cheek and give him water all at the same time. 'You're alive, thank God. You're alive.' And as Callistus tried and failed to say something back, Marcus announced, 'I'm taking you to Victor's. It's only a stone's throw from here.' Too weak to protest, Callistus turned his head into Marcus' breast and abandoned himself to his fate.

Once or twice on the way to the bishop's house Callistus revived sufficiently to note that Marcus had commandeered someone to help him, and that they each had one of his arms around their shoulders. By the time they reached their destination he was more or less conscious and was even trying to walk instead of letting his feet drag along the ground behind him.

Though the bishop was not alone, Callistus and his rescuers were ushered directly into his presence. He had been in conclave with the principal elders of the Church – including Zephyrinus, Urbanus and a fearsome-looking bearded ascetic Callistus did not recognize – and Hermione, Head of the Order of Widows, all deep in discussion about how to handle some inveterate trouble-maker who was worrying the flock with endless doctrinal disagreements. But as soon as they saw Callistus their agenda was discarded.

In spite of his worsening eyesight it was Zephyrinus who knew him first. Blinded still further by his tears he stumbled forward and embraced Callistus where he stood, still supported between the two men who had brought him in. 'God be praised,' Zephyrinus whispered, while Hermione rushed over with a blanket and wrapped it round Callistus' shoulders, for in spite of the summer heat he was visibly shivering. Victor seemed to be struggling to recall who Callistus was, until Zephyrinus spoke his name and declared it a marvel that he was still alive.

'Barely alive, by the look of him,' said the aptly named Urbanus. 'But Bishop, be careful. This man is excommunicate.'

Then to Callistus' deepening dismay the fearsome ascetic whose name he did not know chimed in and began to catalogue for Victor all of his supposed crimes. The feeble flame of hope which Marcus Pollius' compassion had kindled within him was doused; seeing his head loll forward, his rescuers promptly set him down on the nearest couch, filthy from the forum as he was, and Hermione sat beside him with an arm across his back. But all that Callistus was aware of was the rising voice of the ascetic, ever more insistently urging the new bishop to turn the three undesirables out into the street whence they had come.

'Disputes about the divinity of Christ and the date of

Easter will be the least of our worries if Carpophorus finds out that you have had Callistus in your house,' he finished up. And Callistus slumped against Hermione's shoulder preparing himself for the moment when Victor would expel him.

Yet it did not come. 'Let us take our time, Roscius, and not act in thoughtless haste or from fear, as the heathen do,' the bishop said quietly. 'If you had been born in Africa as I was, you would know only too well how it feels to be shunned by those who regard you as a threat to their own assumptions.'

'It's not our assumptions this man threatens!' the ascetic thundered back. 'If you side with him against Carpophorus you'll have the Gentile and Jewish believers at each other's throats within days and the whole Church will be torn apart. He's already caused a riot in a synagogue; he's a threat to everybody!'

'Really?' said Victor. 'A riot, you say? He doesn't look very dangerous to me. Was he trying to get himself killed? To die a martyr's death, perhaps?'

'You wouldn't be the first to accuse Callistus of attempted suicide.' This salient comment came from Zephyrinus. 'After all, the docks at Portus aren't exactly a popular place to choose for an afternoon swim. Yet the mere fact that he has survived the ocean, the treadmill and the mines shows the strength of his desire to live, and that the Lord's hand is upon him. That he should be sitting here with us today is nothing short of a miracle.'

'Miracle? A monumental mistake, more like,' was the grim verdict of a man who hadn't yet spoken, for there were three other elders present of whom Callistus hadn't taken note. He looked up now and saw that the new speaker was a sharp-faced little fellow whose name he seemed to remember as Horatius; to Horatius' right sat a middle-aged patrician called Gaius – well dressed, well groomed and eminently well fed, but whose brow was furrowed in concern – whilst on his left was Asterius, a heavy-featured, taciturn giant of a man who looked more like a block of hewn granite than a pillar of the

Church. 'This boy's name was never on the list of martyrs condemned to the mines,' Horatius forged on. 'There's no reason why he should have been freed with the others. We should simply point out the error to the appropriate authorities and send him back. Legally he has no right to be here at all.'

'Back to the mines? In this condition?' Victor exclaimed, and Callistus felt Hermione's arm go tighter around him.

'It's no better than he deserves,' said Roscius in Horatius' defence. 'Surely we would sooner see this criminal serve the sentence he brought upon himself – harsh though it may be – than allow the whole Church to be destroyed for the sake of one man? It isn't as if there aren't hundreds dying in the mines already. Is it our moral duty to rescue them all?'

For an awkward interval after this no one spoke, and Callistus resigned himself once more to being put on the next ship back to Sardinia. But then Zephyrinus quoted softly into the silence, '"It is expedient that one man suffer for the many",' and Victor, at once understanding the allusion to Jesus' own trial, announced, 'Enough. Callistus will *not* be sent back to the mines, or left to fend for himself like a stray dog. He is a neighbour in need who was once our Christian brother, and though we cannot accept him back into fellowship, neither can we simply pretend we never knew him. A solution must be found which is acceptable to all of us.' Thereafter no one said anything further about handing Callistus over to the authorities or turfing him out into the street.

At length it was Gaius, the patrician with the furrowed brow, who came up with the solution they were seeking. He said unexpectedly, 'My brother owns a seaside house at Antium. I stay with him there in the summer sometimes; sea air's so good for the health. The boy would be company for Titus; he lost his wife many years ago, and Callistus could help with his accounts. He'd be out of the way but provided for, and I know my brother would agree. He's the kindest person you could ever hope to meet, and exceptionally discreet.'

'Well?' said the bishop, turning in obvious relief to Callistus. 'Would that be acceptable to you?'

'To *me?*' croaked Callistus. 'But of course... I mean... thank you...' He gaped at Gaius, Victor and Marcus Pollius in turn, and finally at Zephyrinus, who said to Victor, 'With your permission, Bishop, I shall take charge of him for now and see to it that he's ready to travel as soon as our meeting is over.'

Victor nodded with a knowing smile, but it was Horatius who said, 'Anything to avoid another dose of doctrinal hair-splitting, eh?' as together Zephyrinus and Hermione helped Callistus to his feet.

Zephyrinus declined to rise to Horatius' bait. Instead he turned his attention fully upon Callistus, and again Callistus saw consummate compassion written in the lines on his old mentor's face. 'You see, little prince, the love of God can never be thwarted,' Zephyrinus said. 'Only be patient, and who knows, a way may be found in time for the Church to pardon you altogether.'

As pigs might fly, Callistus thought; yet for as long as he kept his eyes focussed on Zephyrinus' face, anything began to seem possible.

CHAPTER TEN: MARCIA

I

Marcia smiled and shook her head at her handmaid's offer of the last of the honey-coated dates they'd all been devouring. Her twittering flock of slave-girls bobbed with excitement along with most of the crowd, but in spite of her best efforts Marcia had failed to work up any enthusiasm for the afternoon of carnage which was coming.

Today was the first of fourteen days of the annual Plebeian Games, and Marcia and her girls were sitting with Hyacinthus in the elevated box which the emperor had bestowed upon her in the first flush of his infatuation. Whenever he pressed her into coming with him to the amphitheatre the two of them would still sit apart, even though it was now four years since the banishment of Bruttia Crispina to Capri. According to Hyacinthus His Excellency would always be much too busy placing bets and discussing the gladiators' form with his sparring partner Narcissus to want Marcia and her ladies distracting him.

Currently it was break time, and the blood-letting had

ceased while the spectators ate their lunches. In the arena down below there was a comic fight going on between clowns and dwarfs armed with wooden swords; the clowns were dressed as foxes and the dwarfs as chickens, and they were all running round in circles to the accompaniment of horns and trumpets. The morning programme had consisted of bloody re-enactments of events from Roman history, involving the slaughter of large numbers of condemned criminals. In the afternoon there would be contests between pairs of highly-trained gladiators; these bouts featuring experts judiciously matched were always the ones which the crowd – and Commodus – relished the most.

But at present there was no sign of His Excellency at all. From her privileged position Marcia could see the imperial box quite clearly, but Commodus' seat had been unoccupied since the lunch break began. This was unusual. Normally he wouldn't miss a moment of even the most inane knockabout comedy except to empty his wine-bloated bladder now and again. Perhaps his absence had something to do with the surprise he had promised her when he'd come rushing to her chambers early that morning in a state of feverish excitement and made her agree to attend today's entertainments. His mood had unsettled her then, and the recollection of it unsettled her now. With a shudder she drew her cloak more tightly about her. It was November after all, and though the weather was clear and crisp it was by no means warm, and there had been no need for the arena's awnings to be unfurled to protect the crowds from the sun.

Commodus' surprises seldom brought Marcia the pleasure he expected them to. One day not so very long ago he had told her of some wonderful news he had received which he would share with her that evening during a special banquet he had arranged, just for the two of them, to celebrate the apotheosis of their all-conquering love. The news turned out to be that Bruttia Crispina had been privily executed in accordance with Commodus' orders. So much for the emperor's clemency. He had simply bided his time until most people had forgotten about his ex-wife's existence, and then had her sputtering lamp snuffed out.

'But *this* surprise will be like nothing that you or any of my subjects have ever witnessed before!' Commodus had enthused this morning, his eyes dancing like a schoolboy's at Saturnalia. 'You will love it, my darling, and so will my people. They have always loved the Games I have given them, but after today they will love me more than they ever loved any of the emperors who came before me, and you too will love me more than you ever have until now.' And Marcia had stroked back his hair and kissed him, and told him she could never love him more than she already did.

Her words made him clasp her to his bosom in a paroxysm of joy. But he still hadn't married her, even though Crispina was no more. He persisted in avowing that he would never marry again.

Not that this made much difference to Marcia's standing at court or in the eyes of the populace. She was increasingly referred to, or even addressed directly, as Augusta, though the title had never been conferred on her officially. Commodus seemed reluctant to bestow any more grand titles upon anyone since the demise of Cleander.

Marcia still couldn't quite believe that he was gone, or how quickly it had happened. There had been a shortage of grain in the City, and Cleander had been suspected of buying up huge amounts of it himself to inflate the price. A riot had broken out at the Circus Maximus and the enraged – and hungry – mob, baying for Cleander's blood, had swarmed out of town towards one of the emperor's villas where Commodus and Marcia had been staying at the time. Cleander had ordered the Praetorian Guard to drive the horde back, but the City police force – the Vigiles Urbani – under Pertinax the new Urban Prefect, had joined in on the side of the people. Messengers had come one after another to warn Commodus of what was happening but he had taken no notice until Marcia herself had forced him to listen. Then he had swung from denial to panic; capitulating immediately to the rioters' demands he'd had Cleander executed on the spot, no questions asked.

All of which would have been a cause of unspeakable relief and rejoicing to Marcia, except that in his terror and rage Commodus had had little Ursulus, Cleander's son, eliminated too. Soldiers from his private bodyguard had done it, repeatedly smashing the child's head into the ground. Cleander's head had ended up on a pole, being paraded about by the mob like the captured eagle of a legion.

Commodus would never again make the mistake of letting someone else rule the empire on his behalf. It was just a pity, thought Marcia as she contemplated his unoccupied seat, that he wasn't rather better at doing it himself. He had driven venerable senators to suicide with the crippling taxes he had imposed upon them in order for him to dispense extravagant handouts to the common people. He had put an obscene number of his former friends to death due to irrational fears that they were plotting against him. Perhaps some of them were, but many were guilty only of being wealthy and successful and therefore not dependent on *him*, thus rendering them impervious to bribes or to blackmail. So even though Cleander was no more, the climate of fear he had created remained as his legacy.

'Where do you suppose His Excellency can be?' she enquired of Hyacinthus, whose eyes, like her own, kept darting back towards the imperial box. 'Do *you* know anything about this surprise he says he has planned for me?'

Hyacinthus grunted in the negative, but looked distinctly uncomfortable. Sometimes Marcia was convinced that he knew things which he wasn't telling her, yet she was equally sure that he only kept them from her because he knew she had enough to worry about already.

Perhaps some fresh crisis had arisen which Commodus had been called away to address? Crises were currently arising on a daily basis, but Marcia found it hard to imagine one serious enough to make Commodus miss out on the spectacle which the first afternoon of this major festival of butchery was likely to provide. For a while after Cleander's downfall Commodus *had* stayed away from public entertainments, it was true; he hadn't really gone anywhere at all. Now he had swung to the opposite extreme, manifesting himself to his marvelling subjects not only at the Games but in the theatre, at concerts, in religious processions, and on any other occasion which afforded him an excuse to grant mortal beings a glimpse of his glory.

This might have been all to the good had he not begun to appear to them dressed as his hero Hercules, complete with lion-skin and club. Recently he had given orders on a number of public occasions that he should actually be addressed as Hercules, Son of Zeus, rather than as Commodus, and he had commissioned statues of himself in the guise of Hercules to be put up in prominent locations all over the City.

Not that he had ceased to own the name Commodus altogether. Far from it. His new child favourite – who could have been taken for Ursulus' double – he called Philocommodus, so that even the little boy's nickname signified the love for the emperor which was demanded of him. In his escalating megalomania His Excellency had even decreed that Rome should henceforth be known as Colonia Commodiana, on account of his having 'refounded' it after a devastating fire had swept through the city centre. Meanwhile he had ordered the months of the year to be renamed after his own imperial titles, including 'Exsuperatorius' – the Supreme, a title previously reserved for Jupiter, King of the Gods – and 'Amazonius' in recognition of Hercules' taming of Hippolyta, Queen of the Amazons. He still called Marcia his Amazon Queen, and regularly made her dress up in her Amazon costume. Thankfully he hadn't had her do *this* yet in public, but surely it was only a matter of time. After all, for some minor misdemeanour he had made one of the Praetorian Prefects, Julius Julianus, dance naked in front of the imperial concubines, Marcia included.

But many of his subjects had begun to see the fire as an omen of worse to come. For the Temple of Peace had been destroyed, as had the Temple of Vesta which housed the sacred objects brought from the ruins of Troy by Aeneas. Commodus' days were numbered, they said, because he'd begun to go the way of Nero. Perhaps he had. Perhaps the combination of power and insecurity was bound to curdle anyone's brains.

At least he hadn't yet turned his frenzy upon the Christians in the way that Nero had done. Marcia herself had seen to that. She had freed Christians in their hundreds from prison, from mines, quarries and the arena, all of which had a voracious appetite for 'noxii' – condemned criminals – of whom there never seemed to be enough. You would have thought, Marcia reflected for the umpteenth time, that by now the Christians would have deigned to acknowledge me as one of their own.

But she knew it would never happen. Sometimes this knowledge tempted her to wash her hands of them utterly and let them all stew in their own juices.

Yet she could never quite bring herself to do so, because in spite of everything she still didn't blame God for what had happened to her. She continued to hope that when at last she stood before him, he might offer her the pardon which his Church was unable to give. After all, even though she had no right to expect help from heaven any longer, had she not been delivered from the evil that was Cleander, and from the danger that he might at any moment disclose to Commodus whatever it was that he knew about her past?

And she did still find herself thinking more and more often about her old friends, especially Corvus and Junia, and even more especially Callistus, who had mysteriously disappeared from meetings of the Assembly just before she'd had to do the same. Callistus had been such a good friend, she recognized now, as well as being as pretty as his name suggested. Something Hyacinthus had chanced to say recently had made her suspect that the eunuch might know something about this mystery too, but despite a good deal of huffing and puffing he had flatly refused to be drawn. This had prompted her to remember the widow who had once told her that a certain Callistus had robbed her of all her money. Marcia had never got to the bottom of that; indeed, she had never really tried to, assuming at the time that the widow must be talking about another Callistus entirely. Now she was much less sure.

Not that she didn't have other friends she could turn to at the palace these days, and one in particular who was every bit as comely as Carpophorus' apprentice. Even the thought of him brought a rush of colour to her face, even here in the amphitheatre with the crowds roaring with laughter all around her at the antics of the clowns and dwarfs down below. For Commodus had a new chamberlain now that Cleander was no more: an Egyptian freedman, impossibly handsome, bold as brass and flamboyantly pagan. This was Eclectus – the first man Marcia had ever loved.

She hadn't recognized him straight away, for he'd been a mere boy in the days when he'd served Quadratus the elderly senator she was meant to love. But now Eclectus had broad brown shoulders to complement his wasp-thin waist, and was as tall as Commodus himself, though he kept his face scrupulously clean-shaven after the fashion of his people and painted his eyelids with kohl. Of course Commodus had always coveted handsome men as companions as much as he prized glamorous women and pretty boys, though nowadays only so long as they harboured no political ambitions. Thank goodness Eclectus never had, otherwise he might have been embroiled in the conspiracy which had cost Quadratus his life. As it was, Eclectus had known nothing about it until after the event, and would never have had cause to suspect Marcia of involvement in it either.

What Eclectus lacked in political influence he more than made up for in rakish charm. Marcia was well aware that men like this were rarely to be trusted, but the two of them had been virtually childhood sweethearts. Surely it could do no harm for them to be friends again, so long as her handmaids and Hyacinthus always acted as chaperons?

As for whether she would like to be *more* than Eclectus' friend... she found herself pondering this question, and not for the first time, as the clowns at last chased the dwarfs right out of the arena and the sand was raked smooth for the afternoon matches to begin. The fact was that Marcia hadn't slept with anyone except Commodus since taking her vow of chastity before the Church, though she'd had any number of offers.

Now that the arena had been cleared, the afternoon's proceedings ought to have been getting under way. Yet nothing could happen until the President of the Games gave leave for it to do so, and there was still no sign of Commodus. Marcia, who had acquired an acute sensitivity for such things, could feel the mood of the crowd around her shifting. Anticipation was becoming impatience, and this was distinctly undesirable.

Suddenly a fresh wave of expectancy surged up, as from the several gateways into the arena a veritable army of men ran onto the sand carrying stage-blocks which they proceeded to deposit and set about fastening together with pegs. Whatever could it mean? They were apparently constructing two wide cross-walls right across the floor of the amphitheatre, intersecting in the middle. Were there to be four separate events taking place at the same time? There didn't seem to be a great deal of point in that. And still Commodus hadn't come back.

Once the curious structure was complete, an announcement was made that before the listed bouts began there was to be a special unscheduled item. Hercules the Hunter would demonstrate his prowess by pitting himself against a pack of ferocious wild beasts.

Thereupon bears were released into each quadrant: not

one into each, but dozens, from gates and from trapdoors under the sand, until there were easily a hundred altogether. Then trumpets blared, and at the end of one of the cross-walls, directly below the imperial box, another trapdoor opened. From it arose a platform with gilded railings, all hung about with purple cloth, upon which three figures were standing.

The man in the middle, wearing a purple robe with golden spangles and a jewelled crown and carrying a mighty golden sceptre, could only be one person. Of his two companions, one carried in his arms the infamous club and lion-skin, and the other a sheaf of javelins. With a shiver of horror Marcia realized that the former was Eclectus. The latter was Quintus Aemilius Laetus the new Praetorian Prefect; the disgraced Julius Julianus had died some time ago, possibly at his own hand. A huge roar of acclamation went up from the crowd as Commodus held his sceptre aloft, beaming with childish pleasure. Meanwhile Marcia was left cringing in dismay, as were the occupants of the seats reserved for senators.

Using the cross-wall as a walkway, Commodus advanced with his two companions to the centre of the arena. There he handed his sceptre, crown and robe to Eclectus, the Emperor of Rome standing before the entire populace of the City clad in nothing now but a minimal athlete's tunic. Over this he donned the lion-skin, and taking javelins from the arms of Laetus, he began hurling them one after another at the rampaging beasts.

He was a good shot, there was no denying that. In fact no one had ever seriously tried to belittle Commodus' prowess as a sportsman, or his impressive physique. At first his task was easy enough, since there were so many bears marauding about in each of the quadrants that he was almost bound to hit one of them, and by running to and fro along the cross-wall he could ensure that he never had far to throw. But even as his challenge got harder he rose to it valiantly, leaping and twirling and never missing his target, to the cacophanous delight of the plebeians and mounting mortification of the senators. Laetus had to keep running backwards and forwards as well, with fresh batches of javelins to replenish the emperor's supplies.

But as time went on and the bodies of the bears piled up, even the howling mob seemed to lose its stomach for the spectacle. The few bears left alive looked pitiful rather than dangerous as they padded about in their fallen comrades' blood awaiting the inevitable. They may have outnumbered the emperor a hundred to one to begin with, but since he was raised up out of their reach on his walkway they had never stood a chance of bringing him down.

Marcia herself felt physically sick. She wasn't sure if it was the sight and smell of the blood, the senseless waste of life, the destruction of so much nobility and beauty – for there *had* been something noble about the bears as they died, and they were undeniably beautiful creatures in their own way – or simply acute embarrassment on Commodus' behalf. Probably it was all these things put together, but whatever it was, she sat with one hand clamped to her belly and the other to her mouth, and prayed for the whole thing to end.

Sure enough, once all the bears lay dead, their corpses and the cross-walls were removed, and Commodus, Eclectus and Laetus disappeared from view as their gilded platform sank once more into the bowels of the amphitheatre. But then another announcement was made. There was to be a second special feature before the scheduled fights began.

Presently Commodus and his two companions entered the arena again, through one of the regular gates this time, though by their demeanour both Eclectus and Laetus gave the distinct impression that they wished one of the trapdoors would open up and swallow them of its own accord.

Commodus, in contrast, beamed like an urchin invited to a banquet of the gods. And whilst his glossy golden head was bare, from the neck downwards he wore the costume and gleaming armour of a gladiator.

There were many varieties of gladiator, but naturally Commodus would fight as a secutor, the most glamorous kind of all. Laetus had been detailed to carry his long convex shield and the short stubby sword with which secutors were equipped, which resembled those used in the legions; Eclectus bore the flanged full-face helmet with its staring eye-holes through which the secutor was obliged to look upon his opponent.

It soon became apparent who Commodus' opponent was going to be. From the gate opposite the one by which the emperor's party had entered bounded a well-known retiarius known to the crowds as the Lynx. Lightly armed for manoevrability, he carried his own net and trident, the only weapons this type of gladiator was allowed. Audible gasps went up on all sides; surely neither the emperor nor this long-standing favourite of the masses was going to be permitted to squander his life down there in the bloody sand merely for the sake of novelty?

As things turned out no one need have worried. Emperor and gladiator had clearly been training together for some time; on account of their skill and mutual understanding their display was more like a dance than a fight, and not a drop of either man's blood was shed. Equally odd was the fact that Commodus held his shield in his right hand and sword in his left, because for some perverse reason he was mightily proud of being left-handed. Round and round the two performers circled, pouncing, dodging, feinting, for all the world looking as though at any moment one would inevitably send the other hotfoot to Hades whether he intended to or not.

Predictably the extraordinary spectacle ended with a victory for Commodus, who magnanimously spared the Lynx without hesitation and then helped him to his feet, a calculated gesture which had the crowd yelling in jubilation. Commodus went on to make an exaggerated show of kissing both Laetus and Eclectus without removing his helmet. Then he did remove it, and in spite of her disgust Marcia could not help but marvel at how radiant His Excellency appeared as he revelled in his subjects' adulation; briefly he seemed to her to shine more brightly even than Eclectus. The only real difference between an emperor and a common man, she thought, was the number of people who had to love him in order for him to feel affirmed.

As Commodus stood there exulting, the arena's several gates sprang open at the same time and from all directions gladiators of every type came running, to form a circle around the emperor and his companions and his vanquished opponent. Commodus then took inordinate pleasure in pairing them up personally in readiness for the afternoon's contests. Of course it would have been decided in advance who would fight against whom, but Commodus either remembered the pairings perfectly or changed them as he saw fit. Only after the combatants had taken their gladiatorial oath in front of him and saluted him right there on the sand did the emperor at last make his way up to the imperial box, with Laetus and Eclectus still flanking him as he walked.

When Commodus took his seat, Marcia must have been the only person in the whole arena who was looking at one of his companions rather than at the emperor himself. She could only be grateful now that she hadn't been invited to sit with them, and therefore wouldn't be expected to fawn over His Excellency and offer him her congratulations.

She couldn't avoid him that evening, however, when he came straight to her chambers from his supper, like a little boy fresh from winning his first race who runs to his mother desperately wanting her to be proud of him. He was still all but speechless with excitement yet at the same time bursting to tell her of some dream he'd once had where he'd seen himself fighting in the Flavian Amphitheatre, and how it had finally come true for him today. Even as he was struggling to string his words together, Marcia was recalling that she had heard about this dream before, from Corvus' brother. How Caelus and Cottia had laughed at the thought of an emperor dreaming of glory in the arena, as if he didn't have enough of it already! Nonetheless she did her best now to give Commodus the affirmation he was seeking, and thankfully he was too full of himself to detect her insincerity.

'Today was merely my debut!' he informed her. 'In the coming days you will see me do deeds of heroism far more remarkable than anything you witnessed this afternoon!' Then he flung his arms around her and fell to smothering her with kisses. Knowing that she would not escape until he had spent his euphoria inside her, Marcia rose to the occasion and strove with him almost as valiantly upon her bed as the Lynx had done in the sand. She tried hard not to pretend that he was Eclectus.

Commodus proved true to his word: at each subsequent session of the Games he entertained his gawking subjects with ever more bizarre and extravagant displays of butchery. Daily he dispatched lions, tigers, elephants, rhinoceros and even a hippopotamus or two, mostly from the safety of his walkway but occasionally by stepping out onto the sand himself – though any beasts which were genuinely dangerous were led to him in nets. One day he laid low a whole flock of ostriches as they ran about squawking and flapping; lopping off one of their heads he waved it around in front of the senators' benches as some sort of threat, though most of the senators were more embarrassed than afraid and afterwards some were said to have stuffed leaves from their festive garlands into their mouths to stop themselves laughing out loud. Their plucky hero even took down a giraffe, which turned out to be a serious error of judgement because although everyone agreed that the creature was exotic, it was also very obviously harmless. Even the Roman mob at its most savage could find little to enjoy in watching such a gentle and graceful animal quietly expire in a welter of gore.

But this kind of blunder on the emperor's behalf was quickly forgiven and forgotten by the majority when he appeared once more in his secutor's armour and helmet and opened each afternoon's proceedings by taking on another of the City's favourite fighters. Retiarii, Thracians, hoplomachi, scissores... he fought – and beat – them all.

Though the crowds continued to cheer him on with more or less enthusiasm, most of the senators would have ceased to attend the Games altogether had they not been forced to show their faces – as would Marcia. For throughout the fortnight during which the Games lasted, Commodus persisted in visiting her chambers every evening and boasting of his exploits before vanquishing her in her turn, so that she soon came to dread the ending of the daily schedule as much as its beginning. After the first few nights she could no longer play the part of the gushing admirer with any conviction. Soon she ceased even to try, and applied herself instead to persuading him that enough was enough.

'Surely you have nothing left to prove, my darling?' she cooed as he sought to cover her lips with his own to prevent her from saying anything he didn't want to hear. 'Everyone is convinced now of your heroism, and I do worry so much that you might be injured, or worse.'

'Oh, but there is no need at all for you to worry your pretty little head over me,' Commodus assured her. 'There is no gladiator sufficiently brave or skilled – or foolish – to make even the slightest mark upon my divine flesh. You must remember that as Hercules reborn, my veins run with the golden ichor of the gods, so toxic to a mere mortal that the tiniest splash of it can strike a man dead.'

'I don't worry when I am awake and able to hold these truths at the front of my mind! It's when I sleep, my precious, I suffer the most dreadful nightmares...'

But Commodus wasn't remotely interested in hearing about Marcia's nightmares. He was interested only in pinning her to her bed so she could not move a muscle, and pumping her rigid body full of his celestial juices.

She hadn't been lying about the nightmares, however. She had woken up in a cold sweat more than once every night since the Games began. But she hadn't been dreaming of Commodus dead or wounded. Rather she had been seeing herself driven into the arena with him, in the guise of the Amazon Hippolyta, or even of Megara, the wife of Hercules' youth whom he had torn to pieces in a frenzy.

The final few days of the Games saw a number of the senators' seats remain empty; they must have decided that come what may they could take no more. On the penultimate day – the thirteenth – it wasn't merely the senators who voted with their feet. Many of the commoners stayed at home too, for the rumour had gone around that Commodus intended to shoot poisoned arrows randomly into the crowd in imitation of Hercules' sixth 'labour', the Slaughter of the Stymphalian Birds. This rumour was less preposterous than it sounded, because on the twelfth day Commodus had gathered together all the beggars he could find who had lost their feet and lower legs through disease or accident and had them fitted with what looked like serpents' tails pulled on over their knees. He'd armed them with sponges to represent stones and then proceeded to kill them all with blows of his club, pretending that they were the Titans who had once thrown rocks at Jupiter.

Fortunately the rumour about the poisoned arrows turned out to be unfounded; on the thirteenth day Commodus contented himself with killing a hundred lions with a hundred arrows instead.

But that evening, when one of Marcia's maids opened the door to receive him as usual, it wasn't the emperor who stood outside.

CHAPTER TEN: MARCIA

II

'Eclectus?' Marcia whispered. Instinctively she looked round for Hyacinthus. He was fast asleep in his chair.

Eclectus held a finger to Marcia's lips. Without a word he walked her through into her bed-chamber where they were quite alone, and closed the door. Only then did he say, 'His Excellency is indisposed after all his exertions, my lady, and is reluctant to perform for you at less than his best. He sent me to give his apologies.'

At a loss for a suitable reply, Marcia could only swallow and nod as she searched Eclectus' face for any clue as to his own feelings or intentions. When she read there the same warring emotions she was battling with herself she moved towards him unreservedly and let her head fall forward onto his shoulder.

And how wonderful, how incredible it was, to be folded in the arms of someone who wasn't likely to crush her ribs when he took hold of her, or make her lips bleed when he kissed her, or tear her flesh in its tenderest places by using his manhood as a weapon of war. How exhilarating to be embraced by someone whom she desired without fearing, someone who rekindled the instincts within her which Commodus' cruelty had all but extinguished. How thrilling to be kissed by someone who she truly believed respected her, valued her, might even love her... in short by someone, perhaps anyone, who wasn't Commodus.

If Eclectus had sought to steal everything that belonged to his master there and then, she would almost certainly have consented regardless of the consequences. But this wasn't what he had come for.

Framing her face between the palms of his hands, Eclectus parted his lips from hers and looked deep into her eyes. Then he said, 'Marcia, I cannot live this way any longer.' And in that moment of profound mutual understanding, they were united more completely and more irrevocably than they could have been in any other way.

After that, though there was no real need for him to do so, Eclectus could not be deterred from expressing in words the disgust which the emperor's worsening behaviour had evoked within him. And as he went on ranting and she went on listening, the man Marcia held in her arms was no longer Eclectus the flamboyant Egyptian dandy. This was Eclectus the abused and tormented victim, his soul stripped bare as an unwrapped mummy torn from its sarcophagus. Yet the more defiled and damaged he revealed himself to be, the more intensely Marcia found herself loving him. With mounting agitation Eclectus described the indignities to which Commodus had subjected him: every evening during the Games, after inflicting himself upon Marcia, Commodus had returned to his own chambers and there violated Eclectus too, then made him watch while he did the same to his sparring partner Narcissus or the wretched little boy he called Philocommodus. Even so, none of this had been as harrowing as being made to accompany Commodus into the arena and witness at close quarters the mindless bloodshed in which the emperor exulted.

'I couldn't feel more polluted if I had slain all those men and beasts with my own bare hands,' Eclectus finished up, and his hands were visibly trembling as he spoke. 'Oh, I have congratulated Commodus on his heroism a thousand times over, and no one is more adept than an Egyptian at masking his feelings with face-paint. But I cannot do it any more.'

'Nor can I.' Marcia took hold of Eclectus' hands, but hers were no steadier. 'I'm afraid even to sleep sometimes, because of the things I dream about.' She shuddered, suddenly nauseous, but was comforted to feel Eclectus' hands grip her own more tightly. 'You know,' she continued with a grateful little smile, 'They say the Amazon Queen was so smitten with Hercules that she would have given him her girdle of her own free will if only he hadn't tried to take it by force and caused a bloodbath. Now I can't help thinking what a climax it would make to the Games to have female fighters slaughtered just like her warrior maidens, with the Queen herself the last to fall! And I dread that Commodus will read my mind, that my fears will become his fantasies, then part of his plans. If only there were something we could do.'

'There is *something*,' Eclectus murmured, and regardless of his initial intentions he began kissing her face and neck as though there were no tomorrow. Indeed there probably *wouldn't* be, for them at any rate, Marcia was thinking as she let him draw her down onto her bed after all, so what did it matter? At least they would have salvaged something of themselves from the tyrant who ruled them, and given it of their own free will to one another.

Yet at the last moment Marcia felt the desire curdling within her and drew back. And Eclectus released her, uncomplaining, because after everything that each of them had suffered he would never, ever, have coerced her, when at heart they both knew that this wasn't the way they wanted to see Commodus pay for the evil he had done to them.

For even after all this time, at the back of Marcia's mind

was the vow she had made before God and his Church and only ever broken because she hadn't had a choice. Today, lying happy at last in Eclectus' arms, she *did* have a choice, and if the two of them were discovered together and sentenced to die at tomorrow's Games for cuckolding the man they were both supposed to love, she wanted to be able to walk out onto the sand with her head held high because it was not true.

But before she could move to stand up, the door to her bedroom flew open and the bravest and quickest of her own handmaids burst in upon them. Whipping the door shut behind her and leaning hard against it the girl hissed, 'My lady: the emperor! He's here after all!' and in a trice Eclectus was up and dressed and had made his exit by the window.

Did Commodus notice the curtain slowly swinging when he barged his way in just a few moments later, almost knocking the slave-girl off her feet? Did he believe that Marcia had been asleep, and was he convinced by her feigned confusion when she sat bolt upright to find him standing in her doorway? She could not tell, but there was no mistaking the shadow that passed across his face when he asked if Eclectus hadn't been here to see her, since he himself had sent him.

'Oh yes, he did come here, Your Excellency,' said the slave-girl promptly. 'But my lady was sleeping so we sent him away. She hasn't been well since lunch time.'

'You haven't been well, my darling? Is that so?' Commodus advanced toward the bed, his face a shifting stormscape of lust, annoyance and the beginnings of suspicion. As Marcia nodded and did her best to look sick, which was scarcely difficult, he scooped her up and cried, 'Why, you are shivering! You must have a fever. I shall send for my physician at once.'

'No... it is nothing... it is only my fear for you, my lord, it is only my anxious days and sleepless nights which have made me sick...'

'Well in that case you have no reason to be sick any

longer,' Commodus declared with satisfaction, 'Because tomorrow I shall not be fighting.'

'Really?' Reaching up to wind her arms about his neck she prayed that her brimming eyes expressed relief rather than bewilderment and escalating terror.

'Really and truly. You see, I have considered the distress which it causes you, my sweetheart, so for you I shall not step out onto the sand tomorrow. Instead I shall sit all day in the imperial box, and you shall sit by my side in the empress's place from dawn to dusk so that the whole of Rome may recognize you as her mother and mistress and love of their emperor's life!' With that he tossed her back among her pillows and set about demonstrating his devotion in the way he had been doing every evening for a fortnight.

Should she be grateful that his lust had apparently prevailed over his suspicion? She could only hope now that the slave-girl who had already saved her skin would have the wherewithal to go after Eclectus and ensure that their stories matched up. The girl would certainly be rewarded for her initiative; but then again, most slave-girls had their own reasons for becoming adept at covering visitors' tracks.

As for Commodus' promise that he would have Marcia sit beside him tomorrow in the Augusta's seat at the Games… this *was* something new. Whether it was wise was another thing entirely. Though he had escorted her to the amphitheatre in person more than once, they had never sat side by side throughout like a royal couple, and she knew that some of the senators would be incensed – if they turned up – even though none had any reason to bear her a personal grudge. She had never intrigued against any one of them, and had won concessions and mercy for many.

That night Marcia had no nightmares, because she did not sleep. She lay staring up into the darkness, agonizing over what the promise might mean. Might His Excellency be planning to marry her after all? Might he even propose to her in public in front of his adoring fans? How like him that would be; and yet it seemed equally likely that he might denounce her in front of them instead and then have her executed just like Crispina. How horribly ridiculous it was, to be lying awake wondering whether your lover meant to kill you or to marry you and make you mistress of the mightiest empire the world had ever seen.

In the event, the final day of the Games passed off without either proposal or denouncement, though Marcia did get to sit in the Augusta's seat and wear a gold and purple robe and a crown exactly like the emperor's. Behind them sat Eclectus and Laetus; with Eclectus' eyes boring into her back and the eyes of so many senators and people fixed on her face, she thought how ironic it was that she could be the object of so much hatred and envy when she herself would gladly have given up everything to live happily ever after in obscurity with an Egyptian catamite.

Once the Games were over, life in the City returned to what passed for normal, but Commodus did not. Marcia hardly saw him, which was a relief in some respects whilst deeply worrying in others. According to Eclectus, whom she saw much more often than she should have been doing, the emperor was spending long hours in conclave with Games managers and gladiatorial trainers or brooding on his own, and only left his private apartment in order to hone his own gladiatorial skills against various exponents of the art imported into the palace for the purpose. One was the famous retiarius the Lynx, against whom he had fought on the first day of the Plebeian Games. Another was a prodigiously enormous and well-endowed murmillo with a filthy temper, known to his admirers as Vesuvius. But Commodus' favourite sparring partner was still the athlete and wrestler Narcissus, with whom His Excellency had trained regularly ever since Marcia had first come to the palace. It was said to be Narcissus with whom Commodus was now sleeping most nights too, though allegedly Narcissus hated every moment he had to spend in the emperor's company whether in bed or anywhere else.

Marcia was somewhat surprised to find this out, but Eclectus assured her that Narcissus had always regarded his bizarre existence as a living hell.

When at last Commodus did come to visit Marcia once again, he was restless as a chained panther; so much so that he broke off in the middle of renewing their physical acquaintance and took to pacing up and down by her bedside instead.

'My darling, what is wrong?' she beseeched him, and there was no need for her to feign anxiety. 'You are troubled beyond endurance; come, share your burden with me.'

'Marcia, darling, how well you read me! It is true that I am too preoccupied just now for my own good or for yours; yet I am not distressed! Quite the reverse, my dear, quite the reverse. For I have put so much work into preparing myself and my comrades-in-arms for the next great festival in our calendar, and now it will be upon us in a matter of days.'

'The Saturnalia?' Marcia was confused. 'But Saturnalia celebrations don't include games.' For indeed they didn't, as a rule. Saturnalia was the festival of the turning of the year, when Janus, January's god-with-two-faces, was honoured for sheltering the ousted god Saturn from Jupiter who had stolen his throne. Gifts would be exchanged and festive meals enjoyed in people's homes, but nothing special went on in the arena. The only ceremonial events which took place were the public acclamation of the two new consuls – who this year would be Erucius Clarus Vibianus and Pompeius Sosius Falco – and a sacrifice at Janus' temple.

But Commodus would not be drawn any further on the subject and left soon afterwards, with his aborted erotic mission still unaccomplished.

The following morning Marcia summoned Eclectus to attend her as soon as he could make his escape. While Commodus grappled with Narcissus in whatever fresh way took his fancy it was easy enough for Eclectus to evade him; as for Hyacinthus, he was becoming too slow and sleepy to react very much at all to Eclectus' increasingly frequent comings and goings. Eunuchs age early and his years were weighing ever more heavily upon him.

'Whatever madness can Commodus have dreamt up now?' Marcia asked fearfully as she and Eclectus sat side by side upon her bed, the one place where they could talk without being overheard. On any other day his nearness would have thrilled her, but not today.

'I only wish I knew.' Eclectus' kohl-rimmed eyes were deep black pools of dread. 'Morning and night I beg my gods to strike him dead, but they do not listen.'

'Eclectus...' Marcia moved up closer and covered his hands with her own. 'I am going to tell you something which I have never confessed to another living soul. You must repeat it to no one, ever. Do you understand?' And when Eclectus nodded without taking his eyes from hers she plunged on, though without knowing why, 'You remember the failed conspiracy to kill him which ended in the deaths of his sister and your old master Quadratus?'

'Of course I remember. But I didn't think *you*...?'

'Oh yes. I knew about it, though at the time I did not understand how a woman could bring herself to engineer the death of her own brother. Now I understand only too well, and it wasn't because she wanted to see her own husband made emperor in her brother's place, nor even because she wanted what was best for Rome. But that's not all.' Marcia swallowed hard, for suddenly her throat was as dry as a drainage ditch in a drought. 'I didn't merely *know* about the conspiracy, Eclectus. You see... Quadratus hated Commodus so much for stealing me from him – he was his cousin, after all – and I did feel sorry for him, because he had never treated me badly, not like Commodus did. So... it was I who found out for the conspirators exactly when Commodus would be leaving the palace for the Games that day. All that was needed then was for Lucilla to have her nephew arrange an ambush at the entrance to the Colosseum. If only the little fool hadn't started waving his dagger around and shouting, "This is what the Senate has sent you!" Lucilla and your master would not have died. But Commodus would.'

For a long time after that, neither of them said anything more at all, though they continued to search one another's eyes. Then Eclectus said quietly, 'I must go now, or my absence will be noticed.' Gently he prised her hands away from his, and without another word he was gone.

As soon as he had left, Marcia was engulfed by self-reproach. Why had she told him her secret, something no one should ever have needed to know? And when he had heard it, why had he proceeded to excuse himself so quickly? What a fool she was, what a stupid, suicidal fool...

The following day was the last one in December, New Year's Eve. Early in the morning Commodus fetched up on Marcia's doorstep before she had even started breakfast, and in a rush of near-delirium divulged to her his Saturnalia plans in all their ghastly detail. In the midst of the New Year festivities he had resolved to have the incoming consuls Clarus and Falco put to death, and then to appear himself before the people as both sole consul and secutor. Nor would he issue forth from the imperial palace on New Year's morning in the customary fashion. Instead he would come from the gladiatorial barracks, clad in his secutor's armour instead of the imperial purple. And as he led the solemn procession to Janus' temple for the New Year sacrifices he would be accompanied not by Praetorians, but by a bevy of his fellow gladiators.

'Oh no, my darling. Please, no, I beg of you!' Marcia burst into tears and threw herself at his feet as though it was she who faced summary execution. 'Do not do this dreadful thing! Don't bring disgrace upon yourself and your principate by this senseless killing. Don't entrust your own protection to desperate men who would turn on you without a second thought.'

Far from being moved by Marcia's outburst, Commodus

flew into a rage, slapping her and knocking her away from him so brutally that she hit her head hard on the leg of a table. When she recovered her senses she was lying on the couch by her breakfast table with a bandage wound round her temples and Eclectus kneeling at her side.

'Marcia, thank the gods… oh Marcia, both Laetus and I have tried to change his mind, but he is impervious to all reason! He has ordered us to arrange for him to spend tonight at the barracks so that he can proceed to Janus' temple from there first thing in the morning.'

'And did he tell you that he would slaughter the new consuls in cold blood?' Marcia whispered once she had remembered where she was. 'Why would he do such a terrible thing?'

'Because he cannot abide the thought that his people's attention might be diverted for even a second away from *him*. And because he is an evil, impious monster who deserves nothing more than death himself.'

As Marcia listened to Eclectus' impassioned words and noted the glint in his eyes, it came to her that she had been right to tell him of her part in Lucilla's conspiracy after all. Impulsively he took her hand and squeezed it tightly, then rose to his feet and said, 'I must go now and meet with Laetus; it may be that we can find a way to warn Clarus and Falco of what is in store for them, or even induce the gladiators to restrain him… and you must lie still until the physician I sent for has been and given you permission to get up.'

'Yes. Yes, I must,' Marcia agreed readily enough, for she did feel horribly dizzy and nauseous. When Eclectus left she must have drifted out of her senses again straight away, for the next thing she knew was the insistence of someone tugging at her clothing; she revived with a start to find Philocommodus standing by her couch with his thumb in his mouth and his big round eyes fixed on her face.

Just like Ursulus before him, Philocommodus loved

Marcia and would visit her often when he was wandering freely about the palace, flagrantly naked like a fat little Cupid. As Marcia drew him towards her to give him a hug he dropped a small wax tablet which he'd been trying to keep hold of while sucking his thumb and attempting to prod her awake all at the same time. Instinctively Marcia leaned over and picked it up. She saw at once that the writing on it was Commodus'.

Naturally Philocommodus would play with all sorts of things which the emperor left lying about in his chambers. Since by now it was way past noon and Commodus was probably either at the baths or sleeping through the siesta, his little bed-fellow must have been bored enough to start picking through the morning's detritus.

But as soon as Marcia made sense of what His Excellency had written – the blow to her head was causing the words to run together and spill off the sides of the tablet – she felt twice as sick as before. For she was holding in her hand the latest list of individuals who Commodus had decided must forfeit their lives that night. Not only were Clarus and Falco to die, but so were all the senators who had stayed away from his Games. But added in a scribble right at the top of the list was her own name, followed immediately by those of Laetus and Eclectus.

So sharp was Marcia's cry of dismay that it brought all her handmaids and even Hyacinthus running, only to be told not to worry; she had merely had another bad dream. So this was to be her reward for enduring Commodus' arrogance and abuse all these years, for showing him nothing but patience and even devotion in spite of his cruelty. And this was how Eclectus was to be recompensed for allowing Commodus to unman him night after night, and for escorting him time and again into the arena of death. Oh, it wasn't hard to see why Commodus had decided to dispose of either of them, but as soon as Marcia had stifled her tortured cry she made up her mind once and for all that it would not be the people whose names were on the list of the proscribed who would die tonight. Commodus' time had come.

She sent straight away for Eclectus, who responded the moment he received the summons, fearing that Marcia's condition had taken a turn for the worse. At once she handed him the tablet, saying, 'It seems that His Excellency has not told us *everything* he has planned for the New Year celebrations,' and then watched Eclectus' jaw drop and his face turn crimson with rage. The emasculated victim was no more; in his place was reborn the indomitable Eclectus with whom Marcia had first fallen in love. Furthermore she knew that he had already come to the same conclusion she had already reached about what they must do next, and that there was no time to lose in doing it.

Eclectus sealed up the tablet securely and sent for his trustiest slave to take it to Laetus. They did not have long to wait before Laetus arrived in person, accompanied by the wrestler Narcissus.

'Hyacinthus,' said Marcia, pushing herself up from her couch and moving with difficulty to the chair where the eunuch was dozing, 'The four of us are planning a special surprise for the emperor this evening, and no one else must know of it in advance. If anyone comes here this afternoon – the emperor especially – you must not admit them or everything will be spoiled. I know you won't let me down.' And she hugged the old eunuch with such fervour that he was quite overcome and had to fan himself with a napkin. Meanwhile Marcia took her three visitors into her bedroom and closed the door.

The plot was hatched so swiftly that it was almost as though Eclectus' gods had decided to answer his prayers after all and reveal it fully formed. Commodus had already announced to Eclectus his intention to visit Marcia that evening. All it would take to see him off would be for Marcia to poison the wine she was accustomed to offer him on his arrival; Eclectus, Laetus and Narcissus would follow the emperor to her apartment in secret and then be on hand to ensure that events took their course. They did discuss briefly who would rule over Rome when Commodus was dead; perhaps it was high time that the right of making emperors reverted to the Senate. But there was nothing to be gained – and all to be lost – from debating such questions now.

To begin with everything went as smoothly as the conspirators could have hoped for. Commodus fetched up on Marcia's threshold already drunk, so it was simplicity itself for her to induce him to drink the poison which the physician sent by Eclectus to examine her during the afternoon had been instructed to bring with him. Thus when the imperial couple retired to Marcia's bedroom to lie together before His Excellency left for the gladiators' barracks Commodus was already drowsy and disoriented, and he passed out as planned without having time to undress. Meanwhile Hyacinthus had fallen fast asleep in his chair and didn't even stir when Eclectus, Laetus and Narcissus arrived to spring their surprise.

But presently, as Marcia kept fretful vigil by his bedside, the emperor started to moan and writhe, then to retch, and to vomit so violently and loudly that Eclectus, who had been sitting just outside the bedroom door, could stay in his seat no longer. He rushed into Marcia's bedroom to find the emperor being spectacularly sick in his sleep, with Marcia crouched beside him, frozen with fear.

'Hyacinthus?' said Eclectus, aware that the eunuch had awoken and followed him into the bedroom, 'His Excellency is ill. Call Laetus and Narcissus in here at once.' And as soon as the bewildered eunuch had bustled off to do as he was bidden, Eclectus set about rolling Commodus onto his back in the hope that his vomit would choke him.

It didn't work. By the time Laetus and Narcissus had rushed in, and shut Hyacinthus out, it seemed that Commodus might even be regaining his senses, having expelled most of the poison from his system.

'We have to finish this now,' Laetus grunted, after cursing

vehemently under his breath. 'Narcissus? Strangle him. You know best how to do it.'

The athlete did not need telling twice. Springing forward he wrapped an arm about Commodus' throat in a chokehold he must have used a hundred times before to gain a submission when they'd been wrestling. But this time he did not let go when Commodus' eyes began to bulge and then to glaze over and stare like the eyes of one of his own statues. Only when the imperial heart had long stopped beating did Narcissus loosen his grip. Then while athlete and Praetorian commander were exchanging nods of grim satisfaction, their two co-conspirators wept in each other's arms.

CHAPTER ELEVEN: CALLISTUS

Callistus sat reading on the balcony of Titus' villa. Perched on a rocky promontory jutting out into the sea, the house boasted one of the finest views in Antium. Although it was New Year's Day and most people would have thought it far too cold to be sitting outside, Callistus had made it his habit to wring the most out of every daylight moment he was allowed to spend in this glorious place. The sun was already beginning its descent into the sparkling water, but Callistus' thick cloak kept the cold at bay, and each time he looked up he was struck again by the beauty which surrounded him. Antium's beaches were golden, its hillsides wooded, and soon the spring flowers would burst into life to remind him that he too was alive, and once again pleasing to look upon. His cough was almost gone, his sunken flesh was filling out, his shaven hair had grown back glossy and thick and he was still only twenty three years old.

Many young men of his age would have reckoned Antium intolerably dull, and it was true that Callistus felt lonely here from time to time. Titus was often away, and his slaves kept their distance, having been told that the master's new friend was recovering from a personal tragedy and must not be disturbed. But it was so wonderful to be able to fill his mending lungs with fresh sea air and not to have to hack at rocks or grind up grain every hour God sent that he could never be unhappy for long. He could stroll through parkland and town at will, go to the baths or the exercise ground whenever he liked, and aside from casting a critical eye over Titus' accounts from time to time nothing was expected of him at all. For the first time in his life he was no man's property; he was accepted simply for being himself, and this was so foreign to his experience that he had to pinch himself hourly to be sure that it wasn't one of his daydreams.

Titus himself was a congenial companion when he was at home. A wealthy widower without children, he was glad to have Callistus around just as his brother had predicted. And although he wasn't a man who wore his heart on his sleeve, he clearly enjoyed having someone with whom to share his love of edifying books. He brought Callistus a fresh crop of scrolls and even the odd codex whenever he came back from the City – Christian books among them, when he could get them. Some of these were copies of works written by the earliest apostles or their companions, which the Church was coming to regard not only as inspired Scripture but as the completion of the Bible inherited from the Jews. Callistus was surprised at how fascinating he found them.

Never before had he been privileged to study such precious documents for himself. Even though Carpophorus had acquired a couple of Gospels and stashed them away in his library, his slaves had never been allowed to touch them. Titus, however, actively encouraged Callistus to learn as much as he could about God from any and every source, and to seek him deep in his own soul. To Titus what really mattered was making your own personal peace with your Father in Heaven; you could worry about your status in the eyes of His Church on Earth later on. Their long conversations, often conducted on this tranquil balcony after dinner over a flagon of wine from one of Titus' own vineyards, gave Callistus a great deal to think about on the days he spent alone.

Titus' business empire was prodigious. He owned a ship, and several workshops near his town house in Rome which were managed by his freedmen and employed large numbers of poor freeborn citizens, some of whom would otherwise have been needier than many slaves. In addition to houses in Rome and Antium Titus owned a sizeable farming enterprise and some smaller estates in the Tuscan countryside which supplied food to his own and other men's businesses in the City. Some of his fellow Christians begrudged him his riches and said he should give them all away, but according to Titus it was how you used your money that was important, not how much you had. He himself had always striven to use his surplus resources for the glory of God and the relief of other men's suffering, and so far as Callistus could see God must be pleased with him, for the more philanthropic projects Titus financed, the richer he seemed to become.

Many of Titus' most enlightened ideas came from the writings of a Christian scholar known as Clement of Alexandria, one of whose books Callistus was reading this evening. He had begun it the day before, and might have finished it in a single sitting if he hadn't been distracted part way through the afternoon by the unannounced arrival of a visitor. The interruption had disturbed him in more ways than one.

Deeply engrossed, Callistus hadn't registered at first that there were footsteps approaching. Besides, he was so accustomed by now to the sound of Titus' distinctive flat-footed gait and his frequent comings and goings that he'd quite forgotten that his host was away in Rome. So when he sensed that someone was standing behind him, and looked round to see not Titus but Gaius, he almost dropped Clement's scroll on the ground.

'So sorry, my boy; didn't mean to startle you,' Gaius said; even his voice was a lot like his brother's. 'Only *I* was a little startled to find it was you and not Titus all muffled up out here in the middle of winter with your nose in a book. Just as well I wasn't tempted to creep up and pounce on you like I used to do to him when we were both knee-high to grasshoppers. But he did the same to me often enough. We both loved our reading.'

Callistus smiled; little wonder the learned churchman had been taken aback to find that a hard-bitten ex-convict apparently shared his enjoyment of literature. Then again, Gaius didn't know that Callistus' ability to scan Virgil's hexameters on sight had set him on the road to freedom. 'I'm afraid Titus is in Rome,' Callistus told him. 'He didn't say when he would be back. Is something the matter?'

'The matter? Oh no... well, not especially. It's true that there's a mighty strange atmosphere in the City just now; nothing I could put my finger on, you understand, but enough to make me think that a few days in Antium might be just what I'm in need of. When I last saw Titus he said he'd be spending the New Year here. I suppose I should have checked to see that his plans hadn't changed.'

'You'll be staying here tonight, Master Gaius, all the same?'

'No, no, I'll wait while the grooms see to my horses, but if Titus doesn't appear by and by I have friends in town I should like to look up; I shall probably stay overnight with them. In the meantime it's good to have an excuse to talk to *you*.'

So saying, Gaius ensconced himself in Titus' chair, making Callistus feel suddenly guilty for not having invited him to do so earlier. He wasn't really sure if he should be playing the host or the guest in any case, but when he offered to send for refreshments, Gaius waved one hand and said, 'The kitchen lads are fixing something up for me already. Now tell me, young Callistus: are you feeling any better for getting some fresh sea air into your lungs? You're certainly *looking* much better than last time I saw you. And if you're managing to settle to some study already, that's a very good sign, I have to say. Now what's this book that's got you so riveted I could have pulled the chair out from underneath you before you'd noticed I was here?'

'Clement of Alexandria,' Callistus said when he could get a word in. 'Do you know his work, Master Gaius? Titus tells me he's still alive, and no more than forty years old.'

'Yes I do, as it happens; and yes he is – and still in Alexandria so far as I know. He teaches there I think. But none of his books is what you'd call light reading, Callistus. Don't you find him rather hard-going? Oh – thank you,' he said, breaking off to take a bowl of bread and stuffed olives from a slave who handed it over before darting away without a word.

'No,' replied Callistus. 'I find him inspiring.' And as Gaius' eyebrows went up he plunged on, 'I didn't know books like this existed, you see. It's not a commentary on the scriptures, nor is it philosophy of the kind my old friend Hippolytus used to read. Somehow it seems to combine the best of both.'

'I suppose it does,' Gaius acknowledged, looking still more impressed. 'Though I have to admit that Titus was always the philosopher in our house. I preferred the poets and the odd tragic play to help me drown my sorrows whenever a pretty girl abandoned me.' Gaius pulled a mournful face, which was rapidly subsumed in a beaming smile as he asked with disarming simplicity, 'So which of Clement's teachings appeals to you the most?'

Callistus wasn't fooled; having worked so long for Carpophorus, he knew when he was being appraised. 'Well...' he began, then continued with growing confidence, 'I do like the way he pictures the Church as a school, whose pupils have all been accepted onto the register, but who are all very different when it comes to ability and application. They pursue the same course of study, but they're bound to make mistakes as they go along. It seems to me that if more bishops and elders thought like Clement, they could set the highest standards of conduct for every believer to aspire to, yet also keep forgiving and restoring those who let them down. After all, no school expels its pupils simply for getting their sums wrong or their grammar mixed up.'

'Ah yes. Yes indeed,' Gaius said, no doubt concluding that this unlikely novice student with his dubious past had every good reason to find such a doctrine attractive.

So Callistus explained, 'It's not just for myself that I like the sound of this approach so much, Master Gaius. It's for the whole Christian Church. Clement thinks it should be neither a showcase for saints nor a sanctuary for scroungers bent on taking advantage of God's mercy. It should be a school whose doors are always open, but whose teachers never stop working for their pupils' improvement.'

Gaius said nothing to this, merely nodding and stroking his beard; Callistus suspected he was acquitting himself rather well in his impromptu examination. In point of fact he hadn't even straightened out in his head what it was about Clement that he found so compelling until Gaius' canny questioning had forced him to express it.

'You see,' he went on, warming to his subject as his ability to find the right words expanded, 'I couldn't really grasp what philosophy was *for* until I started reading Clement. He says that philosophy's like the Jewish Law, only it's for Gentiles; it's one of the masters in his 'school', whose task is to point each pupil to Jesus. He admits he was brought up on Plato and Aristotle. Yet he doesn't see the need to choose between embracing philosophy wholesale or rejecting it out of hand. He says you just have to accept it for what it is and use it in moderation like anything else.'

'Aha.' Gaius said, with another beaming smile. 'You've hit the nail on the head there, young Callistus. Those who understand these things far better than I do say that this is what makes Clement such a great thinker. He's well known for blending Jesus' ethical teachings with the Greek idea of the Golden Mean. So he says the same sort of thing about wealth as he does about philosophy.'

'Yes, that's what Titus told me, though I haven't come to anything about money so far in this book. Maybe it's in one of his others.'

'I'm not sure where it comes, but I know he says somewhere that we don't need to choose between the two extremes of aspiring to be hermits who live in caves on nothing but locusts, and believing that a man must be as rich as Croesus to demonstrate that God is blessing him. All that's required is a generous, unpretentious lifestyle lived in gratitude to God, and a healthy respect for his creation. Whenever I go to a banquet and someone gives me a garland I'm reminded of Clement's advice that it's better to leave beautiful flowers to grow and flourish in the garden than pick them to weave into wreaths which have wilted before you've even finished your dessert. Not that I don't relish the odd banquet now and again, and why not? Jesus enjoyed a good party after all.'

What wisdom there was in all this, Callistus had marvelled while Gaius was speaking; and he was still marvelling now, long after Gaius had gone on his way and Titus still hadn't come home. If only Gaius hadn't soured the sweetness of his reflections by hinting that something was amiss in the City. Callistus could only trust that Titus – and Marcia – would be all right.

Then, while he was watching the sun sink slowly into the sea, the slave who had brought Gaius his bread and olives yesterday rushed out again onto the balcony and said without preamble, 'I'm sorry, Master Callistus, but I thought you would want to be told this news straight away. His Excellency the emperor is dead.'

At once the winter chill cut through Callistus' warm clothing, and his conversation with Gaius was forgotten. 'Dead?' he repeated. 'Commodus? How so? Did someone kill him?'

'I don't know, Master Callistus. Some are saying he was poisoned, others that a gladiator stabbed him. The story from the palace is that he passed out after the New Year's Eve celebrations and never woke up. Pertinax the Urban Prefect has been acclaimed as his successor.'

'Pertinax... Heavens above. I see. Well – I mean... thank

you; you did well to tell me.'

As the slave bobbed his head and departed, Callistus' mind was already turning cartwheels faster than an acrobat in the marketplace. He was desperate to find out more, but this was Antium, not Rome, and without Titus here he could not think who to ask.

In spite of the pandemonium into which the empire was now bound to be plunged, this was not what concerned him the most. As the late emperor's mistress, what would have become of Marcia? Clement's book lay discarded on Callistus' chair as he paced up and down in mounting panic. Should he take one of Titus' horses and set out for Rome straight away to look for Marcia himself? But he had given his word to Victor that he would stay away from the City, and besides, it would soon be pitch dark. While he was still casting about in his mind for a practical solution to his predicament another slave came out to corroborate the report he had already received, and noting the young master's distress set about convincing him to do nothing until tomorrow when undoubtedly Titus would return. Anyone with the means to do so would be getting out of the City as quickly as possible.

Sure enough Titus did reappear the following day, though not until nightfall, having been on the road since early morning. He arrived by carriage with his personal valet and a great many goods and chattels, for he intended to remain in Antium indefinitely while the chaos in the capital subsided.

'Is it true that the emperor was murdered?' Callistus demanded of him almost as soon as he had sat down. 'And what of the rest of his household?'

'Almost certainly he was murdered,' Titus replied when he had got his breath back; being a man of generous girth he often gave the impression of being a good deal more flustered than he really was. 'Though not by supporters of Pertinax. By all accounts the poor fellow was as surprised as anybody else was when he was hailed as emperor. If you ask me, he's far too old and sensible to satisfy the populace for long. What is the matter, Callistus? You don't seem interested in Pertinax at all.'

Thankful that the thickening twilight would be veiling his blushes, Callistus answered, 'I'm sorry. It's just that I'm rather concerned for someone else…'

'The fair First Lady Marcia, you mean? Oh don't be coy, now, Callistus; you've mentioned her often enough for me to know you have a soft spot for her, though I can't imagine why. You see, they say that Marcia may have been one of the murderers – she and Eclectus her lover, and Laetus the Praetorian Commander. It was they who arranged for the handing of power to Pertinax, at any rate… Callistus? You look like a man who's seen a ghost.'

But Callistus was no longer listening. Marcia, a murderess? And she had a *lover*? It was debatable which was worse. In a single moment the bottom had fallen out of Callistus' newly reconstructed world, for surely even Clement of Alexandria would struggle to find forgiveness in his heart for a sinner such as Marcia had allegedly become. And what would be the point of riding off to Rome to rescue her when she was already involved with someone else?

'Callistus, are you ill again? You're white as a ghost yourself.'

'No. No, Titus, honestly, I am perfectly well. Just a little tired, that's all. If you don't mind, I think I shall retire.' And he went to his room and lay down, but his head was spinning like a hoop and he did not sleep.

Over the course of the next few days more news reached them. Every morning Titus and Callistus went together to the forum where official reports were posted and other news got around the most swiftly, though it was still predictably difficult to establish what was really going on.

It was confirmed that Pertinax had indeed been made emperor; since he had been prominent in Roman politics for many years and even been consul, Callistus knew him by sight as well as by repute. He was an elderly, dignified-looking man, if a little corpulent like Titus, with wiry grey hair combed back severely from his face. Known for his integrity and respect for discipline he was a man of many civic and military accomplishments, though he had started out as a teacher and was reputedly the sole survivor of those wise tutors and counsellors with whom Marcus Aurelius had surrounded his wayward son. Having abandoned education for the army – as so many did, if they wanted to make a decent living – Pertinax had distinguished himself in the field many times over, yet never allowed success to go to his head. In short he was about as different from Commodus as it was possible to get, which was no doubt why people were so pleased and relieved that he had replaced him. Rome no longer had to be referred to as Colonia Commodiana, the statues of Commodus in the guise of Hercules or even of Jupiter were being pulled down, and even in sleepy Antium some of Commodus' inscriptions had been defaced. Pertinax himself had already made a start on remedying the injustices of Commodus' reign, though this would be an uphill struggle.

But Callistus could find no answer to the question which plagued him the most. He asked anyone and everyone who came to Antium from the City what had become of the emperor's mistress, but no one seemed able to tell him anything until eventually a middle-aged couple recently received into the Roman Church arrived to take refuge in Titus' house because their own country estate was undergoing renovation. The wife, who could have gossiped for glory had it been an Olympic sport, patted Callistus on the wrist over dinner and said, 'Why, young man, she and Eclectus will go down in history as heroes once their story gets out, and their love-affair will be as famous as Antony and Cleopatra's! They married straight away once he was dead, you see, since it was only Commodus who stood between them. Some of my friends are saying their story is *so* romantic, and it *is* in a way, since Eclectus was Marcia's first love when they were scarcely more than children. What Marcia's admirers *don't* say is that the little trollop was already having an affair with Eclectus' master, so she must have been enjoying her pretty painted Egyptian right under the gullible fellow's nose! But then the master himself – Quadratus, they called him – was almost certainly carrying on with the emperor's sister Lucilla, because they were executed together for trying to kill Commodus a *very* long time ago. What a household, I ask you! But that's probably the sort of life you've got to have led if you're going to take it upon yourself to slay a tyrant. You haven't got to care what anyone thinks of you. Young man, whatever is wrong?'

There was no reply. While Titus' eyes were starting out of his head and the woman's husband was glowering at her in icy disapproval, Callistus pushed away his plate and rushed out of the dining room with one hand to his mouth. Clearly the couple must be quite unaware that Marcia had once been Melissa, a member of their own Christian congregation. But if the news they'd brought with them were true, surely not even God would be able to forgive her now. Not only had she trampled her baptismal vow and her vow of chastity underfoot, but she had drenched them in the blood of her own consort – the emperor himself – whom she had murdered in her lust for his chamberlain.

Having disgorged his dinner into the impluvium in Titus' atrium, Callistus staggered out onto the balcony for some fresh air. It was then that he saw to his horror the scroll containing the wisdom of Clement still lying on the chair where he had left it several days before; thank God there had been no rain! Scooping it up, he flung himself down where it had lain and sat in a state of shock with it spilling open across his lap.

But almost at once it was as though Clement's words came seeping out of the scroll to inspire him afresh. What if there were no unpardonable sin at all? What if even *now* Marcia could repent and be washed in Christ's blood all over again, instead of being eternally stained by that of Commodus?

Along with the thrill of this possibility there dawned upon Callistus the realization that he ought to go to Rome and attempt to see her after all. For even though she and her accomplices might be the heroes of the hour, Pertinax' position was surely precarious, and if he fell his champions would fall along with him. Should Marcia face death without having been invited to ask for God's forgiveness... if the unthinkable happened, Callistus knew that he would never, ever forgive himself.

He went to bed with this fresh resolve fully formed in his mind and slept like a stone until morning. But when he awoke, the whole idea of seeking out Marcia in Rome seemed as futile and ridiculous as it no doubt was. How could it possibly be an act of kindness to insinuate himself between Marcia and her childhood sweetheart and thus rob her of the one chance of happiness which fate had sent her way? What use was pie in the sky when you died, compared with love and life here on earth, fragile though these might be?

So he didn't go. Even when Titus went back to the City, Callistus remained in Antium mindful of the promise he had made to the bishop and elders of the Roman Church to stay out of their way.

Initially Pertinax made good progress in righting Commodus' wrongs. Modelling himself on Marcus Aurelius he sought to restore dignity to the Senate and keep the greed of the Practorians in check. But predictably enough, though many people had reminisced fondly for years about Commodus' late lamented father, now that Marcus' defunct Golden Age was showing signs of recovery they didn't like what they saw. For a start, Pertinax had cancelled the extravagant Games which Commodus had been planning as an adjunct to the New Year festivities. Furthermore, few of the senators were worthy of the respect in which Pertinax wanted them to be held, because they were upstarts aggrandized by Commodus. Meanwhile the Praetorians reckoned that since Pertinax could not hope to hold onto his position without their support, he ought to be behaving much more generously towards them than he was.

Given that Pertinax had been a successful general, perhaps he should have realized that it was a mistake to try to fight on too many fronts at once.

As for Marcia and Eclectus, Callistus was duly informed that since Commodus' erstwhile chamberlain was now employed in the same capacity by Pertinax, Marcia was still living at the palace, albeit in more modest circumstances. Whether she was happy with the situation, or even with Eclectus himself, Callistus had no way of knowing. Certainly she wouldn't be enjoying the considerable influence she had once exercised over imperial affairs, even though she was one of those who had placed supreme power in Pertinax' hands. Callistus wondered how long it would be before Pertinax acquired Marcus Aurelius' antipathy towards the Christians and began to blame Rome's troubles on Marcia's indulgence of these renegades who showed such contempt for the traditional gods.

At the beginning of March there was an attempt by Pertinax' enemies to make the consul Sosius Falco emperor in his place. The plot was betrayed and the coup foiled; Falco himself was pardoned by Pertinax in an exaggerated demonstration of clemency. But perhaps the magnanimous master of the empire should have been thinking less about his image and more about his survival, for early one evening at the end of the month Titus returned from Rome in a state of advanced agitation. The inevitable had happened: Pertinax had been slain.

This time Titus had the full story in all its gruesome detail. Three hundred soldiers had stormed the gates of the emperor's palace, and his guards, complicit in the plot, had simply let them in. Eclectus had counselled Pertinax to flee for his life but he had resolved to stand his ground and attempt to reason with his would-be executioners. Of all his companions and servants, Eclectus alone had stood with him for the confrontation, but both emperor and chamberlain had been battered to death despite putting up a spirited defence. Pertinax' head had promptly been chopped off and paraded about the City on a spear. No one knew what had happened to the body of Eclectus.

'And Marcia..?' whispered Callistus, nauseous and shaking. 'What happened to her?'

'Marcia? You're still obsessed with her?' Titus exclaimed. 'I thought you might be at least a little interested in who had been installed as your new emperor.'

'Yes. Yes, of course… well who has?'

'It was a farce,' Titus informed him with a snort. 'Falco didn't want anything more to do with the idea, nor did Clarus his colleague, nor anyone else the conspirators might have thought of choosing. So there was an auction at the Praetorian camp, with supreme power on offer to whoever promised the Praetorians the highest reward! The top bidders were Pertinax' father-in-law and a senator called Didius Julianus, who has lots of money but absolutely no principles. You can guess who won. The whole thing was over so fast, they say, that Julianus ate Pertinax' dinner while it was still warm – and so was his corpse, which was lying there headless on the floor.' Then when Callistus had said nothing to interrupt him, Titus finished up, 'I don't know what happened to Marcia, Callistus. I didn't think to ask.'

Callistus nodded faintly and wandered out onto his balcony. Poor, unlucky Marcia. When it seemed that at last she might have found contentment, it had been snatched from her again in the cruellest of ways. Eclectus had ended his days heroically, it had to be said, but this would be of little consolation to his widow. Surely now he, Callistus, would *have* to go to Rome to find her, though he wouldn't know where to start searching because she wouldn't be living at the palace any more. Might she have tried to go back to Corvus and Junia's? To her own parents, if they were even still alive? He really had no idea.

Nor had he any idea where he would stay while he looked for her. He couldn't use Titus' house in the City; Victor and the elders had made it perfectly clear that the Church authorities would only continue to support him if he didn't advertise the fact that they were doing so. There was no one in Rome who would want Callistus under his roof, and he couldn't sleep rough; his health was still too delicate.

With all these thoughts churning in his head Callistus hadn't noticed Titus moving up quietly behind him, until he felt a tentative pat on his shoulder and heard his host's voice venture, 'Unlikely though it seems, Callistus, I can see that you and Commodus' mistress must have meant something to each other in the past. I'm sorry. I didn't mean to be unkind.'

Still gazing far out to sea Callistus said, '*She* meant something to *me*. She meant everything. But I don't think I ever meant anything to her. I see it all too clearly now. To her I was just another slave-boy with a pretty face. She was nice to me, that was all, and we were friends for a while when she was living in hiding as a member of the Church. But when she went back to Commodus…'

Suddenly overwhelmed by the strength of his own suppressed emotions, Callistus was appalled to find himself breaking down in tears where he stood. More embarrassed even than Callistus was, Titus patted him again on the shoulder without speaking, until Callistus recovered enough to implore him, 'What should I do, Titus? She may have no one left but me to care about her in all the world. And now that both Commodus and Eclectus are dead… perhaps she could start to love me, even if she never did before?'

'Perhaps. But then…' Unused as he was to offering anyone this kind of counsel, Titus was struggling to find anything appropriate to say. 'By your own account Marcia turned her back upon her vows, her faith, and you… in short, on everything that had made her the girl you loved. You cannot expect just to pick up the pieces where you left off.'

'I know. And it's not as though my friend Hippolytus

wasn't trying to tell me what kind of person she was all along. But Hippolytus himself let me down when I needed him the most. Perhaps I'm just a very poor judge of character.'

'Well,' said Titus uncertainly, 'You could always pray for her. That avenue at least is never cut off.' Then patting Callistus affectionately once again he shuffled away and left him to his thoughts. Alas, thought Callistus, Titus had been far out of his depth, which was no doubt why his brother was an elder in the Church while he was not.

In the days that followed Callistus did pray for Marcia all the same, or at least he tried to. But he was no more used to praying than Titus was to counselling, and besides, he didn't really know what to ask. Everything was so confusing, and he could barely settle his mind enough to think, let alone pray. Perhaps Marcia had been no more than her father's daughter: a callous manipulator who had used her gullible Christian friends solely for her own ends. Perhaps he, Callistus, was no better. He was a liability, who had ruined his own life and many others through the pursuit of stupid dreams. He should face reality at last and forget that Marcia had ever existed, because the Marcia of whom he had dreamt for so long never had.

It was a stormy afternoon in late spring when everything came to a head. The weather had been sultry all week, much too hot for the time of year, and Callistus had had a throbbing pain behind his eyes for several days. Today he was attempting to tidy his room, which was littered with scrolls and codices he'd begun to read and then tossed aside. While he was standing in the midst of them, incapable even of thinking about what should go where, Titus walked in through his open door and closed it softly behind him. He said, 'Callistus, you had better sit down. I'm afraid I have some very bad news.'

Instantly Callistus' bones turned to liquid, like sand in an earthquake. He sat down hard, and Titus blurted while he still had the courage to do so, 'Marcia is dead, and Laetus too.

They were executed for the murder of Commodus, whom Didius Julianus deems it his duty to avenge. Anyone and everyone responsible for putting Pertinax on the throne is being hunted down and killed. I'm sorry, Callistus. I really am.'

To begin with Callistus simply sat and stared at Titus as though he had no idea who he was. Then as Titus moved to sit beside him, he sprang up and bolted from the room.

He didn't go to his balcony. He ran right out of the house and onto the promontory where angry waves were crashing on the rocks below. It wasn't raining but soon would be; the wind was raging, and thunder was already rumbling further inland.

If only Antium's cliffs had been steeper! thought Callistus. Then he could have thrown himself into the ocean and ended it all, as Hippolytus had once accused him of trying to do. He no longer had any reason to live, and didn't believe he deserved to. The window of opportunity for him to get Marcia to safety had been open for days, and all he had done was sit by the sea reading books. Now she was dead, and worse still, dead in her sins. Callistus would never see her again in this life or the next, for now she had been denied not merely happiness on earth but a place in the world to come. How could he have let this happen?

And more to the point, how could *God* have let it happen? As the implications of this question rushed upon him the noise that was roaring through his head was no longer merely the crashing of the waves or even the clamour of his thoughts, but his own voice shouting, 'I hate you, God! I hate you more than I hate myself! Strike me dead, send me to hell, I don't care! But even from hell I shall curse you.'

Just then there came such an intense flash of lightning that Callistus fell on his face, convinced that his latest prayer at least had been answered. But he was still all too horribly alive; enraged by his curses' impotence he found himself beating on the ground with clenched fists until his strength was exhausted and he lay motionless with his face in the dirt.

Never in all his time on the treadmill or down the mines had he given up deep inside in the way he gave up now.

So he didn't notice straight away that all had gone quiet around him. But presently he became aware that the wind had dropped and he could no longer hear thunder or the breaking of waves against the rocks. Lifting his head he opened his eyes just as the clouds out to sea let slip a single shaft of sunshine, whilst the conflict in his mind had given way to a solitary voice which was saying: *I don't hate you, Callistus. I love you. I always have.*

It was so much like an audible human voice that he looked around to see who was speaking, but no one was there. There *had* been a voice, though, quite unlike the accusing voices which had driven him out of the house, and quite unlike his own voice which had been screaming into the wind. And now as he lay and listened, it came again. *I love you, Callistus. Take my yoke upon you, for I am gentle and humble in heart, and you will find rest for your soul.*

It was then that the rain began to fall: not a violent, squally rain or a depressing drizzle but huge, warm, heavy drops like the falling of tears. Heavier and heavier they came, like a blanket settling over him; he felt not so much soaked to the skin as deluged by the wholly unexpected love of God. He had never experienced anything like it, nor imagined that anyone could, for none of his daydreams had remotely resembled this. Lying on the ground in the pouring rain he found himself laughing and crying aloud. Though he knew he could have got up and walked away if he had chosen to, he did not, because all that he wanted was for this unmerited and unlooked-for experience to last for ever.

Not that he didn't have questions surging through his head along with the flood of divine love, but each one seemed to have been anticipated before he asked it. What could he have done to deserve such a blessing? *Nothing. No one has ever deserved the love of God. It is a gift, which cannot be earned.* So why now? *Because you had not come to the end of yourself before. You have spent many long hours seeking after truth in your books. But rather than searching for ways to save yourself and others, what you really needed was for me to save you, just as only I could save Marcia.*

'*You* could save her?' Callistus cried aloud. 'Then why didn't you?'

I did. Like the thief on the cross she cried out to me for mercy, and today she is with me in Paradise. You too will be with me for ever if you give yourself to me unreservedly. Will you do so, and be reborn?

'I was baptized years ago. Did I not become a new person then?'

You have never been reborn, not as Jesus meant it. You have never truly sought my forgiveness, because you doubted my willingness to give it. Remember the things which my servant Zephyrinus told you. Baptism is a visible sign of invisible grace, but only if that grace is willingly received within. Will you not be reborn today?

'Yes. Yes I will.' Too exhilarated to lie where he was any longer, Callistus lurched to his feet and stood with hands held out as though to catch God's Spirit along with the rain. He knew that this was his true baptism, but that it was only the beginning. A new seed had been planted inside him which was even now being watered and brought to life. For Callistus the storm itself had become a sacrament, quickening and indescribably holy.

Afterwards he could not have said how long he stood there in ecstasy. But presently he was inflamed with a desire to return to his room and search the scriptures afresh, for now he knew that God could indeed be found there – just as he could be found in nature or in music or in anything else once you knew what you were looking for – if you realized that *he* was already seeking *you*.

Scarcely able to see where he was going, Callistus nevertheless found his way unerringly back to the house. Having regained his room and closed the door behind him, he was confronted by the same jumble of disordered books he had run away from. But one of them seemed to call out to him from the chaos and he picked it up in trembling hands.

It was the Gospel of Matthew, and it had come open at Jesus' Parable of the Wheat and the Tares. It took but the briefest of glances to remind Callistus of the story: an enemy sows weeds among a farmer's crop and his servants want permission to pull them up, but the farmer insists that the crop be allowed to grow to maturity lest the wheat be rooted up too.

Now Callistus saw the parable's meaning in a whole new light. He had always known that there were two kinds of people in the Church, yet without understanding the distinction between them. Now he saw it clearly: rebirth in the Spirit was the key, as Jesus had said to Nicodemus. *This* was why so many members of the Church continued to struggle with sin after baptism. If all those who called themselves Christians were truly regenerate there would be no need to fear Hippolytus' rising tide of immorality or to worry about what it was that should distinguish the Church from the pagan world. Those who knew God would *want* to grow more like him every day, and his Holy Spirit would be working within them to bring this about. Yes, they would still make mistakes from time to time, even big mistakes. But there could be no doubt as to the direction in which they were heading.

However it was no one's business to set about purifying the Church by attempting to identify the tares and ripping them out by the roots. Wheat and tares must be left to grow side by side, Callistus saw now, until the Judgement when it would become all too obvious which were which, for those whose souls had never been quickened would perish in the fire which destroys all that is not eternal in its nature. It was the task of the Church to restore the penitent and misguided – not once or twice, or even seven times, but seventy times seven, as Marcia herself had once taught him – to nurture them and pour God's love into them like the rain which had poured over Callistus today. No one who had ever come to Christ would be living in fear of rejection or excommunication, for fear itself was what the Church should be expelling, not the lost or the doubting. The Church was a field containing both wheat and tares, just as it was a school with many kinds of pupils, for what God loves best, and what Jesus died to bring us, was life in all its fullness.

What Jesus died to bring us... sitting down with the Gospel still in his hands Callistus realized that the reason for Jesus' death was another thing he had not understood until now. Like any so-called Christian he could parrot the formula – Jesus died for our sins – yet he had never truly appreciated what this meant. Jesus had died for *everyone* – once for all, for the baptized and the unbaptized, the saint and the sinner – and all that *anyone* needed to do to be forgiven and start afresh was to ask. It really was that simple, because no amount of penitential discipline or amassing of good works had ever changed a single heart.

How could I possibly have attended the Assembly every week for all these years and never known this before? Callistus was asking himself as he sat and gazed about him, knowing now that whichever one of Titus' books he chose to take up would scream the same message at him loud and clear. On the day he had first noticed Marcia at the Assembly some eight years ago, Bishop Eleutherius had been reading a letter from Irenaeus, who claimed no peculiar divine authority for his words, yet even he had written that Jesus hadn't merely *died* for our sins, but had broken sin's power in the lives of those who were reborn. It's true, Callistus thought now: anyone who experiences what I have experienced today will never *want* to sin again. But if and when he stumbles, God will pick him up and set him back on his feet like a father training a little child to walk.

Very much later Callistus opened his eyes to find that night had fallen around him. He must have passed directly from ecstasy into sleep, a sleep so deep and dreamless that he now felt more awake than he could ever remember feeling before. For now he *did* have a reason to live: he would live to serve God, to bring the Gospel of Christ to his Church all over again, because so many of its members had never received it. Some of them knew too little, whilst others – Hippolytus perhaps – arguably knew too much. Either way, they needed what Callistus now had, and he would make it his mission to share it with them.

How he was going to bring this about when he was despised, reviled and excommunicate, he had no idea. Concerning his own future, two things alone he was sure of: that God would be with him, and that he would never marry. Marcia had been, and would remain, the only woman he would ever love.

Part Two:
Callistus Alone

CHAPTER TWELVE

The summer sun was already setting when the last of the slaves drifted away from Callistus' room. On Sunday afternoons almost every member of Titus' household, whether slave or freed, would crowd in together to sing, pray and study. Now Callistus leaned on the balustrade of his balcony drinking in the view he had come to love so much and looking back with pleasure on today's session, which had seen the shyest of the slave-girls pray out loud for the very first time.

Callistus himself was still officially excommunicate, though six years had passed since his revelation on the rocks below – the experience which he described to anyone who asked him about it as his conversion. Titus' servants had been so struck by the unexpected change in their master's friend that they had insisted on learning his secret, and thus the Sunday gatherings had come about. Few of those who attended would even have called themselves Christians at the outset, and most were still not baptized. But each of them, one after another, had gradually come to accept the Gospel as Callistus explained it. And several now attended the small but growing church which met in the centre of Antium on Sunday mornings under the auspices of an elder – or presbyter – sent from Rome. The presbyter himself might have disapproved of their studying with an excommunicate, but nothing he could have said would have convinced them that Callistus was not a true man of God.

Certainly he had changed out of all recognition since first arriving at Antium as Titus' guest. He was now almost thirty years old: healthy, fulfilled, even happy, all of which meant that in appearance he more than lived up to his name these days – at least, the younger slave-girls seemed to think so. Of course there was a quiet melancholy corner set aside in his soul for Marcia. But he rejoiced to believe she was at peace.

Though Callistus had remained in Antium since her death and found deep consolation in doing what he did, lately he had begun to sense that more change was on its way. He could smell it like the salt in the air as he stood in his favourite place and relished its tranquillity. For six years all that his God had required of him was to pray, grow, and learn, and teach others when they asked him to do so. Like Moses in Midian he had bided his time, only too aware that to strike out on his own initiative when what he wanted most was to be God's instrument would spell disaster. Forty years Moses was said to have waited for the moment when God called him from the burning bush to become the leader of his people. Jesus himself had spent forty days and nights in the wilderness after his baptism preparing to undertake his ministry, and before that he had worked for years in obscurity as a jobbing carpenter. Callistus would be returning to Rome to face whatever awaited him there, he was sure, but only in God's good time.

Meanwhile, in addition to studying and shepherding his little flock, Callistus had continued to assist Titus with his accounts, and increasingly with the oversight of his many businesses. Titus himself still spent much of his time in Rome – though presently he was visiting relatives down in Naples – but it had been his privilege and delight to note the growth in

Callistus' spirituality each time he came back to Antium. Poor Titus' heart had been in his boots when he'd had to bring Callistus the news of Marcia's death, and especially after Callistus had then run out like a madman into the storm. Only on the following day had Callistus seen fit to explain to him that what he'd experienced out there in the rain had been nothing less than an encounter with God himself.

'I heard his voice,' Callistus had said, trusting that Titus would be pleased, yet half afraid that he might think him mad after all. 'That's to say: not like a human voice, though it *was* like that in a way. I mean, I knew it must be coming from inside my own head, but the things it was saying were things I'd never heard anywhere before. Well, maybe I'd *heard* them, but never understood...' Accepting that he must be making no sense at all, Callistus had broken off with an apologetic shrug, only to find Titus grinning at him from ear to ear and assuring him that he knew what he meant exactly.

Nowadays Callistus was entrusted not only with Titus' accounts and records, but with visiting his vineyards on a regular basis to ensure that the highest standards of viticulture and wine-production were being maintained and that the slaves and hired men were being decently treated by their foremen. Callistus would have been the first to admit that he'd known next to nothing about wine-making when he started out, but he'd learnt plenty since.

Along with Titus' commercial enterprises, Italy as a whole had been enjoying a welcome growth in prosperity since the accession of yet another new emperor, Septimius Severus, in the year of Callistus' conversion. Small of stature but bristling with authority, Severus was a seasoned soldier from Leptis Magna in North Africa, the very city where Bishop Victor had been born. Just as Victor was the first African Bishop of Rome, so Severus was her first African-born emperor. He had seen off the greedy and ineffectual Didius Julianus and several other rivals for the imperial throne in a matter of months during what had already become known as the Year of the

Five Emperors.

Not that many Italians had so far set eyes on their new ruler, for he had been busy conducting vigorous military campaigns abroad in an effort to sort out some of the troubles on the empire's frontiers which Commodus and his short-lived successors had preferred not to think about. As a result the Church had been enjoying good times as well, for Severus had better things to do than poke his nose into the religious beliefs of some of his most peaceable subjects. Severus himself, in common with many soldiers, was reputed to be incongruously superstitious.

Although Callistus was now spending a fair amount of his own time touring the countryside, his visits were mostly welcomed rather than dreaded by those he was sent to inspect. He was invariably quick to praise and slow to find fault, which was what Titus wanted, for it was how he liked to do things himself. But as Titus was getting on in years and his business empire was still expanding, he could no longer make the rounds of it in person as he would have done in the past. So he had come to rely on Callistus more and more, and Callistus had blossomed as his talents were appreciated. Gradually he had regained the confidence with figures which his disastrous mistake with Shadrach had cost him, and now he was more like Titus' right-hand man than his dependant. In fact the Church in Rome had long since ceased to contribute to his keep; these days Titus was more than happy to accommodate Callistus at his own expense and would have paid him a handsome salary into the bargain had Callistus been willing to accept it. But whenever Titus brought the subject up, Callistus would merely grin and shake his head. This would invariably cause a great swathe of his thick black hair to fall promptly into his eyes, much to the slave-girls' merriment.

'I don't want your money, Titus,' he would say, and genuinely mean. 'What would I spend it on, when you let me live here with you in the lap of luxury already?' Only lately he'd begun to wonder how much longer he would be doing so.

Callistus' days had become so much busier that it was only in the evenings now that he could find time to pursue his own studies in theology and philosophy, and in particular to become thoroughly familiar with the Gospels, Epistles and other works which the Church increasingly referred to as the Bible's New Testament.

Callistus marvelled to think that books written barely a century ago had already been recognized as having the mark of divine inspiration upon them in exactly the same way that the ancient books of Moses had. Yet whenever he read the letters of Paul, or the Gospels of Mark and Matthew and the like, he could see at once why it was so. Divine authority permeated their words just as silver pervaded the seams of lead he'd been digging out in Sardinia, and there had been remarkably little disagreement among Christian scholars as to which of the books that had come down to them were thus inspired and which were not. Two letters attributed to the apostle Peter had not yet gained universal acceptance, but Callistus was sure that they should and would do – unlike some of the far-fetched so-called gospels penned even more recently by charlatans who had known neither Jesus nor any of his associates.

So how could it be, Callistus asked himself frequently, that the Church authorities who so reliably recognized the word of God when they read it had come to lose sight so spectacularly of the message of grace of which it spoke?

It hadn't taken him long to discover that the Church empire-wide had not been quite so blind. In the Greek-speaking eastern provinces they had been happily granting remission from every kind of sin, whether committed after baptism or before, for thirty years at least. Bishop Dionysius of Corinth had famously written that *no* one should be permanently excluded from communion provided that he or she had shown true repentance. The good news of God's grace had only been marginalized in the west – and in Rome in particular – because many years ago the notorious heretic Marcion had taken it to a ridiculous extreme, claiming that the wrathful God of the Jews and the merciful God of the Christians were two completely different deities.

This showed only how little of the Jewish Bible Marcion had actually understood or even read, Callistus thought, for the vein of God's mercy ran right through it. Yes, God had exhibited intolerance and even ruthlessness on occasion, in the Books of Moses, but only because the people with whom he had had to deal had initially been so primitive. Warfare and aggression could not be eradicated overnight, any more than a wayward toddler can be disciplined by logical reasoning. The fate of Pertinax demonstrated all too graphically what can go wrong when a ruler attempts to reason with men who understand only violence.

But Marcion had died over half a century ago. Surely enough water had passed under the bridge since then for the balance to be redressed? Yet Callistus knew full well that if he'd rushed back to Rome and started throwing his weight about the Church there when he was persona non grata already he would have righted no more wrongs than Pertinax had done. As the sun at last sank serenely into the sea, Callistus reminded himself that God never did anything in a hurry.

Soon after taking his breakfast the following morning Callistus was surprised by one of the slaves announcing that a visitor had arrived to see him and was awaiting his pleasure in the atrium.

'Is it someone we know?' asked Callistus, who had eaten alone in the fragrant summer dining room which looked out onto the garden.

'I didn't recognize him, Master Callistus. But he says he's a deacon from the Church in Rome,' the slave replied. 'Shall I tell him you're on your way?'

'Yes. Yes, of course,' said Callistus, but his heart was

already racing. What could a deacon from Rome want with him? Had something happened to Titus? Or might he, Callistus, be in trouble for discipling converts when he was excommunicate? It was perfectly possible that word of his activities had reached the bishop and elders in the City.

But the face of the visitor who greeted him was wreathed in smiles, and to Callistus' astonishment he flashed him the Christians' secret sign. Though secrecy was scarcely an issue these days, the gesture still had worth as a mark of acceptance. Then the man sprang forward, embraced him, and had kissed him fervently on both cheeks before Callistus registered who he was: Clemens, the imperial freedman who had long been accustomed to liaise between Carpophorus and his clients at the palace. He was sprightly and dapper as ever, though there was rather more grey sprinkled through his neat little beard.

'How well you look!' Clemens exclaimed, holding Callistus at arms' length and regarding him with obvious pleasure. 'The sea air must be suiting you. Zephyrinus will be so relieved.'

'Zephyrinus?'

'Yes, I'm here to take you to see him. He's just been made Bishop of Rome, and he wants to receive you back into communion.'

Callistus stared at the freedman in blank amazement on three counts: firstly that Bishop Victor must be dead; secondly that the loveable but aged and unsophisticated Zephyrinus had been chosen to replace him; and thirdly that the new bishop should have found a spare moment to remember *him*.

'Victor's health declined very rapidly,' Clemens explained in answer to the first of Callistus' unvoiced questions. 'So there was no obvious successor waiting in the wings. The other men who might have fancied their chances were all scholars but not pastors, and too obsessed with theological controversy. The most spiritual of Victor's advisers was probably Hermione, so it's just as well that she died before he did, or there might have been some folk asking, "Why not?"' Clemens grinned broadly as Callistus' expression grew more and more incredulous. 'Most people I talk to are tired of debates about the date of Easter and how Christ could be divine and human at the same time. It was obvious to anyone with an ounce of common sense that what was really needed was a peacemaker who cared more about people than about intellectual hair-splitting, and Victor actually mentioned Zephyrinus' name just before he died. The bishops of Ostia and Praeneste have invested him already, and there will be no shortage of men eager to offer him their counsel: that opinionated young egghead Hippolytus for one. But Zephyrinus has refused to listen to anything Hippolytus has to say until he's sorted out his differences with *you;* he says he cannot even look upon Hippolytus' face without picturing the pair of you together arm in arm as he used to see you when you were boys.'

Shocked at last into speech, Callistus said, 'But I was excommunicated for fraud. That's a deadly sin in the Church's book.'

'Did you commit it?'

'No.' Callistus' denial was prompt, but then he averted his eyes momentarily to add, 'Though I did steal some money when I tried to run off to Greece...'

'Petty theft is not unabsolvable. Zephyrinus knows that you were excommunicated unjustly. Will you come back with me and meet up with him as he desires?'

'Tomorrow,' Callistus promised. 'Tonight you will stay here as my guest.' And he called at once for refreshments to be brought and a guestroom prepared.

By the time they arrived in Rome by carriage the following afternoon, Callistus was already thinking that he shouldn't have come. During his convalescence at Antium he had forgotten what a noisy, dirty place Rome was. The rattling of wheels on cobbles, the cries of hawkers, the piles of stinking rubbish left out in the sun to rot... he was grateful at least that Zephyrinus' modest home was near enough the centre of the city to fall within the zone where wheeled vehicles were banned during hours of daylight. The last stretch of their own journey had to be made on foot.

But why was he feeling so nervous about seeing his old mentor once again? He didn't think it had anything to do with Zephyrinus' abrupt elevation to ecclesiastical pre-eminence. He decided it was probably because he didn't want to give the unlikely bishop any cause to regret sending for him, in the way that he himself was already regretting having come.

He needn't have worried. As soon as Clemens had delivered him safely to his destination and Zephyrinus' failing eyes had made out who he was, the bishop came forward with arms outstretched and embraced him, crying, 'Callistus, little prince, my prayers for you have been answered once again! Even *I* can see that your health is restored. The Lord's name be praised, for I have wept day and night over the injustices that were done to you in the name of Christ. Now at last I can make amends.'

'You have already done more than enough for me,' Callistus tried to say, though it took him several attempts to get the words out through his tears. 'If you hadn't spoken up for me when Marcus Pollius dragged me out of the gutter I should probably be dead.'

'I did what I could, it is true. But now by the grace of God I can do so much more! Restoring you to fellowship will be one of the happier tasks I must undertake in the first few weeks of my episcopacy, most of which will be nowhere near so congenial, I can assure you.' Zephyrinus motioned for Callistus to be seated, and lowered himself with an old man's carefulness to sit down beside him. 'Many things have deteriorated in the Roman Church during Victor's years at the helm,' he continued when the pair of them had made themselves comfortable. 'Not that Victor was personally to blame. Disputes about Christ's nature have blighted meetings and destroyed friendships, and are no nearer to being resolved today even though Victor excommunicated a number of the stubbornest troublemakers. My own inclination is simply to say that we don't *know* how exactly Jesus could have been God and man at the same time, yet it seems that sooner or later I shall have no choice but to tackle the issue head on before it tears the Church apart. And the whole business of absolution and restitution... you know better than anyone that I have never supported the uncompromising approach which the Church of Rome has taken in recent years. Victor didn't like it either, but he was prevailed upon to take a much harder line than he would have wanted to.'

'All of which makes me more grateful than ever that the hard-liners didn't get their own way when I got back from Sardinia and the dispute was all about me.'

'You will be the cause of a good deal more controversy all too soon, I fear, yet this is a storm which must be weathered by us both if God's will is to prevail. I know that Victor was deeply committed to seeing unity restored to the Church for which he was responsible, but it has to be said that he didn't always go about promoting it in the wisest way. For one thing, all those who would not accept that Easter should always be celebrated on a Sunday were in the end told to toe the line or leave; and other western churches were exhorted to take the same approach. They didn't like it; many of the bishops already felt that Victor was getting too big for his boots. Even Irenaeus in Gaul protested, and he's usually perfectly happy to follow Roman practice.'

'Irenaeus.' Callistus repeated the name with a wistful smile. 'I remember that a letter of his was being read out on the day I first saw Marcia. I also remember Hippolytus being much impressed by its wisdom.'

'Yes, I remember that day too.' Zephyrinus took both of Callistus' hands between his own and pressed them together. 'I was so sorry to hear of Marcia's death, Callistus, so very, very sorry. And Hippolytus... he was so impressed by Irenaeus' words that in the end he got his parents to send him to Gaul to study with him in person.'

'To Gaul? So he isn't living in Rome any longer?'

'Oh, he's been back now for quite some while – more's the pity, some would say. Irenaeus is a good man as well as a formidable scholar, and I did think that in the time they spent together Hippolytus might have mellowed a little in his views, but... well, you will see for yourself. Still, Irenaeus certainly brought him on as a theologian. Hippolytus has written several books already, including some weighty commentaries on the Jewish Scriptures.'

'Hippolytus has written books? Then I'm surprised Titus never brought me any; he's been bringing me Christian books from Rome all the time I've been staying at his house.'

Zephyrinus released Callistus' hands and clasped his own together in thought. 'Somehow I don't think Titus would encourage you to read Hippolytus any more than I would,' he said ruefully, but then ardently: 'Oh, if only I had more evidence that the way of unlimited forgiveness is the way that God wants us to walk in these degenerate days! If only I could be sure that his people are ready to hear it...'

'*I* am sure,' said Callistus, and prompted by this cue he proceeded to describe in detail his experience on the rocks at Antium, and the revelation he had been granted regarding Jesus' parable of the wheat and the tares. By the time he had finished telling Zephyrinus about the studying he'd been doing since, and about the many members of Titus' household who had also come to faith as a result of his experience, the old man's tears were running into his beard and he was hugging Callistus to his breast all over again.

'Callistus, you are reborn, truly reborn! You know God! And you have become a scholar into the bargain... not only have my prayers for *you* been answered, but you have become an answer to prayer in your own right. For you can help me, Callistus. You can help me find the safest path through the controversies which beset me. Together we shall restore the Church of Rome to its senses and preach the Gospel to its members afresh.'

'Together? Aren't you forgetting that I'm still

excommunicate? That I'm not even meant to be in Rome?'

'I'm not forgetting anything, my little prince. This Sunday you will come with me to the Assembly and be received there as a penitent – not that you would even need to do penance if it were solely up to me, especially since you have been punished a thousand times over for your naïveté already. But there is no point in our making more trouble for ourselves than we need to. And besides, we must give the elders and people time to see for themselves what manner of man you have become, and how God himself has restored you, before we require them to accept that a sinner once ejected for fraud can rightfully be welcomed back into the fold. Once they recognize that the Church is only ratifying what God has already done, they will find the step a lot easier to take.'

'*You* would re-introduce me to the Assembly? You would let me be seen there openly, with you? And so soon?'

'But of course. The longer we postpone your grand entrance the harder it will be for you, and for me too, since I have every intention of beginning my episcopacy in the way that I mean to go on. You will be officially received among the penitents before the catechumens and penitents go out for their instruction, for this has become our custom. No doubt you'll have to contend with some hostile stares, but God knows, you have suffered worse, and no one will dare to challenge my authority in public. Then you must stay on in Rome to advise me. Who can say, one day we may even get away with ordaining you as my deacon.'

At this Callistus laughed aloud and shook his head. Pushing back the hair from his eyes he said, 'Now we really *are* running away with ourselves! But seriously... I don't know, Zephyrinus. Titus needs me to work with *him*.'

'You need not sever your connections with Titus. You can lodge at his house in Rome and continue to help him with his accounts and visit his estates. You see, I have already talked with him about this, and he's perfectly happy for you to assist me as well.'

'But – Titus is in Naples, visiting family.'

'Not any more.' Zephyrinus beamed, his faded eyes dancing. 'But you may return with him to Antium and talk and pray the matter over with him there if you feel that you should.'

'No. I don't think that will be necessary.' Callistus spoke with resolution now, for suddenly he knew exactly what his decision would be. 'If truth be told, I have been expecting something like this to happen for quite some time. With Titus' permission I *shall* come back to live in Rome; in fact if he is back in the City already I shall stay with him tonight and make my arrangements straight away.'

'Praise the Lord, Callistus. Did I not tell you that God would find a way to restore you? Yet not even I could have anticipated just how complete or far-reaching that restoration would be. Go now with my blessing; I shall see you again on Sunday.' So saying, Zephyrinus laid his hands briefly on Callistus' head, kissed him on the brow, and he was dismissed.

Standing by the road outside Zephyrinus' front door, Callistus was far too distracted to head straight for Titus' town house, for in his excitement he would surely have lost his way even though Clemens had given him clear directions. He knew now what all his study, prayer and patience had been preparing him for. And best of all, he wouldn't have to leave Titus in the lurch; in fact he might be destined to see more of him than he had before. For Titus had become so much more to him over the past few months than a protector or an employer.

It was while he was standing there silently thanking God for Titus' friendship and for the promise of its continuation that all of a sudden Callistus found himself staring straight into a face about as unfriendly as it was possible to imagine. No doubt its owner been on his way to see Zephyrinus about something else entirely, but whatever it was had suddenly become profoundly unimportant and the man had stopped dead in his tracks. His eyes narrowed and he said one word:

'You.'

'Hippolytus?' Callistus spoke the name with some hesitation, because the man looked so different from the boy he remembered. Though no older than Callistus, the hair had already begun to recede from Hippolytus' forehead and he had a pasty indoor face to go with his gawky body, making him look more serious and studious than ever. 'Whatever are you doing here?'

'What am *I* doing here? Surely it is *you* who should be giving an account of yourself.' Hippolytus' face was turning whiter by the second.

'I am here because Zephyrinus sent for me. You may be sure I would not have come otherwise.'

'Zephyrinus sent for you? I don't believe it. What reason would he have to suppose that you were even still alive? You were sent to the treadmill, then to the mines. Anyone else would have been dead and buried long ago.'

And how you wish I was, Callistus realized, with a fresh rush of grief. Aloud he said only, 'Hippos, we need to talk.'

'Don't *do* that to my name! I always detested it; I'm not a horse. Besides, I have nothing further to say to you. But I shall certainly have something to say to our illustrious bishop.' As if to prove his point Hippolytus made to push past Callistus into the house. But Callistus reached out and caught him by the wrist, causing Hippolytus to start as though he'd been touched by a spectre in a cemetery.

'Hippolytus, please. If you intend to talk to Zephyrinus about me, at least do me the courtesy of hearing what I have to say to you before you do so. I'm sure you will recall that both our Lord Jesus himself and Paul his apostle commanded us that if we have anything against a brother we should talk to him about it before we talk to anyone else.'

'So *you* would presume to lecture *me* about Christian doctrine? You are not my brother. My quarrel is with Zephyrinus, who is evidently now consorting with an apostate. Now let me pass.' Shaking Callistus' hand from his wrist, Hippolytus strode past him and proceeded to hammer on Zephyrinus' door.

Callistus was distraught. The last thing he had wanted on coming to Rome was to rock Zephyrinus' boat when it had only just set sail, yet the storm had started already. Hostile stares would be the least of Callistus' worries once Zephyrinus concluded that he had made a terrible mistake in launching his episcopacy on a sea of dissension. Perhaps he should go back to Antium now, before things got any worse.

But straight away the voice of the Spirit was speaking within him, saying: *would I have sent you here only to snatch you away again before anything had been accomplished?*

So he gritted his teeth and set out for Titus' house before he could change his mind a second time. Clemens' directions proved reliable and he found the place without difficulty: a large urban mansion not unlike Carpophorus', and not very far away from it. Nonetheless Callistus had to muster all his courage to make himself knock on the door and not slink away.

Titus' greeting quickly restored his equilibrium. 'Of course, you are every bit as welcome to stay here as you are to retreat to my house in Antium whenever you need to! You must come and go as you please, just as I do myself.'

'But there are many who will disapprove. They are making trouble for Zephyrinus already, and may turn on you as well.'

'I'm sure we shall win them over in time, Callistus. And after all my years in business I have learnt to look after myself tolerably well, thank you. The day when I feel more threatened by those within the Church than those outside it will be the day I resign my membership, but somehow I don't think it will be dawning any time soon.'

I only hope you are right, Callistus thought, but all he said was: 'Thank *you*, Titus, once again. I shall never be able to thank you enough.'

'Nonsense, you already have. What would I do these days without you to keep my accounts and my estates in order?

You are gold dust, Callistus, gold dust. Never forget it.'

During the course of the next few days Callistus brought most of his things – the bulk of which were books – from Antium back to Rome. He could have arranged for servants to fetch them, but he wanted to pack them up in person, and to say goodbye to the members of Titus' Antium household with whom he had forged such fruitful bonds.

'You must run your own Bible studies from now on,' he exhorted them. 'You know enough now to carry on your meetings without me. Demetrius and Gorgo will lead you.' Demetrius and Gorgo were a young married couple who were responsible for the upkeep of Titus' Antium gardens; as slaves the state wouldn't have regarded them as married at all, but Titus and the Antium Christians did. They had been among the first to attend Callistus' Sunday gatherings, and it would be hard for him to leave them behind. But he knew that they needed to spread their spiritual wings just as he did himself.

All the same, as Sunday came closer, so Callistus' sense of foreboding grew worse. When the day arrived he donned the long sackcloth tunic which penitents were required to wear for Assembly, and daubed ash fresh from the hearth in Titus' kitchen on his forehead. Titus went with him to Zephyrinus' house, and the bishop studiously avoided any mention of Hippolytus' visit.

Then the three of them set off for the Assembly together on foot; Zephyrinus never travelled by litter and had no escort aside from his single manservant. Titus had brought no slave at all today, at Callistus' insistence. He didn't want them witnessing any ugly scenes.

For it was inevitable that everyone would stare. A new penitent whom few – thankfully – would recognize, and arriving in company with the bishop... who could fail to wonder what sins the mysterious stranger might have committed? And some undoubtedly *would* work out who he was, and react as aggressively as Hippolytus had done. One of these would almost certainly be Carpophorus.

The Assembly was held in the same great house Callistus remembered – Piso and Valeria's – something of a surprise in itself, for he would have thought that in all the time he'd been away the Church would have grown enough to need somewhere even bigger. When they arrived, the congregants were still milling about and talking, but as the bishop and his companions passed them their conversations ceased and they drew back, all eyes upon Callistus. Some no doubt noted his good looks, but many more would be seeing only the sackcloth and ashes and asking themselves who this could be. All too soon one of them would put two and two together.

Titus made straight for the place where he usually stood with a group of his friends; Zephyrinus greeted the men already there and embraced each one briefly before heading off to meet with his elders. More of Titus' friends appeared one by one, and Titus introduced Callistus to them as his assistant from Antium, newly arrived to live and work with him in the City. If any of them recognized him from his past life they were too polite to say so, or to remark on his penitential garb. Once surrounded by these prosperous and congenial fellows Callistus was at last able to stop thinking only about himself and take in more about the congregation which, if all went according to plan, he was soon to rejoin.

To begin with, far from being no larger than it had been over ten years before, if anything it had shrunk. Of course the Quarterdecimans – those who insisted on celebrating Easter on the same day as the Jewish Passover – had been expelled, but Callistus doubted that this alone accounted for the Church's apparent failure to expand. Furthermore the congregants who remained seemed much more segregated by status than Callistus remembered. He was surrounded by the wealthy, whereas those less richly dressed stood apart from them, and mostly further back. Jews were more sharply divided from Gentiles, and women from men; again the Jews and the women and children were predominantly further from the elders' dais than the Gentile men were. Naturally the unmarried youths and maidens had always tended to form single-sex groups of their own, but in the past whole families had worshipped together, with friends of both sexes clustered around them. Now a married couple standing together seemed to be more the exception than the norm. None of this struck Callistus as healthy; on the contrary, he feared that the Church might be losing sight of the very thing which had made it so appealing to him as a boy. There was no sign at all of Carpophorus.

Then, worse than anything else, before the service began a fierce quarrel broke out between two men standing not far from Titus' friends. Both appeared to be men of North African descent, like Victor and the emperor himself, and each was surrounded by a gaggle of supporters. Their argument was becoming increasingly heated, though they were striving to keep their voices down, and whatever they were saying was clearly being taken personally. At least it meant that no one was any longer looking at Callistus.

'Who *are* those men?' he whispered to Titus when he had recovered from his shock.

'Sabellius and Tertullian.' Titus' expression was grim. 'Sabellius is a Libyan, but he's been here long enough to have been made a junior elder. Tertullian's from Carthage, a kinsman or family friend of Victor's who came over when Victor was ill and who's now helping sort out his estate. He used to be a pagan and has a temper as hot as Vesuvius. He trained as a lawyer I believe; he's very clever, and sees a lot of your old friend Hippolytus. He and Sabellius argue all the time.'

'Really? What about?' There was no longer any need to whisper, since first Tertullian and then Sabellius had already lost the battle to keep their anger under control.

'The same thing most arguments in the Church are about these days: the nature of Christ, and how his manhood and godhead related to each other when he was here on earth. You can tell all this dissension really upsets poor Zephyrinus, but he doesn't seem to know what to do about it. Victor would have had those two silenced; any more arguments in public and they would have been thrown out of the Church. Zephyrinus doesn't like to suppress free speech, but their incessant bickering is getting seriously out of hand.'

Thankfully at this point the bishop made his formal entry, accompanied by various representatives of the Church's leadership: elders, deacons and Hermione's successor as Head of the Order of Widows, whose name was Anastasia. Callistus recognized a number of the elders: Gaius, of course, and the refined but unassuming Urbanus, both of whom had served in this capacity for many years, and some of the others who had been present on the day Marcus Pollius had dragged him into Victor's house. But walking in their midst was Hippolytus.

'Hippolytus is an *elder?*' Callistus mouthed to Titus as the congregation – even Sabellius and Tertullian – fell silent.

'Yes,' Titus whispered back. 'He's a highly respected scholar, you know; he's written books.'

'So I'd heard.' Callistus might have said more, but then before the service itself got under way, Urbanus stepped forward and invited anyone present who wished to be received today as a new catechumen or penitent to make his way to the front and take his place on the Seat of Mercy.

The Seat of Mercy? Callistus knew the phrase; the Mercy Seat was the name by which the Jews had referred to the lid of the Ark of the Covenant. It had formed a symbolic throne for God in the sanctuary of the Jerusalem Temple, and on the Day of Atonement it had been sprinkled with sacrificial blood by the High Priest to atone for the people's sins. But never in Callistus' experience had a piece of furniture by this name played a part in meetings of the Assembly, making new catechumens and penitents into even more of a spectacle than they already were. He didn't like it.

Nor did he much like the service when it began, and not only because he felt so uncomfortable sitting on a special bench in his sackcloth and ashes with a number of other men and women who looked similarly ill at ease. Everything seemed more formal than he remembered it: there wasn't the spontaneous singing or extempore prayer; no one prophesied from the floor, or gave a message in tongues or its interpretation. Yes, there was singing, and there were uplifting readings from the scriptures, both old and new, but everything was led from the platform at the front, and none of it by women or children.

The only consolation Callistus found for all this was that Zephyrinus looked no happier about it than he felt himself. Once or twice he caught Zephyrinus' eye, and these were the only moments when the bishop smiled, which saddened Callistus more than ever because in the old days Zephyrinus had smiled all the time.

Yet even though the Service of the Word seemed set to drag on for ever, Callistus was by no means eager for it to end, because then would come the moment he was dreading the most. He began to wish that he had asked exactly how the formal welcome for the new catechumens and penitents would be staged.

When the time arrived, he thought at first that he had worried for nothing. All those who had been sitting with him on the Mercy Seat were simply shepherded onto the platform and Zephyrinus embraced them one by one and pressed a hand against their foreheads in blessing. But after he had done the same to Callistus he put one arm about his shoulders and turned him round gently to face the congregation.

'Brothers and sisters,' he said, 'Some of you will be thinking that you recognize this uncommonly handsome face, and you probably do, for this young man is indeed the Callistus who was barred from communion many years ago for committing fraud. But I declare before all of you here today that his expulsion was unjustified. Yes, he has sinned, just as all of us have sinned and fallen short of the glory of God. Yes, as a boy he acted rashly and perhaps foolishly, as most of us do. Yet not only has he convinced me of the sincerity of his repentance, but he was *never* guilty of the crime for which the Church expelled him and the state sentenced him to a living death. Moreover, those of you who were impoverished as a result of his actions have since been compensated in full by his former master. So we must welcome him back and support him as he undergoes his penance, in any and every way that we can. Fear not, Callistus, for God himself has shown you his mercy.'

Thereupon Zephyrinus kissed Callistus openly on both cheeks and held him in protracted embrace, with the whole Church of Rome looking on.

But all that Callistus could see as he stood with his head over Zephyrinus' shoulder was Hippolytus glaring at him with a face like thunder, so that notwithstanding the warmth of the day or that of the embrace in which he was folded, the bishop must have felt him shiver.

CHAPTER THIRTEEN

Once the Roman Christians learned where he was living, Callistus received a steady stream of visitors eager to echo Zephyrinus' words of welcome. Among the first were Corvus and Junia who had offered sanctuary to Marcia. Soon after came Marcus Pollius who had already saved Callistus' life twice over. Then there was the self-effacing elder Urbanus who had cautioned Victor to be wary of him, but who now wanted Callistus to know that he had no further qualms about his restitution. Titus' brother Gaius came next, then Anastasia with two senior members of her order; and Callistus had several visits from Clemens, who seemed to run errands for everyone and have a gift for liaising between his Christian brothers and sisters all over the City as well as with those on the staff at the emperor's palace where he was still employed.

'Zephyrinus says he will give you the rest of this week to settle in, then once next Sunday's Assembly is out of the way he'll invite you round to talk about how you can be of use to him,' Clemens announced cheerfully.

But it was also from Clemens that Callistus learned more about the opposition to which his return had given rise. Not only was Hippolytus quietly seething, but so was his feisty new friend Tertullian and, unsurprisingly, Carpophorus.

'Ah yes. Carpophorus.' Callistus had been strolling with Clemens through Titus' courtyard garden; now he sat down on a shady bench among the rose beds and invited Clemens to sit beside him. 'I didn't see my old master on Sunday. He's still a member of the Church then?'

'Very much so, yes he is. But he found out somehow that you were to be welcomed back publicly by the bishop this week so he stayed away on purpose in protest.'

'You know this, Clemens? It's not just a spiteful rumour?'

'No, I know it for certain because he put it in writing to Zephyrinus and gave him the letter in person, in the presence of several deacons including myself.'

Callistus hung his head and didn't bother to push back the hair that inevitably fell in his eyes. 'I'd already begun to wish I hadn't returned to Rome. And it will only get worse once people find out that Zephyrinus wants me to be some kind of unofficial confidant. Yet in my heart I feel assured that I'm in the right place and doing the right thing.'

'Oh you are, Callistus. You are,' Clemens enthused, patting Callistus on the back, so that he sat up straight once again and at last shook the hair away from his face.

'Thank you, Clemens. You're a son of encouragement indeed.'

'Glad to be of service. There's nothing like finding one's niche.' Clemens grinned and stood up, and the two of them resumed their tour of the gardens.

The following Sunday Callistus had to brave the Assembly without Titus' or Zephyrinus' escort, for Titus had had to go briefly back to Antium, and it would have been asking for trouble had the bishop arrived with Callistus in tow a second time. Today Callistus made straight for the vicinity of the mercy seat where the penitents and catechumens were expected to congregate so that they could leave as a body before the Eucharist.

But to get there he had to walk past the place where

Carpophorus was accustomed to stand, and with quickening pulse he saw that his old master was already there. Unable to pretend he hadn't seen him, Callistus ventured a nod and a smile. Receiving nothing but a glare in return, he forced himself to keep smiling; this seemed to cause Carpophorus considerable discomfort, and it was he who averted his eyes. Callistus would have tried the same tactic with Hippolytus when the latter took his seat amongst the elders on the platform, but Hippolytus would not meet his gaze at all.

The next day Zephyrinus sent Clemens to invite Callistus to his house that afternoon. He received him in private in his courtyard: not a grand peristyle garden like Titus' but a beautiful, restful place nonetheless, with well-watered flowers and herbs growing in profusion in pretty little tubs which the bishop tended himself. Firstly they talked in general about how Callistus was settling in to his new life in the City, and about the mixed reception he'd had from the Church.

Then Zephyrinus said, 'You should know that I intend to receive you back into communion as soon as you have completed forty days of penance, counting from the date of our first meeting. This will have given you quite long enough to demonstrate the sincerity of your remorse, and will be doubly apt, being equal to the length of time which our Lord spent fasting in the wilderness. Until then you must spend at least an hour a day in prayer, and also perform daily acts of charity and service for needy members of the congregation. This way they will not only see that I have imposed upon you more than token penance, but they will get used to having you around, and witness your sincerity and humility for themselves – not to mention your face, which I don't doubt will appeal to some who might otherwise have found you easier to ignore.'

'May I ask quite what acts of charity you have in mind?' Callistus could not help but smile, for there was so much more to Zephyrinus than avuncular affability. He might not appreciate abstruse philosophy or the finer points of theological scholarship, but he understood people.

'Oh, don't worry, I have plenty of useful little chores lined up for you. Prison visiting, taking bread to families in hardship, not to mention assisting them with their budgeting. Anastasia will supervise your rehabilitation on my behalf. Then you will be received into full communion on the third Sunday in September: your sixth since returning to the City.'

Callistus nodded, thinking how soon that suddenly sounded, for it was less than a month away already. Zephyrinus resumed, 'Now much as it pains me to do so, I must explain to you the history of the quarrels which have been plaguing the Church in recent days, so that when you go out among its members you may not stir up a nest of hornets unawares.'

'Very well.' Callistus readied himself to pay close attention, thankful that he had fully recovered his clarity of mind along with his physical health, for the sorry tale proved to be as complex as it was disturbing.

'During Victor's episcopacy a great deal of trouble was caused by one Theodotus the Tanner, a recent convert with little grounding in the faith but very much self-importance. He seized upon every opportunity he could to peddle his theory that Jesus was just an ordinary human being, born like anyone else of human parents, Mary and Joseph, but who lived such a holy life as a boy that when he was baptized the Holy Spirit descended on him in power, causing him to *become* the Son of God in that precise moment. Theodotus maintained that this was no different from what happens in the sphere of politics where some of our emperors have taken to "adopting" promising young men so that they might become their legitimate successors.'

'You mean, like Julius Caesar adopting Octavius before he became Augustus?'

'Exactly that. So it's not surprising that Theodotus and his admirers became known as Adoptionists. But his theory clearly *was* heresy, not just philosophical speculation. It contradicted everything which the apostles taught, in particular the stories about Jesus' birth related in the Gospels of Matthew and Luke. Victor warned him to stop spouting such nonsense, and many of the elders, myself included, sat him down and tried to show him the error of his ways from the scriptures. But he kept on saying that since Mark and John didn't include the birth stories in their Gospels, they were probably just pious fiction – which really *was* beyond the pale, of course, but it was undermining the faith of many simpler folk who weren't equipped to follow the arguments for themselves, and with whom I have every sympathy. So eventually Victor had little choice but to expel him from the Church.'

'I'm guessing this wasn't the end of the matter?'

'Far from it, Callistus, more's the pity. Theodotus was very eloquent for a fellow with no rhetorical training, and popular into the bargain. He'd convinced a number of equally plausible mischief-makers that he was right: another Theodotus – known as Theodotus the Moneychanger to avoid confusion – and two flagrantly ambitious characters by the names of Asclepiodotus and Natalis. They set up their own rival congregation of which Natalis was persuaded to call himself bishop and even granted a stipend of a hundred and fifty denarii a month. They took with them a significant number of our own congregation as well, as a result of which Rome no longer has one church but two. And I don't mean one mother congregation with daughters in the suburbs whose presbyters are accountable to me, such as we've been planting for years. I mean two churches whose bishops deny one another's legitimacy and whose members are barred from taking communion in each other's Assemblies. It has even become necessary in some circles to refer to our congregation as the "Catholic" Church of Rome in order to distinguish it from the other one.'

'But this is inconceivable. How can Christ's body be divided up like a corpse ripped open by jackals?'

'A graphic way to describe it, my little prince, I must say:

all your reading has evidently given you a ready way with words to match your facility with numbers. But regrettably this is not the first time such a thing has happened. You probably don't know much about the history of heresy at all, because it is not something the Church is keen to expound to young believers, nor am I proud of the way in which some alleged heretics have been treated by my predecessors. It has never been easy to maintain a balance between the preservation of truth on the one hand and the encouragement of free thinking on the other. Ugly dissension in our ranks sends the vilest kind of message to the pagan world, yet perceived suppression of ideas and debate goes down even worse. And unfortunately the expulsion of the Adoptionists didn't even end the dissension within the congregation which does still accept my authority.'

Callistus shifted uncomfortably in his seat. He was beginning to think that a spate of old-fashioned persecution might be more straightforward to deal with than the kind of wrangling into which it seemed that the Church was prone to descend whenever the outside world left it to its own devices.

'You see,' Zephyrinus continued, 'While Theodotus the Tanner was still a member of our own congregation, a vocal minority took it upon themselves to enter into formal debate with him, a bad idea because it only provided the fellow with a bigger platform. It also caused his opponents to take a stance which was too extreme in the opposite direction. They started saying that the earthly Jesus *was* God, in all his fullness, the very Father himself descended to earth in human form. This earned them the nickname "Patripassians" – "the Father suffered" – because they seemed to be saying that God the Father himself had been crucified, though they preferred to call themselves Monarchians. They were led by a certain Epigonus and his right-hand man Cleomenes – disciples of one Noetus of Smyrna – both of whom have since left the City, I'm glad to say. But one of our elders became their disciple, and he's still here, and still promoting their teachings even though Theodotus is no longer around to take issue with him. His name is Sabellius.'

'Sabellius the Libyan? I heard him arguing with Tertullian last week.'

'He argues with Tertullian incessantly, and with anyone else who dares to contradict him, and doesn't seem to care who he upsets in the process. But his theology is much more difficult to dismiss as outright heresy than Theodotus' was. Most people of discernment have a deep-gut feeling that it's wrong, as I do myself, but it isn't easy to put one's finger on where – at least, not for those of us without the time or disposition to study philosophy.'

'Indeed.' Callistus pursed his lips and shifted in his seat once again. 'Though it has to be said that Tertullian seemed like a quarrelsome character in his own right. And I gather that he is a friend of Hippolytus – '

'Oh Callistus, if only *you* and Hippolytus could be friends again the way you once were!' Zephyrinus eased himself up from his place, then unexpectedly shuffled over to one of his tubs of flowers where he proceeded to pick off some dead heads which must have been vexing him as he and Callistus talked. 'You know, I pray every night that the two of you may be reconciled, because I know that this would be of enormous benefit to the entire Church, not merely to the two of you! To be honest, you see, I'm not convinced that Tertullian and Hippolytus' explanation of Christ's nature is quite right either. They are so determined to separate God the Father from God the Son in their minds that some of the other elders accuse them of believing in two gods: Yahweh – or Jehovah, the God of the Jewish scriptures – and Jesus! You can imagine how well this goes down with the Jewish Christians in particular, for whom the most fundamental of all commandments is to worship one god.

'The whole thing is a nightmare, quite frankly. What I really want to do is address the Church's intolerance towards the weak and the broken, but all this in-fighting over

Christology is threatening to make a wreck of my episcopacy before I have even begun. It's the reason why we can't allow spontaneous prophecies or messages from God to be given from the floor any more during Assembly, because we have had shameless propaganda spouted in public as though it were the inspired word of the Holy Spirit! Nor can I make a ruling that all speculation about the nature of Christ must stop, just like that, because those of our brothers and sisters who have well-educated non-Christian friends *need* properly worked-out answers to this kind of question. A great many pagans have studied philosophy – in fact the overwhelming majority of those with any status or intelligence – and we shall never succeed in attracting or retaining them as members of the Church if its leadership appears to be ignorant of what the philosophers have taught or afraid of addressing the questions they ask. The greatest pagan thinkers – Socrates, Plato, Aristotle – have *always* enquired into the nature of God, and into how he who is Spirit can possibly have created, or ever interact with, physical human beings. Since Christ's incarnation is fundamental to Christian belief we really have no choice but to settle upon a clear explanation as to how it can have come about: an explanation which is both simple enough and meaningful enough for all who call themselves Christians to agree upon.'

Realizing that he had begun to pluck off live blooms along with the dead ones, Zephyrinus sat down again beside Callistus, who for the first time in his life found himself in a position to offer comfort and reassurance to Zephyrinus rather than the other way round. He said, 'I shall help you, my old friend, if I can. But this is not a subject on which we can hope to gain consensus overnight. If we are to resolve the issue once and for all, many wise thinkers will need to come together, from Irenaeus in Gaul to Clement of Alexandria, and produce between them a statement to which every Christian believer can subscribe.'

'I'm sure that *will* have to happen, sooner or later,' agreed

Zephyrinus. 'But the most important thing of all is to persuade the leaders of the various factions that our unity as Christians, our love as brothers and sisters for one another, matters very much more than our assent to particular points of doctrine. After all, it is *who* we know that makes us Christians, not *what* we know; and doesn't Saint John's Gospel teach us that before he died our Lord and Saviour himself prayed that his followers might be *one?* This must be our priority, Callistus, and you can help me by preventing men like Sabellius and Hippolytus from pulling the wool over my eyes whenever I have to turn my attention to other things. Once you have completed your penance you must return to your reading, and note down anything which is relevant and might one day assist us in formulating a statement of faith for every bishop and the head of every catechetical school to sign.'

'If the most you are asking of me is that I continue to pursue my literary studies, nothing could bring me more pleasure.'

'I'm asking you to study, yes, but also to lift my spirits by visiting me as often as you can.' Zephyrinus squeezed Callistus' hands between his own, and bestowed upon him a radiant smile which briefly turned him back into the simple-hearted elder who had befriended Callistus and Hippolytus when they were boys. 'I only have to look at you, Callistus, to be reminded that we have a God who answers prayer. And in return you'll get a goblet of good Italian wine whenever you come here. I have found a particularly dependable supplier, highly recommended…'

'Probably because of the excellent inspector he employs to keep an eye on his vineyards,' Callistus grinned. 'We'll just have to hope that Jesus was being unduly pessimistic when he said that no man can serve two masters. But I'll do my best. I promise.'

And indeed he did. Anastasia soon had him taking food to the hungry, helping struggling debtors get their affairs in order, and visiting believers who had fallen foul of the authorities and wound up in prison on various pretexts now that members of the Church no longer had an advocate in the emperor's bedroom. As Zephyrinus had predicted, Callistus charmed pretty well everyone he met, and even those who had been warned against him by his detractors told their friends that there was no reason at all to mistrust the courteous, well-spoken young man who looked more like Orpheus or Narcissus than an ex-convict; you certainly wouldn't believe he had ever worked in the mines, they said, or even been a slave. Before very long most of the unmarried girls in the Church were in love with him, and even their mothers grew tongue-tied when he called on them with baskets of fruit or eggs from the market. Somehow in between times he did varying amounts of work for Titus and enough reading to keep his mind sharp, and he visited Zephyrinus regularly too. On the fortieth day of his period of penance he was duly received back into communion with the Catholic Church of Rome.

Titus went with him to Assembly that morning – neither plague nor pestilence would have kept him away – and was as happy for his pardoned protégé as a bridegroom's father is for his son at his wedding. Many of those for whom Callistus had run errands of mercy reached out to shake his hand or pat him on the back as he passed them on his way to the front of the gathering. To his amazement Carpophorus was present among the worshippers even though he must have known that today was the day on which Callistus would be publicly absolved of his sins; and not only was he there, but when Callistus nodded and smiled at him as he was wont to do whenever he saw him, for the first time Carpophorus nodded back. Perhaps he had heard about Callistus' charitable deeds and had decided to let bygones be bygones at last? He wasn't a bad man after all, Callistus acknowledged; he had been a better master than most up until the time when Shadrach had taken advantage of both of them.

The one person who was conspicuous by his absence was

Hippolytus. It could have been coincidence, because not every elder was present at every service, but Callistus doubted very much that it was.

Yet not even Hippolytus' telling absence could compromise Callistus' elation when he received the consecrated bread upon his tongue, or damp down the Pentecostal fire which flared up within him the moment Christ's blood touched his lips. The choicest Falernian could not have tasted finer or warmed his soul more deliciously.

A matter of weeks after Callistus' reinstatement, Zephyrinus informed him that he was setting things in motion to facilitate his election as a deacon. To become an elder would have taken very much longer; Callistus would have had to demonstrate considerable spiritual maturity over an extended period of time. But as Zephyrinus pointed out, a deacon's role was much more practical. It could be taken on by anyone who had appropriate ability and who had gained relevant experience in the outside world, regardless of how long he had been a Christian, and the title would give Callistus considerably more credibility when undertaking assignments in the bishop's name. Both deacons and elders had to be elected by the members of the Church, however, so it would be beneficial for Callistus to spend a little longer getting to know them and being known in return, and building up his reputation for informed compassion, before presenting himself as a candidate. But Zephyrinus was confident that by Easter, when the majority of baptisms and ordinations took place, both Callistus and the Church would be ready.

So even though Callistus' penance was completed, he continued with his supervised acts of charity. And along the way he began to gain recognition as a peacemaker rather than being seen as a likely focus of friction. For he successfully resolved a number of long-running disputes between Church members which had blighted countless lives. One woman had not spoken to her brother or her uncle for years because she believed they had been spreading malicious gossip about her husband; Callistus contrived to bring all parties together and after long explanations and amidst copious tears the whole thing was found to have been a misunderstanding. In another case a man had accused the Order of Widows of deliberately leaving his aged mother out of a distribution of surplus cloth provided by a philanthropic merchant; it turned out that the cantankerous old woman had refused to accept anything she regarded as a handout. But she was only too happy to take receipt of whatever was delivered in person by Callistus.

Yet still Callistus' quarrel with Hippolytus remained stubbornly unresolved. Callistus made several approaches to him both directly and through third parties, but all to no avail.

At the beginning of the New Year Zephyrinus gave out that Callistus had been nominated for the position of deacon - with the support of a host of admirers. Elections would be held in early spring; in the meantime anyone who wished to object to the candidate's selection on the grounds of his unsuitability for the post should present his case to the bishop.

The day after the announcement was made, Hippolytus arrived at Zephyrinus' house in a state of high dudgeon. Zephyrinus and Callistus were closeted together in prayer, but Hippolytus barged his way past Zephyrinus' manservant and demanded to speak with the bishop in private.

Zephyrinus said mildly, 'Hippolytus, my brother, I rather think that it is *you* who should be asked to leave, not Callistus, seeing as he and I had arranged our meeting in advance. But as it is clearly Callistus you wish to discuss, perhaps the three of us should sit down and consult together. I do not care to talk about people behind their backs when it can be avoided.'

Briefly Hippolytus seemed incapable of saying anything else at all. He simply stood there thunderstruck with crimson face and bulging eyes. So Zephyrinus said, 'Come, brother. Please, sit down, be at peace. Was not our Saviour's counsel given to us for our own good? When he advised us to take our grievances firstly to those who have offended us it was not because he wanted to make our lives difficult. Quite the reverse; and yet I doubt that you have spoken a single civil word to Callistus since he rejoined our fellowship.'

'Very well.' Hippolytus at last calmed down enough to respond, but not enough to take the seat which was offered him. 'Be it as you wish; perhaps he *should* hear what I have to say, and exactly why I shall do everything in my power to oppose his ordination – though somehow I doubt that he needs me to tell him. His readmission to communion was completely out of order in itself; to ordain him as deacon would make a mockery of everything the Church stands for. He committed a deadly sin, Zephyrinus, on a par with murder or apostasy. How can we allow a convicted criminal to minister on Christ's behalf?'

'Hippolytus, I do not believe for a moment that Callistus committed fraud, and neither would you if you would only take the wool from your ears and the scales from your blinkered eyes. And even if he *had*, did not our Saviour from the cross tell a convicted criminal that he would soon be with him in Paradise?'

'Jesus had power on earth to forgive sin because he was the Son of the Most High God! Deacons have financial responsibility; are we to entrust Church funds to a man who has already shown himself grossly unfit to handle them? Lives were ruined when this reprobate made off with all that money which had been deposited with his master. Innocent Christian women and children would have starved if Carpophorus hadn't compensated them from his own robbed pocket.'

'Callistus did not "make off" with anything, and well you know it. He was a boy of fifteen who was exploited by an unscrupulous profiteer; now he is twice that age and has learnt his lesson many times over, on the treadmill and in the mines of Sardinia.'

'No, Zephyrinus. This may be the story he has told you, but it is a lie. He embezzled that money so that he could flee the country and escape his life of servitude. And when caught he chose to attempt suicide rather than face a trial which would establish his guilt beyond doubt.'

Callistus could not keep silent any longer. Rising to his feet and looking Hippolytus in the eye he said, 'It is *you* who have believed a lie, Hippolytus. I told you the truth on the day I ran away and you refused to help me. Oh, I know you were right: I should have gone home and confessed everything to Carpophorus. But I was alone and terrified, and you would not even give me shelter long enough for me to come to my senses.'

'I would not give you shelter because you were a runaway slave, and like all slaves you are a liar and a thief. Why do you think that a slave's word cannot be accepted in a court of law unless he has been tortured first?'

'Hippolytus, bridle your tongue before you break my heart!' Zephyrinus interjected as he too rose from his chair and laid a hand on each of the younger men's shoulders. 'You are a leader in the Church – a family which accepts all as equals, whether slave or free, Gentile or Jew, woman or man. This is the very thing which the Church should be standing for above all else; it is the essence of the Gospel message.'

'What the Church should be standing for is righteousness in a world of corruption.'

In spite of his passionate words Hippolytus' voice had been growing quieter rather than louder throughout their altercation; by now he was speaking so softly yet so bitterly that Callistus found himself recoiling as though a venomous snake had reared up in front of him.

Yet it was all too clear that he believed every word he was saying; he truly did perceive Callistus to be a threat to everything he valued and loved. And not merely Callistus, but Zephyrinus too, for he added more softly still: 'Which is why I opposed your election as bishop just as I oppose this fraudster's bid to be made a deacon. For some sins cannot and should not be forgiven this side of the grave. Where would we be if all manner of cutthroats and stranglers could receive absolution and then go straight back out and take more innocent lives? Or if all those weak-willed apostates who have sacrificed incense to the emperor during times of persecution could simply be restored to communion as though nothing had happened, while their braver brothers and sisters were being thrown to the lions in the arena? How would the relatives of those martyred be able to share fellowship with men and women who had denied their faith and then casually taken it up again as soon as the immediate danger was past?

'Zephyrinus, you maintain that I should confront the man who offends me; well I am doing it now. *You* offend me, because your readiness to offer absolution to whoever can squeeze out a tear of counterfeit remorse is pitiful. Not to mention your tolerance of that rabble-rouser Sabellius with his half-baked notion that the Father suffered... Every church in the western empire looks to the Bishop of Rome for guidance, yet you with your lack of education and moral courage are rendering yourself a laughing stock instead. It would serve you right if the western churches chose to commune with Natalis rather than with you.'

Had Callistus not been there to hear them he would never have believed that Hippolytus could have spoken such callous words to the man who had once been a beloved mentor to both of them. Zephyrinus was someone who wept easily, and he was weeping now, though Callistus strongly suspected that his tears were not for himself. But more shocking than any of this was the fact that Hippolytus was weeping too.

For it was not unqualified contempt which had made the patrician speak so cruelly, Callistus knew full well. Every bit as strong as his spite was his passion for justice and holiness, and his love for the beauty of the code of behaviour which God had prescribed for his people. Hippolytus might have scales over his eyes with regard to Callistus, and even be something of a stranger to compassion. Yet Callistus could fully appreciate now that Hippolytus, like Zephyrinus, firmly believed God's commandments had been given for his people's good, to enable them to live full and happy lives characterized by mutual respect. Unlike Zephyrinus, Hippolytus feared that all of this was jeopardized if unmerited mercy was shown towards those who failed to live up to the nobility of their calling.

At the same time, Callistus could not stand by and allow Hippolytus to continue haranguing the gentle old man without granting him a moment's respite to defend himself. So as calmly as he could, Callistus began to rebuke the enemy who had once been his friend for presuming to lecture their bishop in such an insolent fashion when Zephyrinus had never once spoken an angry word to anyone in their hearing.

'Sometimes there is a *need* for anger.' Hippolytus was still weeping, but without contrition. 'True courage lies in confronting evil wherever it is to be found, not in condoning it, and that is the kind of courage which is required of a bishop most of all. Yet for all his talk of facing up to those who offend us, this one will not face up to false doctrine, sin or immorality, even when they threaten to destroy the very congregation over which he presides. Instead he does nothing but invite wicked men like you to serve as his deacons. It is unheard-of for the Church of Christ to contemplate making a deacon of someone who has had to do public penance for more than a month, let alone a villain who should never have been allowed to undertake that penance in the first place.'

'You are right, Hippolytus,' Zephyrinus interjected before Callistus could respond. 'It *is* unheard-of to appoint as deacon a man with a past like Callistus'. But our faith is not about what we have done in the past; it is about what God wants to make of us now and in the future. So this is by no means the only shocking step you will see me taking now that I have been granted the authority to do so. For example, sooner rather than later I have every intention of legislating that fraud shall cease to be regarded as a mortal sin altogether. For it is *not* like apostasy or murder or adultery, all of which demonstrate a flagrant contempt for God and for the value of human life, not merely of property. Moreover, the period of penance required of baptized Christians for sins which can be pardoned by the Church already will be reduced in its turn, because no matter how many acts of charity or humility we perform, none of us can *ever* atone for our own transgressions.

'Have you forgotten why Jesus died, Hippolytus? We are *all* sinners, and the only legitimate reason for making backsliders do public penance at all is to give them time to come to terms with what they have done wrong and to make restitution whenever possible to those who have suffered as a result. If in our desire to distance ourselves from the world's wickedness we lose sight of the Gospel message altogether, what will we have gained? The world we are commanded to reach with the good news will only dismiss us as arrogant and overbearing. We are not commanded to demonstrate our superiority, Hippolytus. We are commissioned to point out the way of salvation to men and women who have sinned just as we have.'

'But why should they listen, if we are no better than they are? If the Gospel has not manifestly changed us, why should they want to receive it? It would be like a drowning man pinning his hopes of rescue on one who cannot swim! By all that is holy, Zephyrinus, why should *you* want to listen to the worthless opinions of an ignorant ex-convict and slave, and appoint him to a position for which he is utterly unfit, when I who am an elder already and have studied with one of the finest Christian scholars of our age could give you all the theological counsel you could ever need? Dancing attendance on you all the time, insinuating himself so insidiously back into your affections... Callistus has made a fool of you, Zephyrinus. It's scandalous.'

Neither Zephyrinus nor Callistus answered Hippolytus' latest accusation straight away, but the glance which they exchanged with one another said enough. For although Hippolytus' passion for righteousness was unfeigned, both of them recognized that it had been grafted onto a stem which had its roots embedded in an emotion altogether more primal. Finally Zephyrinus said gravely, 'Perhaps, Hippolytus, if *you* had tried to make yourself useful to me in my first few weeks as bishop instead of adding to my burden, I might have confided in you in the way I have chosen to confide in Callistus. But if we are looking for evidence of the transforming power of the Gospel, we need look no further than the changed life of this man who left us as a fugitive from justice and has returned a saint in the making.'

Hippolytus stalked out without another word, but even though all three of them recognized that he had lost the battle, they knew also that the war had barely begun. Callistus put his head on Zephyrinus' shoulder and said, 'I'm so sorry, old friend. Perhaps I should stand before the congregation on Sunday and say that deeply honoured as I am by so many people's confidence in me, and especially by yours, I do not want to be a deacon. The trouble my ordination would cause you would simply be more than it is worth.'

'On the contrary, Callistus,' the bishop assured him. 'It will be nothing less than the will of Almighty God.'

CHAPTER FOURTEEN

On Easter Sunday Callistus was made a deacon in the Catholic Church of Rome. The ceremony was short and simple and was performed during the regular morning Assembly in the presence of the whole congregation and its leaders – except for Hippolytus and his fellow elder Roscius, who had made a point of staying away.

The taut-lipped Roscius, like Hippolytus, had vehemently opposed Callistus' reinstatement to communion in the first place, and the two of them had expended a great deal of energy campaigning against his ordination ever since. But their efforts had come to nothing. Callistus could only be grateful that they had chosen to miss today's service altogether rather than storming out in the middle of it. As for Tertullian, Callistus had no way of knowing if he had stayed away or not. He wasn't entitled to a place on the platform, and the Easter congregation was far too large for Callistus to inspect it face by face.

But the applause and shouts of acclamation which Callistus received from everyone else more than made up for his enemies' disapproval. Before and after the service he was hugged, kissed and congratulated by gap-toothed widows and strapping soldiers alike, by citizen and slave, pauper and merchant, Gentile and Jew. Even Carpophorus shook him by the hand and said, 'I was wrong in my judgement of you, Callistus. It was *I* who robbed *you*, of the best years of your life, and it's not in any man's power to restore such things as that. I can only beg your forgiveness and say that if you ever need anything which I *can* provide, you must come to me without hesitation.' Callistus embraced his former master with tears and smiles and marvelled at how much better reconciliation felt than resentment.

Had Callistus' ordination been to the eldership, the other elders present would have joined Zephyrinus in laying consecrating hands upon him. In the case of a deacon this was done by the bishop alone. Nevertheless Urbanus and Gaius, Asterius and Anastasia and their peers all rose to their feet while Callistus knelt, to signal their support. Acutely aware of the apostolic authority vested in Zephyrinus, it almost seemed to Callistus that he was being ordained by Saint Peter himself.

'Almighty God, who has created all things and set them in order by the power of your Word,' Zephyrinus was saying, with both hands planted firmly on Callistus' head, 'Father of our Lord Jesus Christ, whom you sent to us as our Teacher and Saviour, grant the Holy Spirit's grace, compassion and diligence to this your humble servant whom you have chosen to serve your Church, so that he may do so with a pure heart and be accounted worthy of his calling.'

It was just as well that Callistus himself was not required to speak, for words would have failed him.

Once his ordination had taken place, Callistus could be entrusted with specific administrative responsibilities in addition to assisting and advising Zephyrinus in private. He was given charge over the Church's new burial chambers on the Appian Way, which quickly became known as the Catacombs of Callistus. These constituted the first public burial place for Christians which the Roman Church had owned, and since they had their origins in ancient mine-workings, Callistus was the ideal person to oversee them.

He was also put in charge of the shrines of Saints Peter and Paul, both of whom had been martyred on Roman soil. Paul's shrine was on the Ostian Way, Peter's on the Vatican Hill near the site of his crucifixion; the story was repeated to Callistus by many eager pilgrims that the venerable old fisherman had asked to be crucified upside down, as he was not worthy of dying in the same way as his Lord. Callistus was only too happy to encourage the growing practice of pilgrimage to these two holy places, because he himself so treasured the writings of both apostles. He was especially keen to see the letters ascribed to Peter accepted into the evolving canon of Christian scriptures in the way that those of Paul had been. For both Peter and Paul made it crystal clear in their writings that grace alone could render a human being acceptable to God, and faith alone could receive it. No amount of penance or grovelling or hauling oneself up by one's own bootstraps could impress the Almighty in the slightest.

Saint Peter's tomb was a modest underground vault approached from the road by a staircase dug down into the hillside. His body was encased in a sarcophagus set in the centre of the space to which the staircase led, and a little monument had already been erected over the top, where three or four pilgrims could pray. Paul's tomb was similar, and Callistus visited both as soon as he was asked to look after them. To stand so close to the earthly remains of these giants of the faith, one of whom had known Jesus in the flesh, sent shudders down Callistus' spine. The chill silence of the underground air and the flickering lamplight dancing over the rough-hewn walls, combined with the powerful personal memories which these evoked, only enhanced the sense of awe with which Callistus, like every other pilgrim, was powerfully struck.

No such attitude of reverence tempered the acrimony between the so-called Patripassians and Ditheists, however.

The two factions were growing more and more outspoken.

'We need to bring Sabellius and Hippolytus together formally, in your presence, and have them debate their disagreements soberly when there are no catechumens or folk of simple faith within earshot,' Callistus counselled Zephyrinus. 'Perhaps if the business is handled skilfully, some compromise can be reached which will allow each party to sign a statement of belief that is both meaningful and uncontroversial? This may yet save us having to convene a Council from further afield. Oh, I know we can't prevent them from furthering their speculations, nor should we try. But we can at least make sure that they confine these in future to confidentially circulated papers in which they must explain that their views are entirely their own, and in no way endorsed by the Bishop of Rome.'

'Don't you mean in *our* presence?' Zephyrinus corrected him. 'Isn't this the very reason why I wanted to make you a deacon?'

'My presence would only add fuel to Hippolytus' fire. I could certainly help draw up the statement of faith, but I don't think it would help at all for me to attend the debate which needs to happen first – at least, not while Hippolytus still hates me so intensely.'

'Oh don't say that Hippolytus *hates* you, Callistus. I'm sure he doesn't, deep down.'

'Only because you persist in seeing the best in everyone.' Callistus smiled sadly and placed an affectionate hand on the bishop's wrist.

So weeks and months went by and still the formal debate did not happen, but Hippolytus and Sabellius continued to snipe at each other in public. And Zephyrinus, because he did see the best in everyone, and because he wished above all to keep the peace, would try to assure both of his quarrelsome elders that there was merit in each of their arguments. But this only made things worse. Hippolytus in particular maintained that Zephyrinus was a weak-minded vacillator who agreed with whoever had petitioned him last.

Meanwhile Callistus' reputation was going from strength to strength. Several of the elders, most notably Urbanus, Asterius and Gaius, argued that Zephyrinus should ordain Callistus an elder as well – or a presbyter, as they were called increasingly, from the Greek – because he was clearly as gifted spiritually as he was in matters more practical. But Zephyrinus resisted their arguments, sound as they were, because if Callistus became a presbyter he would no longer be in a position to act as bishop's right-hand man.

Instead, at the Easter of the following year Callistus was made archdeacon, to whom the rest of the deacons must answer. Although he was the youngest of them all and had served as deacon for a shorter term than any, none of the others complained. For Callistus was as modest as his mentor; yet you underestimated his intelligence at your peril. He had been duped by an unscrupulous manipulator once too often, and wasn't about to let it happen again.

Titus, with whom he continued to lodge, was delighted at what he called Callistus' promotion, and Carpophorus was as proud as if Callistus had been his son rather than his former slave. Hippolytus was furious, but there was nothing he could do about it, because even the staunchest members of his own Christological faction adored Callistus. For who but Hippolytus would not love a man who was so unpretentious and yet so capable, and – for those who were inclined to notice such things – so extraordinarily agreeable to look upon?

Certainly no one could claim that Callistus had earned his grand new title through selfish ambition. He himself found it more amusing than ennobling, and might have refused it altogether had he not believed that only by accepting it could he ensure that the debate which needed to be held between the Patripassians and the Ditheists would be staged sooner rather than later. For Zephyrinus flatly refused to let it go ahead unless Callistus promised to attend, and not even

Hippolytus could object to the presence of such an august personage as the archdeacon at an event of such significance. Once he was confident that Callistus would be there, Zephyrinus was only too happy to let him make it happen – particularly if Callistus himself agreed to chair it.

'I must say that for a weak-minded vacillator you can be remarkably stubborn when you want to be,' remarked Callistus. 'If anyone gives you an inch, Zephyrinus, a mile is the very least you're prepared to take.'

'Did not our Saviour command us that if anyone asks us to carry his burden for a mile, we should carry it two?' Zephyrinus pointed out airily, and Callistus sighed, for he knew that he would be chairing the meeting whether he wanted to or not.

It was scheduled to take place just before Pentecost. Sabellius and Hippolytus would debate head to head, and each would be permitted to bring with him up to twelve supporters to witness that all was done fairly, and to take the floor themselves if they chose to. All these supporters must be members of the Church in Rome – though not necessarily elders – so Hippolytus would not be allowed to bring Tertullian, nor could Sabellius fetch back Epigonus or Cleomenes from whom he had first acquired his doctrine.

Hippolytus made a show of objecting in advance to Callistus being the meeting's chairman, but Zephyrinus assured him that the archdeacon would be offering no opinions of his own. Callistus' role would merely be to keep the peace and ensure that all views were lucidly expressed so that no one present could be in any doubt as to the meaning of what was being said. That way, when a mutually acceptable statement of belief had been ratified by everyone present, no one could complain that he – or she – hadn't understood what he was signing up to. And though Callistus would be chairing the debate, Zephyrinus would be its president. If anyone taking part resorted to insulting the bishop personally, he was to be treated as excommunicate from that moment on.

When the great day came Zephyrinus was as nervous as a bride before her wedding, and as they made their way to the meeting together he leaned heavily on Callistus' arm as though in fear of losing his balance. The meeting was to be held in the house of Piso and Valeria where the Assembly itself still met for worship: the bishop's house was much too small, and apart from the catacombs the Church owned no property of its own.

'Are you sure we are doing the right thing, Callistus?' Zephyrinus asked him when they got there, for the umpteenth time that week. Callistus noted how grey and shaky the bishop looked this morning, and this was before the proceedings even began.

'Yes; and so are you,' Callistus reminded him. 'Have we not prayed about it more earnestly than we have ever prayed about anything together before?'

'Of course you are right as usual,' Zephyrinus admitted, but he didn't look any happier as he prepared himself to wait for the faction leaders and their supporters to appear. Piso's slaves brought them olives and well-watered wine to enjoy while they waited; Callistus declined the wine but made Zephyrinus take some to settle his stomach.

Sabellius and his contingent arrived first. By now Callistus was used to seeing Sabellius going about his business, but only when you studied him closely did you realize how striking his appearance was. He had the swarthy skin and noble bearing of his compatriot Victor, but his eyes were more amber than brown, and seemed somehow like a vent for the fire which burned in his soul.

To support him he had brought twelve of his adherents, the maximum number allowed. None of these were elders or deacons of the Church, and there were several women among them. As the bishop and his archdeacon stood to receive their leader, most of the others watched Zephyrinus and Sabellius embrace and exchange the kiss of peace. One or two could not help looking sidelong at Callistus, but this was only what he was used to.

Hippolytus arrived soon afterwards, and he too had brought twelve supporters. None of these were elders or deacons either – Sabellius' and Hippolytus' peers had wisely avoided taking sides in their dispute – but they were all men.

Having welcomed Hippolytus in his turn, Zephyrinus opened the meeting in prayer, and reminded everyone that they were here not as antagonists but as fellow seekers after truth, Christian brothers and sisters intent on reaching an agreement which would enable the Church to move forward with its mission to the world. 'We *all* recognize that Jesus Christ was and is the Son of God, who took on human flesh in order to show everyone what God the Father is like. We *all* accept that he died as a sacrifice for our sins, and to share with us the new life of his resurrection. These things are the foundations on which our faith is built.

'But in what *sense* a human being could have contained the essence of the Godhead – in other words how divinity and humanity could be combined in a single individual – this is something which has never been satisfactorily explained. Was Jesus of Nazareth half God and half man? Was he fully both at once, and if so, how could this have come about? This is the kind of question we must consider here today.

'So Sabellius will expound first what exactly it is that he teaches on this subject, then Hippolytus will state how and why he believes that Sabellius has erred. Each may then cross-examine the other. After that, any other person may speak in favour of either argument, at my chairman's discretion. Then with his assistance a statement of faith will be drawn up which all can sign. Finally we shall all offer one another the kiss of peace and share bread and wine together. I shall read out our statement before the whole congregation on Sunday and make clear that henceforth no one will speculate any further about it in public or teach any other doctrine in the name of the Roman Church. Does everyone accept my conditions?'

Sabellius and Hippolytus each assented, whereupon their

supporters did also. But none of them looked entirely comfortable.

Without hesitation Sabellius then launched into the speech he had prepared.

'God the Father is invisible and incorporeal and therefore *cannot* suffer. So I am no "Patripassian" as others have called me,' was the essence of his explanation. 'But it is as God the *Son* that he became a man; the Son existed only while Christ was on earth, for there cannot be *two* gods, Father and Son, in heaven, or even three, Father, Son and Holy Spirit. So the Son is "the Father veiled in the flesh," the fullness of God expressed in human form. He *has* to be, since no mere man – or even half-man – could die for other people's sins! The Holy Spirit has no more a separate existence than the Son has, and is only emitted from God as and when the need arises. God is *one* person: Father, Son and Holy Spirit are merely names for the modes in which he operates.'

'What you are saying makes no sense,' Hippolytus countered when Sabellius had finished making his case. 'You *are* a Patripassian, whether you like the name or not. For if God is but one person, and Jesus was the totality of God suffering on the cross, was heaven empty while he was there? By no means, for the Son *prayed* to the Father before his crucifixion, begging him not to let him die! God's nature has *always* been that of a plurality within the One, since the very beginning, though his "logos"– his Word, or Reason, as the Gospel of John and the philosophers would have it – was as yet unexpressed, dwelling within him. But the Father "begat" him before the world was even made, for it was through him that everything else was brought into existence. In the Book of Genesis, don't you recall God saying: "let us make man in *our* image"? He was the only begotten logos of the Father long before he came to earth. Yet this is certainly *not* to say that there are two gods. I am much less a Ditheist than you are a Patripassian.'

'No, Hippolytus. It is *your* argument that makes no sense.

For if God "begat" the logos, as a kind of act of the will, there must have been a time *before* his begetting; therefore God would not be changeless, as we have all been taught that he is. In fact, Jesus was only begotten when he became incarnate in Mary's womb.'

'Not at all! You understand nothing! The begotten logos *did* exist from the beginning of *time*, but not from all *eternity*. God stands outside of time, for time is merely an aspect of his own creation. The Son is *subordinate* to the Father, but equally a part of the Godhead; we must think of God as a sort of three in one – a Trinity, as my learned friend Tertullian has called it. God is three *persons* but all of one *substance*; this is the mystery we must embrace.'

'A mystery? A contradiction in terms, more like! How can something have existed from the beginning of time but not from the beginning of eternity?'

'I did not say the *beginning* of eternity, Sabellius. Eternity can *have* no beginning, any more than God can, just as neither can have an end. That is what the very word means.'

'It seems to me that your words mean whatever you want them to mean. You are merely seeking to confuse us all and plunge the truth into obscurity with fancy philosophical language. Just because you are the son of a senator who could afford to let you spend years doing nothing but reading pretentious books and practising rhetoric – '

Up to this point Callistus had done little but follow each speaker's drift and nod his head or raise his hand to give permission for their dialogue to proceed. Now he had no choice but to intervene, since Sabellius' comments were becoming overtly personal and Hippolytus' colour was rising. Moreover the supporters of each were growing restless and looking daggers at one another. So Callistus instructed Sabellius to be silent; the time had come for the protagonists to step aside and see if anyone else had any light to shed on the subject.

They didn't, or not very much. Several men spoke, and

some women too, but none of their contributions took the discussion any further forward. Yet Callistus was careful to cut no one short; nothing would be solved today if anyone went home feeling that there was more which needed to be said.

When at last no one had any fresh points to make, Callistus got up to gather the threads of their discussion together and draw it to a close.

'Bishop Zephyrinus, presbyters Sabellius and Hippolytus, my dear brothers and sisters in Christ,' he began. 'We can't prove or disprove many of the claims which have been made here today. It may be that in time to come, further scholarship may help us hone our views, or God himself may see fit to send us fresh revelation, for Jesus did promise that the Holy Spirit would lead us into all truth. Or perhaps we shall have to accept that we are enquiring into things which human minds will never fully comprehend. Either way, for the time being here is the wording of the statement on which I propose we agree, which I have been refining while listening closely to what everyone has had to say.

' "As Christian brothers and sisters we believe that God imparted his full and true essence into the human being Jesus Christ, from the moment of Christ's conception in the Virgin's womb. Yet heaven did not become empty when he did so, nor was God in any way diminished, any more than a flame passed on by thrusting a brand into a fire makes that fire burn less brightly. Jesus Christ on earth was fully God *and* fully man; and just as Christ proceeded from God the Father, so the Holy Spirit does the same. The three are distinct and yet one; God *never* changes in essence, yet he can and does change with respect to his interaction with human beings and with creation as a whole." Now, are these truths to which every person here can assent?'

Silence descended as Sabellius and Hippolytus each weighed up what Callistus was suggesting. 'You're welcome to retire and discuss my proposal with your supporters; the debate can be adjourned while you do so,' he offered now.

But Sabellius shook his head.

'There is nothing to be gained from an adjournment,' he said. 'The wording of your statement must surely be acceptable to everyone who calls himself a Christian. But it won't stop some of our less discerning brethren continuing to think of God the Father and Jesus Christ as two separate gods.'

'Nor will the wording be precise enough to satisfy a pagan philosopher,' Hippolytus maintained. 'He would want to know *how* it could have come about that pure soul, the essence of the incorporeal God, could attach itself to human flesh.'

'We don't *know* how it happened,' Callistus said patiently. 'That is the whole point at issue. For the Church to make pronouncements on matters about which it has received no clear revelation would be reckless in the extreme.'

'Then how shall we ever win educated pagans for Christ? To a philosopher, especially a disciple of Plato, it is anathema to suggest that God would taint himself by taking on human flesh. The whole purpose of human life for a Platonist is to learn how to *detach* his soul from his body without destroying both. It would be insanity to claim that God would do the opposite, by choice.'

Even Callistus' patience was now wearing thin. But before he could point out that they were merely going round in circles, since these arguments had already been rehearsed several times over, Zephyrinus rose to his feet and put an end to the quibbling himself.

'The incarnation may seem like insanity to many, Hippolytus, but it is the Gospel, without which we would have nothing to preach at all. Is this not precisely what Saint Paul was saying when he wrote in his letter to the Corinthians that the cross is foolishness to the Greeks? If they do not wish to accept the good news which we bring them, that is their choice and their loss. But *less* than this Gospel we as Christians cannot accept, and *more* we cannot know. Now will you assent to the statement of faith which the archdeacon is proposing, or will you not? The decision is for you – for *both* of you – to make.'

Sabellius and Hippolytus each looked the other in the eye. There was still more wariness than trust in their expressions, but Sabellius' inner fire seemed to be raging less fiercely, and Hippolytus' face was a paler shade of crimson.

'I will sign,' said Sabellius first, 'Though I do not believe that in the long term much will be solved.'

'And I will sign too,' Hippolytus acceded. 'Though I shall not abandon my search for deeper truth, since this is every scholar's quest.'

'Nor would I ask you to,' Zephyrinus assured him. 'So long as you remember that it was unity for which Christ prayed with regard to his followers, not intellectual superiority.'

Meanwhile Callistus had been busy writing out on a sheet of papyrus the document which all would need to sign. Once it was finished he read it aloud; Sabellius and Hippolytus signed it first, followed by everyone else, and each appended a seal impression too. Then Zephyrinus insisted that they exchange the kiss of peace, after which bread was broken and wine shared out, and Zephyrinus declared that today there would be rejoicing in heaven.

Perhaps, thought Callistus, who was as relieved as anyone to see Sabellius and Hippolytus eating from the same loaf and drinking from the same cup of fellowship. But surely there must be at least one angel weeping over the hostility Hippolytus continued to harbour against *him*? Callistus' conscience was clear – he firmly believed he had done what he could to repair the breach – but he was struggling to see how Hippolytus could be so heedless of Jesus and Paul's insistence on reconciliation before ritual. Then again, Hippolytus had maintained from the outset that all the blame for their estrangement lay with Callistus Perhaps, thought Callistus ruefully, his conscience is no more clouded than my own.

The following Sunday there was rejoicing in the Church as

well as in heaven, and not only because of Sabellius' and Hippolytus' momentous agreement. For it was Pentecost, which was celebrated annually as the Church's birthday, the anniversary of the occasion on which the Holy Spirit had fallen on the risen Jesus' followers as tongues of fire. In their ecstasy those astonished disciples had found themselves miraculously able to communicate with others whose languages they had never learnt; there could be no more appropriate date in the Church's calendar for inveterate misunderstandings to be cleared up.

Zephyrinus stood before his congregation shoulder to shoulder with Sabellius and Hippolytus, clasped each of them by the hand and declared, '*This* is the faith of the Church whose birthday we celebrate today: that there is but one God, who became incarnate in Jesus Christ; yet it was as God the *Son* that he suffered and died for our sins and rose again, so that *all* of us might share in his victory over death!' Then he invited Callistus to step forward and read out the statement of faith which the two former antagonists among the eldership had signed. 'More than this we cannot yet say,' Zephyrinus concluded, 'But this much we *can* say, with confidence, knowing that it represents the teaching of the apostles and of our Lord Jesus himself. I adjure both of these men, and everyone else who wishes to remain a member of the Roman Church, to abide by it from this time on.'

Stepping back, the bishop then joined his two elders' hands together, and the men embraced: Patripassian and Ditheist, provincial and senator's son, African and Roman, dark-skinned and pale. Clapping and cheering erupted on all sides, and for the first time since Callistus had returned from the mines spontaneous songs of praise rose up too, and there were even people singing in angelic tongues. Callistus was so happy that briefly he forgot his own differences with Hippolytus and abandoned himself to the mood of the moment. For the first time he understood why the apostles at the first Pentecost had been accused of being drunk.

Afterwards Sabellius and Hippolytus both stood by their vow, and for the time being at least there was no more quarrelling over Christology. But no sooner had one issue been resolved among the believers than others came to the fore. The first concerned ecstasy itself, or more specifically the role which ecstatic prophecy should play in the Church's worship.

It was rare indeed these days for the Holy Spirit to fall upon a congregation in the way Callistus had seen and felt it happen after Hippolytus' and Sabellius' reconciliation. Yet in the earliest days of the Church such outpourings had allegedly happened all the time. And even in Callistus' boyhood much of the worship of the Roman Church had been enlivened by charismatic expression. Since his return Zephyrinus had explained to him frankly enough why unvetted contributions to services had had to be discontinued, but there were those who maintained that this approach amounted to quenching the Holy Spirit. Now things seemed likely to come to a head because advocates of something called the New Prophecy had arrived in Rome.

At least, the New Prophecy was what its adherents called their own movement. Others styled them Montanists after their founder Montanus, a Phrygian who with two women named Prisca and Maximilla had won widespread renown for the ecstatic delivery of all kinds of apocalyptic utterances under the influence, so he said, of the Holy Spirit. He made a great song and dance about the visions God had granted him, while his companions complained that not only was the voice of the Spirit being silenced in the churches, but the voices of women too.

But at the beginning of Lent the following spring, the Montanist controversy was spectacularly overshadowed by a new furore over morality. This was sparked by the arrival on Zephyrinus' doorstep of a family of courtesans, a mother and her four daughters, who wanted to join the Church.

Callistus chanced to be in conference with the bishop

when they were announced – or rather, when they announced themselves. The mother, whose voice was so strident that it would have been the envy of many generals, must have been heard by every resident on Zephyrinus' street explaining who they were and why they had come.

The bishop's servant was all for sending the five of them packing, but true to form Zephyrinus invited them in without hesitation. 'My name is Davina,' the mother informed him, settling her ample body in the chair vacated for her by Callistus while her daughters, equally well endowed, draped themselves about her. 'But everyone calls me Derelicta, on account that my waster of a husband abandoned me with two little daughters to bring up and not a denarius to do it with. How *else* was I to feed them, I ask you, but by doing what every abandoned mother has been tempted to do since time immemorial? And how was I to avoid coming by at least a few other children along the way? I've never held with exposing infants at birth, and besides, once they got old enough my girls have all made their own contributions to the family finances. But we've had enough of men treating us like filth. We want to change; we want to be Christians like you.'

'Davina, God bless you! You shall never be called Derelicta again,' Zephyrinus promised her, clasping her hands in his. 'You shall all be enrolled as catechumens straight away; then you can be baptized at Easter along with the rest of those receiving instruction.'

And indeed no one *did* call Davina Derelicta any more, at least not in Callistus' hearing. Instead he heard her addressed increasingly as Dilecta, Beloved, because she was so keen to tell everyone – Christian and pagan alike – how much God loved her in spite of the life she had led, and how much he loved them too.

But it was all too much for Hippolytus. For as long as he had been preoccupied with Christology he hadn't had much energy left over for pursuing his moral crusade. Now he resumed it with a vengeance.

'Surely you cannot believe that a mere six weeks is long enough to create lasting transformation in the heart of a woman like that?' he demanded of Zephyrinus at a meeting of elders for which Callistus was taking notes.

'Since when has sin committed *before* baptism required lengthy penance?' Zephyrinus asked him in return. 'Christ is our atonement. The thief on the cross was told by our Lord and Saviour: *today* you will be with me in Paradise.'

'But that thief was about to die! *He* could hardly be tempted to go on sinning after his conversion.'

'Then reflect upon Zacchaeus the repentant tax-collector who was told: today salvation has come to your house. Our Saviour didn't wait to see if *he* kept all his promises.'

'And the woman taken in adultery, not to mention the Samaritan woman Jesus met at Jacob's well,' added Anastasia, who as Head of the Order of Widows was more confrontational than Hermione had been, but no less highly respected. 'Do we hear Jesus saying to these women: prove that your life has changed, and *then* I will accept you? No. He welcomed them at once. And besides, anyone who looks at Davina's face can see at a glance that she *has* been changed, out of all recognition.'

'Davina perhaps,' Hippolytus acknowledged. 'But what of her daughters? Davina was once respectably married, but *they* have known no life but whoredom. How can you expect them to adopt Christian behaviour overnight, or even understand what it entails?'

'They haven't been selling their bodies on the streets because they *enjoy* it,' Zephyrinus reminded him. 'The Widows will support them. The girls will be given food and a little money to live on until they find husbands prepared to overlook where they have come from just as God does, and Davina can join the widows' order in her own right.'

'No,' said Hippolytus firmly. 'They will fall, Zephyrinus, and keep on falling, and drag other women down with them. Brides of Christ will become harlots, and what kind of message will *that* send to the world? What sort of reputation will the Roman Church be saddled with then?'

'I doubt that any one of *us* is spreading the Gospel as effectively as Davina is at the moment,' said Gaius, brother of Titus. 'Was Christ thinking about his own reputation when he spoke to the woman at the well? Or when a sinful woman anointed his feet with perfume and dried them with her hair?'

'Heart-warming stories, I grant you,' said Hippolytus. 'But it's unlikely that Jesus met either of those women ever again; he didn't need to worry about whether they went on sinning after he forgave and affirmed them.'

'Perhaps not, but he did accept Mary Magdalene into his band of companions, and from what we are told, her reputation was worse than that of any other woman he encountered. Didn't she have seven devils driven out of her?' This final example came from Zephyrinus himself, and there was nothing more that Hippolytus could say. In the end he went home defeated, but as he left predicted that Zephyrinus and those who had taken his part were only making trouble for themselves which they would live to regret.

'He's probably right,' Zephyrinus admitted to Callistus later. 'Yet something tells me we are only doing what our Saviour himself would have done.'

'Not *something*, Zephyrinus. The Holy Spirit,' said Callistus, and Zephyrinus blessed him with one of his knowing smiles and a cup of wine from a jar of Titus' best, which they settled down to enjoy together as they often did.

Only a few weeks after this, a fresh crisis arose which threatened to re-ignite the animosity which perpetually smouldered these days between the Jewish Christians and the Gentiles. A believing Gentile freedman, a gaunt, undernourished-looking fellow by the name of Lysias, was dragged bodily before Zephyrinus by one of the Jewish Christians, who was demanding the wretch's excommunication. Apparently he had been found guilty by a secular law-court of defrauding his patron – who was the

Jewish Christian's cousin. He had already been flogged and made to pay back his ill-gotten gains, but surely if he had committed fraud he should be permanently excluded from church membership?

Callistus had been helping Zephyrinus prepare for a deacons' meeting, and was on the point of leaving so the bishop could take a siesta before the session began. Having learnt the substance of the Jewish Christian's complaint he hovered on the threshold, not knowing if he should go or stay. His heart was thumping in his chest and he suddenly felt very sick. An eloquent look from Zephyrinus convinced him to sit down.

'Well, Lysias, is it true? *Did* you defraud this man's cousin?' the bishop enquired of the freedman, who was cowering at his feet.

Lysias did not respond at once. He was clearly caught in an agony of indecision just as Callistus had been. Eventually he stammered, 'Yes. It's true.' And when Zephyrinus merely watched him and waited for more, he blurted, 'I was responsible for collecting outstanding debts from his clients and I kept some money for myself. But only because he wouldn't pay me a living wage, and my little boy and I were threatened with eviction by our landlord because we couldn't pay our rent. We were better off when we were slaves; my master only freed us so he wouldn't have to keep us under his roof any more after he beat my son so badly that he couldn't do any work.'

'And the boy's mother..?' probed Zephyrinus gently.

Taken aback, Lysias looked from Zephyrinus to his accuser, and then at Callistus, who was trembling all over as long-buried memories of his own past surged up into his throat from the pit of his stomach. 'She's still a slave,' Lysias managed at last. 'She's a Christian like me; we'd said vows and lived as husband and wife, and neither of us ever went with anyone else. But my master had no more time for slaves' marriages than Roman law has, and after I was freed he sold her. I haven't seen her for months.' Tears streamed down Lysias' sunken cheeks; on an impulse he seized hold of the bishop's knees and wept, 'Please don't expel me from the Church! I know I've done wrong; I was too proud to ask for help when I needed it, then too scared to confess what I'd done, because there's no forgiveness for fraud. But now I have no job and no home, and nowhere else to turn.'

Unable to tear his eyes from the suppliant's face, Callistus was sweating and shivering alternately as everything he had suffered himself overwhelmed him afresh. Then as though from very far away he heard Zephyrinus saying, 'Don't be afraid, brother Lysias. You and your son will live here in my house while this matter is addressed. I'm afraid you won't be able to receive communion for the time being, since your accuser's case is proven. But I promise you that once I have done what needs to be done, you will.'

It was obvious that Lysias could not believe what he was hearing. Neither could his accuser, who stood open-mouthed, being told that he had won yet somehow knowing he had lost. Callistus felt like a drowning child to whom someone has thrown a line but who is not sure whether he has got a grip on it or not.

'My boy and I can stay *here*?' Lysias whispered. 'Do you really mean it, my lord?'

'Your lord? I'm your brother, as you are mine,' Zephyrinus reminded him. 'But yes, I do mean it. On one condition: that *you* help *me* as well.'

'I, help you? Of course, anything... but how?'

'I'm not exactly sure as yet; we must wait and see how events turn out. But you may be able to help me accomplish something I have been meaning to do for many months and am only sorry I have not done already.'

So Lysias and his son duly moved in with Zephyrinus, who until now had lived with only his aged manservant for company. Not that there was any requirement for a bishop – or indeed for a presbyter or deacon – to be unmarried, though it was becoming increasingly common. From time to time Callistus wondered whether perhaps Zephyrinus had once loved and lost, just as he had himself. He still dreamed of Marcia at night, and in the daytime his thoughts would all too frequently stray after her.

Once Hippolytus found out that Zephyrinus had excommunicated a man for fraud and then straight away welcomed him to live in his house, he was as incredulous as he was incensed, and this time he was by no means in the minority. Few people understood why the bishop would want to extend hospitality to a delinquent like Lysias who was guilty of fraud by his own admission and had only escaped being sent to the mines because he was too decrepit already to make it worth the state's while keeping him alive until he got there.

'Callistus will have made the bishop take him in,' Hippolytus was persuading anyone who would listen. 'We all know that he was once excommunicated for fraud himself, and that he's got Zephyrinus wound around his little finger.'

Because Zephyrinus had such a reputation for gentleness and mercy, there were some who were willing to give him the benefit of the doubt and say that he must know what he was doing. But many more were convinced that Callistus – who was comely and charming enough but far too clever – must be taking advantage of the bishop's gullibility.

Callistus himself was distraught. 'I should never have come back to Rome,' he told Zephyrinus over and over again. 'If it weren't for me, none of this would have happened.'

'Nonsense,' was always the bishop's response. 'What has your coming back got to do with how Lysias' ex-master treats his dependants? No, my little prince, you and Lysias have provided me with the courage and opportunity I needed to right some very long-standing wrongs, of which the Christian community should be deeply ashamed.'

But it was only when Carpophorus went out of his way to visit Callistus at home and offer him and Zephyrinus his unqualified support that Callistus ceased blaming himself.

'Lysias' old master is a monster,' Carpophorus informed them. 'His mother may have been Jewish, but his father must have been a demon from hell. He treats his slaves and freedmen worse than he treats his wife, and that's saying something.'

Nevertheless, Hippolytus had no trouble collecting enough signatures from members of the Church to present a petition to Zephyrinus demanding that Lysias – and therefore his son as well – be expelled from his house just as he'd been barred from communion. It made no sense whatever for a man who was excommunicate to be living with the bishop.

'Hippolytus, I would no sooner ban Lysias and his son from my house than I would ban you, who were once one of the little princes I looked out for just like Callistus. So for you I am prepared to call a special meeting of the presbyters and deacons and widows' leaders, where you can present your petition before us all. But know this: I shall speak against it, and Lysias and his son will be present throughout the proceedings.'

Thus it was that Lysias and his son came to play a pivotal role in Zephyrinus' plans. Not that they made any effort to tug at anyone's heart-strings, as defendants were wont to do in the secular courts. Well fed now, and tidily dressed, they sat without cowering or commenting while the ministers of the Roman Church, who numbered more than fifty altogether, scrutinized them like a panel of jurors. But when Hippolytus had presented his petition amidst audible murmurs of approval, Zephyrinus rose to his feet and silenced everyone with the gravity of his expression.

'Brothers and sisters in Christ,' he addressed them. 'I have longed for an opportunity such as this since the moment you elected me your bishop. You honoured me with this position, I believe, because you were tired of the fruitlessness of my predecessors' approach to the pastoral dilemmas which beset them. Yet until very recently I have been burdened by theological disputations, the complexities of which I confess have sometimes been beyond my understanding.

'But forgiveness will *never* be beyond me. And so we meet here today not merely to decide the fate of one unhappy man and his innocent child, but because the whole question of the significance of sin committed after baptism must be addressed without further delay. As most of you know, my archdeacon Callistus was convicted of fraud after baptism, and only because he convinced you that his conviction had been unjust does he sit among us today. But supposing I told you that it would have made no difference to me if he had been guilty as charged? When he knelt at Victor's feet just as Lysias knelt at mine, I saw his need and I saw his repentance; and God saw them too! And it is God who has called me as your bishop to lead you further along the road of forgiveness than you have ever believed it possible to go.

'For Jesus offered forgiveness and absolution to *everyone*, and not merely once, for sins committed before they became his followers. Jesus himself baptized no one, yet forgave his apostles again and again. Did not Peter deny him three times? And surely apostasy is a graver sin than fraud! Yet upon the rock of this repentant apostate's faith the Church of Christ was founded. Seventy times seven, Jesus said, *that* is how often we must forgive those who stray from the path prepared for us.' And Callistus' heart missed a beat, for he could never hear those words without remembering that he had heard them first from Marcia.

'It's in love and mercy that we must surpass the standards of the world around us,' Zephyrinus finished up. 'And it is equality and justice for which we must fight. The poor will always be with us, as our Saviour taught us, just as there will always be tares growing up in the Church along with the wheat.' (Again Callistus' heart skipped a beat.) 'Yet we must take their part, as Jesus did. The Pharisees who challenged him had high standards, but did they earn his congratulations? The hard-working older brother in the Parable of the Prodigal Son had high standards too, but did our Lord have sympathy for him? No; his compassion was always for the sinner who repented, the lost one who was found, the fugitive who returned. His heart went out to the broken, and ours should do the same.'

There was a lengthy silence as the assembled ministers weighed Zephyrinus' words. It was Titus' brother Gaius who broke it by asking, 'Bishop, what exactly are you proposing?'

'If I did not think that it would cause yet another rift in our congregation, I should be inclined to propose the abolition of public penance for some sins altogether and rule that *no* sin, however serious and whenever committed, should be regarded as categorically unforgivable by the Church. However,' – and here Zephyrinus paused to quell the audible consternation with another significant look – 'I propose for now merely that henceforth *no* ritual penance be required for sins committed prior to baptism, but only the standard period of instruction given to catechumens in order that no one becomes a full member of the Church without understanding clearly what he is doing. *After* baptism we should rule that fraud and any sexual sin short of adultery – such as lying with your betrothed before your wedding day, or with some other man or woman when neither of you are married or betrothed already – can be absolved after an appropriate period of penance; and by that, I *mean* penance, not public humiliation! Murder, adultery and apostasy committed after baptism will remain outside the Church's authority to remit, for now, as we seek further guidance from God. But we shall strive to teach *everyone* that the secret of living a changed life comes from new birth, from the indwelling of God's Spirit in our hearts.'

This time no look, however meaningful, would have been sufficient to quieten the disturbance which broke out among Zephyrinus' ministers. But the bishop had a final counter yet to play. He called upon Lysias to stand up and tell his story to those assembled just as he had previously told it to him and his archdeacon.

When Lysias had finished there was silence, for the sincerity of his remorse and of his desire to serve God was obvious to all. So was the innocence of his son, whose legs had been smashed so badly that he could barely walk, let alone work.

'Who am I to deny mercy or communion to this man? Who are *you*?' demanded Zephyrinus, holding out his hands palm upward in appeal. 'Can you imagine our Saviour turning him away from his table? If God chooses to condemn him on the Day of Judgement, and me along with him, then so be it. But that is not the sort of God I worship! So I call upon those who would stand with me on this matter, to do it now. The Church and I will abide by the decision of the majority.'

Gaius stood up at once, closely followed by Anastasia, Urbanus, Asterius and almost everyone else including Callistus. Eventually a mere half dozen – prominent among them Hippolytus and Roscius – remained in their seats.

And Callistus thought: *this* is why Zephyrinus was made Bishop of Rome. He is indeed God's man.

CHAPTER FIFTEEN

At the height of summer the emperor Septimius Severus returned to Rome. This was the tenth year of his reign, but he had spent so long away conducting his military campaigns that this was the first time Callistus had ever seen him.

Today, however, everyone would see him, because a magnificent parade had been organized to celebrate his homecoming. It had also been announced that every member of the Praetorian Guard and every poor citizen eligible for the corn dole would be given ten gold pieces to mark the occasion. So the streets were thronged with people cheering, whistling and waving banners long before the emperor and his entourage came in sight. Callistus and Titus had gone together to the house of one of Titus' friends, Priscus, from whose rooftop there would be a splendid view of the procession as it made its way through the city to the imperial palace on the Palatine Hill.

For the first few years of his reign, Severus had mostly been battling against rival claimants for his throne. Since then he had been dealing with troubles on the empire's eastern border, where he had fought a lengthy and ultimately successful campaign against the Parthians. Two new Roman provinces had been created as a result, and these had had to be tamed and organized before Severus deemed it safe to entrust them to others. On his way back to Rome he had made a tour of Palestine – ever a hotbed of unrest – and visited Egypt, where like all distinguished commanders he had paid his respects at the tomb of Alexander the Great, as well as sailing up the Nile to see the pyramids and the temples of Thebes.

'Don't expect Severus to *look* anything like Alexander the Great, mind you,' Titus remarked to Callistus as they stood on Priscus' rooftop with their host and his wife and children, all enjoying the holiday mood. 'He must be nearly twice as old as Alexander was when he died, and they say that he suffers terribly with gout. He isn't even very tall.'

'Alexander wasn't tall, either, was he? From what I've heard, Severus looked formidable enough in his day. After all, he's always earned the respect of his enemies as well as his friends.'

'That's because of his determination, not his appearance. Once he's got his teeth into something he's like a hound with a hare between its jaws. But at least you know where you are with a man who never changes his mind - and in the case of the Senate, that's firmly under his feet. Firm but fair, though; that's what his soldiers say. He shares all their hardships on campaign, just like Alexander did. No wonder his health is in tatters.'

Just then Priscus' two little daughters started bouncing up and down and shrieking with excitement. 'He's coming, Father. Mother, look! There's his chariot!'

And indeed he was. Preceded by trumpeters and garlanded girls throwing rose petals in its path, the imperial chariot hove into view at the far end of the street below. The crowds' cheering erupted afresh and the trumpets blared, and one of Priscus' daughters leaned out so far over the parapet that her father had to grab her round the waist lest she topple onto the heads of the people lining the road.

If the emperor's health was fragile he hid it well. As his chariot came closer Callistus saw a man who was stocky and stolid, with rugged features, a full head of wiry grey hair and a fine beard to match. He clearly had African blood but plenty of Italian too, and altogether looked like a man you would cross at your peril.

He and his driver were not the only occupants of the vehicle. Beside him was his wife, the striking Syrian beauty Julia Domna, who was noticeably taller than he was. He had married her long before becoming emperor; the story went that he had done so because her horoscope foretold that the man she married would be – or become – a mighty monarch, and Severus was famously superstitious.

Considering that he had never set eyes on her, so it was said, when he proposed, and had known almost nothing about her, Severus had netted himself a remarkably impressive catch. For Domna was a woman as capable as she was glamorous, and the couple had been happily married for over fifteen years. She went everywhere with him, even on campaign, and was reputedly even more beloved of the soldiers – who called her 'Mother of the Camps' – than he was. This was quite an achievement for an exotic eastern enchantress who was the daughter of a high priest of the Syrian sun god Elagabal. Julius Bassianus, as her father was known in Latin, was a scion of the ancient dynasty of priest-kings of Emesa, but today his daughter was dressed as a respectable Roman matron and wore her thirty-five-or-so years with an appropriate dignity and consummate grace. You would never have guessed her origins had you not known them already, and whenever she was addressed as Augusta, or Empress, it was as much in recognition of her own imperial qualities as those of her husband.

'The empress looks *so* majestic!' Priscus' younger daughter enthused, leaning alarmingly over the parapet once again. But her older sister's eyes had already been drawn by the occupants of the second chariot in the procession: the emperor's adolescent sons. Fourteen and thirteen years of age respectively, Antoninus and Geta looked like a pair of young gods: olive-skinned and curly-haired and already as tall as their father, they could readily have been taken for Bacchus and Apollo. It was perhaps unfortunate that by all accounts the two of them had no more in common than Bacchus and Apollo had, and hated each other with a passion. Today they were smiling, however, and basking in their parents' reflected glory.

Behind the two boys, a third car carried Julia Maesa, Domna's older sister, and her husband, the eminent Syrian-born senator Julius Avitus. But it was the fourth chariot's passengers who caught Callistus' eye – or rather, one of them did. She was Maesa's daughter Mamaea, and she looked so like Marcia that she could have been taken for her twin.

She was much younger, of course, than Marcia would have been by now, but in Callistus' mind Marcia would for ever be in the prime of her womanhood as Mamaea was today. She rode in the shadow of her sister Soaemias, who was beautiful and knew it, and visibly despised her. But Mamaea had such sad-looking, downcast eyes in her quietly lovely face that Callistus could not tear his away.

So he scarcely noticed that Titus and Priscus had begun talking disparagingly about Plautianus, Commander of the Praetorian Guard, who had been with Severus on all his campaigns and who marched behind the imperial family's chariots at the head of a detachment of his troops.

'I *said*, he's a dangerous man,' Titus repeated when Callistus made no response to a remark addressed to him. 'He would never get away with exhibiting such greed or violence if Severus were in better health. Don't you know he lives in far greater luxury than the emperor? And he certainly throws his weight about a lot more. We can only hope he'll have more pressing things to keep him busy now he's back in Rome than persecuting Christians, which seems to have been a favourite hobby of all too many Praetorian commanders in the past.'

'I doubt he'd get away with *that*,' Priscus put in. 'Severus is far too superstitious to risk offending *any* god, and the Praetorians are all his own veterans, Plautianus included. Don't forget, Severus dismissed the whole of the existing Praetorian Guard when he became emperor, because they'd failed to defend Pertinax. Their replacements are his to a man.'

'It's not surprising that they are unswervingly loyal to him when he pays them so well,' said Titus with a grimace.

In fact Severus could be credited with enhancing the financial circumstances of a great many of his subjects, not merely the Praetorians, because of the stability which his stalwart leadership had brought to the empire and its economy. And the largesse being distributed to Rome's poorest this very day amounted to the most generous sum ever given away on a single occasion by any Roman emperor. No wonder that Severus was being acclaimed as a hero.

Nor was today's parade the only spectacular event being staged in honour of Severus' homecoming. Seven whole days of festivities had been planned, to celebrate not only the emperor's return and the tenth anniversary of his accession to the throne but also the betrothal of his elder son Antoninus to Publia Fulvia Plautilla – the daughter of Plautianus. Notices were posted in the forum that there would be wild beast fights and gladiatorial contests in the Colosseum on a scale not seen since the heady days of Commodus. Sixty wild boar (paid for by Plautianus) tearing each other to shreds would be one of the highlights; there would also be lions, panthers, bison and ostrich strutting their stuff, along with countless other creatures to which many of the spectators would be hard pressed to put a name. Apparently seven hundred wild animals would be running around the arena at the same time, slaughtering and being slaughtered both by one another and by trained beast-fighters.

At least Severus had given no indication of wanting to fight in the arena himself.

'Will you and Callistus be going to the Games?' Priscus asked Titus as the imperial party passed by beneath them. Titus pursed his lips.

'I've no stomach for all that blood these days,' he answered. 'To be honest, very few of the Christians I know best are happy with that sort of entertainment. And who can blame us, when you think that in the past it was our own friends and relatives who were being torn apart by lions for the crowd's amusement.'

'Ah yes. Quite so.' Priscus, who wasn't a Christian himself, must have been wishing he'd thought twice before asking his question. But Callistus, who would normally have run a mile from any celebration of violence, was equally embarrassed to find himself thinking that Mamaea would be at the Games, and wondering if he might contrive to find a seat there from which he would be able to enjoy watching *her* instead of the show. At the same time he couldn't quite believe the direction his own thoughts were taking: he couldn't recall even noticing a woman in that way since Marcia's passing. Luckily Priscus' daughters were too engrossed in discussing which of Severus' sons was the more handsome, or they might have realized that Callistus was still gazing distractedly after Mamaea's retreating back.

During the course of the next few days while most of the populace enjoyed Severus' and Plautianus' generosity, Callistus was finding out, without really intending to, a little more about the niece of the emperor's wife, and why she had looked so sad. The poor girl couldn't have been much more than twenty, but she was already a widow and it wasn't very long since her husband had died.

Antoninus, on the other hand, was officially betrothed a few days into the week of general merrymaking. An enormous banquet was thrown in the forum in the happy couple's honour, to which all members of the Senate were invited, but anyone seated close enough to Antoninus to see his face said afterwards that it looked like thunder throughout the proceedings. Rumour had it that Plautilla was horrendously spoilt and that Antoninus had no desire to be her husband whatever, even though she came with a dowry sufficient to provide for several regular princesses. The obscenely extravagant betrothal gifts which her father had seen fit to lavish upon her and her dashing fiancé were paraded around the forum for all to see, carried by an army of Plautilla's personal servants who were all allegedly eunuchs, castrated on Plautianus' instructions. This might not have been true, but the fact that it was widely believed said a great deal about the sort of man Plautianus was.

Titus was not alone among Callistus' friends in his anxiety about what Severus' and Plautianus' return to the capital might mean for the Church.

'Severus' thoughts about religion must be so convoluted,' Zephyrinus pondered aloud as he and Callistus sat sipping wine the next day in the cool of the bishop's tiny courtyard. 'He may be from Africa as Victor was, but his family's part Italian and part old Carthaginian; his first language is Punic, and no Roman emperor has ever spoken Latin with an accent like Hannibal's before. But then he compounded everything by marrying a Syrian.'

'Well, the Carthaginians hailed from Phoenicia, didn't they? That's not so far from Syria, either geographically or in its culture. Perhaps he just wanted to rediscover his roots.'

'Certainly his wife is firmly attached to hers. She may dress like a Roman lady when the situation demands, but I have it on good authority that she's very much a priestess of the Eastern Sun in private.'

'*I'd* heard that she's interested in a great many religions and philosophies, our own included,' said Callistus, immediately regretting that he'd been so frank about his own interest in the women of the imperial family.

But it wasn't long before Domna's fascination with philosophy and religion of every kind was common knowledge. A woman whose cultural sophistication was fast becoming more celebrated even than her beauty, she had scholars and mystics buzzing about her like bees round a lavender bush. She had taken to hosting intellectual symposia in her chambers at the palace to which every aspiring writer and thinker in Rome hankered to be invited. Not merely spiritual matters but art, poetry and ethics were hotly debated at these postprandial gatherings. While Severus spent his evenings nursing his ailments and Plautianus indulging his gluttony, tickling the back of his throat with a feather to free up more space in his swelling stomach, Domna was having her intellectual ears tickled by the silveriest tongues in Rome.

Then out of the blue the bishop of Rome and his archdeacon were invited to one of Domna's symposia themselves.

Once he had recovered from the shock, the years fell from Zephyrinus' shoulders like a sodden cloak and he became as excited as a schoolboy let loose in a pastry shop. 'What an opportunity!' he marvelled, seizing Callistus by the forearms as though they had been invited to a dance rather than a debate. 'To preach the Gospel to the empress herself and to the elite of Rome's pagan literary establishment all in one go! This is more than an answer to prayer. I should never have dreamt of praying for it in the first place.'

'Well, I'm sure Saint Paul himself said that God is able to do far more for us than we ever think of asking,' Callistus replied with a grin, doing his best not to be swept off his feet. 'But surely it's not so very surprising that such a thing should happen. Our faith has more adherents than any of the other non-native cults in Rome. Why *wouldn't* Julia Domna want to hear about it from those who are most qualified to enlighten her?'

'I'm only glad you're going to be coming with me.' Zephyrinus began to consider the implications of their invitation more seriously once Callistus' measured words had brought him back down to earth. 'I shouldn't care to be cross-examined by all those scholarly hair-splitters without you there to keep me on track. Christians who think too much are trouble enough, but intelligent pagans... perhaps we should see if we can take our friend Hippolytus along with us.'

'He wouldn't come,' said Callistus with a mirthless laugh. 'Intelligent women offend him *whatever* they believe. I think that by the grace of God we shall cope quite adequately on our own.' But in spite of his efforts to inject some moderation into the old man's excitement, Callistus was no less thrilled than Zephyrinus to have been furnished with an excuse to visit the ladies' wing of the emperor's palace. He told himself that the reasons for his enthusiasm were exactly the same as the bishop's.

As the appointed evening drew closer, however, Callistus' own excitement began to be tempered by anxiety. Supposing this were some kind of trap orchestrated by Plautianus to kidnap and dispose of the bishop and his archdeacon at one fell swoop, thereby robbing the Roman Church of both its senior leaders and its faith in God's providence into the bargain? Also they had been informed of the motion to be debated at the symposium, namely: who was the greater, Jesus of Nazareth or Apollonius of Tyana? Apollonius' cause was to be pleaded by one Philostratus, an ardent and erudite admirer of the man as well as an author of some repute. He would be no inconsiderable opponent.

'Apollonius of Tyana? I don't know anything about him. Who on earth was he?' Zephyrinus confessed. 'I can't see how he can have been all that great if I'm not convinced I've ever heard of him.'

'*I've* heard of him,' Callistus said grimly. 'He may not be very well known in Rome these days, but he gets plenty of attention in some of the books I've read about the religions of the east. He lived about the same time as Jesus, but was much more famous during his lifetime. He travelled round a lot more, too: Greece, Asia Minor, Italy, Spain, Mesopotamia and even India, so they say, teaching and doing miracles just like Jesus did.'

'So we're not looking at a debate so much as a calculation of how many miracles each of them did, and how many places they preached in, and how big the crowds were who heard them? Sounds more like arithmetic than philosophy.'

'Somehow I don't think that's the kind of discussion Julia Domna will have in mind. Though if it did come down to a comparison of their miracles, no one ever produced evidence that Apollonius rose from the dead. That's no doubt why his cult hasn't gone on growing in the way that Jesus' has. But he still has his disciples, and their teaching still seems more acceptable to many philosophers than ours does. After all, we believe in a God who "defiled" himself by taking on human flesh, whilst they believe in the power of the mind, which they call "nous" and reckon to be humanity's single most important attribute.'

'*Your* mind may be your finest asset, Callistus, but *mine* is feeling distinctly punch-drunk already. I think you had better do all the talking as far as our cause is concerned, unless our Lord is gracious enough to impart to me some pearl of special revelation and prompts me to drop it into the conversation right at the crucial moment.'

'Well it wouldn't be the first time if he did, would it? You can but ask him. Whereas according to Apollonius, although God is the most perfect and beautiful being we can imagine, he cannot be influenced by prayer or sacrifice at all and has no desire whatever to be worshipped by human beings.'

'I see.' Zephyrinus stroked his beard and looked again at the tablet containing their invitation to Domna's party. 'So what do you know about this fellow Philostratus who is going to be fighting Apollonius' corner? Is he anywhere near as clever as you?'

Callistus pulled a face. 'A good deal cleverer, I shouldn't wonder. Apparently Domna has commissioned him to write a book about Apollonius' life, of which he has completed the better part already, so he'll certainly be in command of his subject. But don't worry; we'll give him a good run for his money so long as we both keep our heads. And if you're generous with your beatific smile, any philosophers present who are scrutinizing us for signs of stress which would cast doubt on Jesus' claim to give us peace which the world cannot give will be well satisfied that he can deliver on his promises.'

Zephyrinus pulled a face of his own which was anything but beatific, but he knew full well what Callistus was implying. Several of the philosophers who belonged to Domna's circle were Stoics, who were noted above all for their ability to master negative emotions and soar on unruffled feathers above the storms of everyday life. To them, and to many other philosophers of similar schools, a system of belief was only as good as its success at enabling its adherents to live happy and harmonious lives.

However, when the evening of the symposium arrived and Zephyrinus and Callistus were shown into Domna's sumptuous dining-room, Callistus realized straight away that keeping a clear head was going to be well nigh impossible. For Domna was not the only woman present.

The opulent triclinium had been furnished with couches to accommodate a dozen diners, of whom six had already taken their places when the Christians made their entry. Two were men whom Callistus knew, though only by sight: Galen, the aged physician from Pergamum – whose distinguished career had begun way back in the reign of Marcus Aurelius with setting the broken bones of gladiators – and Cassius Dio, an eminent historian who was known to be working on a multi-volume chronicle documenting contemporary events even as they were unfolding. There was one other man there whom Callistus didn't recall ever having seen before: he was subsequently introduced as their opponent Philostratus. The other three people present were women.

Julia Domna herself was already reclining in her place at the head of the table. From close quarters she was as handsome a woman as she had appeared at the parade, with her strong features and distinctive centrally parted hair – a style which Rome's leading ladies of fashion were already scrambling to emulate. To her left was a young woman Callistus did not recognize, but who was very simply dressed in a plain white robe with her hair twisted back in an austere-looking bun. To Domna's right was her niece Mamaea.

Much as Callistus had privately hoped she might be there, he hadn't really expected that she would be. Like the other young woman she was simply and modestly dressed, though her hair was artfully coiled on top of her head, with a few stray tendrils softening the alabaster smoothness of her face. But because her eyes were downcast just as they had been when Callistus had seen her at the parade, she gave no sign of having noticed that any new guests had come in.

Domna, on the other hand, gestured graciously for Callistus and Zephyrinus to take their places, on the opposite side of the low central table from the three other men, and by the time they had got themselves settled the remaining guests had arrived. These were four elderly gentlemen none of whom Callistus recognized, but who were each dressed in the standard garb of the philosopher: a homespun mantle which left one shoulder bare. Their beards were fastidiously unkempt.

Domna proceeded to make appropriate introductions and to apologize for the preponderance of men over women. 'My sister Maesa is much cleverer and better at arguing than I am,' she said with a smile. 'But unfortunately philosophical discussion does not rank very highly on her list of exciting things to do after dinner, and I regret that her elder daughter Soaemias rather takes after her in that respect. In any case, Soaemias has recently returned to Syria to be married, so she would be unable to join us this evening even if she cared to.' A ripple of discreet amusement spread through the room at this; clearly Soaemias' new husband was going to have his work cut out for him if he were to avoid becoming an object of amusement in his own right. 'Soaemias' younger sister, on the other hand,' their hostess continued, 'has always been much closer to her dear Aunt Domna than to her own mother. May I present my niece, the Lady Julia Mamaea.'

At last Mamaea raised her eyes with a slight, shy smile, and apart from Marcia's they were the loveliest eyes Callistus had ever seen. Momentarily they chanced to connect with his own, and Callistus was undone.

So he almost missed Domna's introduction of her second female companion entirely. Eventually he recovered himself sufficiently to glean that this was the eminent Platonist philosopher Arria.

The formal debate was not due to commence until after the meal which was subsequently served by Domna's slaves: all dark Syrian beauties, both male and female, though Callistus didn't notice any of them. The meal itself was unusually modest as imperial entertainments went, in recognition of the preferred lifestyle of most of those dining: eggs, fish and lightly boiled vegetables were followed by rabbit and chicken, and for dessert there were figs, nuts and cheese. Several of the philosophers ate only sparingly of the vegetables and fruit, spurning the fish and meat altogether. But they didn't stint on discussion. The veteran doctor Galen in particular questioned the men reclining to either side of him incessantly, demonstrating a voracious appetite for knowledge and wisdom on every topic under the sun. In defiance of his seventy or so years he was still especially fascinated not only by physiology, his own field of expertise, but by mental health, the nature of the soul, immortality and the afterlife.

When at length the plates had been cleared away and her guests were contentedly sipping their watered wine – or water on its own, according to their inclination for austerity – Domna introduced the motion for their debate.

'I myself come from a corner of the world where Syrians, Phoenicians, Greeks and Hebrews have lived cheek by jowl for a very long time,' she explained. 'Not always peaceably, it has to be said, for interest in old creeds and new in those parts is intense. Fearing that I might lack for intellectual stimulation here in Rome, I have therefore brought many illustrious scholars and mystics from the east to the imperial court since I arrived here with my husband some few weeks ago.

'But this evening I was wanting to enquire into the fastest growing faith in the City, to hear its beliefs expounded by individuals who have espoused them, and to have them subjected to cross-examination by experts who deem them erroneous. To frame this enquiry in the form of a contest between Jesus of Nazareth and Apollonius of Tyana was the suggestion of my niece here; and an excellent suggestion it was too, in my opinion, for there is nothing more riveting than single combat between mighty men of valour. However, since neither Jesus nor Apollonius can do battle any longer on his own behalf, each has provided a champion. Ladies and gentlemen: for Jesus, we are privileged to welcome Zephyrinus, Christian – or to avoid confusion should I say Catholic – Bishop of Rome, to address us; for Apollonius, his official biographer Philostratus.'

There was a general round of applause, but before things could proceed any further, Zephyrinus directed everyone's attention toward Callistus and said, 'With your permission, Lady Julia, ladies and gentlemen, I should like to appoint a champion of my own. I think you will find my archdeacon Callistus here a far more competent exponent of the Christian faith than myself, and certainly much better looking.'

For all his thirty years, Callistus found himself blushing, and then stealing a glance at Mamaea to see if she had noticed. She had.

Afterwards he could not remember a single word of what he had said in defence of his beliefs, but it must have been appropriately eloquent because he was bombarded with compliments, questions and objections in equal measure. He did manage to listen attentively enough to Philostratus' own exposition to engage in some verbal sparring with him when it was over; inevitably the general discussion which followed homed in on the question of whether truth could be found more reliably in philosophical reasoning or from divine revelation. Both Jesus and Apollonius were supposed to have received the latter, but Apollonius had written much about the former as well, which led Arria to suggest that Apollonius was therefore the greater of the two after all. Whether or not one accepted that divine revelation was a legitimate source of understanding, Jesus' and Apollonius' shared access to it must of necessity cancel out its influence upon each of them.

This argument met with considerable approval, notwithstanding that its advocate was a woman. But then Mamaea spoke up for the first time to offer an opinion of her own.

'Surely,' she said, 'One cannot simply assume that both Jesus and Apollonius had *equal* access to divine wisdom. Even supposing that either of them was listening to anything other than his own inner voice, one may have been more receptive than the other. Indeed, they may not even have been communing with the same God.'

Her argument was sound enough. But Callistus found himself still more impressed by the musical quality of her voice, the care with which she chose her words, and the way she tilted her head ever so slightly while she was speaking them, disturbing the loose tendrils of hair which brushed her cheeks. She made no further contribution to the discussion, in which Callistus could not help but be thoroughly involved, but was he just imagining it when he fancied that she looked at him more intently when he spoke than she looked at Philostratus?

The debate ended inconclusively, as Callistus had suspected it would, though as the guests went their separate ways into the night, each guided by the light of his own torch and wisdom, they were still chewing the fat. But Zephyrinus was delighted with the way things had gone, and Callistus too was high on his own success. For he knew that he had held his own and caused some of the philosophers at least to view the Christian faith through fresh eyes.

Still, the eyes he remembered were Mamaea's, and it was her voice that he heard in his head when he lay down to sleep that night still exhilarated by the cut and thrust of the evening's verbal combat. He began to think that this was what all his years of study had been preparing him for, and that they had certainly been more than worth while.

As a result of his prowess in this initial contest Callistus received invitations to participate in a number of similar symposia over the course of the following weeks, in a succession of rich men's houses. But exciting as these opportunities undoubtedly were, for Callistus none of them could hold a candle to that first time at Domna's dinner party. He told himself that this was only because a new experience is always more stimulating than something to which one has grown accustomed, but deep down he knew that if Mamaea had shown her face on any of these subsequent occasions his earlier excitement would swiftly have been rekindled.

Of course he reminded himself frequently that there was nothing to be gained by wasting wistful thoughts on Domna's protégée. Not only had he promised himself that there would never be another woman in his life after Marcia, but Mamaea, widow though she was, was even less attainable for an ex-slave with a criminal record than Marcia had been for a besotted boy. Mamaea was the emperor's niece by marriage, not a mere concubine, and of royal blood in her own right. Yet none of this made any difference when Callistus' daydreams ran away with his reason.

However, any hopes he might have harboured of making a name for himself as a Christian apologist in highbrow pagan circles were dashed later that same year. For Emperor Septimius Severus, despite – or perhaps because of – the complexity of his own spiritual and ethical background, had decided to reinvent himself as the defender of traditional Roman religion and values, which according to the most strait-laced of his Stoic friends were what had made Rome great. To counter the decadence which had been rampaging through Roman society like a virulent infection since the accession of Commodus, new-fangled and alien beliefs and teachings must therefore be kept from spreading beyond the bounds of the ethnic communities in which they had originated. It was perfectly acceptable, Severus decreed, for Syrians to worship Syrian gods and Britons to worship British ones; he even permitted men born Jewish to enter political office without renouncing their ancestral religion. But proselytizing was something else altogether. Henceforth, particularly for Roman citizens, there would be severe penalties for converting from paganism to either Judaism or Christianity, and for attempting to persuade others to do so. This, notwithstanding the fact that Severus had practising Christians in his own household and among his closest associates, including one Proclus who was said to be a gifted healer and to have practised his gift successfully on Severus himself on more than one occasion.

'Well, old Severus didn't get where he is today without being shrewd as well as superstitious,' Titus responded when Callistus remarked on this apparent irony. 'Not only does he not want to risk offending any god by robbing him of the devotees he already has, but he knows that flagrant persecution all too often achieves the opposite of what's intended. You can't put out fire with fire, but if you prevent a conflagration from spreading into new territory, in time it will burn itself out.'

'Do you think he truly believes that Jupiter and Juno, Mars and Venus and the rest, are any more than figments of human imagination?' Callistus wondered. 'Though I've been spending more time with non-Christians recently than I ever have before, I'm yet to encounter an intelligent pagan who views the old gods as anything other than quaint literary devices. There may still be ignorant peasants who see deities in every grove and river, but among the educated it's only poets these days who regard the Olympians and their like as relevant.'

'Ah, but if there are no gods on Olympus, there are no

dead emperors there either, nor can live ones be worshipped as divine. And if there's one thing Severus needs, it's to unite his subjects in their devotion to *him*. *We* may never be compelled to sacrifice to his statue, but he can't afford to let refusing to do so become the fashionable thing to do.'

This was no doubt true, but even though Severus himself might understand that threats and coercion rarely caused true believers to renounce their religion permanently, the more volatile of his own admirers were seldom so astute. In the great cities where Severus was especially popular and the Christian Church especially assertive – Carthage and Alexandria, for example, both of which were already cultural and philosophical melting pots – riots broke out in which many Christian believers lost their lives. The sand of those cities' arenas was also stained afresh with Christian blood, and many heart-rending stories of courage in the face of martyrdom emerged. Particularly affecting was that of Perpetua and Felicitas, a Christian mistress and her slave-girl who faced death together hand in hand in the arena at Carthage. Their friendship, as much as their fate, brought tears to Callistus' eyes.

It wasn't long before violence against Christians began breaking out in Rome itself. Mostly these were isolated incidents sparked by personal hatred, but their increasing frequency amounted to a worrying trend. This cloud was not without its silver lining: Natalis, who had been 'bishop' of Rome's rival schismatic church, unexpectedly returned to the Catholic fold. He'd been imprisoned and tortured for spreading his own dissident brand of the Christian faith, and said that he had subsequently received a number of visions admonishing him to abandon the heretics and return to his orthodox roots. When he fell at Zephyrinus' feet in sackcloth and ashes, he maintained that he'd been whipped for an entire night by an angel.

Whatever the nature of this remarkable religious experience, Zephyrinus was only too delighted to welcome

Natalis back into his flock. He would have to do appropriate penance; whatever Zephyrinus' own views might be on the subject, most of his fellow elders would accept nothing less. But even this represented a huge step forward. Previously such schismatics had been regarded as apostates, who could never be received back into communion with the mother Church however convincingly they grovelled.

Nevertheless, Zephyrinus and Callistus recognized only too swiftly that soon it would not merely be schismatics seeking reinstatement to the congregation they had forsaken. If Christians continued to be imprisoned and tortured by the state – albeit as a result of personal vendettas – soon there would be full-blown renegades hammering on the bishop's door begging for readmission, just as there had been in the days of Nero and Domitian. What was to be done about those turncoats who had been so thoroughly intimidated that they had sacrificed to the emperor or even renounced the name of Jesus in public? If *they* were offered restitution, this could not help but make a mockery of the steadfastness of heroes and heroines such as Perpetua and Felicitas who had been prepared to stay their course to the bitter end. For the moment at least Zephyrinus was persuaded that any suggestion on his part that outright apostates might ever be considered for readmission to full communion would be tantamount to tipping a cauldron of boiling oil over his own head.

Early in the following year Lysias the pardoned fraudster was arrested for proselytizing in defiance of the imperial decree, and so was one of his converts. Lysias was simply so grateful for what his Lord and Saviour had done for him that the gospel leached out of him whether he meant it to or not. When he and his latest proselyte – a freeborn Roman citizen – were arrested, they were both told that they would be released straight away if they performed the standard sacrifice to the emperor, but both refused. Callistus toyed briefly with the idea of begging Domna or even Mamaea to intervene on their behalf but before he could act on his inclination it was reported that the two prisoners had been strangled in their cells. Lysias' son passed into the care of the widows, and the outrage horrified not only the whole Church but many outside it as well.

Not very long after this, Davina and her daughters were denounced to the authorities as proselytes too. In fact they had become Christians long before the edict forbidding conversion had been published, but this did not deter their enemies from making trouble for them. Neither Callistus nor Zephyrinus could find out who these enemies were; the first they heard about the matter was when Anastasia informed them that all five women had been thrown into prison. A distinctly unwelcome suspicion formed itself in Callistus' mind, but he made himself toss it away before it had chance to take root.

'I shall go to the prefect Papinianus myself with their certificates of baptism,' he vowed to Zephyrinus. 'That way we can prove that they became Christians before conversion was made illegal.'

'You certainly won't,' Zephyrinus rebuked him. 'It would be asking for trouble, and you are far too indispensable.' Then, once again before Callistus could translate his intentions into action, events moved on ahead of him. It emerged that the women had already been released – but not before the youngest of them, Daphne, had in terror made sacrifice to the emperor of her own volition the moment she had set eyes upon his statue.

'Poor Daphne,' said Zephyrinus on hearing of what had happened. 'She's a timid little thing, so unlike her mother and sisters.'

'And so used to having had to do whatever men asked of her all her life, whether or not it was to her liking,' Callistus added grimly. 'But what are we to do about her now? What's done is done; she has committed apostasy, and no two ways about it.'

'Surely it's perfectly clear what we must do.' Zephyrinus was quite capable of being decisive when he saw a dilemma as pastoral rather than doctrinal. 'Daphne cannot be allowed to receive communion, but she must be encouraged to attend Assembly, and be treated as a member of the Church in every other respect. Moreover on a Sunday she'll be permitted to stay with her mother and sisters until the service is ended, and when they receive communion she will come forward for a blessing at my hands. Any believer who threatens or insults her will forfeit his right to communion as well; at all costs Daphne must be kept from falling back into her former way of life.'

When the bishop's decision was conveyed to Davina she was over the moon, having feared that her now conscience-stricken daughter would be debarred from the congregation altogether and denied any further support. There were plenty of detractors who thought that she should have been. But none of them dared speak ill of her in public, lest they finish up excluded from the Church themselves.

And all the while, rather than fizzling or foundering as Severus had presumably hoped it would, the Church was once again growing larger and stronger by the day – not only in Rome, but in Carthage, Alexandria and other centres of persecution as well. In spite of the differences of opinion among its members on matters doctrinal and ethical, whenever the climate in which it existed grew hostile it gradually closed its ranks, and those on the outside looking in could not fail to be impressed by what they saw. Under circumstances like these there was no need for any of the believers to proselytize intentionally at all.

But no one seemed able to tell Callistus what Domna or her niece thought about the Christian faith any more. Whether their interest in it had dwindled or they were merely deferring to the emperor's wishes, there were no more symposia devoted to examining the claims of exotic religions or philosophies. Poets and playwrights continued to receive invitations to the emperor's table, but not mystics or clerics or pedlars of eastern wisdom, or anyone else whom Callistus could casually question. Not that he made any more conscious effort to find out about Mamaea than he did to win new souls for Christ in these trying times, but it just seemed to happen all the same… until one day he learned that, just like her sister Soaemias, Mamaea had gone home to Syria to be remarried. She was now the wife of a Syrian promagistrate by the name of Marcianus – how ironic it was that even his name echoed Marcia's – and Callistus had to accept that he would never see her again.

He did not know whether to be happy or sad, relieved or distraught. He knew he should not be any of those things; he should merely be pleased that the desolate young widow once again had someone to love and protect her. Instead, he swung wildly from relief to despair and back again a hundred times a day.

Meanwhile Septimius Severus had some new things to worry about quite apart from the growth of the Church. For no sooner had his wife's two nieces remarried than his own son's marriage fell apart. Antoninus, who was still in his teens, had disliked Plautilla from the outset; refusing to sleep or even eat with her, he had threatened more than once that when *he* became emperor he would have no hesitation in exterminating both the bitch herself and her bully of a father. In the end he got fed up with waiting, and prevailed upon three centurions to inform against Plautianus, claiming that he was plotting the emperor's downfall. It might have been true – Plautianus had certainly tried and failed in the past to bring down Julia Domna – but whether it was or it wasn't, Plautianus was put to death and his body thrown into the street for the mob to tear apart. Plautilla was sent into exile on the island of Lipara, and it went without saying that she too would eventually be put quietly out of her misery, just like Commodus' Crispina.

Equally embarrassing for Severus was the startling rampage of one Bulla Felix, a notorious criminal who caused a sensation by assembling a horde of some six hundred outlaws and robbing well-to-do travellers in broad daylight within a day's march of Rome. Flamboyant and cocksure, Bulla and his merry band of runaway slaves and vagabonds remained at large for many months, spending their ill-gotten gains with royal abandon on cheap women and wine. Their reign of exuberant terror over the travelling public would not have lasted anything like so long had they not been highly organized as well as preposterously daring; they seemed to know in advance exactly when their chosen victims would be on the road. If they were in want of armour or utensils they would pounce upon some unsuspecting artisan with relevant expertise and force him to make what they needed; if he turned out to be a needy man himself they would send him on his way loaded with presents. On one occasion Bulla succeeded in freeing two of his own men from prison by posing as a magistrate. Another time he personally kidnapped a centurion by pretending to be a deserter from the bandit army and promising to guide the gullible officer to his former leader's hide-out. When they got there, the centurion was subjected to a farcical mock trial where his head was half shaved like a convict's and he was released with a message to the masters of Rome that they should treat their slaves better if they didn't want them running away to be robbers.

Bulla was eventually captured, just as he had lived, by trickery, but he retained his ebullience to the end. Gleefully describing the swaggerer's arrest to Callistus, Titus said with ill-disguised admiration, 'When the pompous old prefect Papinianus asked him why he had become a thief, Bulla quipped, "I'll tell you if *you* tell *me* why *you* became Urban Prefect".' The outrageous brigand was subsequently thrown to wild beasts in the arena, but whilst the wealthy – Titus included – could not help but be relieved that their business trips would be a good deal less hazardous in the future, many a covert tear was shed because such a colourful character had met such a grisly end. 'They could at least have put a sword in his hand,' Titus said, to Callistus' astonishment, for Titus as a rule had no time at all for gladiators. 'Then he could have provided entertainment in his death as he did in life.' Callistus said that such a scandalous sentiment was scarcely worthy of an upstanding Christian, but found himself smiling as he said it.

An equally astonishing piece of news which reached Callistus' ears during the time that Severus was resident in Rome was that Tertullian, the fiercely strait-laced Carthaginian who had been befriended by Hippolytus while attending to the late bishop Victor's affairs in Rome, had left the mainstream Church in Carthage and become a Montanist.

'A Montanist?' Callistus repeated, incredulous, when Zephyrinus told him. 'You mean an advocate of the New Prophecy? A follower of those wild-eyed fanatics who babble delirious oracles all the time and give the Holy Spirit himself a bad name with their ravings?'

Zephyrinus shook his head sadly and said, 'Perhaps if we Catholics could find a way to accommodate the moving of the Spirit in our worship in the way we used to, those who dream dreams or see visions would not conclude that they need to look elsewhere for acceptance. It may be that Tertullian has been blessed with the very awakening we crave for Hippolytus, and realized that baptism in the Holy Spirit is the key to seeing sinful lives changed and immorality conquered by the Kingdom of God.'

'Amen to that,' conceded Callistus on reflection, recalling as he often did the day on the cliffs at Antium when he himself had received the same blessing and had his life changed for ever.

Then six years after his arrival in Rome, Emperor Severus left the City once again and never returned. Deciding that his handsome but increasingly dissolute sons Antoninus and Geta were in danger of being permanently ruined by living in indolence and luxury, he'd resolved upon taking the pair of them to the bleak windswept island of Britain. There, instead of expending their energies on hating and sniping at one another — for in Rome, his sons each had his own faction of flatterers, gladiators, pimps and women, and it was all that their mother Domna could do to keep the boys' hands from each other's throats — they could channel their adolescent aggression into helping him crush a rebellion. The unruly tribes which infested the moorlands just to the south of Hadrian's Wall, and were little more civilized than the Caledonians beyond it, were currently stirring up trouble which could not go unchecked. Severus was minded to penetrate right to the northernmost tip of the island and subdue it in its entirety. He would head up the campaign himself; his two sons would be his deputies, and if this did not make responsible men of them, nothing would.

But his mission was doomed before it began. As Titus pointed out, hadn't the great man Hadrian himself warned posterity that any attempt to extend the already unwieldy Roman empire further to the north was likely to bring the whole rickety edifice tumbling down? Besides, the emperor's health was failing, and rumour had it that he himself, on his astrologer's authority, believed he would die before he saw Rome again. He did achieve some successes early on: he and Antoninus — who was fitter and fonder of fighting than his brother, and like his father an avid admirer of Alexander the Great — led an army a long way north from their base in York driving all before them, whilst Geta was left behind to take charge of the province. But ultimately all came to nothing. No sooner had the northern tribesmen scattered and vanished into the haunted glens than they formed up again somewhere else, and no matter how many were killed, there always seemed to be more where they had come from. Severus and Antoninus returned to York frustrated, and having instructed his sons to rule his empire jointly when he was gone, Severus died.

Callistus, like everyone else, awaited the brothers' return with bated breath. It seemed blindingly obvious to all that

Antoninus and Geta would never, ever, succeed in ruling together, since they couldn't even share the same couch at a meal without coming to blows. No one could imagine what their dying father had been thinking of when he had made them joint heirs to half the world.

If Julia Domna had had her work cut out for her before, the task she faced as Severus' widow was surely unachievable.

CHAPTER SIXTEEN

The homecoming of Antoninus and Geta was no less spectacular than their father's had been nine years earlier. Once again Callistus and Titus were invited to watch the parade from Priscus' rooftop, though his daughters were grown up and married by now with children of their own. Once again the crowds turned out cheering and waving branches of laurel. The two young men, both still handsome and both clad in imperial purple, headed up the procession through the City, with the year's consuls following on bearing Severus' ashes in a silver urn. 'Imperator! Imperator!' the people were shouting, as was the custom; this was the cry with which soldiers had once hailed a popular general who had led them to victory. Perhaps they should have shouted 'Imperatores' in the plural under the circumstances, Callistus thought, but this would only have emphasized how very irregular the new arrangement was.

Then Callistus' heart turned over as he saw who was riding behind the consuls. For not only was Julia Domna, the joint emperors' mother, conspicuously present with her sister Maesa, but Maesa's daughters had travelled with their husbands from Syria to take part in the homecoming too.

Soaemias glittered as brilliantly as ever, though like Priscus' daughters she was now a wife and mother herself, with a boy of six or seven who was riding in his parents' chariot and holding fiercely to their hands. But today Mamaea too wore gold and jewels as befitted her rank, and rode with her head held high. Her husband, whose dark good looks made his toga seem impossibly white, had wrapped a proudly protective arm about her shoulders, whilst she in turn had her hands upon the shoulders of two little children, a girl and a boy. Callistus decided that these were without question the prettiest children he had ever seen, with their smooth olive-brown cheeks and jet black hair. Then, as his eyes were drawn inexorably back to Mamaea herself, she tilted her face towards her husband's and kissed him lightly and easily on the lips. Callistus looked away, and when the chariots of the imperial family had gone by, he went inside. Suddenly he had lost all interest in following the proceedings any further.

The next few days would be given over to public mourning rather than celebration. This was only fitting following the death of an exceptional emperor who had succeeded in retaining the respect of the vast majority of his subjects to the very end of his reign.

'Rather inconsiderate of our Severus to die abroad, though, and deny his grateful subjects the pageantry of a big state funeral,' Titus remarked when Priscus' daughters and their children had gone home. He and Callistus had been pressed into staying for dinner, and still sat with Priscus – and a jar of his favourite wine – on his rooftop while their meal was being prepared. 'I shouldn't imagine much was made of his cremation, up there in the wilds of northern Britain. It's a wonder they could even get the pyre to light, with all the rain they have in those midge-infested bogs and forests.'

'Don't you believe it,' Priscus said with a grimace. 'That canny old soldier has always known how to have his cake and eat it. Grand cremation in Britain, and even grander ceremonial to come here in Rome, you can bank on that. And those two bonny boys of his aren't going to waste such a golden opportunity to strut their stuff in front of the masses, either, by the look of them. More wine, Titus old man? Yes, I knew you'd like it. Sup up now, Callistus, you've barely got started on yours.'

'It won't exactly be easy to stage a flamboyant funeral without a body, though, will it?' Titus persisted. Callistus went on staring at his wine but not drinking it.

'A minor technicality,' said Priscus with a wave of one hand. 'You can rest assured that Domna and her redoubtable duo will come up with something. I guarantee it.'

And indeed they did, very shortly afterwards. Callistus and Titus could only marvel along with everyone else at the skill of the craftsmen who were called upon to fashion an exact likeness of the late emperor all in wax. Unlike stone or bronze, the colour and texture of the wax they used bore an uncanny similarity to living – or rather, dying – flesh, for the effigy was meant to represent Septimius Severus in the closing days of his final illness. When completed, it was clothed in imperial robes and placed on an elevated ivory couch in public view. For seven days every member of the Senate was required to sit in silent vigil on its left while the women of the emperor's and senators' families sat with his widow on its right. Physicians would visit frequently and examine the image as though it were the failing emperor himself lying on his deathbed, and they would announce each day that His Excellency's condition was worse.

Naturally there was no custom which dictated that the archdeacon of the Roman Church should visit too... Yet Callistus found his regular business somehow taking him past the ceremonial couch several times a day. For there among the women sat Mamaea with her little daughter Theoclia, and her husband nowhere in sight.

When the doctors at length declared the waxen emperor to be dead, the effigy was carried through the streets of the City to the Campus Martius where an enormous pyre had been erected, resembling not so much a bonfire as a great stepped ziggurat complete with mouldings, paintings and tapestries. On top of this construction Severus' double lay for several more hours while the City's assembled populace was treated to elaborate cavalry and chariot displays, and choirs sang hymns in honour of the gods of the Roman state pantheon.

Finally it was the task of the emperor's successor – or in this case successors – to put a torch to the pyre, as from its summit an eagle soared high into the sky, supposedly conveying the deceased ruler's soul from earth to heaven so that he could assume his place among the immortals. Many Christians stayed away from these flagrantly pagan proceedings on principle; Callistus stayed away too, and told himself that this had nothing to do with the fact that the imperial women played no part in the rituals of deification.

With Severus ensconced on Olympus, his all-too-human sons took up residence in the palace he had left them – each in his own private wing, as far from the other as he could get.

'It scarcely bodes well,' observed Clemens, who still kept Zephyrinus and Callistus abreast of developments on the Palatine. 'Especially when I tell you that they've blocked up all the doorways between the two wings and stationed so many guards along the frontier you'd think they were back at Hadrian's Wall.'

'I can't see how having two emperors at once could work even if they liked each other,' Zephyrinus said glumly.

'Well, Rome always did have two consuls.' Callistus offered Clemens a second cup of wine, which he refused on the grounds that he must soon be going. 'That seemed to work tolerably well in the days of the Republic, when the illustrious men of old somehow got by with no emperor at all.'

Clemens downed the dregs of his drink with no manifest pleasure and said, 'But the consuls haven't as a rule been brothers in their twenties who begrudged each other the very clothes they stood up in, as Caracalla and Geta obviously do.'

'Caracalla?' enquired Zephyrinus and Callistus

simultaneously.

'That's the nickname Antoninus' soldiers gave him, after the ridiculous patchwork cloak he took to wearing in Britain,' Clemens explained. 'I think he must have got it from some conquered tribesman, but it wouldn't surprise me if *everyone* is calling him Caracalla before long, since he's been flaunting the hideous thing here in the City as well. You'll know that Severus instructed both his sons to befriend the legions and have no regard for anyone else, and Caracalla at least seems to have taken his counsel to heart. The soldiers love him.'

'Whereas most of the Christians who have met him seem to prefer his brother.' Zephyrinus plucked a handful of straggling weeds out of one of his pots of flowers and frowned at them distractedly before dropping them onto a plate of discarded olive stones.

'Geta is certainly the more intellectual of the two, and perhaps the more open to spiritual things,' Clemens agreed. 'But in Caracalla's eyes that only makes him the more contemptible. I can't think he'll get much of a look-in when it comes to running the empire.'

'We'll just have to pray that our two glorious leaders expend so much energy sniping at one another that they don't have any left over for antagonizing the Church,' said Callistus; but in the event Clemens' analysis of the brothers' relationship proved so accurate that no such prayer was needed. For by the end of the year Geta was dead at Caracalla's hands.

On one level the news surprised no one, so blatant had the brothers' mutual hatred already become. Yet on another it was still deeply shocking, even in Rome, whose foundations had been laid on fratricide when its first king Romulus murdered Remus his twin.

'To kill your own brother...' Zephyrinus kept repeating, when the news was fresh and the shock still raw. 'How could anyone do such a thing? When they had played with the same toys, slept in the same cot, suckled at the same breast...'

'Perhaps we can only truly hate those we once loved,'

Callistus sighed, so sorrowfully that Zephyrinus could not fail to appreciate that it wasn't merely Caracalla's hatred to which he was referring. 'What's harder to understand is how he can have pulled it off, when the pair never went near each other, and neither went anywhere at all without an escort of armed guards.'

They soon found out, as the facts of the matter emerged. Caracalla had given out that he was heartily sick of the war of attrition he and Geta had been waging on one another for half their lives, and had invited Geta to meet him in their mother Domna's chambers, with no one but the three of them present, so that they might talk and be reconciled once and for all. Geta had believed him – no doubt because he desperately wanted to – but on his arrival he'd quickly discovered that Caracalla hadn't in fact come alone. He'd brought half a dozen centurions with him, who rushed at Geta with drawn swords, literally driving him into his horrified mother's arms. There he'd expired screaming in a welter of blood, but Caracalla had forbidden his mother to shed even a single tear for the fruit of her own womb. Considering what a formidable woman Domna had always been, Caracalla's success in enforcing this ludicrously callous edict in the days following the murder was a chilling demonstration of his iron will.

'It hasn't slaked his lust for blood, though,' remarked Clemens grimly, after telling Callistus and Titus the full story of Geta's demise. 'Now Caracalla's in sole charge of the empire he won't need to resort to trickery to rid himself of those who stand in his way. The Tiber will soon be running as red as the Nile did when Aaron struck it with his rod.'

Clemens' fears were well founded. Caracalla at once embarked upon a killing spree of blistering efficiency, massacring anyone and everyone he remotely considered a threat. This included anyone who had been a supporter or even a passing acquaintance of Geta. For those of his subjects with long enough memories – Callistus included – it felt like living under Commodus at his most capricious all over again, except that deep down Commodus had longed only to be loved, whilst Caracalla's dream was for his name to strike fear into every heart. The more integrity you had, the more likely you were to forfeit your life to his henchmen – at the table, at the baths, in the street – because you were that much less susceptible to blackmail.

His exiled wife Plautilla was among the first to bite the dust, closely followed by Papinianus the Prefect, and four Vestal Virgins convicted of immorality – a particularly eye-watering injustice, Callistus reflected, since it was Caracalla himself who had deflowered them. Altogether several thousand people were said to have perished, all in the space of a fortnight after Geta's demise. Some of them were Christians, though no one could say for sure whether or not they had been martyred specifically for their faith, since none of Caracalla's victims was given a trial.

'Perhaps I should arrange for you to flee the City,' Callistus suggested to Zephyrinus after a Sunday Assembly which noticeably fewer folk had attended than usual. 'It's only a matter of time before someone tells Caracalla that the Christians favoured Geta over him, and it's you his thugs will target. I could take you to Titus' place in Antium.'

'Flee the City? What kind of shepherd deserts his flock the moment the wolf attacks?' said Zephyrinus in dismay. 'Besides, I'm getting too old to think of fleeing anywhere.'

Perhaps this was true; sometimes these days when Callistus caught a glimpse of the bishop from the corner of his eye it took him a moment or two to recognize this bent and increasingly frail old man as Zephyrinus at all. And not until recently had a single weed dared show its face among the bishop's beloved flowers.

But Callistus did find himself wondering from time to time how well he himself would cope if he were called upon to suffer for his faith. It hadn't really occurred to him since coming back to live in the City that this might ever happen.

His life had been harsh enough in the past but latterly his circumstances had been all too comfortable and he had grown used to being esteemed rather than abused. He shuddered to think that if arrested and threatened *he* might make the sacrifice to the emperor, just as poor Daphne had done.

As the weeks went by, however, the likelihood of this happening lessened once again, for it emerged that Caracalla did not share his late father's enthusiasm for traditional Roman religion. He was half Syrian after all, and had been brought up by Julia Domna to whom all plausible religions and philosophies were equally worthy of respect. To Caracalla they were all equally irrelevant, and although the decree against making converts from Roman paganism was never revoked, it wasn't invoked either. Bizarrely, the only quasi-religious group which did come in for some serious persecution was that of the Aristotelians, since Caracalla believed that the philosopher Aristotle had somehow been implicated in the death of the one idol he did worship: Alexander the Great.

'Our glorious leader's fixation on Alexander is starting to look a lot too much like Commodus' obsession with Hercules,' Titus remarked to Callistus as they stood together in the forum contemplating one of the many new statues of the emperor which were springing up all over Rome. Like most of the rest of them, this one depicted Caracalla in the guise of Alexander himself, wearing unmistakeably Macedonian armour and carrying a distinctive, bizarrely apexed Macedonian helmet under one arm.

'Well, you have to admit, the real live Caracalla does bear Alexander more than a passing resemblance. He's pretty good looking after all, and has an equally impressive head of hair.'

Titus raised an eyebrow but passed no comment on the unlikely interest Callistus seemed to have taken in the emperor's personal appearance. Instead he quipped, 'The same could be said for you, though, couldn't it? But I must say I can't begin to imagine what a statue of *you* dressed up as

Alexander would look like. Exceedingly odd, at very least.'

'Nothing like as odd as the portraits Caracalla has commissioned showing half of his own face alongside half of Alexander's.'

'Ah yes; I've heard about those. *And* that he's planning a new regiment for the army called Alexander's Phalanx. All its members will be Macedonians, and they'll all be equipped with historically authentic paraphernalia. Even those silly helmets that look like Phrygian peasants' hats. Still, when you're the richest and most powerful man in the world and can indulge your most ridiculous fantasies to your heart's content without anyone daring to tell you how stupid your ideas are, your people will see all the more rapidly what a liability they've been saddled with.'

'So you would think. Yet they say the legions still love him.'

'Little wonder, is it, when he's told every man jack of them that he's due for a fifty percent pay-rise. Curious how much he enjoyed his time as a soldier boy in Britain, after the lackadaisical life he lived before he went there, I always think. But come now, Callistus. We both have better things to do with our day than spending it gawping at self-indulgent sculptures. I'll see you back home for dinner. Have a good day now; don't do anything I wouldn't do.'

Caracalla too seemed to have come to the conclusion that there were many important things that he needed to achieve as matters of urgency, quite apart from liquidating his own personal enemies. In particular he'd evidently decided that it was his bounden duty as emperor to conduct aggressive military campaigns against Rome's restless neighbours along all the frontiers of the empire. So he concocted plans to do exactly that, and made it known that he would be setting out at the head of his troops just as soon as he had consolidated his position in the capital.

This, however, might prove easier said than done.

For unlike his grateful soldiers, the Senate had begun to

hate Caracalla with a passion. Not content with butchering its brightest and best, His Excellency was now grinding down the survivors with punitive taxes and requisitions after the fashion of Commodus in order to fund his payouts to the legions and his own imperial lifestyle.

'He wants mansions built for himself in every province so that when he tours them he can be sure of being accommodated in quarters appropriate to his station,' Titus grumbled when Callistus brought the subject up. 'He wants new amphitheatres and race-courses too. He's almost as obsessed with Games as Commodus was.'

'At least he doesn't fancy his own chances as a gladiator,' said Callistus. 'No doubt we should be thankful for small mercies.'

'No doubt,' Titus agreed with a grunt, for although Caracalla had declined to fight as a gladiator, he had been known to drive a chariot for the Blues in the Circus Maximus (Geta had supported the Greens). He had also embarked on building an enormous bathing complex on a freshly cleared site not far from where Callistus had lived as a boy in the house of Carpophorus.

Soon not even the senators' wealth was enough for him. A year or so after murdering Geta, the announcement was made that Caracalla intended to confer Roman citizenship upon everyone in the empire who hadn't been born into slavery – just so that they too could be forced to pay extra taxes.

'No, of course that's not the official explanation,' Titus said crossly when Callistus pretended to think that this was what he was telling him. 'Our magnanimous sovereign wishes to "unite all his subjects under one set of laws and forge them into one people with a common culture, language and outlook." That's what he says. But anyone with an atom of intelligence can see what he's up to.'

Nevertheless, to some extent the decree's ostensible purpose was achieved. Individual foreigners had long been eligible to have citizens' rights conferred upon them, but henceforth free men from all over the empire could aspire to high political office in the capital, regardless of their place of birth.

Satisfied now that all were in awe of his statesmanship, Caracalla set off on his travels to show the world he was a mighty general as well. And he wasn't a bad one; reports soon came in that he was making significant headway against the Germans, whom he had taken on first, and winning appreciable respect for marching on foot with his men just as his father Severus and his idol Alexander had done before him. Julia Domna was back in her element too, so it was said, for notwithstanding his brother's liquidation she went with Caracalla everywhere, handling the day-to-day business which bored him rigid.

Yet Titus heard other rumours which were more disturbing: that Caracalla had begun to be haunted by his murdered brother's ghost, and had been frequenting tribal shrines and outlandish healers in search of absolution.

Having done what he'd set out to do against the Germans, Caracalla headed east, through Thrace – where he visited Alexander's birthplace – and on to Asia Minor and Antioch, apparently winning acclaim from all and sundry along the way. But when he turned his face towards Egypt, intending to visit the most famous of all the Alexandrias his hero had founded and to venerate his tomb, the ghost of Geta took its grisly revenge.

This time the Christians in Rome had no need to rely on rumour to apprise them of their emperor's outrageous conduct. For a young Alexandrian scholar arrived in the City as a refugee and told them what he had seen with his own eyes.

'Callistus? Meet my new friend Origen,' Zephyrinus announced when Callistus called at the bishop's house one afternoon for his daily visit. 'He's come from Alexandria, and I've invited him to stay with me until it's safe for him to go home.'

Callistus smiled and tried not to look too taken aback at the unexpected apparition of an effete and pallid young man who sat nibbling bread and olives in the bishop's courtyard. Anyone less Egyptian-looking was hard to imagine – Alexandria's population was famously multicultural – and though the stranger could not have been more than thirty years old there were already furrows in his high scholar's brow. But his eyes were as sharp as a magpie's, and he leaped to his feet at once in deference to Rome's archdeacon. Callistus embraced him; Origen was slight as a youth half his age, and no taller than a girl. 'We don't stand on ceremony here,' Callistus said. 'Welcome to Rome, my friend, for anyone who is Zephyrinus' friend is certainly mine. Now won't you take a little wine to wash down your olives?'

'Oh, not for me, thank you,' said Origen, resuming his seat; Callistus sat down too, thinking how high-pitched Origen's voice was for a grown man. 'But I wouldn't say no to a cup of boiled water if it's not too much to ask.'

'I can't imagine this young fellow ever being much of a burden on anyone,' Zephyrinus remarked in a wry stage whisper to Callistus, while nodding at his manservant, who hastened to comply with Origen's request. 'He takes no wine whatever, and barely eats enough to keep a gnat alive.'

'Frugal habits come in useful when you have to flee for your life with little more than the clothes you stand up in,' said Origen, accepting his cup of water with touching gratitude. 'Though I have to admit it was curiosity about the Church of Saints Peter and Paul that persuaded me to trek all the way to Rome when I left home rather than just going to ground in the first place I felt safe. I really must visit their tombs while I'm here, if I can brave the crowds of pilgrims who flock there.'

'Well, Callistus is your man for that,' said Zephyrinus. 'Caring for the shrines of the saints is one of the many responsibilities he has lifted from my ageing shoulders.' As if to supply evidence of his failing health Zephyrinus succumbed at that moment to a protracted fit of coughing; when it was over he apologized and explained that he'd had a head cold for several weeks which he couldn't seem to shake off. 'Just don't let me pass it on to you,' he counselled Origen. 'You're much too thin already to risk getting ill.'

Origen inclined his rather oddly-shaped head and said he wouldn't be thin for very long if Zephyrinus and Callistus kept on trying to ram food and drink down his throat.

'Now, can you bear to share with Callistus the things you told me about our emperor's exploits in Alexandria?' Zephyrinus entreated him at last. 'Or would you rather I told him myself while you take a siesta? You must be worn out after all your travels, and no one could blame you for not wanting to go over such painful ground all over again.'

'No, of course it is my place to tell him,' Origen said, as though he deemed any attempt to shirk pain thoroughly reprehensible. And as he launched into his story, which became more and more astonishing the longer it went on, so his bird-bright eyes glittered more ardently and the pitch of his voice rose higher still.

'You see, the Alexandrians were only too happy to welcome Caracalla with open arms when he arrived, because he said he wanted to honour their heritage and worship at the Temple of Serapis where Alexander the Great had done obeisance. He threw a great banquet for the leading citizens, too, and seemed determined to be everyone's best friend.

'But then he got wind that some of the people were making fun of him behind his back, joking that his nickname ought to be Oedipus rather than Caracalla, because he went everywhere with his mother, whom he addressed by name as though she were his wife. And though he hadn't murdered his father, he *had* killed his own brother…'

'… a joke which His Excellency can scarcely have found amusing, given what we've heard about his terror of Geta's ghost,' said Callistus drily.

'He didn't find it funny at all,' said Origen. 'He fell into a frenzy and instructed the Alexandrians to stay inside their homes, then sent his soldiers to from house to house kicking in doors and slaughtering everyone they found. It went on for days; there was looting and raping as well as outright killing; casual visitors to the city were butchered as well, while Caracalla directed the whole proceedings from the roof of Serapis' temple, foaming at the mouth like a hell-hound. Afterwards he dedicated to Serapis the sword he had used to kill Geta, thinking to appease both god and ghost all in one go.'

'His demons must have driven him completely mad,' said Callistus, while Zephyrinus seemed on the verse of tears even though he was hearing these things for the second time.

'Perhaps so,' Origen admitted. 'But if he *has* lost his wits, it's more likely his craving for absolution which has robbed him of them than any demon or spectre. If only men would realize that in Christ alone can true forgiveness be found!'

'You believe that even bloodshed on *this* kind of scale can be forgiven as a result of what Christ did on the cross?' asked Callistus, leaning forward.

'The blood of Christ has the power to wash away every sin committed since the world began,' Origen answered. 'If we say that any one sinner is too evil to be redeemed, we belittle the power of God himself, which is surely blasphemy.'

At this, Callistus and Zephyrinus exchanged glances; despite his youth Origen was clearly a theological force to be reckoned with.

'I wasn't born a catechetist's son for nothing,' Origen said by way of explanation. 'My father Leonides taught at the Christian school Pantaenus established for enquirers and new believers in Alexandria, which has always attracted some of the finest minds in Greece as well as in Egypt. But they say that I asked *much* harder questions than his other students, even before I could read, which Father would always try to answer as honestly as he could.'

'He must be a very wise man,' Zephyrinus commented,

glancing at Callistus again.

'He *was*,' Origen sighed, and momentarily his bright eyes clouded. 'He was martyred during the persecutions that broke out when Severus made it a crime for Christians to spread their faith. Father was a Roman citizen and so were some of his converts, which was what brought the authorities crashing down on his head. When they came for him it was all my mother could do to stop me running out in the street and begging to die alongside him. She had to steal my clothes to keep me in the house.'

Callistus almost laughed, but noting the look in Origen's eyes succeeded in suppressing his reaction in a cough. Zephyrinus coughed again too, but not for the same reason.

'In the end I had to accept that she'd done the right thing,' Origen continued. 'It was up to me to provide for her and my brothers from that time on, which meant selling a lot of Father's books to keep the wolves from our door. But I was also persuaded to take over his classes, though I was barely seventeen. I even ran the school for a while. That is, until... until...'

'And the authorities left you in peace all those years while you did so?' Zephyrinus probed gently as he laid a comforting hand on Origen's forearm.

'Yes. Yes they did, because I was the child of a mixed marriage and not a Roman citizen myself. But now, thanks to Caracalla's... generosity, I am.'

'So you'd begun to fear for your safety even before the massacre began?'

'Oh yes, and as much as anything because word was going around that Caracalla hated *all* philosophers and teachers as a result of Aristotle's betrayal of Alexander. I had my bags packed as a precaution before Caracalla arrived in Alexandria; not that this takes very long when one owns almost nothing. I managed to slip past his soldiers when they were too intent on raping and pillaging to notice a skinny scholar dashing from one hiding place to the next carrying nothing but a bundle of scrolls.'

'Heaven preserve us!' Callistus exclaimed. 'We can only be grateful that you were better at evading capture than *I* was when I was on the run from the authorities.'

Now it was Origen's turn to register surprise; Callistus merely smiled and promised to tell him his story, too, one day.

'But Heaven *did* preserve me, I'm sure of it,' Origen resumed. 'And it was God who led me to Rome rather than to Jerusalem or Antioch or any other centre of scholarship to which I might have been attracted. You see, much as I respect the churches of the east, I do find them somewhat lax in their morality.'

'Now here's a pretty paradox for us to ponder,' said Zephyrinus who – like Callistus – seemed to be finding Origen a paradoxical figure in himself. 'You boast of your belief that Christ's blood can wash away all sin, yet now you begin to sound like Hippolytus.'

'Hippolytus? Ah yes, he's one of your elders here, is he not? I have heard many impressive things about him.' Origen's eyes were bright as a songbird's once again. 'I've even read one of his books. I do hope I'll get to meet him, not least because he studied with Irenaeus, and also on account of his knowledge of the Jewish scriptures. So many Gentile Christians are ignorant of them entirely, yet they constitute one of the strongest pillars of our faith! I have even begun to learn Hebrew so that I can read them in their original language and write with authority on them myself.'

Before Callistus could be tempted to launch into his own story there and then to Hippolytus' detriment, Zephyrinus said, 'Yes, Hippolytus is a very learned man, though it has often been said of him that he does not suffer fools gladly. But perhaps, like him, you consider this to be a strength rather than a failing?'

Understandably thrown by this interruption, Origen nevertheless pressed on regardless. 'I believe passionately in the efficacy of Christ's blood over any and every sin committed by a repentant man, woman or child, and that as soon as that sinner's soul is offered to God it is flushed clean of every stain. But this doesn't mean that once we have become Christians our way of living shouldn't be radically distinct from that of the world we have left behind. I learned that lesson afresh when I had to flee Alexandria, losing the few creature comforts on which I had relied. Life is *so* much simpler, so much *purer* if you are not weighed down with houses, servants, businesses and the like. None of these things are necessities for the holy man who puts his trust in Christ.'

'Perhaps not,' Zephyrinus conceded. 'Yet it's just as well some Christians have yet to scale this pinnacle of holiness, or else saintly men such as yourself or even our spotless Lord Jesus himself surely *would* have nowhere to lay their heads. But if you prefer it, you may sleep in the street tonight. I should hate to stand in the way of your spiritual progress.'

Origen's eyes had gone wide as saucers at this; then they narrowed once again as he saw that bishop was smiling, and had been baiting him benignly in an unsuccessful effort to make him smile too. But Callistus graciously permitted him to mask his embarrassment by asking him if he knew Clement, the Alexandrian scholar whose description of the Church itself as a school he had found so inspiring. 'If my good friend Titus hadn't brought me Clement's books when I was finding my feet as a Christian, I doubt I would be who I am today,' Callistus admitted. 'It helped me so much to think of other Christians as pupils, all with their own strengths and weaknesses, and bound to make mistakes as they go along. Viewing the Church as a school means that we can encourage high moral standards *and* keep helping the fallen to get up again, as often as it takes them to learn how to rely on God for themselves.'

'Yes, I did know Clement when I was a boy; he took over *our* school from Pantaenus for a while. But he left Alexandria during the persecutions in which Father died. I think he went to Antioch.' Origen took another sip of his boiled water; it was obvious to Callistus that his grief for his murdered father was still raw, proud of him though he was, and afraid to seem weak by comparison. 'Clement is a great writer as you say, archdeacon, but a little too fond of worldly pleasures and the pagan poets for my liking. And very keen on strange doctrines like cosmic cycles and the equality of women with men, and on extolling the beauties of nature, when we know that this world is destined for destruction.'

'But it is life's simplest and most innocent pleasures that Clement exhorts us to enjoy,' Callistus could not help but counter. 'He never recommends greed or indulgence. And according to Genesis, God himself delighted in the beauty of the world he had fashioned, exclaiming in pleasure at the end of each day of creation. Didn't Christ himself exhort us to consider the lilies? And Saint Paul reminds us that in Christ there is neither male nor female.'

'I see you are well read and a thinker too, Brother Callistus.' The tone of Origen's voice was distinctly wary now, but in his eyes there was tentative respect. 'So perhaps you find Clement's "logos" theology helpful too, as I do myself, and as I know for a fact that Hippolytus does. Greek philosophical terms *can* be helpful to Christian thinkers provided that we don't use them unguardedly. Philosophy was to the Gentiles what Moses' Law was to the Jews after all; it prepared them to receive the Gospel of Christ.'

'And here was I thinking it was the Holy Spirit who prepared human hearts to receive from God,' Zephyrinus said with pointed irony, the effect of which was somewhat spoiled by another bout of coughing.

'You are right of course,' Origen acknowledged. 'But discipline must play its part too, and we must embrace the whole witness of Scripture if we wish to hear God's living voice, not merely cite proof-texts out of context.'

'Well,' said Zephyrinus when he was able to speak again, 'I must confess that all this edifying conversation and this confounded cough have rather tired me out. So I should like to take a siesta now even if you don't need one. You two may stay here and discuss theology as long as you like, and you're welcome to share my home for as long as you need to, young Origen. That is, if Hippolytus doesn't prevail upon you to stay with *him*.'

Origen thanked the bishop profusely, but in the event did not stay in Rome for very long. He was unstintingly grateful and deferential to both Zephyrinus and Callistus while he was there, but it soon became apparent that he was little happier than he would have been in Antioch or Jerusalem. Some of the Roman Christians were rather rough and ready after all; they found Origen's intensity threatening, and his high-pitched voice grated on their nerves. Some even whispered that he must literally have 'made himself a eunuch for the Kingdom of God' and they weren't all joking. For his part Origen was horrified that Daphne, despite her excommunication, was still welcome to receive a blessing at the bishop's hands during the Eucharist, though he wasn't in the end impressed by Hippolytus, confessing to Zephyrinus and Callistus that in person he had found Irenaeus' disciple narrow-minded rather than upright, and disinclined to discuss things impartially without taking any expression of dissent as a personal affront.

'Well, it's a relief to know it's not just *me*,' said Callistus with a little too much feeling. Then he got on with arranging to take Origen to visit the shrines of saints Peter and Paul before the young Alexandrian risked going back home to pick up the pieces of his school and succour its surviving pupils in the aftermath of the massacre. Reflecting on Origen's reaction to Daphne, Callistus could only hope that none of these students had been bullied into being less than forthright about their faith during the crisis, for there was no way that Origen was going to let such spineless renegades back onto *his* pupil register without some serious self-abasement. Not that reneging on their religion would have done them any favours with Caracalla. The victims of his butchery had died for the crime of being Alexandrians, for being in the wrong place at the wrong time and not running away from it fast enough.

Whilst Origen returned to Alexandria, Caracalla did not come back to Rome. Instead he retraced his steps to Antioch where he began preparing a fresh campaign against Rome's old enemies the Parthians. Meanwhile Julia Domna was gleefully relieving her son of more and more of his administrative responsibilities, sending dispatches all over the empire in both Greek and Latin, commanding her own Praetorian Guards, and loving every minute of it.

At the same time, Callistus found himself taking on more and more of Zephyrinus' responsibilities too, but he was far from happy. Zephyrinus' cough was getting worse rather than better, and he tired easily. Yet he refused to let Callistus fetch a physician or summon the elders to pray over him, maintaining that it was only a cold and would pass in its own good time.

'Then why are you losing weight? And why does the running of a regular Sunday Assembly exhaust you? You haven't weeded your plant pots for weeks, and you're eating so little you're starting to make Origen look like a glutton. Please let me have a doctor examine you, just once; if he agrees that you simply have a cold I won't mention it again.' But Zephyrinus merely patted Callistus on the hand and said he would appreciate it very much if the archdeacon would stop talking about doctors altogether and proceed directly with his resolution not to mention the matter any more.

Meanwhile, pursuing his grandiose ambitions in the east, Caracalla sought the hand of the Parthian king's daughter in marriage. On being refused he flew into another of his rages and unleashed his troops to ravage the Parthian towns and countryside to their hearts' content. Afterwards he holed up in Edessa to enjoy a winter of hunting and chariot-racing and planning more military operations for the campaigning season ahead.

Then there came a Sunday when Zephyrinus couldn't get

out of bed for Assembly at all. The elders were left to run it themselves while Callistus remained at Zephyrinus' side. He had a fever now, and each fit of coughing left him weaker than the last. When Callistus informed him that he was sending for a doctor whatever the bishop had to say about it, for the first time Zephyrinus did not object.

The physician who came was a member of the Assembly himself, a wise and well-respected Jewish Christian who had tended Victor in his latter days. Laying a hand on Zephyrinus' forehead he peered hard into his eyes before pressing his ear against the old man's chest. Then he straightened up, sucked in his breath and took Callistus to one side.

'You must get him out of Rome, Callistus. It's his only hope. The climate here is too unhealthy; there are too many bad vapours from the marshes.'

But whatever else was wrong with Zephyrinus, his hearing was still sharp enough for him to call out, 'I am Bishop of Rome, Callistus, and Rome is where I stay.' Callistus asked the doctor in an undertone whether getting him away from Rome was likely to do much good at this stage in any case. The doctor seemed about to say: it's possible. But with his mouth half open he stopped and shook his head.

As winter gave way once more to spring it emerged that Caracalla had appropriated Edessa as a Roman colony even though the kingdom of which it was the capital was already an ally of Rome and contributed soldiers to Rome's armies quite willingly. But Caracalla had invited Abgar its king to talks and then imprisoned him and taken over his country as a spoilt child will steal his playmates' toys. It was an outrage; the emperor's own mother was furious, and the whole region was in turmoil. The Parthians, Edessans and Medes were reputed to be planning their revenge.

Then in April news reached Rome that Caracalla had been murdered while relieving himself during a bout of diarrhoea. The deed had been done not by his oriental enemies but by order of the Praetorian Commander Macrinus. Apparently an

Egyptian seer called Serapio had predicted that Macrinus would succeed Caracalla as emperor; Macrinus, who had had no intention whatever of plotting against the emperor at the time, had hurriedly advised Caracalla to have Serapio thrown to the lions. When the lions wouldn't eat the unappetizing fellow a soldier despatched him instead, but Macrinus was only too aware that unless he *did* do away with the emperor, his own days could probably be numbered on the fingers of one hand. And so he had set about engineering His Excellency's demise, though he hadn't done the bloody deed himself. But with Caracalla dead, Macrinus had declared himself emperor and paid the Parthians, Edessans and Medes two hundred million sesterces to call off their action. This they were more than happy to do, once they had convinced themselves that Caracalla really was no more.

More surprisingly, Julia Domna was reported to be dead as well, though not at the hands of Macrinus. Some said she had committed suicide rather than face execution, exile, or – perhaps worse for her than either – life as an unsung Roman matron without political power. Others said she'd had a wasting sickness for months and had been dying already.

But Callistus himself had little time to consider the implications of any of this, because Zephyrinus was dying too. There was no room now in Callistus' life or in his head for anything or anyone else. The ailing bishop had been his spiritual mentor for so long that he could not begin to imagine life without him; yet with each passing day Zephyrinus seemed to belong less to this world and more to the next. For the final weeks of his long and inexorable decline, Callistus lived with him, delegating all routine duties to others. Every morning he carried Zephyrinus out into his flower-filled courtyard at his own request and every evening he carried him back to his bed, with distressingly little effort because by now the old man weighed less than a child. Yet Zephyrinus never complained, and rather than frail he seemed almost transparent somehow, as though better to reflect the light of heaven onto the earth he was leaving behind.

'Don't weep for me, Little Prince,' he exhorted Callistus, chancing to spot a tear glistening in the corner of one of his eyes. 'I'm not afraid to die. In fact I am perfectly ready. My only regret is that I didn't have the time or courage to absolve more sinners than I did. If only I could have held out some hope to murderers, adulterers and idolaters who had once known the love of Christ but fallen away! If only I could have found some way to restore little Daphne to full fellowship! But you will be able to do these things when I am gone. You have more courage *and* intellect than I ever had. When *you* are bishop, Callistus – '

'Sshhh.' Callistus laid a gentle finger across Zephyrinus' lips. 'I shall never be bishop!' And the tear which had glistened in his eye began rolling its way down his cheek as he accepted that Zephyrinus must finally be losing his mind as well as his physical strength.

But Zephyrinus only patted Callistus' hand and smiled his knowing smile, and very quietly died.

CHAPTER SEVENTEEN

Zephyrinus' passing drove a stake through Callistus' heart. He badly wanted to rejoice that his beloved mentor was safely home at last, but instead all he knew was a desperate loneliness and loss. He floundered through the funeral in a daze; as Zephyrinus' closest friend he would have been the obvious person to organize it, but he stood by and let Hippolytus take over, which the latter was only too willing to do. Through a blur of tears Callistus watched transfixed as the little corpse was washed and wrapped in its shroud. While psalms of lament rose up around him, Callistus' tongue clove to the roof of his mouth. Though the body was laid to rest in the catacomb for which Callistus was responsible, he was not among those who carried it there. He who had ferried the dying bishop back and forth between his bed-chamber and his garden every day for months now allowed other men to bear his earthly remains to their final destination.

He knew very well that it wasn't Zephyrinus for whom he was grieving. He felt exactly as he had felt when told about the death of Marcia, that he was utterly alone and that life would never be worth living again. For so long his existence had been bound up with Zephyrinus'; now he was like a pen with no ink, an empty chalice, a vine whose trellis has rotted away. For days he sat in Zephyrinus' empty house beside his empty bed, and neither ate, washed nor slept. In the end Titus came and collected him and Callistus went with him without complaint, but only because he was too weak to resist.

Back in his old room, Callistus was at last prevailed upon to attend to some of his physical needs, but in mind and spirit he was broken as a ship smashed against rocks. Finally Titus came to him with Gaius his brother and said, 'Callistus, you *have* to rouse yourself and wake up to what is going on around you. You are letting Hippolytus cast himself in the role of Zephyrinus' successor when it ought to be you.'

Callistus threw an arm up in front of his face to block out the light which had flooded the room when his friends entered. 'No,' he demurred. 'Not me. You don't know what you are saying.'

'*We* don't know what we are saying? We can see only too well what is happening while you lie here wallowing in your own self-pity. Of course you must mourn Zephyrinus; we all must, for he was a man after God's own heart. But do you *want* his Church to fall into the hands of those who despised him? Is that what *he* would have wanted? You know it isn't. You *know* what Zephyrinus wanted.'

'Oh?' retorted Callistus, his tears welling afresh. 'And what exactly is that?'

'He wanted you to be bishop after him.'

At length Callistus condescended to look Titus in the eye, though his head ached like fury and he could scarcely see anything for weeping. But he was beginning to feel the stirring of God's Spirit deep within him; in truth that still small voice had been there all along, whispering: *you are not alone, Callistus. No one born of God is ever alone.* But he had paid it no heed.

'I'm sorry, Titus,' he said, chastened. 'And Gaius. Perhaps because I was born a slave and never even knew my own father's name, Zephyrinus meant more to me than he should have done. I don't know. But it's not for a bishop to choose his own successor. We all know that.'

'True enough,' agreed Gaius. 'But he can make a recommendation, just as Victor recommended Zephyrinus. And it *is* for the body of elders to nominate a new incumbent, and only if several eligible alternatives present themselves, to arrange for an election by the Church. In this case our choice is you.'

'But you are not the body of elders. Unless I am very much mistaken, you are one not especially influential elder and his brother.'

'That may be so, but we speak for every elder except Hippolytus, and for the widows too. Even Roscius is with us.'

Roscius, the stern ascetic who had been all for turfing Callistus out on his ear again after Marcus Pollius had rescued him from the gutter..? With s brief, bitter laugh Callistus said, 'I can only apologize for my scepticism, Brother Gaius, but you're not exactly making it easy for me to believe you. Why aren't these people here to speak for themselves if they are all so keen to endorse my nomination?'

'Because they are loath to intrude upon your grief! But even Sabellius is with us, because you stood up to Hippolytus over his Christology. And even those elders who favour Hippolytus' Christology know that he's no pastor.'

'Except for Hippolytus himself. He would say that there is no one better to lead the flock of God than a man who knows his own mind and will never change it. He feels that he was unjustly passed over even when Zephyrinus was elected. How much more will he think so now.'

'And yet he would be no more fitting a choice now than he would have been then,' Titus put in. 'All he has gained in the meantime is eighteen years' worth of hard-heartedness and intolerance. The pastor is meant to *care* for the flock, to model Christ's love and compassion to his people. Everyone has heard of your clemency; everyone has seen the gentle way in which you go about your work, the depth of your spirituality and understanding. Since you *were* born a slave, you know how to find joy in serving others in the way few freeborn men ever can; you will never be the sort of shepherd who lords it over his flock instead of nurturing it. Not only that, but you are truly born again. I know that for a fact, and your Christian brothers and sisters have seen ample evidence of your regeneration for themselves.'

'There is no better man than you to take up and put on Zephyrinus' mantle,' declared Gaius in summary. 'In fact, if you will not accept the elders' nomination, frankly we don't know where to look next.'

A long silence followed as Callistus studied the brothers' faces and accepted that they spoke not only in earnest but with the weight of the Roman Church's Council of Elders and Widows behind them. Finally he said, 'But I'm not even an elder myself. I'm just a deacon; I can't even preside at communion. And the only reason I am a deacon is because Zephyrinus wanted me to be one. Now I want nothing more than to surrender my office and return to being a simple follower of Christ. I'd like to go back to doing your accounts, Titus, and visiting your estates. I'd like to live at Antium again in your house by the sea, and leave the politics of the City and its Church behind me.'

In fact he hadn't known what he wanted; these words had tumbled from his lips as though of their own accord. But as soon as he had spoken them Callistus knew two things with certainty: that this *was* what he wanted, but that it wasn't going to happen. For, as Gaius explained patiently, 'Your ordination as bishop would elevate you to the presbyterate automatically. Besides, Callistus, deacons are not *inferior* to elders. There are even those who say that deacons should be regarded as being of *higher* rank than elders – if such a thing as rank should even exist among the people of God. Ignatius of Antioch – a student of the blessed Saint John himself – said that a bishop should be respected as if he were God the Father, a deacon as Jesus the Son, and elders merely as the Twelve Apostles.'

'Oh, Callistus, do let us nominate you to be our shepherd!'

Titus seized him suddenly by both hands, convinced that reason could take them no further. 'Gaius will propose you; Urbanus or Asterius will gladly second his proposal; we shall send word to the bishops of Ostia, Perusia and Capua to request their endorsement too. Then the Church members will be asked if they support your consecration, and they will leave you no choice but to accept that this is God's will for your life! After that, bishops will come from all over Italy – Anathalon of Milan, Agapitus of Ravenna, Probus of Naples, and their colleagues from Genoa and Capua and maybe even from Sicily – and they will lay hands on you and you will know that you have taken your rightful place in a line which can be traced back without interruption to Christ's companion Saint Peter himself.'

It was in vain that Callistus tried to protest again, to point out that clearly his friends had not been listening; all he wanted was to return to his little study by the sea, and restrict his pastoral responsibilities to shepherding the little flock of slaves who had been accustomed to meet and study the scriptures there with him on a sunny Sunday afternoon.

'But why would you want to do that, when they don't need you and we do? When Demetrius and Gorgo who you left in charge have led them from strength to strength so that their group could no more squeeze itself into your apartment now than the Church of Rome could meet in your catacomb? Antium will soon need a bishop of its own!'

'And why would *you* want me to let you have your way, when my work in Rome is done? When God called me here to serve Zephyrinus, and now my task is complete?'

Another silence ensued, which ended only when Titus and Gaius got up to take their leave. 'Well,' said Titus, 'Surely you can promise us one thing at least: to think and pray over what we have discussed. We shall return at this time tomorrow to learn of your decision, bringing other elders with us if you still persist in doubting that we speak on their behalf.'

'Very well. I shall think and pray and await your return, but you needn't bring anyone with you. If you say that you know the elders' minds, then I have to believe you. You are both men of your word; I must grant you that.' So saying, Callistus collapsed against the back of his couch, all at once more exhausted than an athlete who has given his all, yet lost his race.

But he himself had little intention of keeping his word. He lacked the energy to think or to pray, let alone the will. Having eaten little and slept even less since Zephyrinus' passing, he let his mind wander where it would, and in fitful half-waking dreams he was back on the treadmill or labouring in the mines, while his muscles went on wasting away as Zephyrinus' had done, and his head was full of fog, like the evil yellow vapour which rose from Rome's marshes every year when the sun was at its hottest, as it was now, and the storms most torrid. Hovering between consciousness and oblivion, the robust imagination on which he had so often relied for sanity during his youth now threatened to divorce him from it entirely. Now he was seven years old again, curled up with Hippolytus at Zephyrinus' feet; now the two boys were playing a noisy game of hide and seek among the crowds loitering after a Sunday Assembly, while Zephyrinus sought to pacify them with treats bought for them from the marketplace. And now he was sitting in some quiet little spot with Marcia – disguised as Melissa – hanging on her every word and wishing he had the courage to reach out and touch her hand or even kiss her boldly on the cheek. When he emerged from a shockingly vivid reverie in which he *had* kissed her, and then the two of them had lain together as husband and wife while Zephyrinus recited the wedding blessings over their heads, he began to think he must have come down with the summer fever which the yellow fog brought with it, and which had probably played no small part in Zephyrinus' decline.

It was only after his imagination had worn itself out just as his body had done that Callistus finally fell sound asleep on his couch and slept there fully clothed, shamelessly and dreamlessly, whilst all those things which had been, and which might have been, but never would be again, flowed like the Tiber out to sea taking their pollution with them. When he awoke, it was morning, and he knew what he must do.

So when Titus and Gaius returned they found Callistus bathed and changed, his oiled hair shining; he had eaten both breakfast and lunch and spent the time in between deep in prayer. Nor had it been the kind of prayer which comes hard, wrenched from the gut with great labour and groaning. As soon as the brothers set eyes on him they knew there was no need even to ask their question, so they embraced him instead and the three of them rejoiced and worshipped together. Gaius then left to pass on the good news to his fellow elders while Titus went off to instruct the cook to prepare a special dinner for him and Callistus that evening and open a jar of their finest wine.

When he went to bed very much later Callistus slept as soundly as he had the night before, but this time he did have a dream: Marcia came to him radiant and smiling and no longer in disguise, and he told her that when he was bishop there would be forgiveness – seventy-times-seven times over – for all who sought it. At this Marcia opened her cupped hands and the white dove of God's Holy Spirit soared up from between them and flew in circles above their heads before coming to rest on Callistus' shoulder. So he knew that God was smiling on him too.

Callistus took no part in the formalities regarding his nomination to the bishopric, nor in canvassing for his election. He had made up his mind that if it was the will of God for him to be made Bishop of Rome, then God must bring it about; it was not for the nominee to go around blowing his own trumpet like a candidate for a quaestorship. He merely signed and attached his seal to the requisite documents when they were brought to him, and spent the weeks which went by while neighbouring bishops' endorsements were sought working for Titus as he had done in the past, even visiting some of his estates in the Tuscan hills. Here the slaves and freedmen who laboured in Titus' vineyards greeted Callistus like a long-lost brother – which to the Christians among them he effectively was. In Zephyrinus' final days Callistus had had precious little time to spare for Titus or his employees, and once he was bishop – assuming that this was the way things fell out – he would have even less. Titus had already promoted others to take on some of Callistus' workload temporarily. Now it seemed likely that these men would have to remain in post for the foreseeable future.

Though Callistus put pressure on no one during those long days of waiting, he had plenty of visitors keen to put pressure on him. Some merely wanted to encourage him to persevere in his purpose, others to warn him about obstacles or opposition he might run into along the way. One of the first lobbyists to fetch up on Titus' doorstep was Sabellius, the quick-tempered elder whose altercations with Tertullian and Hippolytus had caused Zephyrinus so much heartache. Though Hippolytus and Sabellius had both finished up signing the statement of faith which Callistus had composed, now Sabellius made it all too obvious that the tension and mistrust between them remained.

'Callistus, you have to put a stop to Hippolytus' scheming now, before he destroys the Church!' Sabellius insisted, amber eyes flashing in his fervour. 'He's spending his every waking moment stirring up trouble, reminding people about your past and undermining your campaign by convincing them that you're not worthy of their confidence.'

'But I don't have any campaign for him to undermine,' responded Callistus with a smile. 'And so far as I know, I don't have a rival for the episcopacy in any case. Hippolytus can't drum up enough support even to get himself nominated, let alone elected.'

'Not yet, but that may change if you are not prepared to

show us what you're made of! You can't just sit back and let others decide your future for you.'

'That's not what I'm doing. I intend to let *God* decide my future.'

'While Hippolytus is busy intriguing and poisoning people's minds and looking for ways to blackmail good men into taking his part? He's a heretic with *two* gods, and the same blind faith in them as you have in yours.'

'If the people he approaches are truly good, they won't be susceptible to blackmail, will they? And don't forget, Sabellius: Hippolytus signed up to the same creed as you did. He may be intolerant, but he's no more a heretic than you or I. I won't have it said that I deliberately sought to prevent him standing against me, if that's what he wants to do. Especially when everyone knows that he's my enemy.'

'Then let *me* deal with him on your behalf. I'm more than happy to do so, provided I am confident you will not listen to any rumours which present me in an unfavourable light, or start asking awkward questions.'

Callistus felt his jaw drop visibly. He said, 'Sabellius, you are an elder in the Church of Christ. I trust you will never do anything which could possibly lead me to do either of those things.'

'But surely you don't want Hippolytus to be bishop?'

'No, Sabellius. I don't.'

'Good.' Sabellius stood up and made ready to leave. 'That is all I needed to know.' Then he pressed Callistus' hand and was gone.

Afterwards Callistus was sorely troubled. Three days later he learned that his anxiety had been well founded, when he was told that another visitor was awaiting him in Titus' atrium. It was Hippolytus himself, and he wasn't alone. When Callistus emerged from his room to receive him, he found his latest guest accompanied by two ex-gladiators – unarmed, but they didn't need to be.

'Hippolytus.' Beyond his name Callistus had no idea what

to say to him. In all the time he had been archdeacon Hippolytus had never once spoken to him civilly, and he had evaded every attempt on Callistus' part to initiate a conversation since the fateful day on which he had driven the fugitive slave from his parents' mansion. He didn't look any friendlier now.

'Callistus, I demand that you withdraw your ridiculous claim to the bishop's seat forthwith,' Hippolytus said without preamble; Callistus was surprised that he even deigned to use his name, but recognized that for Hippolytus, addressing him as 'brother' or even 'archdeacon' would have left a still fouller taste in the mouth.

'You demand?' he responded, as mildly as he could manage. 'And what gives you the right to demand that, or anything else, of me?'

'The fact that I have been threatened by your thugs, that is all.'

'Threatened? By *my* thugs? I assure you that neither I nor any associate of mine has threatened anyone.'

'No? Then how come these past three days there have been men trying to prevent me from leaving my own house? How come I now need a bodyguard whenever I wish to go anywhere?'

Callistus' heart sank, for it was obvious that Hippolytus was telling the truth. Watching his patrician features distorted by anger, Callistus tried hard to see behind them the sweet face of his boyhood friend, which he had seen all too clearly in recent dreams and daydreams. But all he could discern behind the anger was jealousy, hurt and betrayal.

'Hippolytus, I think I know who is responsible for these outrages, and if I do become bishop I shall deal with him swiftly and decisively. But you have my word that it is not I. Nor shall I withdraw my candidacy, because I know when I am doing the will of God.'

'The will of God?' Hippolytus spat the phrase so venomously that Callistus winced. 'You know no more about

God now than you did when you were a snivelling slave – which by rights you should still be today, since you were never legally freed. With you at the helm, this Church would be filled with adulterers, fornicators, thieves, villains and demoniacs of every hue! Things were bad enough under Zephyrinus; as God is my witness, I will not stand by and see everything Saints Peter and Paul built here in Rome systematically demolished.'

Callistus said softly, 'Yet wasn't it Jesus himself who reminded us that it is not the healthy who need a doctor, but the sick? And wasn't his own entourage in Palestine composed of exactly the kind of people you describe?'

'So is the world, Callistus! So is the world! What is the *point* of the Church if its members are no different from those outside it? People who become Christians from backgrounds in violence and depravity need discipline to help them change, not indulgence; rules and regulations are all they understand! Indiscriminate love and forgiveness only confuse them; they need boundaries, just as children do…'

Hippolytus' voice had been rising; suddenly it failed him entirely at the height of his passion. This was when Callistus saw that his old friend's eyes were brimming with tears, as he had seen them do once before, and that once again these were not tears of anger.

'Hippolytus, please… sit down. Let us discuss these things as Christian brothers. Let the servants bring us wine, let us share bread together…'

But Hippolytus only seized hold of the back of a chair to lend himself support. His knuckles were white and taut as a straining rope.

'I'm not your brother, Callistus, and I shall never accept your hospitality. As Tertullian warned me, you are bent on destroying not only the Church of Rome but all that Christ came to earth to achieve. Christ gave us hope: the chance for men of good will to come together and present a different way of living to a desperate world, to rebuild humanity in the way God wanted it built in the first place! His insistence on our obedience to his commandments was always for our own good, not for his; he made us, and he knows what we must do to be happy. Isn't a life of order and serenity what *every* true Christian wants? Isn't it the dream of everyone who truly loves God?'

Never before that moment had Callistus understood Hippolytus so well; never had he felt such compassion for the man welling up within him. Hippolytus *did* love God, and he was consumed with determination to see God's world changed for the better. How glorious it would be if the two of them could work together and weave their two visions into one! Callistus rose to his feet and ventured to approach him; Hippolytus was weeping openly now and his knuckles were trembling as he went on gripping the back of the chair as though his life depended on not letting it go. But he started backwards as soon as Callistus came near, leaving him no choice but to go on appealing to reason when he would far rather have taken Hippolytus in his arms.

'Yes it *is* my dream; more than anything I want to see my brothers and sisters modelling the abundant life which Christ came to bring us, a life free from malice, deceit, infidelity and spite. But we do not build the Kingdom of God by banishing from it the very people most in need of its protection. We build it by encouraging them to allow the Holy Spirit to change them from within! Is that not why your friend Tertullian has left the Catholic Church and become a Montanist? Do the Montanists not decry our unwillingness to let the Spirit do the work of God in our hearts, burning away our sinfulness from the inside out with the flame of his holy fire?'

It was such a long time before Hippolytus replied that Callistus dared to hope he might have won him over. Hippolytus stood with his head hanging forward from heaving shoulders as though the weight of the thoughts which churned within it had become too much to be borne. Then he raised his brimming eyes, fixed them on Callistus' face, and said, 'Tertullian left the Catholic Church because he no longer believes that it represents Christ to the world, and if you become Bishop of Rome I shall have to conclude that he is right. You know as well as I do that every congregation in the western empire looks to the Bishop of Rome for its lead; how shall we escape on the Day of Judgement if we lead half of God's people astray? Know this, Callistus: I shall *never* be found as a member of a congregation which has placed itself under your leadership. But it won't be I or those who support me who will have left the Church. We will *be* the Church; it is you and your feeble-minded followers who will be the schismatics.' Then with tears still pouring down his cheeks, Hippolytus turned and walked out, with his bodyguards lumbering behind him.

Drained and defeated, Callistus went back to his room and fell upon his bed. What Hippolytus had said about the Day of Judgement had shaken him harder than he might have expected: could he, a mere man who had once been a slave, presume to know the will of God in anything? One thing was certain: he would not be able to serve as Rome's bishop if he could not. And only if he found space in each day to spend as much time in God's presence as he had in the past week would he stand any chance of doing so. Yes, he would have to deal decisively with troublemakers like Sabellius, but at the same time he must retain his humility lest his passion for change spiral out of control as Hippolytus' had done, and maybe Tertullian's too. All must be done for the glory of God, not for the honour of Callistus.

When the day came on which nominations for the bishopric were to close, there was still only one candidate in the running for the post. Hippolytus had failed in his bid to find another elder prepared to put his name forward, therefore no election was needed. Instead there would simply be a public acclamation of Callistus during the following Sunday's Assembly, ahead of his investiture which would be held some weeks after that.

So it was that Callistus found himself that Sunday morning standing on the leaders' platform before the congregation of the Church of Rome, flanked by a beaming Gaius and Urbanus, his ears ringing with applause and cries of, 'Callistus! Callistus! Callistus for bishop! We choose him!'

But he was much more acutely aware of the silence emanating from Hippolytus and his resentful little knot of supporters, who crowded as close as they could get to his seat among the elders. On such a significant occasion no elder's absence would have been tolerated. Whether Hippolytus would absent himself permanently from the congregation after Callistus' ordination, as he had threatened, remained to be seen.

CHAPTER EIGHTEEN

The courtyard of Piso and Valeria's mansion was already bursting at the seams an hour before the service began. Children had to sit on their fathers' shoulders to avoid being crushed, while latecomers found themselves jammed into the sweltering atrium or even spilling out into the street. Valeria and her handmaids had strung swags of flowers between columns and over doorways, and the dais where Callistus, the elders and the bishops who would ordain him would sit was festooned with garlands. As soon as Callistus was sighted the cry went up: 'Hail Callistus! Callistus of Rome! Callistus of Rome! Hail the heir of Saint Peter!' and the children on their fathers' shoulders pushed themselves higher to catch a glimpse of the man of the moment or even to reach out and touch his garments as he passed, as though he were Peter in person or the emperor himself.

There was nothing imperial about Callistus' appearance – he was bare-headed and dressed in a plain white robe – but he could not help but smile and wave and clasp the hands that reached out to him as, flanked by Gaius and Urbanus, he followed a pair of officious young deacons who forged a path for the platform party through the crowd. Behind him walked

Anathalon the Bishop of Milan, whose church had been founded by Barnabas, companion of Saint Paul, and the Bishop of Sicily whose church owed its existence to Saint Peter. After them came other bishops from every major city in Italy, for there was no urban centre on the Italian peninsula which could not now boast a Christian community of its own. The rest of the elders of the Roman Church brought up the rear – including Hippolytus, who had said no more about leaving if Callistus became its bishop. Whether he had swallowed his pride or was merely biding his time until he could use his shock announcement to maximum effect, Callistus did not know.

The first part of the service proceeded as a Sunday Assembly always did, though the singing was more exuberant and the prayers of thanksgiving longer. Then before the breaking of the bread the visiting bishops gathered around Callistus and laid their hands upon his head and shoulders, and the oldest, Anathalon, spoke over him the words of consecration.

'O God of truth, who sent the Lord Jesus Christ for the gain of the whole world, and through him chose the apostles, and then ordained holy bishops for your Church, we ask now that you make this your servant Callistus their worthy successor! Grant him grace and your divine Spirit; bestow upon him the wisdom he will need to shepherd your flock, and may he continue blamelessly and honourably in his sacred office from this day forward; amen.'

'Amen!' echoed Anathalon's peers. Then one by one they embraced and kissed their new colleague and he embraced them in return, overwhelmed to think that one such as he should have been elevated to serve God as vicar of Christ. Inside he did not feel very much older or worthier than that slave-boy who had stood at the back of the Assembly with the latecomers so many years ago and first noticed Commodus' concubine listening rapt to the reading of Irenaeus' letter. Indeed, though he was now only three years short of fifty, he was still the youngest of the bishops gathered, his hair was almost as thick and black as it had been in his youth, and there were many in the congregation who were still more than happy to have an excuse to feast their eyes upon him without having to pretend that they weren't.

If only Marcia could have been there among them, Callistus wished fleetingly. Once again reality had outstripped his boyhood fantasies; once again God had blessed him beyond anything he could have believed possible. Whatever trials and tribulations his new role might bring with it, they could wait until tomorrow. Today was a day for rejoicing, and nothing was going to rob Callistus of the happiness which had flooded his soul.

Once the formal proceedings were over, it was time for all who could get near him to offer Callistus their own congratulations. Amongst them was his old master Carpophorus: well-nigh bald these days above his snow-white beard but as portly and pompous as ever, he took noisy delight in reminding everyone within earshot that Callistus owed his entire Christian upbringing to him. But having long since repented of misjudging him, Carpophorus was genuinely thrilled to see Callistus' potential fulfilled. There were hugs and kisses from Davina and her daughters, as well as from Anastasia on behalf of the Order of Widows; Jews and Gentiles, rich and poor, Roman and provincial, slave and free... those who surged forward to wish him well came from every walk of life and represented every shade of opinion – except for Hippolytus'.

Callistus knew full well that as soon as it was feasible he must set about implementing the reforms which Zephyrinus had longed to introduce. Of course it would be a mistake to attempt to change too much too quickly, but hesitancy would serve him no better than rashness. What mattered most was discerning God's timing in everything and moving neither too slowly nor too fast.

One or two serious issues did need to be tackled straight

away. The day after his ordination, in the presence of Gaius, Urbanus and Asterius – the three elders with whom he felt the most affinity – Callistus sent for Sabellius and asked him if he were responsible for intimidating Hippolytus in the days before nominations for the episcopacy closed.

'I should prefer it to be said that I helped him put things in perspective,' Sabellius replied with a wry smile, as though he expected to be thanked for making such a crucial contribution to the success of Callistus' electoral campaign.

'Then it is my sad duty to inform you that you can no longer serve as an elder in the Roman Church. I'm sorry, Sabellius, but I made it very clear to you that I would not have it said by anyone that I had deterred Hippolytus from standing against me.'

Momentarily Sabellius was too stunned to respond. Then he clenched both his hands into fists and expostulated, 'This is outrageous! Anyone would think you had *wanted* Hippolytus to get his way! *He* was the one using inappropriate tactics, not I! I never *heard* such ingratitude!'

'So you think it was appropriate to station men outside his house to restrict his movements? You think it was appropriate to – '

'They were *not* there to restrict his movements! They were there to observe them, that is all! How dare you question my actions, when I was already an elder while you were hacking at rocks under ground in Sardinia? How dare you – '

'Sabellius, please. If you continue to talk like this you will leave me no choice but to excommunicate you as well as deposing you from office.'

'Excommunicate me? I'd like to see you try! The Christians of Rome will soon regret putting *you* in charge if you throw your weight around like this on the slightest pretext, just because that dim-witted Zephyrinus thought the sun shone out of – '

'That's enough, Sabellius. If you would be so kind as to close the door on your way out, I would very much appreciate it. You may consider yourself excommunicate until such time as you repent of your unseemly actions and attitude and apologize for reviling me as *no* believer – bishop or catechumen – should be reviled by any other. When you are ready to show remorse you may return and be restored without further recriminations.'

Patently unable to believe what he was hearing, Sabellius turned in fury to Gaius and then to Urbanus, but neither man's expression offered him any encouragement. As for Asterius, he seemed about to pitch in energetically on the bishop's behalf. Before he could do so, Sabellius turned back to Callistus and bellowed, 'You can keep your repentance and your restoration and your Hippolytus with his two gods! Congratulations on banning your first Christian brother from fellowship less than twenty four hours after your installation! So much for tolerance and forbearance! So much for the clemency of Callistus!' And he strode out of the room without a backward glance, slamming the door behind him.

Callistus put his head in his hands, but at once felt the hands of his companions laid on his shoulders.

'You only did what you had to do,' Gaius said. 'Sabellius has done nothing but cause trouble since he first fell out with Tertullian. Sometimes a line must be drawn in the sand, as gladiators say, and you have drawn yours in the right place.'

'The last thing I wanted to do was give anyone cause to say I had stifled free speech by preventing Hippolytus from putting obstacles in my path. Now I shall have Sabellius telling everyone I muzzled *him*, and the next thing we shall hear is that all the Africans in the Church have turned against me.'

'I don't think we shall.' Urbanus' cultured voice was as soothing as the hand he had laid on Callistus' shoulder. 'The Africans in the Church know Sabellius as well as they know you. To those who are born of the Spirit, a man's integrity and spirituality will always matter more than the language he speaks, or the colour of his skin, or whether or not he has been circumcised, or any other such distinction by which the ignorant and carnal set store.'

'Let's pray for Callistus now,' Asterius suggested, his hand still resting on Callistus' other shoulder. 'A leader's life's a lonely one. He'll need good friends to support him. Same as he supported Zephyrinus.'

So the three elders lifted their voices to God on Callistus' behalf, and slowly but surely Callistus' spirit rose along with theirs. When it was over, as Callistus studied each of his companions' faces in turn he understood why he had been drawn to them. They all knew what it meant to allow the Holy Spirit to remake them from the inside.

This was where the likeness between them ended, however. Gaius was in his sixties, podgy, round-faced and genial-looking like his brother. Urbanus was younger, very dark, urbane by nature as well as by name, a smart son of the City and patrician to his finger-tips. Asterius was the son of a warehouse manager from Ostia, big-boned, loose-limbed, heavy-featured and gruffly laconic, just about as dissimilar to Urbanus as it was possible to get except in age. But to Callistus in that moment these three very different individuals meant as much to him as Peter, John and James had meant to Jesus.

'We must pray like this every day,' he said to them. 'It will make all the difference. I know now what made Zephyrinus summon me from Antium.'

Gaius patted him on the wrist, a gesture so reminiscent of his brother that Callistus had to smile. 'We'll be here every morning,' Gaius promised him. 'Though it's to be hoped that not *all* of our meetings will begin with an excommunication.' He was grinning as he spoke; Callistus' smile broadened too, and the four of them parted with lightened hearts and easy laughter.

Callistus knew that he must also meet often with the body of elders and widows' leaders as a whole. At the first of these sessions he explained to those assembled that he would be praying daily with Gaius, Urbanus and Asterius in private, because even Jesus had needed a close circle of friends with whom he could share his innermost thoughts. He then explained that Sabellius would not be attending any meetings at all because he was no longer an elder, and was excommunicate from the Church until further notice.

Hippolytus' jaw dropped visibly, and Callistus could almost see his rhetorician's mind tying itself in knots as he sought to unravel the message which Callistus was trying to send him. It simply hadn't occurred to him that Callistus' expulsion of Sabellius might have nothing to do with personal enmity, or even with rival approaches to belief or morality. In the end he could hold his silence no longer, and demanded that Callistus explain precisely why Sabellius had been expelled.

Callistus answered levelly, 'Because his antagonistic attitude towards anyone who disagrees with him was a threat to our fellowship. As Saint Paul admonished us: love doesn't puff up, it builds up. And unity amongst his followers was the one thing for which our Lord Jesus prayed on the night before he gave his life for them.'

Hippolytus made no further comment. But for the next few days he went about impressing upon everyone he met that Callistus must be frightened of him, and had expelled Sabellius in a pathetic attempt to keep him – Hippolytus – sweet. 'You shouldn't trust Callistus any further than a dog can throw a discus, that's what Hippolytus is saying,' Asterius told Callistus indignantly when they met for prayer on the Friday morning.

'I really don't want to expel Hippolytus too,' Callistus said with fervour. 'Even though he does seem to think it his mission to be my personal thorn in the flesh.'

'We should just hold our nerve and allow him to blow off steam for a while,' Urbanus advised him. 'No one takes him seriously when he prances about on his high horse like this.'

'You're as wise as you are unflappable, Urbanus. I think I must take you with me everywhere I go, to ensure I always think before I act.'

'So long as you don't make me archdeacon as well as an elder. I might get delusions of grandeur myself.' The corners of Urbanus' eyes creased with a hint of mischief, and the more so when Callistus told him he was archdeacon in all but name already. Whether anyone *could* be archdeacon and elder at the same time was another matter. Since there had been no such thing as an archdeacon before Callistus, the question had never arisen.

'How I wish we could get rid of these titles altogether,' Callistus sighed. 'Was Peter an archdeacon, or Paul a presbyter? Even Jesus was happier to be called the Son of Man than answer to anything grander. Oh, I know we have to put up with them now that our churches have grown so large; but don't worry, Urbanus. We have quite enough deacons already, who will inherit the care of the catacombs and the shrines of the saints, and all the other things I won't have time for any more. So long as you continue to keep my eyes fixed on Christ and my feet on the ground I shan't expect any more of you than you're already doing.'

On the Sunday following his ordination Callistus preached his first homily as bishop, to a congregation almost as large as the one which had gathered the week before. He spoke on the story of Nicodemus, the Jewish enquirer told by Jesus that he must be born again to enter God's Kingdom even though he was already a senior official in the synagogue. Along the way Callistus described his own conversion in Antium: how he had considered himself a Christian all his life, but learned that day that he had never truly known God at all.

'My beloved brothers and sisters,' he finished up. 'In the weeks to come I shall be introducing you to other scriptures which have gone into making me the man I am today. If you take them to heart you too will be changed, and so will our Church. Most of you have been baptized on the outside, but was it really a sign of inner grace, the invisible action of God's Spirit upon your soul? If any of you here, baptized or not, know that *you* still need to be reborn, please, come to me for prayer when the Eucharist is over.'

After the service so many people crowded forward that Callistus had to call upon others to help him with the prayer and counselling. Gaius, Urbanus and Asterius were instantly at his side; Anastasia and two of her widows ministered to the women. There was weeping and laughter as men, women and children opened their hearts to God in a way they had never done before.

The following Sunday Callistus took as the text for his homily Marcia's favourite passage from Matthew's Gospel, in which Jesus tells Peter that the number of times he must forgive someone who has offended him is seventy times seven. Along with it Callistus told his hearers Marcia's story, just as he had told them his own the week before.

'Most of you knew her as Melissa,' he reminded them, 'And most of you believe that she abandoned her faith, along with her disguise, without a second thought. Because of the rules by which our Church has bound itself – rules which Jesus would never have condoned – she died unabsolved, cut off from the friends she had loved. Yet God loved her to the end, and so did I.' At this point Callistus broke down, and the congregation looked on in mingled horror and awe as their new bishop bared his soul before them. 'Do we *want* to deny God's mercy to the weak and broken?' he appealed to them through tears. 'Do we want to let Jesus' message of hope be swamped by rules and regulations? I tell you, even if we neglect to preach the true Gospel, the very stones will cry out that God is love and cannot be mocked or thwarted by human arrogance. Now any one of *you* who is holding a grudge against a fellow Christian whom he or she needs to forgive must seek out that person here and now and be reconciled before we share communion, as Jesus and Paul both taught us.' Then he sat down and wept unashamedly.

But already there were others weeping too, and soon throughout the Assembly there were people who had not spoken to one another in years embracing each other and weeping openly together. It was only when the Eucharist was ended that Asterius informed Callistus that Hippolytus and his supporters had left in undisguised disgust.

The next Sunday after that, Callistus preached on Jesus' parable of the Wheat and the Tares, where the tares are allowed to grow up with the crop until harvest time lest the wheat be ripped up with the weeds. He explained how he had come across the works of Clement of Alexandria, to whom the Church was no showcase for saints but a school for sinners. Its pupils may benefit from discipline, and in extreme circumstances it may be necessary for one to be expelled. But how are they ever to learn if they are permanently excluded, with no hope of restitution?

'Therefore a change will be made, from today, in the way we do things here in the Church of Rome,' Callistus concluded, gazing out upon the sea of expectant faces. 'Henceforward the possibility of absolution will not be denied to anyone. With repentance, and after doing penance, a former brother or sister who has committed adultery or murder or even apostasy after baptism may seek readmission to communion. All that my fellow elders and I will require before enrolling them as penitents is evidence of genuine remorse, along with a willingness to face up to the consequences of what they have done and to make restitution wherever possible. Thus we shall all grow up in Christ together, and if there are tares among us whose repentance is false, that is for God to determine. To show that I mean what I say, I call upon Daphne, daughter of Davina, to come up to be accepted as a penitent here and now.'

The silence into which he had spoken was shattered as murmurs and then cries of incredulity erupted from every side. For a long time it seemed that Daphne would decline his invitation; timid at the best of times, to respond to Callistus' challenge would require exactly the sort of courage which had failed her when confronted by the emperor's statue. Yet she knew that Callistus had always believed in her just as

Zephyrinus had done.

So she made her way forward through the multitude and ascended the steps to the platform. When she knelt at Callistus' feet, and her unbound hair spilled out over his sandals, no one could fail to be reminded of the sinful woman who had won affirmation from Jesus by anointing his feet with perfume and using her hair to dry them. Thus no one presumed to object when Callistus laid his hands on Daphne's head in blessing, then drew her up and invited her to take her place on the penitents' bench.

'Know this, too, my brothers and sisters in Christ,' Callistus continued, when Daphne had sat down and the woman beside her had grasped her hand in affirmation. 'Henceforth all acts of penitence will be done in private. There will be no public humiliation for those awaiting readmission to communion. The wearing of sackcloth and ashes will not be enforced; it will be a matter for the penitent to decide before God. Finally, I would have you understand that none of these changes stem from newfangled notions I have dreamed up for myself. They are all reforms which Zephyrinus longed for years to introduce, yet could not, because you were not ready. Then when the time might at last have been ripe, he had become too ill to see his vision through. So now it falls to me to enact the dying wishes of the godly man whom it was my joy and privilege to serve.'

No one said a word in protest; by his own choice of words Callistus had effectively tied their tongues. He could not help but cast a sideways glance at Hippolytus, who remained seated with the elders where he had always sat; he looked distraught but did not speak. Then, before normal proceedings could resume, another young woman ventured onto the platform, uninvited, and she too fell on her knees at Callistus' feet. He did not know who she was; the Roman Church was now much too large for him to be able to put a name to every face, though he was working hard to learn as many as he could. But enough of those present did know who she was for fresh murmurs of disapproval to be rumbling all around; besides, what right did *any* woman think she had to present herself before the bishop in the middle of a service without his asking her to do so?

Yet Callistus saw only the desperation in her eyes, and the flicker of hope which his sympathy for Daphne had ignited there. He took hold of the hands she held out to him and asked how he might help her.

'Bishop Callistus, may God bless you for your kindness! I have been denied communion since the days of the blessed Victor because my husband beat me so badly that I left him for another man. But he beat me too, so now I'm with someone else, and so ashamed of how my life has turned out. I never wanted to break my marriage vows. I never wanted to run away from trouble the way I did. I just want to say how sorry I am – to God, to all my brothers and sisters…' She could not go on; Callistus said tenderly, 'Come, my daughter. You too will be offered absolution.' And he guided her carefully down from the platform into the waiting arms of Daphne.

Meanwhile the murmurings against him were growing louder, but there were also cries of 'Praise the Lord!' and 'Blessed be Callistus!' rising above the disquiet. Then all at once there were other conscience-stricken sinners pushing forward through the crowd, some of whom were not even excommunicate because their wrongdoings had never come to light and they had never dared confess them. Now they could keep their secrets to themselves no longer; confessions tumbled from their lips as they stretched out their arms to touch Callistus' garments or fall on their faces in his shadow. One by one he raised them to their feet; one by one they went to join the penitents until there was no more room on the bench and they stood in a throng at the foot of the podium calling out, 'God bless Callistus! God bless Callistus of Rome!' until finally Hippolytus could take no more.

'Callistus, you must put a stop to this travesty at once!' he demanded, starting forward and seizing Callistus by the shoulders as if to shock him back to his senses, despite not having touched his old friend in thirty years. 'It's a disgrace. This will make the Church of Rome a laughing-stock in every city of the empire.' Then he thrust Callistus aside and interposed himself between the bishop and his suppliants. 'I will have *no* part in this mockery, and neither will any of *you*, unless you want to forfeit all chance of forgiveness when you stand before God's throne on the Day of Judgement!' he announced to those still attempting to climb onto the platform. 'What good will it do you to hear empty words of absolution from a man who has no right to utter them, if you are rejected by Almighty God? What is the point of enjoying acceptance for a few brief years on earth if you end up damned for eternity in hell?' His deep orator's voice grew more and more resonant as he piled his rhetorical questions one upon another. Soon Asterius was on his feet as well, motioning others to help him eject Hippolytus from the Assembly, but Callistus noticed and had him sit down. In any case there was no one else attempting to mount the dais now. No one was blessing or cursing Callistus except for Hippolytus himself, and once his diatribe was over, the whole congregation stood cowed into silence. Callistus then said quietly, 'Let us pray,' and proceeded to go on with the service as though nothing were amiss.

But when the time came for communion, Hippolytus refused to receive it. He said, loudly enough for many in the congregation to hear, 'I will not take bread and wine from a man whose hands defile these holy gifts and whose words of consecration mean nothing! His own consecration as bishop was meaningless; he is an impostor bent on bringing darkness where there was light and misery where there was hope. How can he presume to say that the elements he holds in his filthy hands represent the body and blood of our Saviour? Callistus is crucifying Christ all over again.'

This time when Asterius stood to escort Hippolytus from

the platform, Callistus merely nodded his head. Gaius and Urbanus stood too, and Hippolytus went with them without another word, his face set and head held high. Those men who regarded themselves as his supporters left as well. But no one else refused communion at Callistus' hands.

When the service was over, Callistus longed only to be alone. But Hippolytus was waiting for him in the atrium when everyone else had gone except a handful of his supporters and Gaius, Urbanus and Asterius, who stood by with arms folded and expressions grim.

'This was the last straw, Callistus,' Hippolytus said without preamble. 'You have appropriated rights which belong to God alone. That is to say: you are a blasphemer. You leave me no choice but to resign as elder and abandon this congregation to its fate.'

Callistus sat down wearily on a couch and bade Hippolytus be seated too; predictably he refused. 'Why then did Jesus give to Peter the keys of his Kingdom?' Callistus enquired of him. 'Why did he promise that whatever Peter bound or loosed on earth would be bound and loosed in heaven, if he meant nothing by it?' Callistus' voice betrayed no anger; in fact to those who were listening he sounded to be seeking Hippolytus' opinion in all sincerity. But Hippolytus was implacable.

'It's too late for discussing theology now. My mind is made up, though my heart is broken. But make no mistake about this: it is you who are the schismatic, not I. Those few righteous men who perceive the truth as I do will form a church of their own with me as their bishop, and small though it may be to begin with, it will soon eclipse the one you have ruined, and when other bishops find out what has gone on here, it is my church with which they will choose to commune. Your sect, which you are so fond of likening to a school, will be called exactly that: the School of Callistus. Certainly that is what *I* shall call it. Goodbye, Callistus. Somehow I do not think that you and I shall have cause to speak to one another again.'

Callistus made no response. He didn't want to say goodbye and could think of nothing else worth saying. Nor did he make any move to prevent Hippolytus from leaving; noting his acceptance of the situation Gaius, Urbanus and Asterius stood aside while Hippolytus and his tight little knot of supporters departed. Once more Callistus put his head in his hands; once more his friends laid their hands on his shoulders in intercession. But this time his sorrow was too deep for their prayers to penetrate.

There were times in the following months when Callistus began to think that Hippolytus' bleak predictions might be coming true. A letter was received from Origen in Alexandria to say that he was gravely troubled by reports he had received from Rome, and informing Callistus that in spite of the rift of which he had heard, he remained in communion with Hippolytus. But he did not go so far as to say that he would not commune with Callistus, nor did he refer to the Church over which he presided as 'Callistus' school'. And Callistus' heart began to lighten at last when other bishops or their representatives made a point of journeying to Rome to carry out their own assessment of the situation – and found much about the mainstream Roman Church which impressed them profoundly. Some of them even resolved to remodel their own churches along similar lines when they got home.

So it was that Callistus found the courage to press on with his reforms whatever the cost to himself, for he knew how much depended on his not looking back having once put his hand to the plough. And as time went on he found himself establishing precedents which had little to do with what Zephyrinus had wished for and everything to do with needs he could see for himself. For one thing, it had been growing increasingly fashionable for Church elders to be celibate like the Order of Widows; not only were unmarried elders being discouraged by their peers from taking wives, but those already married were coming under pressure to set their wives aside and live as though they had never been married in the first place. This, said Callistus, must stop. 'Did not Saint Paul instruct us that an elder must be the husband of one wife?' he pointed out to those who objected. 'Polygamy he abhorred and divorce broke his heart, but even Paul who was never married himself could see that marriage was a gift from God and a rich means of his grace.'

'But Saint Paul also said it was better for all to remain in the marital state they had been in when called to serve Christ,' the response came back. 'We accept that the married should perhaps stay married, but those who were single should stay that way too.'

'Just as he stated most emphatically that it is better to marry than to burn,' Callistus rejoined, in a tone which suggested that he would brook no further protest. 'We must remember that Saint Paul believed that the world as we know it would come to an end within a matter of years, or even months, rendering arrangements for betrothals and weddings a pointless distraction. As for me, I have reasons of my own for choosing not to marry, and you may have yours, into which it is not my business to enquire. And it's true that for many a conscientious servant of the Church, the demands of wife and family have proven overwhelming. But enforced celibacy will give rise to many more problems than it solves.'

Callistus' verdict prevailed, for the time being at least; he had based his own thinking on an argument much favoured by Origen, that in seeking God's guidance one must weigh the whole balance of Scripture, not seize upon isolated verses and use them as proof-texts. Privately Callistus suspected that Origen himself would argue in favour of clerical celibacy if he were asked about it, as would Hippolytus and Tertullian, so the irony was not lost on him. But he didn't think that any of these three men's reservations about marriage had much to do with their reading of Scripture.

In similar vein but more controversial still, Callistus refused to accept that clergy who committed serious sin should necessarily be barred from office indefinitely. So long as they repented and took steps to repair any damage they had done, why should they not be restored and reinstated just like anyone else? Had not King David himself committed adultery and later repented, without forfeiting his right to rule over the people of God?

'*All* of us are human,' Callistus reminded the elders and widows gathered around him for their regular meeting. '*None* of us can afford to allow ourselves to be put on pedestals like marble statues immune to corruption. We may be regenerate, but we aren't yet perfect. Any of us may fall and need to start out afresh.' So it was that this change, too, was duly approved, as was Callistus' proposal that no man be barred from becoming an elder simply because he'd been married more than once, provided that his first wife had died, or that he had thoroughly repented of the failings which had caused his first marriage to founder.

'But surely we can only sanction this if he remarried before he was baptized,' a number of elders had protested before the decision was taken. 'Baptism alone can wash away a sin as grave as a marriage which should never have been.'

'Baptism in itself is not what changes us,' Callistus explained yet again. 'Besides, it is not the *marriage* which was sinful and in need of washing away.'

Meanwhile Hippolytus might have made up his mind not to speak to Callistus again, but this did not stop him sending a stream of vitriolic letters to the elders and widows denouncing Callistus' wickedness, and signing himself the Rightful Bishop of Rome. Letters came from Tertullian too, reviling Callistus as 'Pontifex Maximus' – the title of a pagan high priest – and proclaiming that even if every other bishop in the empire agreed with his programme of reform, 'the Church of Christ is not a conclave of bishops but a manifestation of the Holy Spirit!'

Reading this out to Gaius, Urbanus and Asterius, Callistus gave a mirthless laugh and said, 'Well, on the last point at least we can agree with our Montanist friend.' Then he laid the letter aside and studied each of his companions in turn. '*Am* I just being arrogant?' he asked them. 'Please, I need you to tell me if you think I am overstepping the mark.'

'Oh, we shall tell you, have no fear,' said Urbanus with his crinkle-eyed smile. 'But it is those who would deny a sinner forgiveness who are arrogant and out of step with the Holy Spirit. As Jesus said: let the one who is sinless cast the first stone.'

'Thank you, Urbanus. Once again you have set my mind at rest,' Callistus sighed; but he had barely finished his sentence when one of Titus' slaves appeared in the doorway to tell him that an anxious young couple from the Church had fetched up at the house and asked to see him. If it was not convenient just now they were quite prepared to wait, but seemed to have every intention of remaining on the premises until it was.

'Show them in,' said Callistus, sighing again; the slave bobbed out, and returned a few moments later with a young man and woman in tow.

The woman was fashionably dressed, with her hair piled up and her manicured hands betraying the fact that she had never washed a dish or scrubbed a floor in her life. The man wore the homespun tunic of a slave.

The reason for their visit was obvious before either of them opened their mouths. They stood hand in hand, and every glance they exchanged betrayed their illicit love. Callistus knew very well that it was not uncommon in Roman society for a master to fall in love with his slave-girl and set her free so that they could be legally married. And committed relationships between couples both of whom were enslaved had long been recognized as marriages by the Roman Church. But a relationship between a well-born woman and a slave was something else altogether, and as Callistus studied the lovers' faces he was transported disconcertingly back to his own adolescence. Of course he had been much younger than Marcia, as well as being a slave; he had accepted by now that

Marcia herself would have described his forbidden feelings for her as infatuation rather than love. But if they had been closer together in age, if she had loved him in the way he'd loved her...

'We have been in love since we were children,' explained the young man, whose name was Terentius. 'But by the time I have earned enough money to buy my freedom, Cordelia will be too old for us ever to have children of our own. If only we could be married in the eyes of God in the way that we could if she were a slave like me...'

'But your parents would disown you, surely?' Callistus said, turning to Cordelia whose brimming eyes were already fixed on his face in entreaty. 'You would bring grave dishonour on their house. And any grandchildren you gave them would be regarded by the courts as illegitimate.'

'No,' she said. 'Because I have no parents. They died when I was little, and the aunt and uncle who brought me up are Christians who have known Terentius as long as I have. They care only that we are happy, and would adopt our children themselves if it were the only way to give them legal status as their heirs.'

'Could *they* not buy Terentius' freedom?' Urbanus suggested hesitantly, evidently unsure if it was appropriate for him to speak yet too concerned to stay silent.

'They would, if his master would sell him. But every time they offer he puts up the price,' Cordelia told him, then turned directly back to Callistus. 'Oh, Bishop Callistus, if only you could see your way to giving our union the Church's blessing! Then at least we could live at peace with ourselves and with God. Or is it really not true after all that in Christ there is neither slave nor free?'

Callistus clasped their joined hands between his own. 'It is true,' he assured them. 'Come to Assembly on Sunday with your aunt and uncle to vouch for you, and you will have the blessing you seek.'

Heedless of propriety, Cordelia threw her arms around

Callistus and Terentius both at once, and when presently the young couple went on their way, Callistus was still grinning so foolishly that Urbanus said, 'Perhaps you should get married yourself, Callistus, if hugging attractive young women brings you such pleasure.' Callistus turned red as a radish and threatened to throw Urbanus in Titus' fish-pond.

Terentius and Cordelia were duly married in the eyes of God and his Church, and it wasn't long before Cordelia was carrying Terentius' child. No one could have been happier for them than Cordelia's aunt and uncle – except perhaps Callistus.

Cordelia might have been the first freeborn woman to marry a slave in the Roman Church but she certainly wasn't the last. The Christian faith had always appealed most strongly to the oppressed and the dispossessed, so it wasn't surprising that the Church's register of members listed more slaves than senators and more women than men. As a result there were never going to be enough men of appropriate status for the freeborn women to marry, and there were many parents who would have been happier for their daughter to marry a slave than a pagan. Naturally there were some unmarried women in the Church who would rather have stayed single than marry someone they considered beneath them. But as Callistus reminded everyone in his homilies, celibacy wasn't for everyone. There were even some who argued that women, like men, should be allowed to hold office in the Church if they were married. But this would have been a step too far even for Callistus to take; he could not see how a woman would ever be able to juggle the demands of a husband, a family and an official position in the Church successfully.

Not that he expected women to go on bearing children if they were not in a position to feed, house or care for them adequately, or if they had been forced into wedlock or concubinage against their will. He brought down another deluge of protest on his own head by refusing to reprehend women who – as Marcia had done – sought to avoid becoming pregnant when they made love. Surely, he argued, it is better not to conceive a child in the first place than to resort to a dangerous abortion or expose an unwanted infant by throwing it out with the rubbish? No, thundered Hippolytus by return of post, it is not; all three are abominable – and while we are on the subject of unacceptable practices which it's your business to condemn: you should tell the members of your congregation not to attend heathen Games or eat at heathen banquets either.

'I certainly do discourage the sheep of my flock from indulging in sinful practices,' Callistus wrote in reply. 'But since neither medicinal herbs nor competitive sports, nor accepting hospitality from our neighbours, came in for any criticism from Moses or Christ, I shall make no pronouncements concerning them. After all, you have invariably been one of the first to complain whenever you have suspected me of appropriating God's authority before. Some things are for a believer's own conscience to decide. No one is going to make *you* go to chariot races or noisy parties if you don't want to.'

And gradually once again most of the other Italian bishops came round to Callistus' way of thinking. Better still, the entire schismatic Church of Theodotus decided to return to the Catholic fold en masse now that Sabellius was gone, following the example of Natalis who had come back in the days of Zephyrinus. Overjoyed, Callistus welcomed them with open arms, eliciting Hippolytus' angriest letter to date.

'You would feed Christ's body to *pigs,* provided that they grovelled at your feet and made your head swell with their flatteries!' he wrote. 'Anyone would think you were the late great Caracalla himself, granting citizenship to all and sundry just to make himself look good. It's no wonder your School is so popular, when its pupils can strut around like cockerels calling themselves Christians when in truth they are swine wallowing in the mire.'

'It's only too obvious what he's afraid of,' said Urbanus

when Callistus showed him the letter. 'He's afraid that *his* disciples will desert to you, if they think they can do so without penalty. Let's pray that they *will*, and the sooner the better, before we lose any more sleep over his wild accusations.'

The following Sunday Callistus preached on Jesus' encounter with the woman taken in adultery. 'The way we live our lives *does* matter,' he reminded his flock, which grew every week and lapped up every word he spoke. 'Yes, Jesus forgave the woman without reservation, but we must not forget that he admonished her not to sin again.

'Yet we must remember too that this was for *her* good, not for his! God *does* want us to change and live holy lives, but not in order to earn our own salvation. Salvation is the gift of God, and holiness is the result of his Spirit's work in our lives, lives that we offer up to him in love and gratitude for his love for us! Let us live in love, my brothers and sisters, for love is of God, and it is by this love that the world will know us, and one day know him too. Then the Kingdom of God will extend to the boundaries of the empire and beyond, and the human race will at last fulfil the destiny which God planned for it.'

Part Three:
Callistus and Mamaea

CHAPTER NINETEEN: CALLISTUS

As the torrid Roman summer mellowed into autumn, notices were posted in the forum announcing that the emperor's son Diadumenianus would shortly be celebrating his ninth birthday and that a spectacular horse racing event would be staged at the Circus Maximus in his honour.

'I didn't know the emperor *had* a son,' Callistus said when Titus told him, barely looking up; he was working his way through a heap of correspondence while chewing on a hunk of hard cheese for lunch.

'You're not the only one. Some folk aren't even convinced we've got an emperor. He's a bit *too* much like a god, they say: it's not as if they've ever seen him.' This was true, Callistus acknowledged; since the demise of Caracalla, his nemesis Macrinus had been in no hurry to return from his military campaigning on the empire's eastern frontier. 'Then again,' said Titus, 'We shan't have a bishop much longer either if you don't start feeding yourself properly. The cooks would be only too eager to rustle up something saucy to tickle your tastebuds if you asked them to. No wonder you're thin as a bulrush.'

'You're only jealous because I can still touch my toes while you can't even see yours over your belly.' Callistus tossed the tablet he'd been reading onto a pile that needed replies and moved on to the next one.

'Come, come, Callistus. How is anyone to believe you're not a grumpy old ascetic if they never see you enjoying yourself? Come with me to the birthday races; you need a break from all this bureaucracy, and what better way to demonstrate to the likes of Hippolytus that there's nothing sinful about attending the odd sporting engagement than by being seen at the Circus in person? It's not as if there are going to be hulking great gladiators knocking the living daylights out of each other and spraying each other's blood and guts all over the front row seats. What do you say? We could go with Priscus; he's always glad to have company.'

'All right,' said Callistus because he wasn't really listening; but when the appointed day came he had little choice but to honour his offhand agreement.

Taking his seat between Titus and Priscus as the spectators were gathering he did feel unexpectedly excited, in a slightly guilty kind of way. Carpophorus had always denounced horse racing – along with chariot racing and gladiatorial combat – as the kind of Gentile frivolity which no self-respecting son of Abraham should have anything to do with, and Callistus had never felt any pressing need to research the matter for himself. Now, surrounded by the noisily expectant crowd, the cries of sausage-sellers and the ferocious arguments over form and odds, he began to think that Titus had been right: some undemanding entertainment and the chance to let his hair down a little would do him the world of good. He even thought about placing a bet on one of the horses himself, but decided that this would be a step too far.

From the place where the three of them were sitting, they had a good view not only of the race track below but also of the canopied platform reserved for the imperial party. The emperor was still away on campaign, but his wife and son were there, along with a buzzing swarm of retainers to fawn over them, and a detachment of Praetorians for their protection. The woman was as fair as her husband was famously dark; Macrinus' family came from the province of Mauretania to the south of the Pillars of Hercules. Thus the birthday boy, who was tall and slender for his age, was uncommonly striking to look upon, with his carob-brown complexion and incongruously tawny hair. He had been elevated to the rank of Caesar – heir apparent – soon after his father had assumed the imperial throne, and his loose-limbed elegance and confident demeanour were entirely appropriate to his station.

However, the longer Callistus sat drinking in the atmosphere, the more aware he became that all was not quite as it should have been. The sense of anticipation was undeniably exhilarating, but he noticed by and by that it had a brittle edge to it which didn't feel entirely healthy. Too much time seemed to pass with nothing happening on the race track, yet there had been no announcement apologizing for the delay. The spectators' excitement was souring into annoyance; a few rows behind Callistus and his friends a couple of old men were swearing loudly, complaining that none of Rome's emperors had known how to stage a decent show since that ungrateful bitch Marcia had murdered good old Commodus. Even Diadumenianus, who until now had been more than happy to be the focus of everyone's attention, was starting to look distinctly uncomfortable, turning round frequently to his mother, who sat stock-still in her high-backed chair.

'The poor lad can't have seen much more of his father than we have these past few years,' Titus remarked, offering Callistus a handful of the roasted grain he had bought on their way into the arena. 'The Senate was all too willing to extol Macrinus' virtues when he rid us of Caracalla, but its support for him won't last long unless he stops gallivanting around winning glory for himself on the fringes of the empire and starts facing up to his responsibilities here in Rome.'

'I'd wager Septimius Severus spent more time abroad than he did in Rome, and no one held that against *him*,' said Callistus. 'Mind you, he had so many rivals to eliminate in his first few years, he didn't have much choice. But even so – '

'I don't think Macrinus is winning much glory or eliminating anyone that matters,' Priscus cut in. 'From what my friends in the military tell me, with Caracalla out of the way he could have defeated the Parthians once and for all if he'd had anything about him as a general. Instead he squandered a fortune buying them off, when he could have been replenishing the treasury with Parthian gold *and* breathing new life into the slave trade at one fell swoop. Everyone knows how much the common soldiers loved Caracalla because he made a show of sharing their hardships. But Macrinus wafts around in a litter, with a golden fillet in his hair and his beard curled like a Persian's.'

'That must look rather out of keeping with the hoop they say he wears through his ear,' said Titus, somewhat inaudibly because his mouth was full of corn.

'Oh, I don't suppose he wears anything like that any more, if he ever did,' said Priscus. 'He's no more a painted savage than Severus was; his family's been steeped in Roman culture for generations and his father was an equestrian. Still, they say Marcus Aurelius is the emperor he tries to emulate; that's why he boasts such a big curly beard. And he sits there staring into space whenever anyone asks him a question, then replies in an undertone, in the hope of sounding philosophical. It doesn't work. The few men I know who have met him say it just makes him seem even more stupid than he is.'

'*Is* he stupid? Brutal perhaps; he's certainly not slow in obliterating his opponents.'

'Well he doesn't seem intelligent enough to see that if he keeps on trying to claw back the privileges Caracalla heaped upon the soldiers without giving them some proper victories to boast of in return, he's in for a pretty rough ride. And he'd be well advised to take more notice of the omens the gods have sent him, too. It can't be coincidence that the Colosseum was struck by lightning only weeks after his accession so the gladiator fights had to be moved here to the Circus. Or that the Tiber rose so high in the storms that the forum itself was knee deep in water. You could have staged a naval battle there, no problem at all.'

'Come now, Priscus. You know better than to talk to Christians about omens and portents in the heavens – or indeed the Colosseum. It's in Almighty God that we're meant to trust, not bizarre climatic phenomena.'

But the friends' good-natured banter was abruptly cut short by Callistus gripping each of them by the wrist, because the mood of the crowd was growing uglier by the moment. The two old men behind them who had been swearing loudly enough before were now shouting out their profanities and brazen criticisms of the emperor with such gusto that their neighbours were joining in. 'Where's your yellow-bellied father on your special day, then, Diadem Denis?' 'Are you sure you've even got one?' 'The birthday boy's a bastard! The birthday boy's a bastard!' they were yelling, embellishing their catcalls with obscenities such as Callistus hadn't heard since his escape from Sardinia.

'Jupiter save us! We have no emperor!' cried someone else off to their right, and swiftly this chant was taken up by others too. All around the arena frustration was erupting into open hostility; from every quarter anger surged like lava from Vesuvius. Close to the imperial platform a brave clutch of senators was attempting to stay the swelling tide by shouting, 'Hail Macrinus! Hail his heir! Hail Macrinus! Hail his heir!' but no one much further away than Callistus could have heard them in a stadium which held a hundred and fifty thousand people, many of whom were now up on their feet bawling and punching the air. Diadumenianus' mother – who was probably just about old enough to remember the riot in this very stadium which had ended in the death of Commodus' henchman Cleander – clutched at her son in terror. Though their armed Praetorians surrounded them and spectators were forbidden to carry weapons, if the chanting and yelling ripened into violence the Praetorians were few, and the size and fury of the mob formidable.

'We should leave while we still can,' Titus said. His voice was shaking, and he had spilt what was left of his roasted grain all down his toga. 'I'm sorry, Callistus. I never should have brought you.'

'Leave?' repeated Priscus, indignant. 'But the racing's about to begin. Look, they are bringing in the horses. This racket will stop once the punters have something to watch.'

Callistus was inclined to think Priscus might be right, but Titus' face had gone white as his toga and he had clearly lost all interest in showing his friends a good time. Callistus tried to convince him that attempting to fight their way out of the arena now would probably be more dangerous than staying put; the tumult would subside soon enough, since the Praetorians had resisted the temptation to pour fuel on its flames by drawing their swords. But all in vain. Titus was a nervous wreck, in marked contrast to Diadumenianus who was now gazing defiantly about him like the lone hero Horatius defending his bridge. The treat which his absent father had planned for him might have turned into the birthday from hell, but he wasn't for letting the common people see him cry.

Whoever had taken the decision to go ahead with the races had probably acted wisely, for cancelling them would have disgorged the volatile horde into the streets. As it was, all that was disgorged to Callistus' knowledge was Titus' bellyful of roasted grain. This he spewed spectacularly over the feet of an infuriated sausage-seller while his two companions were striving to bundle him through an exit before he passed out.

Although on this occasion full-scale rioting had been averted, the tension and sense of impending doom did not disperse along with the crowd at the end of the day. As winter closed in, it felt as if Rome herself were battening down her hatches against disaster. There were more fires like the one which had done so much damage to the Colosseum; one of them even damaged the emperor's personal property. Then came a succession of minor earthquakes, which seemed only too obvious a metaphor for political instability and imminent collapse. It began to be bandied about quite openly by senators and slaves alike that what Rome really needed was a strong imperial dynasty in which civilians as well as soldiers could have confidence, so that presumptuous generals seizing power and being toppled in their turn a few months later would be forever consigned to history.

'I must say it would be rather nice not to wake up every day wondering whether I still have the same employer I had at bedtime,' Clemens admitted one morning when bringing Callistus his regular news bulletin from the palace. Though he had worked there as long as Callistus had known him, Clemens rarely expressed a political view; he had more sense. 'A big, strong, stable imperial family with plenty of strapping sons and nephews so there's always one of them waiting in the wings all grown up and ready to come striding on stage when his predecessor gives up the ghost ... maybe *that's* the sort of government we need to hold our sagging monstrosity of an empire together these days.'

'A monarchy, you mean?' said Callistus, smiling innocently at Clemens' sharp intake of breath; he knew very well that by Roman standards he'd uttered a dirty word, for Rome had driven out the last of its kings centuries before. 'Come now, Clemens, you have to admit that the principate is a monarchy in all but name already, whatever anyone says. Die-hard Republicans can harp all they like on the evils of inherited power, and we can all try to pretend there's no real difference between an emperor and those old-time dictators who were only handed supreme power temporarily to steer the state through some short-term crisis. But there's no way we could go back now to rule by the Senate and People, any more than a church could get rid of its bishop and go back to sharing –

and deciding – everything in common, much as I might wish it could sometimes. Everything has just got too big and unwieldy, exactly as you said yourself.'

'Well in the case of the Church we can only thank God that it's got so big so quickly. As for Rome... I have to say I do see the sense of establishing an imperial dynasty with convincing credentials and clear rules of succession. The modern world is the modern world, like it or not. There will never be a time when we don't face one crisis or another, so there will never be a time when we don't need an emperor who knows what he's doing.'

If the rumours concerning her were true, Clemens' view had an enthusiastic advocate in Julia Maesa – surviving sister of the late great Julia Domna, Severus' wife – and Maesa was in no doubt that the dynasty which should be established was her own. No matter that she and all her offspring were as Syrian as the sun god Elagabal, whose high priest her father had been, or that she herself was living in Syria even now. No matter that she had previously shown no interest whatever in the politics of power, or indeed in anything very much except ensnaring handsome, high-status lovers as obscenely rich as she was herself. In fact she was easily as clever and capable as Domna had been, and Domna had admitted as much on more than one occasion.

Maesa had two adolescent grandsons for whom she apparently harboured grand ambitions. One was the son of her promiscuous daughter Soaemias. The other was the son of Mamaea.

Mamaea! It was fully fifteen years since Callistus had first laid eyes on her, when Severus entered Rome; she must be in her mid-thirties by now. Yet when Titus chanced to mention her name as they talked politics over dinner Callistus' heart still leaped in his chest as disconcertingly as if she had just walked in through the door.

'Callistus, are you all right? You look as if you had just swallowed a fish-bone. Was it something I said?'

'No. I mean, yes…'

'You mean you're blushing as red as an over-ripe pomegranate. Ah yes, I remember now. You met Mamaea at that symposium you attended with Zephyrinus, didn't you? I recall thinking when you came home that night that your eyes were uncommonly bright, but I just put it down to the Falernian.'

Callistus opened his mouth to protest, but nothing came out of it. All at once in his mind's eye he was no longer sharing a quiet meal with Titus, but reclining beside Zephyrinus in Domna's triclinium, surrounded by scholars and philosophers so eminent in their respective fields that their names would echo through the annals of history. But he had forgotten every face except one, and every voice except the low musical lilt of Mamaea's. Now once again her lovely eyes looked up to meet his; once again a loose tendril of hair brushed her cheek as she tilted her head just a little to speak; once again her slight, sad smile disarmed him…

But she had been a widow in those days, albeit only twenty years old. Since then she had married again – the poignantly named Marcianus – and borne him two children. Callistus had watched them all ride into Rome together when Caracalla and Geta had brought home their father's ashes. To Callistus Mamaea had never seemed more content, or more unattainable, than she had on that bitter-sweet day.

'She's been widowed again, you know,' Titus informed him now, startling him from his reverie with such a jolt that his wine-cup juddered visibly in his hand. 'Marcianus was murdered on the orders of Macrinus, along with everyone else whose face the upstart didn't like when he pulled off his coup against Caracalla. In fact *both* Maesa's daughters are widows again. Soaemias' husband died when he was Governor of Numidia… Callistus, put that cup down before you spill it and ruin my new mosaic.'

'I'm sorry.' Callistus did meekly as he was told, feeling suddenly and stupidly like a shy little boy caught ogling his mother's handmaid. 'Titus, do you mind terribly if I don't finish my honey-cake? I'm afraid I'm not very hungry.' He got up at once and went to his room, leaving Titus chuckling into his napkin.

That night Callistus hardly slept, and when he did, he dreamed – of Mamaea, of Marcia, of some impossibly beautiful creature who was a glorious amalgam of the two. At first this paragon of womanhood stood motionless on a plinth like a goddess, distant and aloof and dressed in gold from head to foot, elevated so far above Callistus' head that she couldn't even see him. But later on she floated down to the ground – which had inexplicably become Titus' new mosaic floor – and walked towards Callistus with her arms held out. When she was standing almost close enough for him to touch, rather than embracing him she unfastened the brooches at her shoulders, letting her robe pool like golden water at her feet. He awoke in a sweat with damp bedclothes tangled about him, and having sponged himself all over with cold water from the pitcher in his room he spent the few hours which remained until sunrise down on his knees in prayer.

He wasn't a natural ascetic like Hippolytus, he told himself; there was no reason for any man to feel ashamed of his attraction to a woman. But he had vowed after Marcia's death that he would never marry or think about a woman in that way again. Now his feelings were in turmoil, ridiculous as it was. Was he under some subtle Satanic attack, he wondered, an occupational hazard for any prominent ambassador of the Kingdom of God? Or was this simply a temptation of the kind which is common to man, or not even a temptation at all, merely something and nothing, to be brushed aside with a shrug and a laugh with his friends? After all, Mamaea was no more attainable as a widow than she had been as another man's wife. He should simply put her out of his mind, which would no doubt be very much easier to do by the cold light of day than it was now, in the sleepless solitude of his bedroom with the demons of darkness prowling around him.

Yet it was not. When he awoke in the morning having fallen asleep where he knelt, his first thought was of Mamaea, and she was no longer conflated in his mind with Marcia.

Nor did the passage of time do anything to alleviate his distress. Indeed, as winter gave way to spring it became abundantly clear that pretending Mamaea and her family didn't exist wasn't going to be an option much longer for anyone. Every other day, it seemed, Rome was regaled with news of the latest exploits of Mamaea's redoubtable mother Julia Maesa. Having been banished by Macrinus to her ancestral home of Emesa because he feared her influence with the army, she had by no means given up hope of securing imperial power for her daughters' sons. She was busily engaged in grooming them for glory – Soaemias' son in particular, but Mamaea's as well – and she was determined that the Senate and People of Rome should learn how remarkable these boys were.

To begin with, she put it about that both of her grandsons were the offspring of Caracalla. Not enough for Maesa that they should be known as his close relations – which of course they were. For her they must be of his seed, since Caracalla even more than his father Severus had been the soldiers' idol.

It would be easy enough to convince people that Soaemias had lain with her cousin, but *Mamaea*? Surely no one would believe that *she* could have done such a thing, Callistus thought in horror; then instantly started to ask himself why he should care.

But it wasn't merely their connection with Caracalla that made Maesa's grandsons' glorification seem assured. Through Maesa herself they were descended from the ancient priest-kings of Emesa, and the older of the two, Soaemias' son Avitus, already served as priest of the sun god Elagabal in his own right. Resplendent in shimmering gold and purple and crowned with a gem-studded chaplet, this boy of fourteen would dance for his god on the steps of Emesa's magnificent temple, built to house a conical black stone which had allegedly fallen from heaven and symbolized Elagabal's phallus. Enormous crowds – including legionaries of Macrinus – would assemble to watch Avitus perform, for he was said to be such a beautiful youth and such a graceful dancer that surely the ichor of the gods must flow in his veins along with the blood of Caracalla. Such radiance *had* to be more than human, or so said everyone who had had the privilege of beholding his dazzling countenance. It was hard to imagine that the mincing and pirouetting of an exotic dancing-boy would impress the common soldiery very much, but apparently Avitus' facial features resembled Caracalla's so strikingly that his unsettling effeminacy tended to be overlooked.

In April there was an eclipse of the sun, which Maesa declared to be a sign of the sun god's displeasure with Macrinus' rule. Soon after that a comet was seen in broad daylight, which was believed to herald the coming of a saviour. So early in May Maesa made her move.

It was Titus as usual who brought the news to Callistus: young Avitus had been hailed as emperor in the camp of the third legion near Emesa, into which he had been smuggled by his supporters at dead of night. Now it seemed there would be all-out bloody warfare between troops loyal to Macrinus and those who had been ensnared by Maesa's propaganda and substantial financial inducements, for she was unimaginably rich. But this war would be fought far away to the east – about as far east as you could go while remaining within the borders of the empire.

'So whose side will the Senate take?' wondered Callistus, rolling up the scroll he had been reading when Titus rushed into his bedroom.

'Isn't it obvious?' Titus responded with a question of his own. 'The Senate hated Caracalla with a passion, because he pandered only to the army. The senators have already ratified Macrinus' elevation of Diadumenianus to the rank of Augustus – co-emperor, if you like – on the grounds, I suppose, that if their enemies can have a beautiful boy emperor, so can *they*, and so that if anything happens to Macrinus, the next member of *his* dynasty will already be established on the throne. And they have declared war: not only on Avitus – or Elagabalus, as everyone seems to be calling him now – but also on Maesa, Soaemias and Mamaea, and Mamaea's son Alexianus into the bargain.'

'Meaning that anyone in Rome could hack down any one of them in the street, or even the whole family, and earn himself a medal rather than a murder charge?' Callistus tried to swallow but found that his mouth was as dry as a ditch in a drought.

'Quite so, except that none of them are actually *in* Rome. Maesa's daughters and their children – including the divine Elagabalus – are all in Emesa with Maesa, consorting with soldiers legally obliged to fight for Macrinus.'

'Then heaven help them! Julia Maesa has signed her own death warrant, and those of all her kinsfolk.'

'Possibly. But Maesa is no fool, and Macrinus very probably *is* one. He will underestimate her at his peril.'

However, the more Callistus discovered over the next few days about the state of affairs in Emesa – not that he was making any conscious effort to find out – the less likely it seemed to him that Maesa and Elagabalus could win the war which their audacity had provoked. They had crack legionary soldiers on their side, it was true, but their general was apparently Elagabalus' tutor Gannys – reputed to be Soaemias' latest lover – who had learnt all he knew about battles from books.

And should I even be *wanting* them to win? Callistus asked himself repeatedly. Should the Bishop of Rome really be wishing – praying, even – for the victory of a fourteen-year-old pagan priest over an officially recognized Head of State? Then again, Macrinus himself was a shameless usurper who had only come to power in the first place because he had engineered the murder of his predecessor. But so far as

Callistus was aware, Macrinus had no particular interest in religion, which made Elagabalus much the more dangerous of the two. A priest, whose ancestors on his mother's side had all been priests before him, Elagabalus would appreciate all too keenly just how potent a force religion could be. During Callistus' lifetime the most systematic persecution of Christians had taken place under one of Rome's most spiritually literate emperors, Marcus Aurelius, when Callistus had been a very small boy. In almost every respect Marcus Aurelius had been more enlightened than most of his predecessors and any of his successors, yet his understanding of religion's power had led him to regard the Christian Church with deep suspicion and attempt to suppress it accordingly. So Callistus was acutely aware that his heart was almost certainly backing the wrong horse, yet his will was not strong enough to rein it in.

The decisive battle between the troops of Macrinus and Elagabalus' rebel forces took place in June, and Gannys proved himself a surprisingly competent commander. Furthermore, it was reported in Rome that when the battle seemed to be going against him nonetheless, Maesa and Soaemias had taken to the field themselves. They had rampaged around it in chariots and even jumped out of them into the path of men who were deserting, challenging them to stand and fight for the brave son of Caracalla. Meanwhile the glittering Elagabalus demonstrated his own courage by charging up and down on his warhorse wearing a patchwork cloak like Caracalla's and brandishing his sword like an avenging angel. Eventually the tide had turned, and it was Macrinus' troops who were deserting in droves to the other side. Macrinus finished up running for his life, but both he and Diadumenianus, who had gone out to Antioch to join him, were hunted down and executed. Elagabalus, dancer and priest and scion of the royal house of Emesa, was now recognized from Syria to Britain as Emperor of Rome.

It was a noticeably subdued Assembly which gathered in

Piso and Valeria's courtyard the Sunday after the announcement was made. Another new emperor, the third in not much more than a year... it was as though the madness which had broken out on the death of Commodus had flared up all over again, and it was anyone's guess what the accession of Maesa's grandson would mean for the empire's Christians. It fell to Callistus to exhort his fearful flock to trust in the one true God who loved them all and was never taken by surprise; nothing could unseat *him* from his throne. But it was a message which Callistus himself needed to take in and hold on to as much as they did.

At first life in the City continued as before. Elagabalus and his entourage remained in the east, gradually dispersing the legions which had accumulated there for Caracalla's Parthian campaigns and sending them back to their permanent bases, since it was scarcely prudent to have such a vast number of armed men massed in one place with nothing particular to do for any length of time. Gannys was also disposed of; though largely responsible for Elagabalus' victory over Macrinus, the young emperor allegedly found his old teacher insufferably domineering. It was said that he felt the same way very often about his mother and grandmother too, but for the time being he needed them as much as they needed him. And so far he had also refrained from launching full-scale reprisals against former supporters of Macrinus, or lopping off the head of anyone who dared criticize his own actions or appearance. Elagabalus might be flamboyant and eccentric, but at least he didn't seem to be congenitally vindictive.

Then in the spring of the following year, news was posted in the forum that the imperial cavalcade was about to start out on its journey home – which was an ironic way of putting it, since most of those undertaking the journey must have felt much more at home in Emesa than they ever would in Rome. Certainly Elagabalus did. It was rumoured that he would have been much happier to stay where he was indefinitely, exercising the privileges of his new-found authority and indulging a precocious appetite for sexual experimentation, copulating enthusiastically with a succession of muscle-bound men as well as with multifarious women and girls. However, Maesa was insistent that he should not repeat the chief mistake of his predecessor: the population of Rome had never set eyes on Macrinus at all.

The stormy love-hate relationship between Julia Maesa and her outlandish grandson was fast becoming the talk of the town. Apparently the indomitable old lady was intent upon Elagabalus making his grand entry into Rome wearing a respectable woollen toga with his hair close-cropped in traditional Roman style, but Elagabalus was equally determined that his people should embrace him for who he was: flowing locks, glittering golden gown, jewel-studded chaplet and all. When Maesa maintained that the poor benighted citizens of the capital were not yet ready to behold such an awesome epiphany and would be horribly shocked, Elagabalus decided to resolve the problem by sending them a portrait of himself in advance. When it arrived, the reaction of the Senate did not bode well. Elagabalus looked more like a bride dressed for her wedding than an emperor of Rome – rumour had it that whenever he lay with a man he actually preferred to be the submissive partner – and beside him in the picture was the conical black stone from Emesa's Temple to the Sun, which he was bringing with him to Rome to be honoured as the supreme god of the universe.

As the day of His Excellency's homecoming drew inexorably closer, so Callistus' thoughts and feelings grew ever more tangled, and his prayers more intense. He dreaded his own reaction to seeing Elagabalus in the flesh – not to mention the great black phallus – and the furore which the spectacle might unleash among the people of Rome. Yet at the same time he could not stop his heart beating faster when he remembered that Mamaea would be coming home too.

In the event, Callistus acknowledged, nothing could have prepared him or anyone else for his first glimpse of Rome's new master, and no picture could have done justice to the bizarre and preposterous reality that was Mamaea's nephew in his gleaming gilded chariot. By now the people of Rome had grown used to being ruled by emperors born in the provinces: Severus and Macrinus had been from Africa, and even the mighty Trajan and his cousin Hadrian, a hundred years before, had been born in Spain. But each of these foreigners had served his time in the Roman army, where he had assimilated Roman ways and learnt how to command the respect of seasoned Roman troops. Elagabalus looked so young, so effete and so generally astonishing that Callistus even forgot for the moment that Mamaea would be riding close behind him.

'Good God,' was all that Priscus could say; as on similar occasions in the past, he had invited Titus and Callistus to watch the proceedings from his rooftop. Neither Titus nor Callistus could think of anything suitable to say at all. Elagabalus wore so much gold – on his head, in his hair and about his person – that he looked as though he had fallen into a molten vat of the stuff fully clothed. His cheeks were stained with rouge and his eyelids with kohl, and the cloak which cascaded from his neck in a shining torrent to his feet had been made from gold interwoven with silk, a fabric Callistus had never seen a male wearing before. If it were true that his soldiers loved him, thought Callistus, it could surely be only because he made them laugh.

Yet Elagabalus, much as he clearly fancied himself shamelessly and revelled in his own imperial glory, did not take pride of place in the procession. This was reserved for the sun god's great black stone, which was borne along on a flower-strewn stretcher laid across the shoulders of two long lines of priests and surrounded by scantily clad boys and girls dancing, clashing cymbals and playing flutes. Anything less like Roman state religion was hard to imagine, Priscus remarked with disgust. Ribald as some of its pagan mythology might be, Roman religious ceremonial was traditionally conducted with consummate dignity.

While Priscus was still regaling his Christian friends with examples of the benefits which Roman paganism had brought to their fatherland over the centuries, Callistus saw Mamaea. He hadn't even been looking for her, yet suddenly she was there, riding with her two children as she had been the last time he'd seen her, but now with no husband to wrap a protective arm around her. Her son Alexianus was now almost as tall as she was, and as unlike Elagabalus as Mamaea was unlike her sister. At twelve years old his hair was still uncropped, but he wore a simple woollen toga of the kind any well-born Roman boy would wear, and no face paint or jewels. His sister Theoclia was respectably dressed too, as was their mother; yet once Callistus had seen them he could look nowhere else. All three seemed so very different from their kinsfolk, and so much not a part of the extravaganza which was going on around them, that Callistus became suddenly yet profoundly convinced that in this quietly dignified mother and her children lay the future of Rome.

This wholly unexpected revelation was as overwhelming as it was disturbing. Over the years Callistus had learnt very well how to recognize the quickening of the Holy Spirit within him for what it was, and he recognized it now. Nor was the experience a fleeting one. As he stood rooted to the spot with his eyes glued to Mamaea's face, his vision took wings and he saw himself patiently explaining the Gospel of Christ to her and her children in the imperial palace on the Palatine Hill. He saw them accepting the message with joy, and then he saw men and angels rejoicing too as he proceeded to baptize all three in the pool at Piso's house. Finally he saw Alexianus enthroned as emperor of Rome: a scion of the Kingdom of Heaven ruling over the greatest empire on earth.

Not that he intended to breathe a word of what he had seen to another living soul. He knew exactly what they would say, even Titus: that Callistus' imagination was running away with him once again. Perhaps it was. Though he knew that his latest fantasy had sprung out of a genuine revelation from God himself, perhaps his infatuation with Mamaea had seized it from the Holy Spirit's grasp and run off with it into the realms of wild speculation.

But he also knew that imagination combined with prayer is one of the most potent forces in the universe, and that a dream consecrated to God is more likely than any other to come true.

CHAPTER TWENTY: MAMAEA

Mamaea closed her eyes in concentration as the slave-boy read on, his richly accented voice painting an ever more extraordinary picture with the words from her precious new scroll. She sat beneath a rose-decked pergola in the gardens of the emperor's palace on the Palatine Hill, but in her mind's eye she was chained up in a subterranean cavern with half a dozen similarly manacled prisoners, all of whom were watching a bizarre sort of underground shadow-play which was being staged exclusively for their benefit. A succession of everyday objects was being carried along behind them, but all they could see was the distorted shadows of these objects flung against the opposite wall by the light of a fire burning at the back of the cave.

It was a singularly strange scenario to be sure, contrived by the philosopher Plato as an analogy of human life, in which he believed that we are prisoners who perceive only distorted shadows of reality. Beyond the material world, Mamaea understood him to be saying, is a spiritual realm which is far more solid and meaningful than the humdrum world of futility and illusion in which mortals are condemned to live. But as Mamaea whiled the morning away in her arbour, lost in thought, Plato's cave-analogy seemed to her to be the truest, cleverest, deepest insight into human existence – and her own in particular – she had ever encountered.

Perhaps it was the fact that the slave-boy was Greek and therefore reading in his own native language that made Plato's text leap so readily to life. Or maybe it was simply that Mamaea had dreamt of owning a copy of Plato's magnum opus *The Republic* for so long that her excitement at having acquired one at last was breathing fire into its every word.

She could have read the scroll perfectly well for herself, highly educated as she was in both Greek and Latin. But having sent the children off to their tutor for their own daily dose of education there was nothing Mamaea liked better than to relax among the roses, drinking in their fragrance and beauty while someone else did the reading for her. Sometimes she would stroll about as she listened, admiring the perfection of individual blooms. Sometimes she would sit back with her eyes closed, just as she was doing now, and escape entirely into the world of her imagination. Her own pampered existence, hemmed about by imperial protocols and pretensions and blighted by the sneering disdain of Soaemias and her son, often seemed as restricting and artificial as that of the prisoners in Plato's cave.

It was so thrilling, so liberating, for her to imagine that there really might be more to life than politics and power-struggles, wealth and ostentation, in a world where no clear thinker could any longer believe in the myths which had sustained his – or her – ancestors. Poor men might dream of gold and silver, the disenfranchised and downtrodden might dream of imposing their will upon others, Mamaea reflected, but when you had basked in the lap of luxury all your life and grown up surrounded by servants whose only function was to be at your personal beck and call, you knew only too well that these things brought no lasting satisfaction. There was a limit to the number of baths in asses' milk you could genuinely appreciate, and to the range of pointless and humiliating tasks you could set your army of minions to perform – though neither Soaemias nor Elagabalus seemed to have found that limit yet.

Elagabalus, Mamaea knew, believed in the importance of spiritual things at least as much as she did. For a fourteen-year-old boy, he took his duties as Elagabal's high priest very seriously indeed. He was descended from the distinguished priest-kings of Emesa, after all – as was Mamaea herself – and a native of Syria, where many of Rome's most outlandish foreign cults had come from. Half his waking life consisted of offering sacrifices or performing his famous sacred dances for his god's gratification.

Unfortunately the other half consisted of indulging in precocious sexual promiscuity. At fourteen Mamaea had been a timorous virgin about to be married to a man of her parents' choosing, whilst so far as she could tell Elagabalus revelled in lying indiscriminately with men, women and children as the fancy took him. He saw no reason to feel guilty about this debauchery whatsoever, since Elagabal demanded no stricter moral standards of his priests than he did of his regular worshippers.

But Elagabalus' fanciful beliefs and exotic rituals bore little resemblance to the kind of spirituality which interested Mamaea. It was the all-powerful, all-knowing God of the philosophers – and of the Jews and Christians – she found the most intriguing.

Unexpectedly her reverie was interrupted just then by what seemed to be the sound of someone else walking in the garden. This was disconcerting; Mamaea was used to having her leafy haven deliciously to herself in a morning, except for when the slaves who tended it made their scheduled rounds. The palace gardens were extensive but this particular area was private, accessible only from the apartments of Mamaea and her sister, and only the two of them and their children, guests and servants ever enjoyed them. In fact Soaemias rarely did; she was always too afraid that the sunlight might darken her lead-whitened skin, and besides, her elaborate toilette would keep her and her long-suffering attendants busy until lunch-time at least. When the sound did not come again, Mamaea decided she must have imagined it, and turned her attention back to Plato.

She had been fascinated by what the Greeks called philosophy for as long as she could remember. As a child she had always been asking questions: why does the moon get bigger and smaller? where do the stars go in the daytime? how did the world begin? Her aunt Julia Domna who had doted on her, and to whom she had been devoted in return, had found Mamaea's questions delightful, and done all she could to keep them coming. Moreover it had pleased Domna no end that her niece had never been content with trite or fanciful answers involving rivalry between jealous deities, or the great Sky Father copulating with the Earth Mother, or some heavenly warrior vanquishing the monsters of darkness and chaos.

Yet to Mamaea the answers of the philosophers had seldom seemed any more convincing. Had not Thales of Miletus maintained that the earth stayed in place by floating like a log on the ocean? And had not Anaxagoras of Clazomenae held that the sun was a stone, comparable in size to the Peloponnese? Unsubstantiated and bland assertions such as these did not merely fail to convince, but threatened to rob the universe of its mystery into the bargain.

As for the so-called mystery religions from Egypt and Persia which had become so fashionable among the Romans in recent years, these had little more to recommend them than the old gods of Olympus so far as Mamaea could see. They had their clandestine initiations and rituals, and they promised their adherents preferential treatment in the afterlife, but their claims were based on fairy tales no more credible than the mythologies of Homer and Hesiod.

Plato, on the other hand, had attempted to ground his doctrines on rational principles, on what could be deduced by the mind or discerned by the enlightened spirit. And then there were the startling teachings of the Jews and Christians to consider too. Where the mysteries of Isis and Mithras offered fantasy, the Jews and Christians offered history; where the mysteries offered secret ceremonies and wild speculation, the Jews and Christians offered revelations from the Almighty Creator himself, based on scrupulously authenticated texts documenting the experiences of real people over a period of hundreds of years. Furthermore, for both Jews and Christians, ethics and belief went hand in hand, and, unlike the gods of Olympus – or of Persia or Syria – their God had every right to demand good behaviour of his devotees because he was believed to be good himself. Yet these people spoke much of mercy as well as of righteousness, and maintained that their faith enabled them to escape both chance and fate.

So many questions about philosophy and religion continued to baffle and fascinate Mamaea in equal measure that she never ceased to be amazed at how most adults seemed to have grown out of asking them. It wasn't as if they had found any more satisfying answers than she had. Certainly Soaemias hadn't. Probably for most people it was just that other, more urgent, questions got in the way: where will my next meal come from? will anyone want to marry me? will I be able to give my daughter a dowry?

Naturally neither Mamaea nor any of her close relatives had ever had to worry about things like that. But they had known sorrow like anyone else. Wealth didn't exempt you or those dearest to you from being mortal. Still in her early thirties, Mamaea had already been widowed twice, and although both her marriages had been arranged for her by her parents, each of her husbands had been kind to her and she had grieved for them deeply when they died. She had been especially fond of her second husband Marcianus, the father of her two children. She still missed him terribly, so much so that thinking suddenly of him now brought unbidden tears to her eyes.

All at once she heard the sound of unexplained movement

in the garden a second time. Could it be a cat? Just birds perhaps? Somehow she did not think so, but when she bade the slave-boy stop reading for a moment while she listened for the sound again, there was nothing to hear. Perhaps she had imagined it after all.

The one person she still missed more than Marcianus was her beloved Aunt Domna. When Mamaea and Soaemias had been growing up, Domna had always taken far more interest in them than their mother had done. Maesa's daylight hours had been swallowed up in readying herself for the nights when she would entertain her rich and influential lovers, and little girls getting under foot were given short shrift. Soaemias had coped by mimicking her mother's behaviour like a diminutive shadow, becoming obsessed with clothes and cosmetics from an early age and, as she got older, with ensnaring desirable men. She had also enjoyed bullying Mamaea, ridiculing her mousy appearance and bookish habits and boasting that the gods had given *her* – their sweetheart Soaemias – a double portion of beauty, whilst Mamaea had got all the brains, a booby prize if ever there was one. For what manner of man would want a woman who was cleverer than he was? Meanwhile Mamaea had taken refuge in her reading, withdrawing further and further into her private world the more Soaemias mocked her for doing so. When Domna had noted what was happening she had taken Mamaea the Mouse (as Soaemias delighted in calling her) under her wing, assuring her that she was easily as pretty as Soaemias, just as Soaemias was in fact much cleverer than she liked to pretend. Domna had talked to Mamaea by the hour about what they took to calling their 'big questions'; she had given her books in both Greek and Latin and taught her to read them, and even introduced her to the scriptures of the Hebrews, in their Greek translation.

These Mamaea had found particularly enthralling from the outset, just as Domna herself had. The Jewish religion so exquisitely combined a sense of reverence for the Divine with the realism of history. There was mystery without absurdity or wizardry, and the stories of God's encounters with human beings were so very strange that surely no one could have invented them.

Judaism's wayward offspring Christianity was more fascinating still, but Mamaea could never think about this baffling and often secretive sect for very long without being catapulted back in time to the symposium at which she had been introduced to its singularly eloquent exponent Callistus. Most Beautiful, the word meant in Greek, and she still couldn't help thinking that she had never met anyone more appropriately named. Although he'd been the Christian bishop's subordinate, Callistus had done most of the talking, just as Aaron had for Moses, and apparently now he was bishop himself – whatever that meant. She knew that it certainly didn't mean 'priest'. The Christians were at pains to point out that they needed no earthly mediator between themselves and God because Jesus the founder of their cult had been both God and man at the same time.

So compelling had she found Callistus' words – not to mention his gaze and demeanour – that she had subsequently devoted some serious attention to finding out more about the Christian faith. But it hadn't been easy, when she'd had no one to talk to who knew any more about it than she did. And the few Christians who had crossed her path over the years since then had been frustratingly coy about what they really believed. Although their sect had not been systematically persecuted for a long time, on a local and individual level it could be a very different matter.

Callistus, however, seemed to enjoy nothing so much as expounding his beliefs to others. Although he had struck her as a quiet and even shy young man when he had entered Domna's triclinium with Zephyrinus, once he was given the opportunity to speak about his faith he had bubbled over like a boiling pot with the excitement of doing so. Yet he hadn't been too engrossed to notice *her*. When their eyes met – which had happened much more frequently than it ought to have done during the course of a single evening – the look in Callistus' had been unmistakeable.

As a younger woman Mamaea had never been truly in love. Prior to encountering Callistus, she wasn't even sure she would have known what it meant. Afterwards, she had known all too well that it meant thinking about him every moment of every day, and seeing his face whenever she closed her eyes. Not very much later she had married Marcianus, who had cared for her assiduously, and to whom she had always remained faithful, even after his death. But she had never loved him in the way she knew she could have loved Callistus.

Now that she was back in Rome and a prominent member of the imperial household, she could have sent for Callistus whenever she liked. Yet she did not do so, because she was sure he would regard it as highly inappropriate. It wasn't that there was any other woman in his life – she had found out that much at least – but she had been told by several of her acquaintances who claimed to know these things that most Christian clergy were celibate, and bishops especially.

Would that the same were true of the priests of Elagabal... At least with Maesa his grandmother on hand to rein him in, young Elagabalus' alarming sexual appetite wasn't about to devour the very empire itself. Ever since his accession Mamaea's own mother had been ruler of Rome in all but name. She had even attended meetings of the Senate, and from time to time taken Soaemias with her. (Predictably Soaemias had been bored by the whole affair and subsequently set up a 'women's senate' of her own, to discuss fashion and social etiquette.) But lately Maesa's little puppet – who was rapidly becoming as pig-headed as he was profligate – had succeeded on a number of occasions in outwitting her and getting his own way, just as he had over the manner of his entry into Rome. Most spectacularly he had eliminated Gannys, his mother's lover and his own former tutor, even though the scholar and unlikely warlord had been responsible for leading his pupil's troops to victory over Macrinus, thus winning him the principate.

When the truth came out Maesa had been furious, and Mamaea more distraught even than Soaemias, for Gannys had been a level-headed adviser to the whole family, as well as a surprisingly capable general and an excellent teacher. He had been a good influence not only on Elagabalus but over Mamaea's two children, whom he had taught as well, and since Marcianus' death he had frequently been Mamaea's confidant – at least until Soaemias had grown jealous of their relationship and set about seducing him. But Elagabalus maintained that Gannys no longer pleased him, because he kept trying to tell him what to do – which was completely out of order now that he was ruler over half the world.

The man Mamaea would most have liked to engage as her children's tutor in Gannys' place was Domitius Ulpianus, a distinguished lawyer and scholar of outstanding integrity who had been a friend of Maesa's for many years and taken an avuncular interest in Alexianus and Theoclia since they had been tiny babies. But Elagabalus had already had Ulpianus banished from Rome for meddling in matters which did not concern him. So Mamaea had reluctantly agreed to entrust her children's education to another man of Maesa's choosing.

Just then she became aware that the slave-boy had stopped reading without being bidden, and not only because it was obvious that his mistress's attention had drifted as she had become absorbed in thoughts of her own. This time it was he who had heard something odd, so for a few moments they listened for the sound together. But again there was nothing more to hear, so she bade him read on; the cadence of his voice was so pleasing to the ear even though she was finding it increasingly difficult to concentrate on the words themselves. With philosophy this was all too often what happened in any case: one nugget of wisdom arrestingly expressed by the writer could set off such a meandering train of thought in Mamaea's mind that the rest of the paragraph or even whole columns would have to be re-read because she had lost track of what they were saying.

Because of her own love of learning, Mamaea had resolved very early on that Theoclia would be educated to the same high standard as Alexianus. She was every bit as clever as he was, though admittedly not half so studious. It was curious, Mamaea thought, how the siblings in her family down the generations always seemed to come in pairs of opposites. As a girl Domna had been the bookish one while Maesa was flighty; Mamaea had been like Domna, Soaemias like Maesa; now Alexianus was the scholar and Theoclia the wild child who would no doubt give her mother many sleepless nights as she got older. Perhaps each sibling simply reacted against the other; it was only once Domna was dead that Maesa had calmed down enough to reveal her true ability and ambition.

If only she would content herself with ruling through Elagabalus and leave Mamaea's son out of her scheming! But Maesa coveted greatness for *both* of her grandsons, and was too canny to pin all her hopes on one as volatile as Elagabalus. She had even put it about that both boys were actually the bastard sons of Caracalla, because she knew how the legions had loved him. This had made Mamaea angrier than she could ever remember being: as if *she* would have lain with her own cousin, or with any man who was not her husband! But when she had plucked up the courage to confront her mother about it, demanding to know what kind of woman wants the world to think that her own daughter is a shameless adulteress, Maesa had been quite unable to understand what all the fuss was about. 'Don't you think Alexianus would make as least as good an emperor as Elagabalus?' she had demanded of Mamaea in return, and there was little Mamaea could say to that because it was hard to imagine how he could possibly turn out to be worse.

Apart from when they took their lessons together, Mamaea tried to keep Alexianus away from Elagabalus as much as she could. Soaemias' son had set a bad example to his playmates from early childhood, and since Alexianus was two years the younger, it might have been all too easy for Elagabalus to lead him badly astray. There was nothing the child Elagabalus had liked better than stealing his mother's cosmetics to paint his own face, or spying on her handmaids when they were bathing, or touching them where he shouldn't and making them cry. He would make other boys play games where they had to strip off their garments one by one as forfeits, or get them drunk on stolen wine until they didn't know what they were doing at all. Yet Soaemias found his antics endearing, and had seen no harm in his running round her chambers naked or dressed up in her clothes, or sleeping in her bed with her at night until he was nine or ten years old. Apparently he had even slept there while she was entertaining her lovers, and some said this was how he had acquired his interest in sex at such a tender age. Thankfully Alexianus had always been far too shy to want to do any of the sorts of things his cousin did. But Mamaea was taking no chances.

At that moment the disturbing sound of movement came yet again, so unmistakeably that Mamaea and her attendant both started simultaneously, and Mamaea decided that it would have to be investigated.

Bidding the slave come with her, Mamaea stood up and set out at once in the direction from which the sound had come. There were many formal areas in the palace gardens, with neatly clipped hedges and serried ranks of scarlet poppies standing to attention, but this was not one of them. Rambling roses and rampant jasmine scrambled over archways and trellises; there were fig trees, apple trees and olives, statuesque acanthus and swathes of lavender, all of which could provide ideal cover for someone anxious to avoid discovery. But surely there was no way that anyone who wasn't connected with Mamaea's immediate family could have got into this part of the gardens without alerting their guards?

Emerging from a tunnel of greenery, Mamaea and her companion came within sight of the fish-pond upon which all pathways through the vegetation converged. At once Mamaea caught her breath, for a girl she had never seen before was strolling by the poolside. As Mamaea watched her, the girl dropped to her knees and peered wide-eyed into the water as though her attention had suddenly been caught by the bright metallic beauty of the goldfish gliding in and out among the rushes.

However, when she had been kneeling there entranced for some while, Mamaea realized it was not the fishes' beauty which had captivated the girl, but her own. This was scarcely surprising, for she was astonishingly lovely from head to toe: slender and graceful as the reeds which surrounded her, with skin as flawless as Parian marble and a bright halo of hair which shone like the pool's still water in the brilliant morning sun. The face which the halo encircled was exquisitely painted, the eyes enlarged and drawn up at the outer corners and the lids smokily darkened. Lengthened lashes brushed cheeks as daintily rouged as ripening plums; the mouth was wide, the lips red and full and gently upturned in pleasure as solipsistic as that of the legendary Narcissus himself.

Who could this startling creature be? She was no new slave-girl of Soaemias', that was for sure, for not only was her face made up like a society bride's, but her gown was spun from oriental silk and fastened at the shoulders by heavy golden brooches. She looked more like a statue of Venus commissioned at vast expense by a plutocrat than any sort of servant.

Then as Mamaea stood staring, the girl raised her head and looked straight at her, and she wasn't a girl at all, but Elagabalus.

Mamaea blushed red as a rosehip, but Elagabalus wasn't in the least embarrassed. It was common knowledge that he had enjoyed dressing up in his mother's clothes and using her make-up ever since he'd been eating solid food; why should he care that Mamaea and her slave had come upon him looking as he most liked to look? In fact it dawned on her slowly that he had *wanted* her to see him like this: not as an effeminate boy, eccentric and grotesque, but as a maiden on the cusp of womanhood, as lovely as Mamaea was herself. This was why he was here, at a time when he knew that she would be here too, and this was why he had made sure she would hear him moving about, and seek him out.

'Aunt Mamaea,' he drawled, still smiling, in a voice not artificially high, yet subtly softened to sound unnervingly feminine. Then he rose to his feet with fastidious elegance and walked towards her; ignoring her slave-boy completely, he took her hands in his he looked her full in the face and asked, 'Don't *you* think I look particularly beautiful this morning?'

What was she to say? He still looked just as beautiful as he had when kneeling at the poolside, even though she now knew who he was; he was a vision at once sickeningly beguiling and bewitchingly repugnant. Even more confusingly, there had been no obvious sarcasm in the tone of his question, and as he awaited her response he seemed genuinely to be seeking her approval. Perhaps it was all part of an elaborate joke at her expense, or maybe – and this was the first time the thought had ever occurred to her – just *maybe*, her nephew really *did* wish he were her niece? Finding herself unable to answer his question at all, Mamaea said, 'Shouldn't you be at your lessons? I don't know what you are doing here at this time in the morning.'

'Oh, I don't have lessons any more, Aunt Mamaea. I am the emperor of Rome. No one can presume to be my teacher, *or* try to tell me what to do.'

'No. I don't suppose they can.' Mamaea found herself struggling to free her hands from his grasp, because the intensity with which he was gazing into her eyes was becoming unbearable. But he only tightened his grip and said, 'Don't go away, Aunt Mamaea. We spend so little time together. I thought you might like to walk with me in the garden until it is time for me to meet my friend.'

You've arranged to *meet* someone? Looking like that?

Mamaea thought, but did not say; Elagabalus, knowing exactly what was going through her mind, said, 'Oh yes, this is just how he likes me best.' Then lowering his eyes so that the luscious lashes swept his cheeks he added, 'Don't *you* like me this way, Aunt Mamaea?'

Mamaea was beginning to be afraid that if she could not pull her hands free very quickly she was going to disgorge her breakfast all over them. Not content with shocking her to the core, was Elagabalus now bent on seducing her as well? When at last she had collected herself sufficiently to speak, she heard herself saying, 'I liked you the way the gods made you, Elag... Avitus. I liked you before...'

'Before I found out who they meant me to be? How your words would sadden me if they were true! But I don't believe they *are* true, Aunt Mamaea. I don't believe you *ever* really liked me.' (Was that menace in his sultry voice, or merely regret?) 'Still, it matters not, since Hierocles likes me just the way you see me today. He will be here any minute – he's with my mother now – for I fear that you have stumbled on our favourite trysting place. So if you do not wish to intrude upon our intimacy, I regret that you must go inside after all.'

Hierocles? Hierocles the charioteer? Again Mamaea's mind was reeling, but again she succeeded in curbing her tongue. Hierocles was a Carian slave who had come to Elagabalus' notice when he had fallen from his chariot in the Games; his helmet had been knocked off as he fell, revealing the most glorious mane of tawny hair and handsome face His Excellency had ever seen. After this broken angel had been lifted insensible from the sand, Elagabalus had sent his own physicians to ensure he was properly mended, and later visited him personally during his convalescence. But Mamaea had had no idea that the smitten emperor's interest in the fellow had been anything more than a flash in the pan and had persisted beyond supervising his recovery. Now it seemed that the unlikely couple were pursuing a relationship even more irregular and inappropriate than any of Elagabalus' previous liaisons, none of which had been more than a one night stand.

So it was with relief rather than reluctance that Mamaea did as her nephew suggested, and took her slave and her scroll of Plato back into her chambers. But the philosopher's spell had been broken and she could find no further solace in his words. When Alexianus and Theoclia returned from their lessons they found their mother sitting alone in her bedroom, sunk into a deep melancholy from which she would not be roused. She had allowed herself to wonder where an empire with Elagabalus at its helm might end up, and could see no outcome for the voyage but shipwreck.

CHAPTER TWENTY ONE: CALLISTUS

Callistus stepped out into the freshness of the early spring morning and filled his lungs with its cool clear air. Winter in the City had been damp and unhealthy, summer would be torrid and equally unhealthy, but the Roman springtime had a loveliness all of its own, and there were few finer places to appreciate that loveliness than in Titus' courtyard garden. Here the fruit trees were bursting into bloom, bees hummed along the borders, butterflies flitted to and fro across the pathways, and everything was fragrant with hope and promise. Callistus felt the need of hope very keenly, just as his lungs craved the fresh air, for since Maesa's increasingly independent young grandson had begun flexing his imperial muscles the political atmosphere had begun to feel as oppressive as the winter weather.

An hour or so from now Gaius, Urbanus and Asterius would arrive for morning prayers, as they had done every day since Callistus' installation as bishop. It was these times of deep spiritual fellowship which kept him going, along with Titus' undemanding hospitality and the freedom this afforded him to study, think, and oversee the welfare of his flock. Titus had insisted on Callistus' staying with him indefinitely even though he could no longer find time for visiting his host's vineyards or even keeping his accounts. One of Titus' freedmen did the bulk of that now, on Callistus' recommendation. Callistus would willingly have paid Titus for his own keep from the tithes and offerings which he and his fellow ministers received from the rest of the believers, but Titus would have none of it.

Callistus was happy, on the whole, with the way the Roman Church was evolving under his care. With Hippolytus gone – though there was little he wouldn't have given to win him back – disputes over doctrine were fewer and further between, and much less vitriolic. As a result, not only was the congregation growing in size once more, but the message Callistus had been sharing with it every Sunday in different ways seemed to be hitting home: it wasn't conforming to external standards that mattered, or even participating in rituals such as baptism and communion, but welcoming the Holy Spirit into your heart to change you from within. This theme formed the basis of all the teaching given to catechumens; nor were the baptized believers left to work out their own salvation from one week to the next without the support of others on the same spiritual journey. Many of the elders and widows opened their homes to groups of the faithful who were eager to pray and study the scriptures together in order to keep one another on track and share their joys and sorrows along the way. It was especially gratifying to see men and women, Jews and Gentiles, slaves and free, praying and studying together as equals.

If only he were not so concerned that Elagabalus was about to embark on some harebrained religious campaign of his own... It was less than a year since the emperor and his entourage had returned to Rome, but the atmosphere in the City had changed significantly since then, and not for the better. It had been obvious from the outset that Elagabalus was seriously eccentric; later many had concluded that he was perverted and depraved. But at least he hadn't seemed paranoid or congenitally cruel; he hadn't made it his business to exterminate every last man who had served Macrinus or to silence anyone who ventured to voice his own discontent with the current regime.

Alas, this was no longer true. Since emerging from his grandmother's shadow, Elagabalus had begun to show himself as savage as he was self-indulgent. Having experimented by eliminating his own mentor Gannys, he had since put to death large numbers of people who had dared to criticize his behaviour or displease him in any way at all. Macrinus' supporters were hunted and put down like stray dogs. Governors of provinces were liquidated if they had not at once declared for Elagabalus when he'd made his bid for power. The faintest whisper of conspiracy was enough to seal the fate of anyone whose name was breathed in connection with it. A certain Seius Carus – grandson of the Urban Prefect Fuscianus who had sentenced Callistus to Sardinia's mines – was killed on the pretext that he had formed some kind of illicit soldiers' league. But everyone knew that the young man had died because he was rich, intelligent and influential.

No doubt some people really were plotting against Elagabalus, Callistus reflected, out of sheer desperation. They could not bear to sit back and do nothing when past experience and common sense were telling them all too insistently where the emperor and his administration were heading. Even respectable senators had allegedly contemplated seizing the throne for themselves, not through personal ambition but out of their deep-seated sense of duty to Rome.

So far Elagabalus had not interfered directly in the life of the Church, for which small mercy Callistus could only thank heaven. In fact he had offended Rome's staunchest pagans more profoundly than her Christians, through his promotion of Syria's gods at the Roman pantheon's expense. One of his first independent actions as emperor had been to start building a temple to Elagabal on the Palatine Hill itself – the

Elagabalium – in flagrant Asiatic style. Before it had even been completed he was sacrificing droves of cattle and sheep there daily, in person, and compelling senators and high-ranking officials of every hue to stand in solemn attendance dressed like a chorus of Bacchantes. Military prefects and magistrates wearing gauzy Phoenician robes were made to prance about carrying the entrails of victims in golden bowls while semi-naked boys and girls sang and danced around them or – worse still – Elagabalus danced for them himself.

It was even rumoured that His Excellency had been planning on emulating the dancing priests of Phrygian Cybele who had had themselves castrated in order to render their worship purer and more powerful, until Maesa inconveniently reminded him that all emperors need heirs. So he'd had to content himself with being circumcised instead, which had led some people to conclude that he might be toying with the idea of becoming a Jew.

This seemed to Callistus about as likely as Soaemias becoming a Vestal Virgin, particularly since Clemens the freedman from the palace had recently been to warn him that Elagabalus was thinking seriously of decreeing that every Roman citizen – Jews included – must make a public offering to Elagabal. Callistus found this distinctly worrying, because if Jews, who had traditionally enjoyed exemption from the imperial cult, were forced to comply with a ruling such as this, there was no way that the Christians would escape. Callistus himself might do so, since his irregular legal status meant that he had never been made a Roman citizen. But many of his congregation would not.

So far, however, no such decree had been issued, because Elagabalus had been preoccupied with other more pressing concerns. Maesa's comment about his need for heirs must have hit home, because in spite of his own extreme youth, the emperor had decided to get married. Not that he didn't have bastards in plenty already – or at least, women claiming that their children were his – but to give him legitimate sons he had promptly taken as his wife a high-born woman Julia Cornelia Paula, whose pedigree as a member of the Roman aristocratic establishment was impeccable. What this gently-bred lady made of being wed to a promiscuous Syrian dancing-boy Callistus could not begin to imagine; but receiving the title Empress of Rome presumably constituted a warped kind of compensation.

It certainly did nothing to reform her husband's sexual delinquencies. Not long after marrying Paula, Elagabalus had announced that he had also 'married' his Carian charioteer Hierocles; and as if this were not irregular enough, he had allegedly taken to quitting the palace at night in disguise and selling his body on the streets of the Suburra – quite cheaply, so Callistus had been told – for the sheer thrill of the experience. Whether his customers were men or women, and what gender they thought *he* belonged to when they paid him in advance for his services, was a topic of heated debate in Rome's bathhouses. Callistus had heard it said more than once that Elagabalus' sole reason for lying with any woman other than Paula was so that she could teach him what she knew about pleasing men. (Apparently to please his husband Hierocles even more Elagabalus had also taken up cookery and spinning.)

Quite apart from the business of producing an heir, the conscientious emperor was further burdened with the need to espouse a suitably majestic lifestyle. Like Midas of old, Elagabalus seemed to think that every object he touched or used – even the pot in which he relieved himself – should be made of gold, dyed purple or drenched in nard. The cushions on which he reclined were purple with golden tassels, Callistus had heard, and stuffed with feathers from the underside of partridges' wings. Even in private he reputedly dined on the tongues of peacocks and nightingales, the combs of roosters and flamingoes' brains, whilst his pet lions ate parrots, and his horses grapes. When entertaining his fawning friends, novelty was as important as expense: fish would be served in blue sauce so that they seemed to be swimming in the sea; live birds or even dancing-girls would be concealed under tureens or inside cakes and pies ready to burst forth and assail the diners' ears with their squawking and laughter respectively. By all accounts Elagabalus wasn't without a sense of humour himself; he deemed it uproariously funny to serve his guests rice cooked with pearls on which they would crack their teeth, or present them with elaborate desserts which turned out to be made of wax or clay. He loved sending extravagant gifts to his favourites, but was even fonder of sending them dead dogs or jars of flies. Meanwhile he took delight in appointing hairdressers, acrobats and actors to high office, which many of the common people found almost as amusing as he did. But those to whom the glory of Rome was important were outraged, and pretty well anyone who was capable of seeing anything beyond the end of his nose was becoming increasingly anxious for the fate of civilization itself.

Still, Callistus reminded himself, worry is only misdirected prayer, and though our emperor might wish to seem gifted with the touch of King Midas, it's our God who truly turns all to gold and specializes in transforming tragedy into triumph.

But before he could offer his current concerns up to heaven on this bright clear morning, one of Titus' slaves came out into the garden and called softly from behind him, 'I'm sorry, Master Callistus, but your presence is required in the atrium.'

'Gaius and the others are here already?' asked Callistus; he must have spent longer in unproductive fretting than he had thought.

'No, Master Callistus, it's someone else wanting to see you. A woman; I don't know who she is.'

'A woman? Did she seem distressed?' The members of his congregation knew not to call on their bishop before noon except in dire emergency.

'To be honest she did not, master, but if you'll forgive me, she did seem like the sort of woman who won't take no for an answer. At least, that's what Master Titus said.'

'Very well, Aratus. I will see her.'

Reluctantly he followed the slave back indoors, where the woman was awaiting him – a woman looking not unlike many who had approached him for help, though judging from the expression on her face she expected the good bishop to be much more shocked to find such a one as her fetching up on his doorstep than he evidently was.

For this was no gently-born Roman matron or orphaned maiden in need of the Church's protection. Callistus' visitor was a woman of the streets festooned with gaudy jewellery and swathed in clashing colours; her unbound hair – or was it a wig? – was yellow as egg-yolk and her face was crustily painted. Without giving Callistus space to react, she stepped forward and presumed to take both of his hands in her own.

'Bishop Callistus,' she drawled, savouring each syllable as though it were a smooth rich sauce in her mouth. 'I do believe that at close quarters you seem even worthier of your name than you do when studied from a safe distance. Forgive my importunity, but I need to speak with you alone.' She eyed Titus' slave who was still hovering in the background.

'Speak away, my lady; you have my full attention,' Callistus replied, noting the unexpected elegance of the hands clasping his. It was evident that his visitor was not given to supplementing her income by washing dishes or scrubbing floors. 'I regret that it is not my custom to meet with any woman alone when it can be avoided.'

'Then you must make an exception in my case.' She fixed his eyes with her own; despite the garishness of their setting these were more like diamonds than cheap coloured glass, and disconcertingly compelling. Then switching without effort from Latin into Greek she said, 'Come, let us walk in your garden, for the day is most beautiful too.' Smiling at her own slick pun upon his name she walked uninvited to the peristyle doors which still stood open revealing the paradise beyond. And since she had kept a firm hold on one of Callistus' hands, he found himself walking there too.

Once outside she didn't say anything at all for a while; she simply moved among the spring flowers leading him after her, seemingly enchanted by everything she saw. She paused to admire the drifts of anemones and tiny irises which spilled over the edges of the paths. She took the unfolding bud of an early rose in her free hand and held it in front of her face to relish its fragrance, then poked it under Callistus' chin inviting him to do the same; when he drew back tactfully she only smiled again and sashayed on. She trailed her fingers through the herb beds and cherry blossom, then held their pollen-dusted tips to her nose; her long polished nails were as red as her lips. Lingering by the pool which every peristyle garden must have as its centrepiece, she looked down with obvious pleasure at the reflection of herself and Callistus holding hands. Callistus looked down too, and though he did not feel as embarrassed as he probably should have done, he did find the spectacle disturbing. At length he was led to a shady stone seat where two could sit side by side, but only just. It was surrounded by tumbling jasmine, and here the woman decided that they were sufficiently screened from the rest of the world for her business with him to be conducted.

'You see, Bishop Callistus,' she began – or was she still using his name as an adjective? – 'I have observed you from a distance on several occasions, and found you unexpectedly appealing to look upon. But you need not be anxious: I'm not here to lead you into temptation. For I have also listened to you speak, and been equally impressed by what my ears were telling me. You strike me as a man who knows and loves God just as I do, a man who has found the pearl of great price and, rather than keeping it for himself, delights in sharing his discovery with others. Now don't misunderstand me: *I* am no follower of Christ, since I need no intermediary to liaise between me and my Lord, but I have attended your Assembly in disguise, dressed as you see me today. Oh yes: I must wear many different masks, for how else could I walk the streets of this City and not be known?'

Callistus very nearly succeeded in masking his own incredulity. 'You are...?'

'No; do not say it.' His companion put her – his – blossom-scented fingers to Callistus' lips now rather than his own. 'I am merely a servant of Almighty God, as I believe you are yourself, which is precisely why I have come to see you. For he gifted you prodigiously when he chose you as his vessel, just as he also chose me: you have a winning way with words and with people, which causes the hearts of your audience to be wondrously softened to receive God's Spirit within them. Meanwhile he has given *me* unimaginable power, to inaugurate his celestial kingdom here in the world of men. You and I have been called by Elagabal himself, Callistus, though you may never have called him by that name until today! To work together, to cause his will to be done on earth as it is in heaven.'

Any facility Callistus had formerly had with words spectacularly failed him. It wasn't that he had nothing to say; rather, he could not think where to begin. He was convinced that Elagabalus must indeed have attended the Assembly, and listened long and hard enough to be able to allude to its parables and its best known prayer in his own conversation, but not enough to understand why its bishop was not now sharing his excitement. Elagabalus himself was becoming so feverishly excited by whatever grand vision his god had sent him that his painted eyes were burning like two flaming beacons in his head. Unable to keep his dream to himself any longer His Excellency plunged on, 'Until now, Rome and the world have been noisy with the ranting of rival priests and prophets and the clamour of ignorant men worshipping thousands of deities in as many languages and styles as there are peoples on this planet. Yet they have all been groping in the dark for the truth which only the enlightened few such as you and I have long understood: that there is but one God who is the source of all life and who is worthy of our veneration! Now it is time for the hubbub of the cults to be harmonized, because God has revealed to me that all the people for whom I am responsible – every man, woman and child in the Roman empire – is to honour him by his true name Elagabal, and in his true form as the Sun upon whom we all depend.'

'I see.' So Clemens had been right, as he usually was, meaning that Callistus could no longer afford to sit and listen in silence to Elagabalus' rhetoric. The sweetness of the morning had soured in his nostrils and the vivid colours of the flowers and the butterflies had faded for him as though the sun of which His Excellency spoke had gone behind a cloud. He ventured, 'And you have shared this revelation with the priests of Jupiter too, and those of Isis, and Mithras, and those of the deified emperors who ruled before you?'

'Not with all of them, no, though there are one or two men and women of discernment among them who I am sure will come to perceive its glory and appreciate the sincerity of the one who is urging them to embrace it! But fear not, Callistus – for I perceive that you *are* afraid – I shall not prevent anyone from continuing to worship whatever god or goddess he or she chooses. I shall merely insist on his acknowledgement that each of these deities represents but one face of Elagabal himself, one ray of the Sun's brilliance, as it were. Thus everyone in my empire – and in time, the whole human race – will come to realize that we are all brothers and sisters, children of the same Father! And not merely human beings either, but every living creature that walks or crawls or slides upon the ground, and every plant which grows up toward the source of its existence... all are related to one another, members of the same universal family. Do not the flowers that delight us here in your garden recognize this truth already? Don't they instinctively turn toward the sunlight and open their petals when they feel its warmth upon them? They are wiser than we are, Callistus, because they know without anyone telling them where the true source of their nourishment is to be found. But now, *you* tell *me* why you seem so disconsolate. Is not my vision a fine one?'

'It would be a fine thing indeed for all of humanity to live in brotherhood under the one true God and undertake to care for the world he created,' Callistus conceded. 'But if I have learnt one thing in my limited time as leader of the Roman Church it is that in affairs of the spirit there can be no place for compulsion. We can persuade and perhaps convince, but we must never force. And whilst many preachers, teachers and philosophers would agree with you that, despite his many faces, God is One, concerning his name and nature you will find little unanimity.'

'My point exactly! It is unanimity which has been lacking, and which I am now in a position to supply.'

'No, Your Excellency, with all respect, you are not. Unanimity is not something which can be imposed upon others by any worldly authority. It can never be the bequest of one man, however powerful or benevolent; of all people a Christian bishop knows this, for if it could, the Church's short history would not be littered with the detritus of so many schisms and heresies. But no matter how brutally you coerce us, you will never induce any Jew or Christian who cares about pleasing God to call him Elagabal or equate him with the sun, when he *made* the sun, along with everything else in the universe. I doubt you could even convince the pagans who worship Rome's ancestral gods, and are used to conflating others' beliefs with their own, to start calling Jupiter the King of Olympus by a barbarian name.'

'Why all this talk of coercion and brutality? My dear Callistus, you *do* misunderstand me. I wish to inspire, not to enforce! I mean to educate people into seeing the error of their ways for themselves! And not merely through words – though words are important and those, like you, who can use them well, more important still – but through sign and symbol as well. I mean to take sacred symbols from every temple in Rome and have them dedicated in the Sanctuary of Elagabal; I mean to fill his shrine with the statues of lesser gods so that they may serve as his devoted attendants.'

'You intend to make Jupiter and Juno Elagabal's slaves? Your Excellency, I beg you... please, lay this scheme aside before it is too late. Far from unifying your empire, I fear you may tear it apart.'

'My *scheme*? This is not a scheme; it is the will of Almighty God! I could as soon lay it down as I could cut out my own heart! Mark my words, Callistus the Most Beautiful: Elagabal will be enthroned as the true God of Rome with or without your assistance. And he will have a consort as Jupiter does, a Goddess who will rule over every other goddess just as he rules over the gods. Pallas, Goddess of Troy, will be brought from her shrine in the Temple of Vesta to share his glory, and the sacred fire which the Vestal Virgins tend – the symbol of the greatness of Rome – will be transferred there with her. Oh, you think I could not do it; but I *will*, for the plans are already drawn up, and to seal them I myself will divorce my wife – who has conspicuously failed to bear me a son – and marry the Vestal Virgin Aquilia Severa, so that we may have godlike children together!'

'But my lord... your wife Paula... it is scarcely a year since you were wed! Her family is one of the noblest in Rome; and to compromise an unsullied priestess who has vowed her maidenhead to the gods... don't you know that a Vestal Virgin who lies with a man must be buried alive?'

'Not if the man she lies with is the Ruler of Rome! You come dangerously close to disappointing me, Callistus, for why should you care if I put pagan gods to shame? You should be delighted that I seek to replace the childish habits of the heathen with veneration of the One Almighty God! Nor is the temple I have built for him on the Palatine to be Elagabal's only home in this historic City. I shall build him another temple – bigger and more beautiful still – further from the centre where there is space to erect a structure more in keeping with his grandeur. Every year at midsummer his sacred black stone will be carried there in procession from the Palatine, in a carriage drawn by snow-white horses; I myself will run backwards along the road before it so that all of Rome will know that her emperor lives to bring glory not to himself but to God.'

Awed by the magnificence of his own intentions, the emperor at length fell silent, but his eyes were still on fire and his chest heaved like an overstretched athlete's beneath his harlot's garments. For a few terrible moments Callistus feared that the androgynous creature was minded to swoon into his lap, for he had begun to sway alarmingly back and forth where he sat; could he who believed himself inspired by God even be possessed by a demon? In Callistus' time as bishop he had come across some who were – not many, for typically one had to have delved deeply into occult things and consorted long and closely with underworld gods in order for the simple formula of exorcism pronounced before baptism not to be enough to drive Satan away. But he had rarely conversed with a pagan in the way he had done with Elagabalus today, and besides, Elagabalus was so spectacularly different from any other man – or woman – he had ever met, that there was nothing in Callistus' experience which could supply him with any point of comparison. So he simply sat and waited, in the hope that by and by His Excellency's bizarre seizure would pass, and in the meantime he prayed in silence for God's Spirit to bring the troubled youth peace.

After a while his pent-up chest stopped heaving and some of the fire faded from his blazing eyes, but if anything the vulnerability which came in its place made Elagabalus seem more disturbingly feminine than ever. Once again he reached out for Callistus' hands, not boldly this time, but diffidently, as if it truly mattered to him not to frighten this wary Christian away.

'Think on what I have said,' he implored Callistus at last. 'For I would much rather be your friend than your enemy, and you *are* most worthy of your name... Now I must leave you, before I am tempted to seduce you after all.' And rising to his feet as gracefully as any maiden he darted off before Callistus could offer to see him back to the atrium, and was gone.

When Gaius, Asterius and Urbanus arrived in their turn they found their bishop fallen on his face by the poolside so dead to the world that they dared not rouse him. They knew that he was praying and not sick, because he lay with his arms outstretched as though pinned to an invisible cross. But they also knew that they should not leave him to confront whatever catastrophe had felled him alone. Like Christ in the Garden of Gethsemane he needed his friends close by and their prayers to give him strength, and unlike the faithless disciples they did not intend to let their master down. The three of them knelt round about him, one by each of his shoulders and one at his feet, and waited for him to return to them of his own accord.

When he did so his face was ashen and he could not keep the tremor from his voice. He said, 'My brothers, we must summon the elders and deacons and widows' leaders here without delay, so that we can all fast and pray together for God's intervention. Otherwise we may soon find ourselves facing the worst persecution the Church has suffered since the days of Nero.' And without wasting time asking questions his companions left at once to spread the word among their fellow ministers.

Soon after sunset, as many of the Roman Church's leaders as were able to do so gathered in Titus' atrium. Not every one could come; some being men or women of substance were away from the City on business, whilst others were slaves of masters who did not share their faith and were less than sympathetic towards it. Nevertheless there were more than fifty people assembled, mostly men, but not a few women as well: Anastasia and some of her ablest co-workers. None of those present had eaten since receiving Callistus' summons, and many had spent the intervening hours in private prayer. In the flickering lamplight the ring of faces that surrounded him appeared more pallid and lined than perhaps they would have done by day, yet none looked more troubled than Callistus felt.

As concisely as he could, Callistus imparted to them the gist of Elagabalus' intentions, and asked anyone who might already have received revelation on the subject to share it straight away. No one had. So Callistus announced that all would keep vigil together until the Lord showed them how he meant them to respond to the crisis which the Church seemed destined to face.

As one his audience fell to its knees. Yet as Callistus gazed out upon the sea of bowed heads and upturned palms and listened to the swelling murmur of prayer, he found that he could see much more vividly the kohl-smeared eyes of Elagabalus searching his own, and hear much more clearly Elagabalus' honey-sweet voice dallying over the syllables of his name. What was worse, he could feel the warmth of the emperor's hand in his, and sense on some deep – and deeply disquieting – level the pleasure which His Excellency had derived from contemplating the reflection of the two of them standing side by side. The harder he tried to forget the way that the nearness of the boy had moved as well as upset him, the less he was able to do so. And the more he tried to cast the image of that painted yet beautiful face from his mind, the more tenacious the image became. In the end he was forced to acknowledge the family resemblance it bore to Mamaea's and therefore how powerfully and painfully it reminded him of Marcia's. This was when he fell on his face once more and wept.

Just as his three confidants had refrained from intruding upon his agony that morning, so their fellow ministers let him weep unrestrainedly now, for which he could only be grateful. No doubt they believed that he was weeping in intercession for his flock, and they would not have been altogether wrong. Yet there was more, much more, to his grief than that, and he would never, ever have wanted to explain it to anybody.

But when at last he got up – long after midnight, with most of the lamps gone out and some of his companions now exhausted and sleeping like the disciples in Gethsemane after all – Callistus knew that their prayers had been heard. For he believed that God had indeed revealed to him what needed to happen if the Church – and the empire itself – were to escape the scourge that was Elagabalus. And as he sat in the stillness and mulled over what he had learnt, the grey light of the new day began to seep into the room and he realized that he had received the same revelation once before, when from Priscus' rooftop he had witnessed Elagabalus' sensational arrival in Rome.

'Brothers and sisters.' He spoke softly into the breaking dawn; one by one the elders, deacons and widows raised their heads and regarded him with bleary eyes. 'Saint Paul exhorted us to pray earnestly for our rulers as they seek to preserve order in society, and to do everything in our power to promote peace and good will among men. Yet there comes a time when these ideals begin to conflict with one another, when our consciences tell us that we must no longer pray for the emperor's wellbeing but for his downfall. Elagabalus is not the man who should be sitting on the Caesars' throne. We must pray for his demise, and for the installation of Alexianus son of Mamaea in his place.'

For a long time no one else spoke. It would have been superfluous for anyone to have asked him if he was sure, for his conviction was unequivocal. Eventually Urbanus asked if this message should be passed on directly to the rest of the Church. 'No,' Callistus told him. 'At least, not yet. Not a single word about the revelation I have just shared with you is to be uttered outside of these four walls.' Then he bade the vigilants disperse and go about their business as if today were just another day.

But the following Sunday when the whole congregation came together, Callistus sensed that come what may, he must share his secret with them all. For rumours had begun to fly about the City that Elagabalus was making plans to have every citizen pay public homage to his god. The Jews were already up in arms – metaphorically, thank God – because they had it on good authority that their customary exemption from religious edicts would not be granted this time round. Many Christians too had begun to panic; instead of the expectant reverence with which the weekly Assembly was wont to begin, there was fear in the air, and faces were pinched with foreboding. Before a single hymn was sung or scripture read, Callistus knew that he must address the questions which were at the forefront of his people's minds.

And so he told them what he had told their leaders before them. He warned them too that it would be their own undoing if they boasted to all and sundry that they were counting on their God to strike the emperor dead. Callistus was under no illusions; it was inevitable that sooner or later the cat would get out of the bag. But his revelation had to be shared nonetheless, because every Christian needed to add his or her voice to the cry of prayer which must go up to heaven on Rome's behalf. There was no doubt in Callistus' mind that God was still as able and willing to intervene in human history as he had been in the days of Moses when the Children of Israel had walked through the parted waters of the Red Sea. Yet the effectiveness of the Almighty's intervention seemed to depend very much on the sincerity of his people's determination to do business with him. Had not Christ himself been unable to perform great miracles in his hometown of Nazareth on account of the residents' unbelief?

'So every one of you must pray,' he enjoined them. 'And whoever is able must fast as well, from corn, wine and oil every Sabbath for a year, or as long as it takes, and on other days too if you can manage it. We have to show God and each other that we mean what we pray, that we need him to fight strenuously on our behalf as he fought for the Children of Israel when they sought to recapture their Promised Land from those who had taken it from them. Raise your hand now if you pledge to do what I ask of you.' At once the people complied. They were only too aware that their lives might depend on it.

Yet what if praying and fasting were not enough? That night Callistus was awakened more than once by the thought that perhaps *he* needed to do something more, himself. For the Red Sea would never have parted if Moses had not raised his staff over the waters, and his people would never have won back their land from the idolaters who had occupied it if they hadn't armed themselves for battle. Perhaps he should go in person to see Mamaea and her son and tell them that Rome needed Alexianus to seize his cousin's throne because it was the will of God that he should do so?

But the more he contemplated this course of action in his sleepless hours, the more ludicrous and perilous it seemed. There might come a day in the future, once the Church was larger and more influential, when a Bishop of Rome might hope to be actively involved in affairs of state. But notwithstanding Elagabalus' – and once upon a time Mamaea's – interest in Callistus as an individual, that day had not yet arrived, and his startling prophecy would merely be laughed out of court. More than almost anything else, he dreaded becoming a laughing-stock to Mamaea.

If only Mamaea might take it into her head to visit *him*... of course there was no plausible reason why she should do so, but they *had* shared those meaningful glances at Domna's symposium; he *knew* she had thought about him, albeit so very briefly, in the way he had thought about her. In the morning, when the torments of the night had been put behind him, he resolved to add this prayer to the rest: that if it were God's will for him to speak with Mamaea, their paths would cross again.

Not very long after this, work began on Elagabalus' new temple in the suburbs. Though it was announced all through the City that this would be a temple where one day every inhabitant of Rome could – and would – come to do obeisance to Elagabal, so far no Jew or Christian had been induced to worship the Syrian god against his or her will, even though prominent pagan senators were still being made to tramp up and down the precincts of the original Elagabalium on the Palatine every day carrying the paraphernalia his cult required. Perhaps, Callistus dared to hope, Elagabalus had quietly and wisely decided to exempt the Jews and Christians from his campaign for spiritual unity after all? He certainly hadn't given up on the rest of it. He had divorced Cornelia Paula and married his Vestal Virgin – to the horror of just about everyone including Hierocles his husband. Many pious pagans confidently expected Jupiter to strike Elagabalus dead with a thunderbolt; when this did not happen, the emperor declared with smug satisfaction that this only proved what he had said all along: Jupiter was fit only to be Elagabal's slave.

However, the following summer the Christians began to see evidence that their own God had been inexorably working away behind the scenes. For it transpired that Julia Maesa had prevailed upon the emperor to adopt Alexianus as his son and heir; henceforth the younger boy was to be addressed as Caesar, and to go by the name of Marcus Aurelius Alexander. From a common sense viewpoint this was ridiculous: at thirteen Alexianus – Alexander – was only a few years younger than his adoptive father. But from Maesa's perspective it was a triumph. There was now a recognized heir to the throne who was just as closely related to her as the emperor was, and already becoming more popular. Eventually Elagabalus and his Vestal no-longer-Virgin might produce the godlike offspring they dreamed of, but in the meantime if anything happened to the emperor the future of Maesa's dynasty was secured. For everyone who met him seemed to fall in love with Alexander, if only because in all respects except ancestry he was everything which Elagabalus was not.

Quite why Elagabalus had agreed to adopt him was – Callistus and Titus agreed – another matter entirely. Perhaps he thought he could exercise greater influence over his cousin this way, prising him away from his prudish mother, or perhaps he liked the sound of Maesa's suggestion that Alexander might take over some of the Head of State's more tedious administrative duties, leaving his 'father' freer to dedicate himself to the service of his god. Everyone else knew exactly where Maesa was coming from: she had been growing increasingly dismayed at Elagabalus' erratic behaviour and her own inability to keep him in check. The Senate had never taken to him, and the soldiers who had put him on the throne were starting to wonder how they had ever seen any resemblance between him and their beloved Caracalla. Alexander, on the other hand, was *very* like Caracalla, and out of deference had even taken the name of Caracalla's hero Alexander the Great.

The one person manifestly upset about Elagabalus' adoption of Alexander was Soaemias. Having bullied Mamaea all her life, she wasn't used to perceiving her little sister – much less her sister's children – as a threat. So now she took to humiliating Mamaea in public as well as in private, and to pointing out whenever the opportunity presented itself that Mamaea could no longer legitimately call herself Alexander's mother, since legally the boy's parents were now her own son Elagabalus and his new wife Aquilia Severa.

Alas, the unfortunate Aquilia Severa wasn't destined to remain Elagabalus' wife for very long. Barely a month after adopting his cousin, Elagabalus divorced her, mostly because she had been no more successful than her predecessor Claudia Paula in providing him with a real son of his own. Not that she had been granted any longer than Paula to achieve her prime objective – she and the emperor had been married less than a year. Having attained the advanced age of seventeen Elagabalus now married his third wife, Annia Faustina, who was distantly related to the late and still much lamented Marcus Aurelius. At the same time, the god Elagabal was declared to have divorced Pallas and married the exotic eastern goddess Astarte, with whom Elagabalus cheerfully identified the Phoenician Tanith and Greek Urania.

'Whatever can His Excellency be thinking of?' Titus asked of Callistus when these things came to light. 'Everything he says and does seems calculated to cause offence to someone.'

'Perhaps he wants to avoid being accused of discrimination, by offending all his subjects equally,' Callistus suggested, not quite smiling; prudent men did not joke about Elagabalus even in private. So he refrained from commenting that since Tanith's image was a big black stone too, it would look rather splendid – cute, even – standing beside Elagabal's.

But the emperor's behaviour was frankly incomprehensible. Traditionalists had been horrified enough at the notion of one of Rome's greatest goddesses being wed to the Syrian sun god, but that she should subsequently be rejected by him out of hand was still more scandalous. Was Elagabalus perhaps trying to snub Maesa in some round-about sort of way? Or perhaps *she* was unwilling to wait any longer for the Romans to oust her elder grandson from the imperial throne in favour of the younger, and had goaded him into this reckless course of action to precipitate a coup?

Certainly there was little love lost between the two of them these days, if Clemens was to be believed. Elagabalus was doing just about everything he could to shock his grandmother into an early grave. He wore women's clothes nearly all the time now, allegedly just to spite her, only dressing as a man when he addressed the Senate or heard cases in court, and sometimes not even then. He must have realized that Maesa had stitched him up comprehensively by inducing him to adopt Alexander; apparently he now wanted his little cousin dead, but couldn't find anyone prepared to do the necessary deed for love or money.

'Suppose Elagabalus murders Alexander himself?' Titus mooted over dinner one evening. He was peering morosely into the dregs of his wine as though, like a pagan soothsayer, he thought they might enable him to see into the future.

'When Alexander has every Christian in Rome interceding daily for his protection? It's not going to happen,' Callistus reassured him, feeling almost as confident as he sounded.

Early in the following year – the fourth of Elagabalus' reign – the fickle young emperor stunned his subjects yet again by divorcing Annia Faustina and remarrying Aquilia Severa whom he had divorced the year before. Clemens maintained that His Excellency had loved Aquilia all along and had only divorced her in the first place because Maesa (for whatever reason) had made him do it.

The only sexual partner of whom Elagabalus never seemed to tire was Hierocles his Carian charioteer. Not that their mutual passion did anything to temper the emperor's promiscuity, but he would always slope back to his husband with his tail between his legs after 'cuckolding' him, wailing in remorse and begging to be beaten for his infidelity. Before adopting Alexander, Elagabalus had apparently wanted to proclaim Hierocles his Caesar and heir, but this could only have happened over Maesa's dead body, and the stalwart old battleaxe had plenty of life left in her yet.

Uncannily, Callistus soon discovered that in addition to their monotheistic beliefs he himself shared something else in common with Elagabalus: both were growing increasingly convinced that things were coming to a head and that, young as he was, Elagabalus' days were numbered. Callistus believed this because of the Holy Spirit's witness within him; Elagabalus believed it because a visiting clairvoyant from Syria had told him in so many words that he did not have long to live.

As only Elagabalus would have done, the emperor reacted to the news by making plans for a flamboyant suicide. Not that he had any intention of playing into his grandmother's hands by doing away with himself straight away. All he wanted was to have an array of appropriate exit strategies at the ready for when the storm of rebellion which must surely be brewing finally broke out against him. He ordered silken cords to be spun and made into ropes in case he decided to hang himself or have himself strangled, and swords to be cast with golden blades lest, when the time came, stabbing himself seemed more expedient. He also procured priceless antique chalices from which he might drink poison, and had a lofty gilded tower constructed at his palace from which he might leap to his death onto gem-encrusted decking. Titus was of the opinion that the braggart lacked the courage to do any of these things, but Callistus disagreed. Elagabalus was nothing if not a showman, and would surely contrive to die as ostentatiously as he had lived.

What Callistus did not tell Titus, or anyone else for a very long time, was that he was starting to sense that his own days were numbered too.

Even though the Church's prayers seemed to be having the desired effect, and it was becoming more and more likely that Elagabalus was on the way out, Callistus for some unaccountable reason began to believe that the same was true of *him*. He had no inkling as to why this should be the case. Had Elagabalus perhaps been brooding on his lack of enthusiasm for the Great Universal Religion of Unity and secretly resolved to dispose of him? Or was it that when the two of them had stood holding hands beside Titus' pool, their fates had somehow become fused?

He knew that his presentiment made little sense. He wasn't ill, he wasn't under obvious personal threat, and even if every citizen in the empire were made to offer a sacrifice at one of Elagabal's shrines, Callistus was not a citizen and presumably never could be.

Nevertheless, the feeling grew stronger by the day, until at length he had no alternative but to confront it and put it into words, at least in his private prayers. Was he about to succumb to some dreadful disease, he asked, with which he was already infected? Was some terrible accident going to befall him? Or could God be calling him to martyrdom, the ultimate test – and privilege – for any true follower of Christ?

Perhaps *all* those called to be martyrs felt like this before their time came; perhaps this was God's way of preparing them. But did he want to be a martyr? Was he ready?

One morning when Gaius, Urbanus and Asterius came to pray with him as usual, he kept Urbanus back when the others had gone.

'Urbanus, please do not ask me why I am saying this to you now, because I do not know,' Callistus began, before fear or reason got the better of him. 'But I feel very strongly that you must prepare yourself to succeed me.'

Urbanus stared at him in blank incomprehension. 'Succeed you? As what? What are you saying?'

'Please, Urbanus. Don't be obtuse, you know very well what I'm saying. I don't know what I am being called to face, but I do know that some trial or tribulation is on its way for which I must be prepared, and so must you. You are the wisest, steadiest and most widely respected of my partners in prayer. And the fact that you are the youngest of them too may be no bad thing, as you will have many years to build on the foundations which Zephyrinus and I have laid. It makes perfect sense that you should be the man to take over from me when I am gone, though ultimately that will be for the congregation to decide. But for now – '

'Callistus, you must not talk like this!' The fine lines at the corners of Urbanus' eyes which compassion and humour had etched were sharpened with apprehension.

'It matters not how I talk; it will not alter what I know deep inside, nor will running away from the truth ever take any of us to a better place than the one we have left behind.'

'No, Callistus! You're not leaving anything or anyone behind. We need you. We love you. *I* love you, as my own flesh and blood.' Distraught, Urbanus seized Callistus by the wrists as though to prevent the powers of darkness from snatching him away. His face was crumpling.

'Urbanus, I singled you out for your level-headedness as much as for your knowledge and love of God. Don't make me regret my choice! It is Alexander for whom we must be concerned, and who must be protected at all costs. *He* is the one for whom we must weep, fast and pray, more earnestly even than we have done up to now.'

But Urbanus was not listening. He was weeping unashamedly into Callistus' lap, and Callistus could do nothing but lay his hands on his friend's head in silent blessing and thank God that not all patricians were like Hippolytus.

CHAPTER TWENTY TWO: MAMAEA

Mamaea took up her discarded scroll of Virgil's poetry and tried to find the place she had reached in her reading. But with the words skittering in front of her eyes she had to set it down again with no progress made. In frustration she had her handmaid go to the door and look once more for Alexianus returning from his lessons.

'There's still no sign of him, my lady,' the girl told her, having looked both ways along the passageway outside. Then noting her mistress's hands twisting in her lap she added, 'Would you like me to bring you some warm spiced wine while you wait?'

'No, that won't be necessary,' Mamaea said, too sharply, then: 'I mean... yes, Chloe, if you please. I should like that very much.'

The handmaid bobbed and disappeared, leaving her mistress to fret alone. Where *was* Alexianus? His sister Theoclia had been and gone again already, having wolfed a scratch lunch in between; she spent her afternoons in one of the many palace bathhouses with her air-headed, blue-blooded friends. Mamaea herself had been invited to lunch with the wife of a senator who was celebrating her birthday, but she would not leave the apartment until her son was safely back. She worried about him constantly these days whenever he was out of her sight. And although he was officially one of Rome's two consuls – the other being his adoptive father the emperor – he was still a mere fourteen years old and had yet to complete his education.

That a boy of fourteen should hold what had once been the highest civic office in the Roman Republic said more about how badly the old tapestry of government had come unravelled than it did about Alexianus' maturity, Mamaea knew. But he *was* mature for his age, and she was proud of him. She had supervised his education keenly from his earliest years, and her conscientiousness had paid off. Alexianus – or Alexander, as she must remember to call him now – was well-mannered, well-read and well-spoken. He could converse fluently in both Latin and Greek, without any trace of an accent, and with all the wrestling and training with weapons he did every afternoon his muscles were as honed as his intellect. A healthy mind in a healthy body, that had been the classic Greek and Roman ideal, and Alexander conformed to it as perfectly as any foreigner could hope to do.

Moreover he was as modest as he was accomplished and as kind as he was courageous. If he had any major flaw in his character, it was his gravity – he seldom laughed, and even his smile was not something he used to its best advantage. But anyone who tried to hate him for taking himself so seriously, or for being so good at everything he did, found himself quite unable to do so because of Alexander's total lack of conceit.

Anyone, that was, except Elagabalus, who hated his cousin with every fibre of his being.

It hadn't always been this way. But since the boys' grandmother had manipulated him into adopting Alexander as his son, Elagabalus had been able to see the writing on the wall as clearly as anyone else. He knew full well that Maesa had transferred her favour from him to his cousin, and he had only agreed to recognize Alexander as his heir because if he hadn't, Maesa would have found a way of doing it for him. Even Mamaea had begun to believe that one day her own little boy might be emperor of Rome. For as things stood now, even if Elagabalus and his Vestal ex-Virgin produced a legitimate son of their own, the child would have no more legal right to the throne than Alexander.

Needless to say, Elagabalus would look for a way to unadopt – or worse – his cousin very swiftly if anything should happen to Maesa... At the beginning of January – just over two months ago now – when Elagabalus and Alexander had been proclaimed joint consuls for the year, someone had (no doubt ironically) congratulated Elagabalus on being fortunate enough to share the honour with his 'son'. 'Oh, I shall be more fortunate than ever next year,' Elagabalus had responded, 'when I actually do.'

Speculation had been rife after reports of this remark had got around Was Aquilia Severa already pregnant? Would Elagabalus really make a new-born baby consul? His subjects had learnt to put nothing past him. And he had been surprisingly successful in outmanoeuvring Maesa on several occasions already... Mamaea shuddered, and accepted with gratitude the mulled wine her handmaid held out to her. It was only early spring, but still she felt colder than she ought to have done. Having drained her wine-cup much too quickly, she sent the girl out to look for Alexander once again, but just as before there was no sign of him coming back.

Elagabalus might have learnt a lot about dealing with Maesa, but his grandmother was no longer the sole threat to his independence. Serious rifts had opened up between the emperor and the Praetorians on whom he relied for his protection. The soldiery had brought him to power and had always loved him on account of his resemblance to Caracalla who had been their idol. But these days he looked more like the goddess Aphrodite, with his diaphanous gowns and dyed-gold hair, and the more the Praetorians saw of him, the less they liked him – and the more they liked Alexander.

Consumed with jealousy, Elagabalus had recently tried to strip Alexander of the title Caesar, and sent slaves into the Praetorians' camp with orders to deface the statues of his cousin which had been erected there. But this had led to rioting on such a scale that Elagabalus had been forced to go to the camp in person, with Alexander in tow, to prove that the two were not rivals. Even then His Excellency had only succeeded in pacifying the rioters by agreeing to dismiss from their posts many of the actors, acrobats, pimps and hairdressers he had appointed to high civic and even military office. They had only allowed him to keep his precious Hierocles because he had made them lots of tearful promises, which he had yet to keep.

If Alexander had decided to make a bid for power on his own account, Mamaea was fairly confident that the Praetorians would have supported him. It was widely rumoured – courtesy of Soaemias, no doubt – that Mamaea was already using her wealth to bribe the troops or even the Senate to champion her son's cause over her nephew's. Mamaea did have considerable riches at her disposal, and powerful friends. Yet she was sure it was still too soon, and Alexander himself was content to bide his time until he was older, wiser and more experienced in political affairs. He took his role as consul as seriously as he took everything else, and was learning all he could about government, ready for the day when he must inevitably assume a starring role on the political stage. In the meantime, Mamaea thought, let Elagabalus carry on offending and alienating everyone he should have been cultivating, and elevating his worthless friends to high honours. Let him dig himself a deeper and deeper pit to fall into, for when his downfall came, it would surely be spectacular.

So much for the future, but where was Alexander now? Mamaea had trained him assiduously never to be late, never to give her cause for needless concern. All the more reason for her anxiety today, for she could think of no harmless explanation as to why he should have been held up so long without sending her a message. She sent Chloe yet again to check the hallway, and this time the girl gave a little squeak of alarm, for on the very threshold of the apartment she collided with one of Alexander's personal slaves who called out past her, 'Lady Mamaea, the Praetorians are rioting. The emperor has gone to their camp and taken Master Alexander with him, just like before.'

Mamaea's hands flew to her mouth, and it was just as well that she was already sitting down. Yes, the soldiers loved Alexander, but in the heat of the moment, in the chaos of a crowd... 'Felix,' she said to the slave, 'I must go to him at once. Summon guards to escort me.' And she sent Chloe hotfoot to fetch her outdoor clothes and shoes.

By the time she had thrown on her cloak and Chloe had fastened her sandals, there was already a detachment of Praetorians at hand to accompany her, and her litter-bearers were ready with her vehicle. They all knew better than to try to dissuade her from setting out. In her impatience she would sooner have run all the way to the Praetorian camp on her own two feet than waste time exchanging futile words. Nevertheless, the journey by litter through the urban streets seemed to take for ever even though her bearers were themselves all but running before she left off urging them to go faster.

As soon as they reached the camp she saw that Alexander's slave had not been exaggerating. The parade ground was a seething mass of soldiers yelling and smashing their swords against their shields; Mamaea's escort was instantly swollen by reinforcements anxious to protect her from the volatility of the mob. She could not make herself heard sufficiently to ask what had sparked the riot off, but from the slogans the soldiers were shouting she grasped soon enough that Elagabalus was believed to have made an attempt on Alexander's life.

'What sort of attempt? What did he do?' she demanded of

the tribune who appeared at her elbow, having been detailed to see that she was safely reunited with her son. For months now she had been having Alexander's food prepared by cooks she had appointed herself, and tasted by a slave before he ate it. The slaves who prepared his bath were thoroughly vetted lest they try to push his head under the water, and anyone who visited him at the palace was searched for weapons. But the tribune could not answer her questions. All he knew was that once again Elagabalus had ordered Alexander to stand beside him when he faced the troops, to quell the rumours and to demonstrate that the two of them were still the firmest of friends.

'So did Alexander do as he was told?' Mamaea persisted, as the tribune steered her away from the parade ground by a back route towards the headquarters building where her son had apparently been taken – whether he had gone there willingly or been dragged there kicking and screaming was far from clear.

'Not yet.' The tribune led her inside the building, only to be told that Alexander had already left, having complied with his cousin's orders after all. He was now with the emperor and his bodyguards on the podium of the parade ground; and Soaemias was with them.

'Soaemias? Why would *she* have come here?' Mamaea asked, without expecting a satisfactory answer to this question either, but she received one when the tribune took her to the doorway and she could see for herself what was happening. In the fullness of her buxom beauty Soaemias was standing centre-stage fielding the Praetorians' anger, flanked by her son and her nephew whose arms she was holding aloft. Behind them, standing in a line, were the men of His Excellency's personal guard, all Praetorians themselves.

'Behold, your emperor and his heir!' Soaemias was crying out over the heads of the multitude below. 'All hail Antoninus!' (For this was the name by which Elagabalus was officially known.) 'All hail Alexander! All hail the sons of the mighty Caracalla: cousins, brothers and friends!' Then she joined Elagabalus' and Alexander's raised hands together, high in the air, before stepping nimbly backwards to leave the two of them standing there in front of her, hand in triumphant hand.

There must have been enough loyalty to the emperor remaining, or enough conviction in Soaemias' voice, to shame some of the soldiers into taking up her cry of 'Hail Antoninus! Hail Alexander! Hail the sons of Caracalla!' But it quickly became apparent that whereas some were hailing both cousins equally, others were shouting only for Alexander. Soon it was almost impossible to hear Elagabalus' name being called out at all, but Alexander's was on every man's lips. Mamaea began to feel sick.

But she didn't feel as sick as Elagabalus looked. Swamped by his imperial robes and with the colour draining from his face, he suddenly looked like the very little boy who had first dressed up in his mother's clothing. But even as Mamaea watched him, the vulnerability was eclipsed. Dropping his cousin's hand like a stone he held both of his own high above his head, balled into fists, and screamed, '*I* am your emperor, I, the divine Antoninus, high priest of Elagabal the Unconquerable Sun!'

'Hail Antoninus! Hail Antoninus!' Soaemias chimed in; then noting that Alexander had made no attempt to contradict them, but had rather gone down on one knee before Elagabalus with head bowed in deference, some of the Praetorians began hailing the reigning emperor once again. Thus even at this late hour disaster might have been averted thanks to Alexander's self-abasement. But this was no longer enough for Elagabalus, or his mother.

'You hail him too!' she ordered his bodyguards, who stood impassive in their line according to regular practice. 'Hail him! Hail Antoninus! Do it now!'

Being under no obligation to take orders from anyone who was not the emperor or their own officer, the guards maintained a steadfast silence. Incandescent, Soaemias seized Elagabalus by the arm and shrieked at him, '*You* tell them!' like a distraught child in school demanding the teacher's intervention in a dispute over a broken stylus.

'Yes! Do as she tells you!' Elagabalus enjoined them, but his face was as white as an election candidate's toga and he choked over his words as though there were invisible hands wrapped around his throat. At their officer's nod, some of the guards duly began chanting, 'Hail Antoninus. Hail Antoninus,' but when two of them failed to join in at once, Soaemias yelled, 'Arrest them! Arrest those traitors now!' and the officer decided he had little choice but to carry out her instructions.

But when Soaemias then began demanding that any man present who continued to acclaim Alexander should be arrested as well, Mamaea decided that things had gone far enough. Heedless of the fighting which was breaking out around the foot of the podium, she walked out onto it herself, intent upon calming her sister down before the brawling led to bloodshed.

All to no avail; approaching Soaemias scorned was like trying to tackle a raging inferno with a leaky bucket. Unwilling to let his mother endanger herself on his account, Alexander sprang to his feet and sought to pull her back into the safety of the headquarters building. But the sight of him calm, compassionate and resolute, in contrast to the emperor who was now as hysterical as Soaemias, tearing at his golden hair and robes like an actor in a bad Greek tragedy, left the Praetorians in no further doubt as to which of Maesa's grandsons was the more worthy of their allegiance. In that moment both cousins' fates were sealed. Soon there was no one left at all shouting for Elagabalus; everyone was chanting in unison: 'Hail Alexander! Hail Alexander! Alexander for emperor *now*!'

After that, everything moved too fast for Mamaea to follow quite what was happening. In any case the tribune who had been assigned to oversee her protection soon had so many men surrounding her that she couldn't see past them; they swarmed between her and Soaemias and cut her off from her son at the same time, for they had been ordered to take her directly back to the palace. 'Leave me alone! Let me go! Alexander needs me,' she implored them, afraid that she too was becoming hysterical. But her entreaties fell on deaf ears. With infuriating speed and efficiency she was removed from the podium and bundled back into her litter, and with so much noise and so many armed men crowding around her that she could have been on a battlefield, she found herself being rushed back home as unceremoniously as she had left it.

Despite their haste, her escort barely got her back to the palace in time. For as the fire of rebellion spread, all hell was breaking loose in the City as well as in the Praetorian camp. The messengers she sent out into the crowds to establish the facts each returned with conflicting stories. The emperor was dead; no, he had escaped, along with his mother; no, both of them had been killed in the barracks where they had taken refuge, or in a granary, or a cupboard, or a latrine.

It was Maesa who eventually brought her the news she'd been waiting and dreading to hear. She came in person to Mamaea's chambers as dusk was falling, attended by a minimal escort which she left at the door. With face unadorned and hair loosed in mourning, Maesa sat down beside her daughter and drew her into her bosom – something she had not done for very many years.

'Do not torment yourself any longer, child,' she murmured. 'The emperor is safe.' And when Mamaea raised her head and searched her mother's face with eyes which said: that isn't what I wanted to know, Maesa added, 'I don't mean Avitus. I mean Alexianus.' And Mamaea burst into tears.

Maesa was soon weeping with her, for much as she had been at pains to distance herself from Elagabalus in recent months, he had been the first of her grandsons, and now he was dead. So was her elder daughter Soaemias, whom she had loved in spite of everything. The wretched pair had been hauled out of hiding – whether in a latrine or a storage-chest still wasn't clear – and run through with swords by a pack of Praetorians baying for their blood.

So much for Elagabalus' pre-planned suicide, so much for his gilded tower and silken cords and the priceless antique chalices from which he might sip poison of the choicest vintage! When their heads had been hacked from their shoulders, the bodies of the murdered emperor and his mother had been dragged naked through the streets of Rome before being flung into the Tiber – the traditional fate of common criminals. Meanwhile their severed heads were paraded about the City on the points of spears for the populace to revile, and afterwards there hadn't been enough left of these sorry trophies to make them worth throwing to the stray dogs that harried Rome's seamier streets. Hierocles the emperor's husband was dead too, as was the City Prefect Elagabalus had appointed, and many other prominent citizens besides, some of whom would have deserved their fate a lot more than others. Elagabalus' reign had lasted less than four years, but already folk were saying that this was four years too long. Many were surprised it had lasted as long as it had. Those who enjoyed laughing at the fallen emperor's expense were already referring to him as 'Tibertinus' rather than by any of the grandiloquent titles he had dreamt up for himself.

'And they have made Alexianus emperor instead?' Mamaea asked in a small voice, tears still flowing down her cheeks. Part of her was still vainly hoping that they hadn't.

'When he conducted himself with such dignity throughout the insurrection, how could they not?' Maesa stroked the damp hair from her daughter's face. 'After the Praetorians acclaimed him, they took him straight to the senate house for the Senate to ratify their decision – which it was only too happy to do. It seems that for a change Rome now has an emperor who is the darling of soldiers and senators alike.' A poignant little laugh escaped Maesa's lips to temper her grief. 'It can only bode well.'

'I suppose so.' Mamaea wished she could share her mother's optimism. This was how the old woman had survived imperial politics for so long, Mamaea knew: by always believing that the future would be better than the past. It was true that Mamaea too had often found herself looking forward with longing to the day when Alexander would take his cousin's place. Yet now it was here she marvelled that she could ever have wished such a fate upon her beloved son.

'They have already accorded him the titles Pontifex Maximus and Pater Patriae,' Maesa went on. 'They wanted him to accept the title "Great", as well, but he wouldn't. He did agree to add "Severus" to his name, though, in honour of dear Septimius.'

'Alexander Severus.' Mamaea let the implications of her son's new name sink in. She could not deny that it suited him; not only had it belonged to his great uncle, one of Rome's most effective rulers, but the meaning of the word was 'serious' or 'grave', which summed up Alexander's personality exactly. Yet with every fresh name and title he acquired, he seemed a little less like her Alexianus.

At least he wouldn't be going by the name of Alexander the Great... the hint of a laugh escaped her own lips at the thought of that, surprising both of them. Briefly mother and daughter caught each other's eyes and shared an even briefer smile. Tomorrow was another day, on which they might indeed permit themselves to smile; after all, the boy who had long been the brightest light in both of their lives was poised to become the most powerful man in the world. But for today they must grieve, and their grief would be genuine if not uncomplicated. Soaemias had bullied Mamaea from early childhood, but she had been her only sister. Elagabalus had been her only nephew; perhaps if he had been her niece instead, he might never have become the tortured creature so many had loved to hate?

If Elagabalus had been any other kind of emperor at all, the following days would have been filled with solemn pomp and ceremony, the public paying of respects to his body, then its cremation and the long-winded rites of deification. As it was, not even his closest relatives observed the customary nine days' full mourning which the death of any family member enjoined. Maesa and Mamaea wore mourning clothes, but could ill afford to lose whole days to traditional funereal practices. For in all but name they were now joint Regents of Rome.

Not that Mamaea would ever have wanted to enter the arena of politics in her own right. She had always been secretly grateful that women could not officially do so, since unlike her sister she had invariably sought to stay out of the public eye, and unlike Maesa or Domna she had never indulged in intrigue behind the scenes. Though widely recognized as the cleverer of Maesa's two daughters, her interests lay in philosophy and literature, not in stalking the corridors of power, and all she wanted even now was assurance that her son would receive advice from the right people, and that she would not be kept from seeing him when she needed to. Alexander – Alexianus – still wasn't old enough to shave, and his voice was barely broken.

Fortunately Maesa agreed that their most pressing priority was to put in place a top-flight advisory and executive council for Alexander, comprising men of experience and integrity who would know how best to get Rome back on an even keel after the storm of mismanagement caused by Elagabalus' promotion of wildly unsuitable people to positions of prominence. Singers, dancers, tumblers and actors had been quaestors, aediles and praetors, many of them chosen not even for their skills as entertainers, but one because he had perfectly aligned white teeth and another for his elegant penis. Any who remained in office were to be dismissed immediately and replaced by citizens of good reputation and family, but there were to be no vengeful recriminations. Once pulled down from their pedestals the late emperor's appointees would pose little threat, since most of them were bumbling incompetents, and even those who weren't could be effectively neutralized by sending them into exile – along with the big black stone of Elagabal, which was to be deported without delay back to Syria.

The sixteen men appointed to the new Imperial Council, by contrast, had enjoyed distinguished careers in law, politics and the army, and were all of senatorial rank. Maesa was insistent that the Senate should be accorded the kind of respect it had received in the glory days of the Republic, and that Emperor and Senate should govern the empire in partnership.

She was also every bit as determined as Mamaea herself that power should not go to Alexander's head in the way it had gone to Elagabalus'. Alexander's formal education would continue even now that he was emperor, and at all costs he must be shielded from men – and women – who would flatter or corrupt him for their own advancement. His chief adviser was to be Mamaea's old friend Domitius Ulpianus, who would have been his tutor had Elagabalus not banished him from Rome. Now he was brought back and put in supreme command of the Praetorians over and above their two commanders Flavius and Chrestus.

To the ill-informed, Ulpianus' role might have sounded disturbingly similar to that of Cleander who had been 'Bearer of the Dagger' under Commodus. But as Maesa reminded her when Mamaea raised the issue, Ulpianus was no Cleander. He was a man of unimpeachable sobriety who was intent from the outset on bringing the spoilt Praetorians to heel. He would have his work cut out for him. The Praetorians had got far too used to calling the tunes for far too long, and Ulpianus' background was predominantly in the law, not in the army. But if emperors were to go on being made and unmade according to the whims of soldiers, Maesa said, Rome was surely destined for self-destruction. Happily, for now, Senate, Populace and Praetorians all seemed to be in love with Alexander Severus.

As for Mamaea, she might have found it easier to share her son's love with all these people if she'd still had a husband to lover her as well. With increasing demands being made on her son's time, reluctantly she had to accept that she had come to rely on him for love and support in the way she had once relied on his father Marcianus, and that this had probably never been healthy. Still, she was profoundly taken aback when in one of their brief private moments together during those first few weeks of his reign, Alexander said to her with disarming directness, 'Mother, you are lonely. I can see it in your eyes.' And she had to avert her gaze, because his own was so intense; in fact it was becoming a talking point far beyond the circle of his own family. Suppliants who had had but a single audience with their youthful new sovereign said that his eyes could pierce right into your soul.

Mamaea was more disconcerted still when, a few days after he had made this observation, Alexander began talking to her about Bishop Callistus. 'We should send for him, Mother, don't you think? He could come to dine with us one evening. I have a mind to find out more about the Christian faith, since so many of my people seem to be embracing it, and I know that at one time you were interested in it yourself.'

Mamaea's heart skipped a beat. Had Alexander really meant 'in it', or had he meant 'in *him*', Callistus? Whatever had she said to Alexander about Callistus in the past? Could he really have made this staggering suggestion in all innocence, quite unaware of her feelings?

Somehow she did not think so, and even if he had, she was sure he that he must be aware of them now. For when she began to protest that this really might not be a very good idea at all, Alexander blessed her with one of his rare smiles and said, 'I shall have Ulpianus arrange it at once; we'll invite *him* to dine with us too, for the sake of propriety.' Then kissing her briefly on the brow he breezed off to his next engagement, leaving her to wonder, with a mother's mixture of pride and wistfulness, at how her shy, self-effacing little boy seemed to be taking so much in his stride.

As the appointed evening drew closer, Mamaea found that she could scarcely eat , sleep or even sit still on a chair. It was ridiculous, as she told herself a hundred times a day. She was a grown woman, twice married and twice widowed; Callistus was older still and had never been interested in marrying at all. What did it matter what she wore, or what he thought of her? He probably wouldn't even register that she was there. He would be far too preoccupied with expounding his precious religion to the emperor and his right-hand man.

'You are ill, my lady,' said Chloe anxiously, after Mamaea sent away yet another plate of food barely touched. 'With your leave I will send for a physician.'

'Do I *look* ill?' Mamaea demanded, more abruptly than she meant to; Chloe put down the plate and peered at her as though she were some recently installed work of art. 'Far from it,' she answered on completing her inspection. 'In fact I don't recall seeing you look better.' No doubt, thought Mamaea ruefully, it's because I feel more alive than I have done since Marcianus died. Or perhaps my eyes are just glittering with semi-starvation and lack of sleep. Then she had Chloe fetch a selection of dresses from her bed-chamber so that she could make sure she hadn't changed her mind, for the umpteenth time, about which was the right one to choose.

When the evening came at last, Mamaea settled on a gown of pure white silk, not too sheer, and the simplest of styles for her hair. The barest blush of mulberry rouge had been applied to her cheeks and lips, and a hint of kohl to her eyelids, none of which at the final moment she felt was enough.

Yet as soon as Callistus entered the emperor's private triclinium where the meal was to be served, and she noted the simple robe he wore himself, she knew that her instincts had been correct. She knew it more surely still when their eyes met as he greeted her. Immediately they could have been back at Domna's symposium as though the past twenty years and her marriage to Marcianus had never intervened.

At Domna's symposium, however, there had been many guests, and Mamaea had felt free to observe Callistus at her leisure without supposing he would notice. This evening there were only the four of them present, other than the slaves who came and went, wordlessly attending to their needs. Alexander had stipulated that there should be no unnecessary ostentation or formality – even when giving audiences he had already established the convention of being addressed simply as Alexander – so Mamaea had nowhere to hide.

Still, it was obvious from the outset that Callistus was as taken with her son as he was with her. And watching their faces as Alexander offered Callistus a choice hors d'oeuvre from his own plate, Mamaea found herself seeing her little boy through a stranger's eyes. He had been blessed with the same full and even features as Elagabalus, though Alexander was already handsome rather than beautiful. His skin was clear, and he had a smooth, high forehead which was perfectly complemented by the new way he wore his hair, austerely cropped. The regime of study and exercise to which he had been subjected all his life had not only enlivened the intelligence apparent in his face but had also trimmed any childish plumpness from his physique. His solemnity lent him a presence beyond his years, and his habit of gazing so intently at the person with whom he was conversing made him – or her – feel uniquely valued. Little wonder that he so impressed all who encountered him. Mamaea suspected that Callistus would soon not merely be accepting food from the emperor's plate, but eating out of his hand.

Ulpianus, meanwhile, was content to recline quietly on his couch and let his young protégé play the solicitous host. The boy was well able to speak for himself, and Ulpianus would step in only if he did not like the way the conversation was going. The lawyer's silent vigilance could be unnerving, but Callistus was not visibly daunted.

'It was kind of you to accept my invitation,' Alexander said to Callistus as he set down the plate he had offered him. 'I wasn't sure that you would. Christians are said to be uncommonly secretive. And it's hardly surprising, when one considers how some of those who held your office before you have been treated by some who held mine.'

'How could I refuse?' Callistus sipped the wine a slave placed before him for his approval with the close attention of a connoisseur, and evidently found it to his liking. 'Not only are you my emperor, but your invitation came as an answer to my prayers. Though it's certainly true, my lord, that – '

'Alexander.'

' – Alexander – ' Callistus acknowledged the emperor's graciousness with a courteous nod of his own ' – that since one Roman emperor at least used Christians as torches at his garden parties, a certain degree of caution is advisable.'

'Ah, but those days are long gone.' If Alexander was ruffled by Callistus' bluntness, he did not show it.

'It's not so very long since your – kinsman? father? – Elagabalus decided that we should be made to worship his god.' Callistus seemed determined to test whether what he had heard about Alexander's equanimity was true, though Mamaea suspected he was equally interested in the effect his mischievous probing was having on *her*. 'You see, he too sought me out because he wanted to talk to me about religion.'

'My *cousin*,' said Alexander, still not rising to the bait. 'But I am not Elagabalus.'

'No; most certainly you are not.' Alexander must have passed Callistus' test, for now he enquired with open friendliness, 'So what is it that you wish to know about my faith that neither your books nor your tutors nor your mother could teach you?' He didn't look at either Ulpianus or Mamaea as he spoke, but he didn't need to.

'Well, I have to say that some of my advisers believe it is a danger to national security and should be suppressed at all costs, whereas I know for a fact that my great aunt Domna – who was a serious scholar and philosopher in her own right –

found it highly attractive, and passed on her interest to my mother. I have also heard that not all Christians are in agreement concerning its doctrines, and that there are rival congregations even here in Rome who will not eat bread from the same basket. So I wish to hear – from the man who is surely more qualified than anyone else to inform me – what exactly an orthodox Christian is meant to believe. Your Gospel, as I'm told that you call it. I want you to tell me in a nutshell what it is.'

'Very well.' Suddenly Callistus could not have looked happier if Alexander had offered to bequeath him half of his empire. 'Christians, like Jews and like your late cousin, worship only one God. But he is not the sun, or any other celestial body. He is the one who made them, who is not himself a part of creation at all – which is why he is invisible to anything which exists within it. Yet he loves humanity above all else, and longs so earnestly for fellowship with us that he visited the world himself in the person of a human being named Yeshua – Jesus – not in some mythical past when everything was shrouded in legend, but in the province of Judea in the reign of Augustus. This Jesus was conceived in the womb of an ordinary woman by the quickening of the Holy Spirit, and by the power of the same Spirit he performed many miracles as evidence of his divinity. After his enemies plotted against him he was executed by one of Tiberius' governors less than two hundred years ago. You could read about his case in your own imperial annals if you cared to, and the archives of the Roman Church contain a number of documents written by those who knew him in the flesh.'

'So he wasn't unlike Apollonius of Tyana?' Alexander interposed. 'Apollonius was another hero of Great Aunt Domna's. He had supernatural powers and did miracles too. Surely you must have heard of him?'

'Indeed I have.' Now Callistus could not avoid snatching a glance at Mamaea, and because her eyes were already fixed on his, they inevitably met. 'Your great aunt invited my predecessor and myself to a symposium where Jesus' and Apollonius' relative merits and achievements were the prescribed topic of debate. But with respect, my – '

'Alexander.'

'With respect, Alexander, the two had much less in common than you might imagine. Apollonius travelled all over Greece and the eastern provinces promoting himself and his philosophy; Jesus scarcely went anywhere, and spent most of his time trying to evade the crowds who dogged his every step. Apollonius was frequently accused of being a charlatan; Jesus was accused of many things by those who hated him, but no one could deny that the healings he performed were genuine, or produce convincing evidence of any sin he ever committed. So when he died, it was for the sake of *our* sin, so that we may be loosed from our addiction to destructive behaviour. They say that Apollonius was taken straight into heaven when he died, but Jesus came back to life visibly, and ate food, and talked with his friends, and on one occasion was seen alive by more than five hundred people. Nor was this resurrection purely for his own benefit. He was the first fruits of the new life in the Spirit, so that *all* who put their trust in him may live for ever.'

This time Alexander refrained from making a comment of his own as soon as Callistus paused for breath. Instead he weighed the bishop's words carefully while his companions went on eating in silence, except that Mamaea wasn't eating anything at all. Eventually he said, 'You claim that Jesus committed no sin. What then did he teach about the characteristics of a righteous life? Or had he nothing helpful to say about how *we* should live?'

Callistus' expression showed that he thought the question a good one. 'Far from it,' he replied. 'He said a great deal. He said that all human beings are of equal value to God – slave or free, rich or poor, woman or man, Gentile or Jew – and should therefore be treated as equals among his followers. He said that no one can serve both God and money, and that we should use the resources God has given us to reach out to those in need. He said that honesty and justice matter, whilst mercy and forgiveness matter even more. But he summed up all his ethical teachings in two simple statements: love God and your neighbour with all that you have and are; and do unto others as you would wish them to do unto you.'

'He must have been a match for the very wisest of the ancient Greek thinkers, then,' Alexander exclaimed, and for a boy of his age he was uncommonly well qualified to judge. 'Many seers and sages have said: don't do to others that which you don't wish them to do unto you. I have vowed to live by this precept myself. Yet your Jesus takes it so much further, by turning it on its head and making a negative into a positive, and thereby into something very much more demanding. How can anyone hope to live up to a standard like that?'

'In our own strength we cannot. It can only happen – or begin to happen – by the indwelling of God's Holy Spirit, who must quicken our own spirits in the same way he quickened Mary's womb.'

'Then how does this indwelling, this quickening, come about?'

'A prominent Jewish truth-seeker named Nicodemus once posed that very question to Jesus himself. Jesus told him it was like being born all over again, which comes about when you invite Jesus to be Saviour and Lord of your life. Even so, none of us can ever attain perfection here on earth, and only by the grace of God can we enter his kingdom. Yet you can only receive God's gift of salvation if you choose to do so, by an act of the will, just as you made a deliberate choice to invite me to dine with you this evening. The decision is then sealed by baptism, which symbolizes not only a cleansing from sin, but dying to your old self and rising to a whole new life in Christ.'

'So simple and yet so profound.' Alexander shook his head slowly, as though what he had heard was surely too good to be true. Then out of the blue he looked straight at Mamaea and asked her, 'Mother, what do *you* think of what our good friend Callistus has told us?'

Now everyone was looking straight at her, Ulpianus included. Momentarily Mamaea was confounded, but then she heard herself saying quite coherently, 'I think it is the most beautiful message I have ever heard – if it is true. But to believe that a mortal man who lived a mere two hundred years ago was the Almighty God in human form... this is a difficult thing to accept, Alexander. I think we should take time to find out more about it.'

'And you, Ulpianus?' Mercifully her son directed his own and Callistus' gaze elsewhere.

'Indeed we must find out more,' the lawyer agreed, 'once we have leisure to devote to such abstract pursuits. But for now our political objectives must still take precedence. Establishing stable government concerns me rather more at the present time than pampering my soul, and this must be your concern too, Alexander, until public confidence in the principate has been restored.'

'How right you are, as always,' said Alexander with a sigh. 'And that will not be easy. I believe we have made a good beginning, you and I, in restoring to the Senate the prestige it traditionally enjoyed. But the Praetorians who brought me to power... they are something else altogether. Did Jesus have anything to say to greedy and indisciplined soldiers, Callistus, who were far too used to having things their own way?'

Callistus contrived to purse his lips and somehow smile while doing so. 'I don't recall him giving any advice specifically to soldiers,' he said. 'But his cousin John the Baptist told them to be content with their pay. And as cousins go, Jesus and John seem to have seen eye to eye more consistently than some...'

'Which only goes to prove the old adage that great minds think alike.' Alexander's lips curved ever so slightly upward, the closest he seemed willing to allow himself just then to a smile of his own. 'But if there is anything guaranteed to bring an emperor or even his entire empire crashing down, it is the greed and insubordination of his army. Am I not right, Ulpianus?'

'Certainly,' Ulpianus agreed. 'Though disputes over religion have also played their part in the downfall of many, a certain cousin included. Which is why, fascinating though the Christian faith may be, it would be a mistake on your part to present yourself for the time being as anything other than a pious devotee of the Roman state pantheon.'

'As indeed I shall, Ulpianus, have no fear. But the gods of Rome have ever been welcoming to those of the nations Rome has subdued; just as she herself has done, they have shown mercy to the conquered, which is why Rome's empire has lasted so long in spite of its flawed government, unwieldy size, and heady mixture of cultures.'

'A pity then that the God of the Jews and Christians has not been so accommodating.'

The tone of Ulpianus' remark drew wary glances from Mamaea and Callistus alike; Alexander however fixed him with his most penetrating stare and said, 'Well, there is room in *my* household shrine for *many* gods and holy men whom others have considered unworthy of veneration. Come, Callistus, if you have finished eating: I shall show you my private lararium so you may see for yourself that I am serious and open-minded in my religious quest, and quite prepared to bestow honour where honour is due.'

Before anyone could object, Alexander had swung himself up from his couch and straightened his toga all in one lithe movement, before holding out a hand to Callistus. Mamaea could see all too clearly what was going through Callistus' mind: to be admitted to the holiest place in the emperor's private apartment was almost as intimate a privilege as being invited to share his bed. 'My lord...' he began uncertainly, but Alexander interrupted him, 'Have you *such* a short memory, Callistus? If you will not call me Alexander, I shall insist upon calling you "Father" or "Rabbi", which I've heard that even

Jesus' twelve apostles weren't supposed to answer to. Now come with me; in fact *all* of you must come.'

So saying, Alexander deigned to link arms with Callistus, whom he steered out of the room without needing to check that Mamaea and Ulpianus followed. Mamaea had a disconcerting sensation that Ulpianus would have liked to link arms with *her*, yet did not dare. They had been friends for years, but no more; had he too noticed something about the way she looked at Callistus?

Alexander's lararium, the shrine of his personal gods, had a windowless chamber all to itself where his slaves kept lamps perpetually burning, for he would visit it several times a day. Not for Alexander a perfunctory nod towards a niche in a spidery corner with stale offerings gathering dust like the statuettes of half-forgotten ancestors for whom they had been left. Once again Mamaea studied Callistus' face as he took in the spectacle which greeted him: a plethora of figurines representing deities, holy men and heroes from many lands.

'Look,' said Alexander softly, so as not to spoil the reverential hush which had settled over his companions. 'Here are Jupiter and Juno, King and Queen of the gods of Rome, whom as emperor I must indeed venerate above all others. And here are some of my own heroes from history: Cicero and Virgil from Rome, Achilles and my namesake Alexander from Greece. And some of the best of Rome's emperors: Augustus, Trajan, Hadrian, Marcus Aurelius, and the noble Septimius Severus who can be reckoned as the founding father of my own dynasty as well as one of the greatest emperors of all time. But here too are Cybele the Mother Goddess, and Elagabal, and Apollonius and the Sybil… and here are Abraham and Jesus, for *any* man or woman to whom God has spoken is in my mind worthy of the greatest respect… Callistus? Is something the matter?' For Callistus' jaw had dropped as though one of the little figures had spoken to *him*.

'No,' he answered at length, though he didn't sound very

sure. 'It's just that I have never seen a statue of Jesus before, nor do I know of any Christian craftsman who would make one. Wherever did you get it?'

'From Ephesus. The craftsmen there will make a statue of anyone if they think it will sell. There isn't so much of a market these days for the images they made of Diana when her cult was at its most fashionable. These days there's a lot more interest in Jesus and Mary.'

Callistus continued to stare at the little figure of Jesus as if bewitched; he was plainly trying to make up his mind whether its existence was a good thing or not. It depicted his Lord as a shepherd, complete with crook in one hand and a lamb draped contentedly over his other shoulder. Eventually he said, 'Well, it's true that when the apostle Paul visited Ephesus the idol-makers complained that his new teaching would have a bad impact on sales. But godlike statues of Jesus... and of Mary too, when she was merely a humble peasant-girl, as human as any one of us... The strength of the Christian faith lies chiefly in its close connection to history. If legends are left to grow up like bindweed around the facts, they may squeeze the very life from them, and a few years from now the Church may look as pagan as the Pantheon.'

After that no one spoke until Alexander tugged gently at Callistus' elbow and guided him out of the lararium back to the triclinium, with Mamaea and Ulpianus following. When they had resumed their places round the table for the wine course and Callistus still seemed to be suffering from shock, Alexander said, 'Forgive me, my friend, for I have upset you and that was the last thing I wanted. You are a man of unusual foresight and humility yourself, I can see. The Roman Church is fortunate indeed that you chose to lead it.'

'Oh, but I didn't. The Church chose me, for that is the Christian way, and I accepted only so that someone unsuitable was not elected instead.'

'Ah, now this too is something I have heard about the Christians and which has impressed me very deeply: that *only* reluctant leaders are appointed to the highest offices. And I believe too – correct me if I'm wrong – that before a man is ordained as an elder, any member of your Church may object and say that his lifestyle does not match his credentials. I intend to introduce the very same practice among my magistrates. I want those who hold office under *me* to be incorruptible, to set an example, in the same way that you and your elders do in the Church. I want traders to use fair measurements and not clip their coins. I want all accounts kept honestly, and properly audited, including my own. I want everyone who marries to be faithful to his or her spouse; I would make prostitution illegal if I didn't know that it would merely be driven underground. I would end the Games, too, if I could. All that bloodshed, the wanton waste of life, both human and animal, the destruction of so many noble creatures…'

Now it was Mamaea's turn to stare in astonishment, for she had never seen Alexander so animated or heard him speak with such fervour. There were real tears in his eyes as he lowered them, suddenly aware of Ulpianus' disapproval. 'You know, Callistus,' he finished up quietly, 'No treasure in my entire palace means as much to me as my collection of wild birds. I have a whole complex of aviaries full of them, the only luxury I allow myself to spend more money on than I should, and which would truly hurt me to give up. Some time I will show you *those*, for there is little which makes me happier than sharing my love of nature with someone capable of understanding my passion. But sadly Juvenal the Satirist was no doubt right when he said that the Roman mob needs its "panem et circenses". Have you read any Juvenal, Callistus? Sometimes a satirist can be as wise as the gravest philosopher.'

'Bread and circuses,' Callistus repeated, nodding grimly. 'Yes, I have read Juvenal. I have read much more widely than many Christians would recommend. But God the Father still speaks in divers ways even though his Son represents his most perfect revelation.'

'He does indeed. And how I wish that every one of my subjects could read the words of the wise for themselves as you and I can do! When I have accomplished all those things which Ulpianus thinks I should do first, I shall establish schools in every town and village, and scholarships for the poor, so that a love of learning may be kindled in every child, as my mother ensured it was kindled in me. Even the meanest slave should be taught to read.'

'As I was myself, when I was a slave in the house of a Christian master. Alas, I never really knew my mother.'

'You were a slave? My dear Callistus, I had no idea... But how did your manumission come about? Did you earn your own freedom?'

'In a manner of speaking. But not before I had almost lost my life hacking silver and lead from the mines in Sardinia.'

'God in heaven,' said Alexander, and after that no one said very much at all, until Callistus drank up the last of his wine and begged leave to depart. The emperor gave his permission; both he and his mother rose to see their guest to the door, which neither was obliged by custom to do, and Ulpianus plainly regarded as being well out of order.

As Callistus was leaving, Alexander once again took both the bishop's hands in his. 'Thank you, Callistus,' he said simply. 'I have learned more from you tonight than a hundred books could have taught me.'

'And I have gained more pleasure from our conversation than many hours of reading would have given *me* – Alexander,' said Callistus, raising the emperor's hands to his lips.

Then Mamaea stepped forward as her son stepped back; and on an impulse she took Callistus' hands too. 'Thank you,' she said. 'My son's education and the shaping of his character have always been more important to me than anything else over which I could hope to have influence. You have helped me greatly in my task this evening. I have no words to tell you how much this occasion has meant to me.'

Then for one final moment their eyes met and held. Almost imperceptibly Callistus squeezed Mamaea's hands more tightly, and briefly she dared to hope that he would kiss them as he had kissed her son's. Instead he dropped his gaze and let them go; did he think he had presumed too much already? Without another word he departed with an escort of Alexander's slaves, and the doors closed behind him.

CHAPTER TWENTY THREE: CALLISTUS

At the end of the evening Callistus was provided with an imperial escort – large, liveried slaves with flaming torches – to see him safely back to Titus' house. It was perhaps as well; otherwise he might never have got there.

It wasn't the wine, though he had drunk more than he'd meant to. It was sheer exhilaration, more intoxicating than any drug. Sharing his faith with truth-seekers invariably excited him. To find the emperor himself – and his mother – not far from the Kingdom of God felt like a miracle – the miracle he'd been waiting for ever since the day he had watched them enter Rome in the wake of Elagabalus and his big black stone.

But somehow more miraculous still had been the glow in Mamaea's eyes when she had held his hands and thanked him – actually thanked him – for taking the time to explain his religion to her son.

He tried not to think about Mamaea's eyes as he followed the dancing torchlight home. He thought about Alexander instead, about how wonderful it was that in spite of his youth the emperor was everything Callistus had prayed that he might be – cultured, generous, open-minded – meaning that at last there might truly be grounds for believing that the years of turmoil, when each new emperor seemed to have been more of a liability than the one before, had come to an end. Surely the nagging presentiment of doom which Callistus himself had been experiencing, the conviction that his own death was stalking him, must have been a stratagem of Satan to bring him down when he should have been rejoicing? For if he kept his head and guarded the closeness of his walk with God, he might well see the most powerful man in the world come to faith in Christ. As a child and a slave, Callistus' daydreams had filled his dark world with colour, but never had his imagination run riot in quite the way that it was doing when he fell into bed that night. He knew he would not sleep, and he did not.

He was half expecting to be summoned back to the palace within days to assist Alexander and Mamaea with their spiritual quest, but when this did not happen he told himself not to be unduly concerned. After all, he had long since come to accept that the Almighty's sense of timing was better than his own. And as Ulpianus had rightly said, there were very many more urgent matters requiring the emperor's attention. First and foremost, the economy must be set to rights after the depredations of Caracalla's wars and Elagabalus' extravagance. Alexander must see to it that taxes were raised fairly but promptly, that the poor did not grow poorer while the rich were either bled dry or permitted to live in unbridled luxury at others' expense, and he rose to the challenge with relish.

Just as important as the raising of taxes was the curtailment of corruption, and this too Alexander tackled decisively by putting his own house in order first. A prominent member of the imperial court by the name of Turinus was foremost among those made to pay the ultimate penalty. Condemned for accepting bribes, the mode of his execution was exquisitely chosen: he was condemned to die from asphyxiation by the inhalation of wood-smoke. 'Selling smoke' was the popular name for the crime he had committed.

'You have to hand it to Alexander,' Titus said to Callistus when reports of the incident reached them. 'I wouldn't have thought he had it in him. But the odd show of ruthlessness when it's required will make troublemakers think twice before trying to take advantage of His Excellency's youth and benevolence.'

In particular it kept the Praetorians on side – at least for the present – and their emperor's determination to persevere with his own military training impressed the legions too. Alexander and Ulpianus took pains to reassure them that reinforcements would swiftly be sent to the empire's frontiers to deal with the barbarian incursions which had been causing trouble for border garrisons since the time of Marcus Aurelius. Yet notwithstanding his focus on economic and military objectives, Alexander was already being acclaimed as a champion of education and the arts. This came about almost by default. In striving for stability and integrity in every area of public life, he was simultaneously creating a climate in which those endeavours which thrive against such a backdrop could hardly fail to flourish.

As for Callistus, he wasn't entirely sure whether the Church came into this category or not. Sometimes it seemed to grow more strongly when Christians were thrown to the lions in the arena.

But growing it was, slowly and steadily, and from time to time the emperor's personal intervention in disputes involving Christians indicated that the Church still enjoyed his approval. On one notable occasion when dissension arose over the tenancy of a building in which a cell of the Roman Church had been meeting, Alexander found in the Church's favour. The lease had been claimed by some tavern-keepers, but Alexander decreed that the use of a building for worship had to be preferable to its becoming a drinkers' den.

All in all, Callistus reminded himself whenever he woke from dreaming about Mamaea yet again, it wasn't surprising that Alexander had been far too busy to send for him.

But what of Mamaea herself? What was keeping *her* from inviting him back to the palace, in her own right? It wasn't as if her beloved aunt Domna hadn't set her a precedent.

Perhaps it was Ulpianus who stood in her way? His insistence on Alexander's unqualified support for the old Roman gods made excellent sense, and could easily account for his discouragement of further contact between the imperial household and the Christian bishop. Callistus decided that there was really no need to worry that Ulpianus might have more personal reasons for wanting to keep him and Mamaea apart...

Why am I even *thinking* this way? Callistus asked himself crossly, as morning by morning and night by night he tried to pray the whole thing through but found his thoughts coming full circle once again. Why should it matter to me in the slightest how Ulpianus feels about Mamaea? Why should it upset me so terribly to think that he might be keeping her from sending me greetings?

The fact was, it upset him even more to think that Mamaea's silence might have nothing to do with Ulpianus at all. It might rather be that she regretted looking at their dinner guest so long and hard when they had said goodbye. It might be that she was even ashamed.

If so, she wouldn't be the first person dear to Callistus who had been embarrassed to call him a friend.

Having had his hands full for so many years attempting to pastor his rival flock, recently Hippolytus had taken to flinging mud at Callistus' sheep instead, presumably because his own had begun straying back to their former fold in alarming numbers. Little of the mud he was throwing ever stuck; the overwhelming majority of bishops persisted in communing with Callistus, and Callistus' open-armed acceptance of returning heretics made their journey from Hippolytus' bosom back to his so very much easier than it might have been. But now Callistus learned that Hippolytus had dedicated his latest theological treatise to Mamaea.

'He's done it to spite me, I'm sure of it,' Callistus complained to his three partners in prayer the next morning when they sensed straight away that his equilibrium had been disturbed. 'He's never believed women to be capable of understanding theology at all.'

Urbanus' eyebrows lifted; bitterness was not something he or anyone else associated with Callistus. But Callistus' reluctance to discuss the matter further led to their regular prayer time being cut unusually short. Disunited in spirit, all four of them felt that their prayers were bouncing off the ceiling, and when they took leave of one another to face the day each went away frustrated rather than renewed.

As soon as his friends had gone, Callistus fell into a black mood the like of which he had not experienced since the death of Zephyrinus. He felt completely cut off from God and from his fellow human beings, as though a toxic cloud had engulfed him. Nothing he had accomplished had been worth while; his whole life had been wasted, because the first woman he'd loved had rejected him and all that he stood for, and now the second was being seduced by the man who had once been his best friend but who today lived only to make him suffer. What a terrible person he, Callistus, must be, to have turned those he loved the most so thoroughly against him.

What was worse, as he as he struggled beneath this crushing weight of worthlessness he was assailed once again by the spectre of his own death. Like a netted gladiator he could do nothing to defend himself against the stabbing of his opponent's trident. The end was approaching, he knew it; his only comfort derived from the thought that it would not be long in coming. For the remainder of the day he kept to his room, and when Titus' servants appeared to call him for lunch and then dinner, he sent them away. When at length Titus came himself, Callistus said, 'Titus, please send for Urbanus. Tell him to come here at once. I don't know how long I have got.'

'Callistus, are you ill? Whatever is – '

'Please, Titus! Do as I ask!'

Titus complied without another word.

When Urbanus arrived, having left his evening meal half eaten on the table, Callistus was lying face down on his bed fully dressed, but with bedclothes tangled about him.

'Callistus..?' Urbanus knelt down and touched him tentatively on one shoulder. Callistus responded at once by clamping his arms around his visitor's back and sobbing into his toga. There was little Urbanus could do but embrace him in return, and wait, until presently Callistus recovered himself sufficiently to apologize not only for this unseemly display of emotion but for his conduct in the morning as well.

'Forgive me, Urbanus; you should be able to expect better of me than this. But I have been under such horrendous attack of late, you would not believe. Physical hardship is one thing, and, God knows, I've learnt well enough in my time how to deal with that. But this is different. I can only say what I said to you before, that you must be ready to take over from me when I am gone.'

'Callistus, please. I don't want to go through all that with you again. It is as you said: you are under attack – '

'Yes I am, but that does not alter the fact that I'm going to die, and sooner rather than later. I *know* that now, and you have to believe me, and be ready to take my place. Gaius and Asterius are good men too, and as spiritual as you are in their way, but Gaius is so much older, and Asterius just doesn't have the learning he would need. You are a man apart, Urbanus. Knowledgeable, capable and compassionate, steady – in everything but this! – and you feel things deeply, as I do, and as Zephyrinus did before me. You must pray and fast and enquire of the Lord for yourself whether the future I have in mind for you accords with his will. And Gaius and Asterius must get ready to support you.'

'All right. I shall pray if you insist. And I shall speak to

Gaius and Asterius – '

'You will? You promise?'

'Yes, Callistus. I promise!' Then wincing as Callistus' nails dug into the flesh of his forearms, he added in a different tone entirely, 'Yes. I promise.' And with a great sigh Callistus rolled back onto his bed and fell instantly asleep.

He slept without stirring all through that evening and night. When he woke in the morning the toxic cloud was gone, but not the conviction that he must put his affairs in order as speedily as possible.

He had few belongings; he had never owned a house, land or slaves, and he possessed little of any value apart from his books, which he would leave to Urbanus. But he was desperate not to die without making one final effort to repair his relationship with Hippolytus.

Having agonized for hours over the wording of a brief conciliatory letter, he entrusted it to Aratus, the most reliable of Titus' slaves, but Hippolytus recognized the courier at once and sent him packing without even taking the letter from his hands. Callistus dispatched another slave with a gift, but it was rebuffed. A third slave was deluged with a torrent of abuse from an upper window before even reaching the door. Callistus began to feel like the owner of the vineyard in Jesus' parable who is driven to sending his own son in a last-ditch attempt to gain his tenants' respect – except that if Callistus had had a son, he wouldn't have sent him within a mile of Hippolytus. Eventually he had to accept that you can never be reconciled to a person who has no interest whatsoever in being reconciled to you. *So far as it is up to you, live in peace with everyone,* Saint Paul had admonished his readers, and this was the most that any human being could do. Callistus' own conscience in the matter was clear.

But had Mamaea been taken in by Hippolytus' duplicity? Surely, oh surely not? Surely to goodness she had the wherewithal to see through his flattery and recognize it for what it was? Yet the more Callistus allowed himself to dwell on the subject, the more be became tormented by the possibility that the reason why the emperor and his mother had not sent for him a second time was that they were receiving instruction from Hippolytus instead.

And why wouldn't they? Hippolytus called himself a bishop just as Callistus did; moreover, his father had been a senator whereas Callistus had never known his father, and his mother had been a common slave. Hippolytus was in a position to offer Mamaea considerably more than spiritual guidance – assuming that Ulpianus was not doing this already.

If only he hadn't got things so badly wrong with Marcia! If only *he,* Callistus, had had the wherewithal to recognize duplicity when it was staring him in the face, in the person of Shadrach ben Abner. Then Marcia need never have written him off as a silly little boy unworthy of her affection. And if he hadn't got himself condemned to the treadmill and then to the mines, he might instead have been in the right place at the right time to deter her from returning to Commodus. Of course, they could never have married. The hurdles they would have had to leap were simply too many and too high, and the difference in their ages had been too great. But if he hadn't been so stupid they *could* have gone on being friends – even close friends, if they had been discreet. Then most probably he would never have noticed Mamaea at all, and would never have been bewitched by her resemblance to Marcia, who in reality had probably looked nothing like her.

And Hippolytus might still have been friends with him too.

But even as Callistus was indulging in these pointless regrets, another voice within him was prompting him to let them go, and he knew full well whose voice it was. For the life he had lived was the one which God the master potter had shaped out of all that his servant had had to offer him, and no one could hope for a better life than that. If he were to die without ever knowing a woman, then so be it; after all, he had vowed before heaven that if he couldn't marry Marcia he would not marry at all, notwithstanding that he was a healthy and handsome man still, and that the silver streaks in his hair became him.

If I were to die... In the middle of the next night Callistus awoke in a lather of sweat with these words spinning around his head. There was nothing new about the prospect in itself, which had dogged him for months. But *how* was he to die? Would the end come swiftly and painlessly, or was he destined to regret all too bitterly telling Urbanus that physical suffering was something he could cope with better than most? What if his years on the treadmill and down the mines had merely been a preparation for something worse?

And what would happen to him afterwards? Oh, he would be saved, he would find paradise, he would go to heaven... however you chose to put it, Callistus was in no doubt about his own eternal salvation, because he knew that it depended wholly upon the grace of the God who loved him. But surely he would be required to give some account of himself before passing into glory? The scriptures said so little about how and when the judgement was to take place, or what the afterlife would be like. Would he wake up to find himself standing naked and alone before God in some soaring celestial basilica the moment his heart stopped beating, or would he sleep blissfully in Abraham's bosom until the final trumpet sounded? Would Jesus Christ be sitting enthroned at the Judge's right hand in the courtroom, or standing beside Callistus as his advocate? Would the ghastly catalogue of all his sins be read out aloud for the whole of the heavenly court to deplore, or would his slate already have been wiped clean when his trial began? Would there be terrifying seraphim and cherubim standing guard on every side, with multiple wings, blazing eyes and drawn swords, or would God's presence be so dazzling as to render the rest of his court invisible?

Or perhaps there would be no courtroom at all. Perhaps there would just be a sunny shore where the people Callistus had known and loved and who had gone on before him would be waiting with outstretched arms to welcome him home. But would Marcia be among them? Would he even know any of these people for who they were, or would they have changed out of all recognition? After all, Mary Magdalene had failed to recognize Jesus himself in his resurrection body when he had called to her in the garden outside his tomb, though they had been the closest of friends. Jesus had promised his earthly disciples that whoever had given up brothers or sisters, parents or children for the sake of the Gospel would get back a hundredfold along with eternal life in the age to come; but would any of these be the *same* brothers and sisters, or different ones entirely? And would those such as himself who had given up the chance of having children altogether be given sons and daughters after all?

Exhausted by the bombardment of these unanswerable questions, Callistus fell back into a feverish sleep. But when next he awoke the questions were gone, and a mysterious peace had settled upon him in their place. He knew quite definitely then that it was not for him to worry about such things. No human mind could encompass the wonders of what awaits each one of us once the shackles of mortality have been shaken off. All he needed to do was cling to the promise of Scripture that God would wipe away his every tear. There would be no more sorrow, no crying, no pain, no regrets and no loneliness in the place to which he was going.

When he rose in the morning with a smile on his face and tucked into a hearty breakfast, Titus was mightily relieved. So were Gaius and Asterius when they arrived noticeably later than usual to pray; Urbanus looked understandably wary, since he had spoken to them about Callistus' depression already yet now found him cheerful, alert and well-groomed, as though nothing had ever been wrong. But after the three of them had gone their separate ways once more and Callistus began attending to some correspondence which had been allowed to go unheeded, Titus' slave Aratus came to tell him that he had another visitor waiting for him in the atrium.

'It's a woman again,' Aratus said apologetically, as though it were his own fault, and Callistus recalled that it was he who had announced to him the unknown woman who had turned out to be Elagabalus.

But when Callistus put down his tablets and went out into the atrium, the woman awaiting him could not have looked more different from the flamboyant creature who had confronted him then. This woman sat very still on a couch with her hands locked together in her lap. Her face was completely hidden by the hood of the woollen cloak she had drawn up over her head. She did not look up even when he approached her quite closely and greeted her in the kindest of voices lest his presence should startle her, for she seemed as timid as one of the injured birds he sometimes rescued in the garden. So he knelt on the floor in front of her where he could see her shrouded face, and it was Mamaea's.

'My lady..?' Callistus began, but did not know how to go on after a single tear escaped one of her eyelids and ran all the way down her cheek like the first drop of rain on a window pane which warns of the storm to come. Then when he saw her locked hands judder, and took in how white the knuckles were and how starkly they stood out from the taut skin around them, he said, 'Come.' And against all propriety and common sense he led her back to his private chamber, telling Aratus who hovered awaiting his instructions that they must on no account be disturbed.

Only when she heard the door close firmly behind them did Mamaea slip the hood back from her face. Underneath it her hair was loose, her eyes unpainted and hollow with fright. Her gown, though impossibly fine by any ordinary woman's standards, was no doubt the plainest she could lay her hands on. She had come to him in disguise just as Elagabalus had done, and in desperation, intending absolutely no one else to know that she was here. Not trusting himself to say another word, Callistus sat down beside her and waited for her to tell him of her own accord what was wrong.

But she sat in tortured silence for such a long time that he began to be afraid that she would leave again without saying anything at all. And all the while she was sitting on his couch, seeing the things he saw around him every day, breathing the same air, close enough for him to have taken her in his arms without even shifting in his seat. He could smell yesterday's scent in her hair along with her fear; he could feel the warmth of her body as well as her trembling, he could almost hear the beating of the burdened heart within her breast.

Then, when he had almost decided that he must break the silence himself, Mamaea turned her great haunted eyes upon him and said, 'Dear Bishop Callistus, I know I should not have come here, and neither Alexander nor Ulpianus must ever know that I have. But I am *so* afraid for my son, and for the Rome he is trying to save from herself! I don't know where else to turn but to God, and you seem to know God so much better than any other person I've ever met. Oh, I'm still not sure if he came to earth in the form of your Jesus, but I have seen him in *you*, and I have heard him in your words, not only when you spoke with Alexander, but all those years ago at my aunt's symposium. You're a holy man, I know it. So I have come here to beg you to pray for my son's deliverance from his enemies, and for his very life.'

'His life?' Callistus repeated, his own heart racing. 'But what danger threatens him? Whoever would wish him ill?'

'I don't know that people *do* wish him ill, not directly. But they wish Ulpianus the worst that can happen to anyone, and without Ulpianus, Alexander and I – and even Maesa my mother – would be nothing! Alexander's so young and my mother so old, and it's Ulpianus who keeps the Praetorians under control. But they don't like it, Callistus. They don't like *him*, or the way he was brought in as their commander over Flavianus' and Chrestus' heads. In fact it's Flavianus and Chrestus who have been stirring up trouble against him. I'm terrified that there will be an uprising and Ulpianus will be killed – '

'And you... care for Ulpianus? As well as for Alexander?'

'Care for him?' Momentarily confused by Callistus' question, Mamaea lost her train of thought. Then catching on to his meaning she exclaimed, 'Oh no, not like that! Never like that... It's just that if we lose Ulpianus, it will destabilize everything. He's so capable, and has been given such wide-ranging powers that Rome would founder without him. He's been my lifeline too, it's true, ever since Alexander's accession, but not in the way you're thinking. If Mother were younger we wouldn't have needed him so badly. But I am no politician, and since Marcianus was murdered, Ulpianus is the nearest thing Alexander has had to a father.'

At this point the storm which Mamaea's single tear had foreshadowed broke out with all the violence of five years' grief behind it. While she sat there and wept, head pressed to her knees and loose hair tumbling, Callistus perched beside her in an agony of indecision. Of course he knew he should never have allowed himself to counsel a woman alone; it went against all his customary practice and against the salutary reminders he issued frequently to the elders for whom he was responsible. Perhaps it wasn't too late even now to send for Anastasia or one of the other senior widows who assisted her in her ministry. But *he* was the one to whom Mamaea had turned, and she had made it quite obvious that no one else was to be involved.

Still he held back from putting his arm around her. Instead he offered her a napkin to dry her tears, but when she took it from him their fingers brushed together and she seized hold of his hand with the ferocity of someone drowning. So it came about that he put his other arm around her after all, and rather than pulling away as he was sure she would, she folded herself against him and wept on without inhibition as so much pent-up emotion found its release.

But Callistus' agony only intensified. Suppose someone should walk in on them? Yet there was really no reason why they should. He had given strict orders that they were to be left alone; no member of Titus' household would dare to disobey. And the feeling of Mamaea's body pressed against his own was so indescribably thrilling that he was quite unable to do what he was sure he ought to do, and push her kindly but firmly away.

Then presently he realized that although she was no longer weeping, she still had her head on his breast. Taking hold of her shoulders very gently to coax her into letting him go, he found that he was looking directly into her eyes. This was when he finally accepted that what he had feared she felt for Ulpianus or even for Hippolytus, she had felt all along for him.

Afterwards Callistus could not have explained what kept him in that moment from following the desires of his own heart as he so badly wanted to do. How close their lips were already; she would have allowed him to kiss her, he knew it; nay, she would even have encouraged him. Perhaps in the end this was why he did not act upon his impulse in spite of everything: he feared where it all might lead. There was no barrier in his Church's teaching to a bishop befriending, courting or even marrying the woman he loved, even though there was no shortage of clergy who believed it preferable to be celibate, and plenty who argued that once a woman had been widowed she should never marry again. But there was *every* reason why a bishop should not marry a woman who wasn't yet a Christian, and even more reason why he shouldn't throw caution and convention to the winds and make love to her without marrying her at all. Besides, if Callistus' days were numbered, he could not bear to be responsible for Mamaea's heart being broken all over again.

So instead he said, 'My lady, you came here asking me to pray on your behalf. Will you let me do it now?'

'Now?' Mamaea seemed more confused than she had been over Ulpianus. 'While I'm still here with you? You would call upon your God in my presence?'

'Certainly, with your permission. Whenever a blessing is

invoked over someone's life, the prayer is invariably more powerful if the person is present to receive it.'

'But you don't understand. I'm not holy like you. That's why I came. I'm not worthy to approach your God on my own account.'

'Neither is anyone else. That is why Christ had to die. Besides,' – and Callistus allowed himself a rueful smile – 'I don't suppose you have ever been convicted of fraud. Or caused those who could least afford it to lose all their life-savings in one fell swoop.'

'I have colluded with Alexander in putting men to death! And I have wished a fate *worse* than death upon those who set out to corrupt him or destroy his reputation...'

'*All* of us have sinned and fallen short of the glory of God.' Callistus moved to kneel in front of Mamaea as he had done before in the atrium; now he placed his hands lightly on her bowed head and said, 'Close your eyes, my lady, and together we shall ask him to forgive you and bless you, and bless your son as well.'

'Just like that? We don't need to make a sacrifice? Or even go to your lararium?'

'Every Christian believer is a temple of God's Holy Spirit, whose shrine is the human heart. Jesus Christ himself is the only sacrifice we need.'

'Very well,' Mamaea consented with some hesitation, but her eyes were already closed. Momentarily Callistus was rendered helpless once more, because sitting there so expectantly with her lashes brushing her cheeks and her lips moistly parted she reminded him so poignantly of Marcia the first time he had noticed her at the Assembly in Piso and Valeria's villa that it was all too easy to understand how even the most principled and self-disciplined man of God might suffer a catastrophic fall from grace. Then he succeeded in quelling his emotions sufficiently to begin praying aloud for God to pour his blessing into the lives of Mamaea and her son alike, such that both of them might come to know for themselves the awesome power of the Almighty sustaining them and protecting them from the dangers that lay ahead. The Holy Spirit was touching her even now, he was sure of it, though he had never before prayed in this way for anyone who wasn't yet a Christian.

But the members of his congregation had been taught how to recognize the signs of the Spirit at work; Mamaea had not. Disconcerted by the unfamiliar feelings these prayers had stirred within her, she shook herself and opened her eyes; finding Callistus gazing into them she looked down hastily at her hands, which were once again twisted together in her lap. 'Thank you,' she murmured. 'With all my heart. I must go, but do please continue to pray for Alexander, every day if you can manage it. It will bring me great comfort to think that your God is on his side.'

'I shall pray for *both* of you every day, my lady. Indeed, I already do.'

'Mamaea,' she said, now venturing to meet his gaze. 'Please; you call my son Alexander. Please let me hear you speak my name too, just once.'

'Mamaea,' said Callistus obligingly, then found that once was not enough. 'Mamaea,' he said again, but this time his voice faltered as he lingered over the syllables, and now it was he who had to look away.

'Goodbye, Callistus. I dare not come here again; it would be far too dangerous for us both. But you will never know how much I wish I could.' Then she drew her hood back over her head, got up unsteadily, and fled.

After she had gone, it was not Alexander or even Mamaea for whom Callistus prayed, but himself. Every word Mamaea had said to him was repeating itself over and over in his head and every glance they had exchanged was imprinted on his memory for ever. Yet more overpowering even than any of this was the sense of his own impending doom, which welled up with double the force it had exerted before, and with the certainty that it was inextricably linked with the salvation of the emperor and his mother. *Are you ready,* he sensed the Lord asking him, *to do something for Alexander and Mamaea, as well as to pray? Are you ready to give yourself for them, for me, for the future we all long to see? Jesus' sacrifice was sufficient to blot out the sins of all the world, yet sometimes those who would follow him are called upon give their lives just as he did. You have committed no sin in loving Mamaea. But there is something more important you can do for her than seeking to take Marcianus' place in her life. Are you prepared to do it, Callistus? For her, for Alexander, for Rome and for me?*

'Yes, Lord. I am ready,' Callistus murmured into the cushion he was clutching against him; it still smelled just a little of Mamaea's perfume. Then, 'Yes,' he said again, louder, sitting up and laying the cushion aside. Finally, standing with arms outstretched: 'Yes, Lord. I know it is for this that you have been preparing me all my life. Take me, use me, do what you want with me; only let me die knowing that I have fulfilled my calling.'

You have spoken well, he heard God say to him as clearly as if he were a person who had walked into the room. *Now you must listen very carefully for the voice of my Spirit within you in the coming days. Then you will know exactly what you need to do.*

Less than a week after this, Callistus awoke very suddenly one morning, much earlier than usual. Branded upon his mind was a searing intuition that something was very wrong in the Praetorian camp, and that he must be prepared to go there in person when prompted to do so.

At first he dismissed the notion as folly; it must be the remnant of some dream his jumbled thoughts had conjured in his sleep and then suppressed. Then he remembered what he had heard God say to him so very clearly the week before, and he rose and dressed at once.

He breakfasted as usual with Titus, and prayed as usual with Urbanus, Gaius and Asterius, but mentioned nothing to any of them about the thing he would have to do once they had left. Urbanus sensed the strangeness in his mood straight away, but a single look from Callistus told him that he was to make no comment and ask no questions. So instead Urbanus prayed, with his customary fervour but a very much sharper urgency, that God would grant his dearest friend a double portion of blessing and protection that day for whatever challenges awaited him. Callistus merely nodded his appreciation and gave nothing more away.

When his companions had gone, he knew that it was time for him to leave too. So he walked out into the City alone, having received no indication that he should take anyone with him. This was something he often did in any case; he had not maintained his youthful vigour or physique solely by wrestling with theology.

The Praetorian camp lay at a considerable distance from Titus' house, on the eastern outskirts of the City; it would take him a good while to get there and he had no idea what would happen when he did. Certainly he could not expect to gain unquestioning admission unless God had planned a convenient earthquake to coincide with his arrival. To his congregation Callistus was an esteemed and venerable figure, and since being invited to dine with the emperor and then to pray with his mother he had at last begun to believe that he was not without influence on the Palatine. But to the Praetorians he was no one.

He need not have worried, because the Praetorians came to him. He heard them approaching when he was still some way short of his destination, chanting and beating on their shields and generally kicking up a rumpus the like of which had not been heard in Rome's streets since the murder of Elagabalus. Ahead of them, civilians who had been travelling in the same direction as Callistus along the road were fleeing back the way they had come, terrified of being trampled underfoot. From their cries and gesticulations Callistus gleaned that a mutiny had broken out in the camp at the instigation of the slighted Flavianus and Chrestus, and the men were heading as a body for the imperial palace, baying for Ulpianus' blood.

This was exactly the eventuality Mamaea had feared; no doubt she was more politically astute than she gave herself credit for. Why the simmering crisis should have boiled over on this day rather than any other no one seemed to know, except that it was now high summer, torrid and oppressive, the season when hot tempers always seemed to wax hotter still and there were often riots over taxes, the price of oil, or the corn dole for the poor. But a full-scale mutiny of the Praetorian Guard was another thing altogether.

Briefly Callistus' faith wavered; suddenly he felt like a child who has let go of his father's hand in a teeming market. Should he have set out earlier and attempted to remonstrate with the men before things got so far out of hand? Or should he have gone to the palace rather than the camp, to warn the emperor and his household of what was happening, even though the camp was the place where the trouble had started?

Then the panic subsided as he found his Father's hand once again. There would have been no point in his going to the camp any earlier; he would not have been admitted and there would have been nothing he could have done. If he had gone directly to the palace without seeing evidence of the Praetorians' rebellion for himself, any warning he could have given would very probably have been dismissed. But clearly he must go to the palace now, and arrive well before the Praetorians did. How he would fare when it came to gaining admission there, he did not know, but since the palace guards were Praetorians themselves it was more than likely that regular security procedures had already broken down.

So Callistus turned tail and allowed himself to be swept along by the swelling crowd. He had little doubt but that he would be able to outrun the Praetorians provided that he wasn't knocked sideways into the gutter by stampeding civilians first. Being some of the best-drilled troops in the world, the soldiers were marching, not swarming; Flavianus and Chrestus their upstaged commanders would be only too eager to demonstrate the expertise in maintaining military discipline which they had acquired in the many years of soldiering they had notched up together, and which the upstart Ulpianus did not share. Ulpianus on the other hand would surely be with Alexander when they found him. Callistus knew from Clemens, who still worked in the heart of the palace, that Alexander, Ulpianus and Maesa met together every morning in the emperor's private chambers to ensure that their political thoughts were all running along the same course. He could only be thankful that Mamaea's disinclination for state affairs meant that she would not be with them.

Yet as Callistus rushed on, gradually pulling away from the multitude pressing on his heels, destructive thoughts dogged his every step. He would be too late to warn anyone about anything; there was no point in his even trying, for surely Ulpianus would have his own spies in the camp and about the City who would know better than anyone what was going on, and would already have put him on the alert. Distracted by these fresh anxieties he tripped, and would have fallen on his face and got no further if the two men running behind him hadn't caught him as he stumbled and hauled him along with them. As he looked round to thank them he saw that one of them was Clemens himself, and the other Asterius.

He had neither the time nor the breath to ask how either of them had come to be there, nor did they ask him. Like as not each of them had followed the promptings of God's Spirit within them, and now all three of them found themselves heading for the palace together. In the company of Clemens, Callistus would gain automatic admission, and the presence of the burly Asterius made him feel at least a little less vulnerable to physical attack.

As the palace hove in sight Callistus was powerfully and disconcertingly reminded of the murder of Pertinax, whom Marcia's Eclectus had sought and failed to defend with his life when the Praetorians had come after him. So he sent up a fountain of wordless prayers, not for his own deliverance – he already knew that this would be a waste of mental energy – but that whatever form his sacrifice was going to take, it would not be in vain. Whatever became of him – or even of Clemens or Asterius – Alexander, Maesa and Ulpianus must survive. Rome's future depended on it, as did the happiness and perhaps the eternal destiny of the woman he loved. This time, thought Callistus, I *must* not get it wrong, and with God's help I will not.

CHAPTER TWENTY FOUR: MAMAEA

Mamaea's morning had begun much like any other summer day in the City – torrid, airless, sticky – except that her mother had failed to join her for breakfast. Alexander had breakfasted with Ulpianus at the crack of dawn as usual; Theoclia would not be up for hours, and seldom ate anything before midday. Mamaea would have been quite content to eat alone had one of Maesa's slaves not come to tell her that his mistress was ill.

'She sends her apologies and asks that you take her place when His Excellency and Ulpianus meet to discuss the day's agenda for the Imperial Council, my lady,' the slave finished up. 'She expects to be out and about again by tomorrow.'

But Maesa was never ill. Suddenly disinclined to eat at all, Mamaea went at once to her mother's apartment, leaving her attendants behind. Here she was told that Maesa was still in bed, which was unheard-of; ignoring the squawks of a flock of fluttering handmaids, Mamaea pushed past them into the bedroom, where she found its sole occupant apparently fast asleep. She looked so startlingly small and frail lying there that Mamaea's heart lurched, and only then did she acknowledge how long it was since she had allowed herself to take any real note of her mother's appearance. Having entered her room so forcefully she now approached the bed with faltering steps. But while she was still some way off Maesa opened her eyes and fixed her with a look as sharp as a spear-point.

'Mamaea? What are you doing here? Is the grandmother of an emperor not entitled to a moment's privacy even in her own bedchamber?'

'I – came to see if you needed anything...'

'I do. I need you to be my eyes and ears at Alexander's conference with Ulpianus.'

Mamaea began to say that this wasn't quite the sort of thing she'd had in mind, but the words stuck in her throat when she saw her mother's face twist in pain as she tried to push herself upright on her pillows. It was no passing summer head-cold which had kept Maesa from her breakfast, nor had she become so thin and haggard overnight. Knowing Maesa, she had probably been suffering in silence for months, and Mamaea cursed herself for having turned a blind eye to the signs.

'Don't say anything,' Maesa cautioned her now. 'Especially do not tell me that you have no head for politics, when I know very well that you have. And before long you'll have to start using it whether you want to or not, because I shan't live for ever. You need to find room for *that* morsel of truth amongst all the philosophy and otherworldly offal you stuff it with...' Another stab of pain brought Maesa's lecture to an abrupt end. Wincing again she let herself slide back among the pillows, whence she continued to study her daughter's face intently. But now her own expression was almost tender rather than critical. 'Please, child,' she said when she could speak again. 'For Alexander's sake if not for mine, keep him company this morning. Something tells me you won't regret it.' And a moment later Maesa was asleep once more.

Accepting that she had no choice, Mamaea made her way directly to her son's private chambers.

Though there were any number of magnificent apartments

within the palace complex which previous emperors had commissioned or embellished for their own use, Alexander had chosen to keep the rooms he'd been allocated when his cousin ruled. The only modifications he had made to them on assuming supreme power had been the removal of superfluous furniture and the replacement of the turgid frescoes with fresh white plaster. Friezes of swirling foliage painted in soft blue-green with the lightest of touches were all he had kept by way of decoration. The overwhelming impression you received as you stepped from the modest vestibule into Alexander's atrium was one of cool spring sunshine, a welcome relief from the sultry intensity of the summer outside. But it seemed to Mamaea that the brightness proceeded as much from her son's person as it did from the environment in which he lived.

The doors to Alexander's private peristyle had been thrown open to catch whatever breath of breeze might be passing, and he and Ulpianus sat as near to the garden as they could get without being outside. 'Mother, what a lovely surprise,' Alexander exclaimed as soon as her arrival was announced. Then his face fell as he realized this had to mean that something was wrong.

'Your grandmother feels a little unwell today, that is all,' Mamaea told him. 'It's nothing to worry about, but she asked me to join you in conference this morning as her representative if that is acceptable to you.'

'Of course,' Alexander replied at once; Ulpianus nodded too, adding, 'Though I doubt that our discussions will interest you very much, my lady.' He didn't mean to be unkind or even patronizing, Mamaea knew. He esteemed her as highly as her son and her mother did, and like them he was inclined to think that she did not esteem herself highly enough.

And indeed, as their conversation resumed there was not very much about it that was engaging enough to prevent her from thinking about Maesa instead. She had to keep reminding herself to pay due attention to what was being said, else there was no point in her being there at all. There were problems on the frontiers of the empire and problems in the heart of the City: disputes between governors, disputes between magistrates; barbarian incursions, disaffection amongst the urban poor. So it went on, and would go on for ever, Mamaea thought – an endless tale of woe for both ruler and ruled – as long as human nature remained unchanged. If the empire of her son's namesake Alexander the Great had fallen prey to the jealousy and wrangling of the subordinates who became his successors – which it had – there could be little hope for the long-term survival of any political system under the sun. For that first Alexander's charisma and gift for leadership had never been equalled before or since.

Still, the day-to-day administration of the state apparatus had to be overseen by somebody, and much as Mamaea would have preferred to exercise her intellect in sifting the arguments of Plato or Aristotle and to sidestep the machinations of ambitious men in favour of finding peace for her own soul, these were luxuries she could ill afford at present despite belonging to the richest family in the world.

And so the meeting proceeded, with Mamaea saying nothing, but striving to commit as much as she could to memory so that she might report it back faithfully to Maesa afterwards. Alexander on the other hand had a great deal to say, and his mother marvelled as ever, not only at the ease with which he took things in but also at the astuteness of his comments and suggestions. Perhaps it wouldn't be long, she reflected with a pang of nostalgia, before her little boy became capable of steering the ship of state for himself, without the likes of Maesa and Ulpianus keeping their hands on the tiller all the time to steady his.

Then out of the blue, raised voices from the vestibule through which Mamaea had passed earlier put an abrupt end to her reflections and to any further discussion of routine politics. Alexander started and looked round, frowning; Ulpianus was instantly on his guard. A moment later three men had entered the atrium uninvited, hotly pursued by the slaves they had elbowed aside. The first of the intruders was Clemens, the veteran freedman from the treasury. The second was a stranger, built like Hercules and dressed in homespun, but with an incongruously childlike face. The third was Callistus.

'Forgive us, Excellency; my lady; Commander Ulpianus,' Clemens began with undisguised urgency. 'But you must evacuate these chambers immediately and seek refuge where no one will think to look for you. There has been an insurrection in the Praetorian camp. Your guards are gone; we don't know where they are. But no Praetorian is to be trusted.'

Mamaea's hands went to her mouth and she looked straight at Callistus. The very thing she'd had him pray against had come upon them, yet somehow *he* was here, too, and bizarrely his incongruous presence reassured her. So did the presence of Clemens, and that of the gentle giant who was with them. Alexander seemed about to regale Clemens with questions – a reminder to everyone else that he was indeed only fourteen years old – but Ulpianus said, 'Save that for later, Alexander,' and Mamaea said, 'Come. I have an idea.'

Surprising even herself by her quick thinking, she led the way out of the emperor's apartment, heading straight for her own. Here alongside her bedroom a previous emperor's wife or daughter had devised a hiding place, no doubt for some secret lover she might need to stash away in a hurry: a tiny chamber which could only be accessed through a low narrow door concealed behind a tapestry. It would not foil a systematic search but it would buy them time, and it wasn't far away. They would be unlucky to run into trouble before they got there.

In the event they saw no one at all, until back in Mamaea's apartment they found her handmaids cowering in anticipation of their mistress's return. They knew nothing about the insurrection, but they knew all too well that the guards who should have been doing their duty outside the entrance to her chambers had become conspicuous by their absence, and that something was very wrong.

Mamaea waved her women into silence and ushered her son and the four men past them and on into the hidden chamber. With only the smallest of windows, more like a slit, high up in one of the walls, it was gloomy and airless as a prison cell. Mamaea shuddered and tried not to think that it might all too easily become their tomb.

Only when Ulpianus had pulled the tapestry back into place and closed the door behind them did he allow Alexander to ask his questions, and Clemens to explain what he had seen and experienced on the streets outside. As the picture Clemens painted grew clearer and grimmer, and further details were filled in by Callistus, the boy quietly took hold of his mother's hand. Whether he was seeking reassurance or offering it she could not be sure. But a fleeting thought occurred to her that if either Callistus or Ulpianus had not been present, the other might have offered her his hand as well.

When Clemens and Callistus had told their story as coherently as they were able, Ulpianus concluded, 'Then I am the one for whom the Praetorians will be searching when they get here. I should leave this place at once and prepare myself to face them. It would be safer for all of you, and for Rome.'

'No!' protested Mamaea, more loudly than she had intended; when four of her five companions looked daggers at her she was shamed into silence, but then added, 'I'm sorry, Ulpianus, but for the moment Rome needs you as surely as she needs Alexander.'

'And with respect, Commander, whilst it may have been your appointment and actions which roused the Praetorians' anger in the first place, your sacrifice may be insufficient to slake it now.' This came from Callistus; of all those present he seemed to Mamaea to be the least unnerved by their predicament. He was the one who had spared her the withering look, too, and she felt gladder than ever that he was there.

But Mamaea was not the only one who had found Callistus' speech heartening. For Alexander said steadily into the silence which followed it, 'My friends, it is not fitting that the emperor of Rome should hide cringing in a cupboard in his own palace like a criminal on the run. If the Praetorians are set upon finding us they will certainly do so, and I would sooner not receive them in a ratholc. So it is I who will go out to meet them. If any of you wishes to come with me I shall be for ever in his debt, but I do not demand or even expect that you will do so.'

'No, Alexander. You are still my responsibility and I forbid it,' said Ulpianus at once.

'Your Excellency... remember what happened to your predecessor Pertinax when he acted as you are suggesting,' Clemens added to strengthen Ulpianus' case. 'He was slain by the Praetorians not a hundred yards from this spot, along with his chamberlain.'

'*Alexander*,' the emperor reminded him. 'You know, I do find it hard to accept that men who are famously competent in other respects seem quite incapable of remembering my name. But fortunately I have a better memory than most. I remember all too well how my cousin and his mother died hiding in a toilet. And as for Pertinax, I remember the history lessons my tutors taught me, too.' Acknowledging Ulpianus with a nod he finished up, 'Pertinax's chamberlain was Eclectus, as I recall, the soul mate of Commodus' concubine, but a braver man than all the Praetorian Guard put together. The most that any wise emperor could ask for is to be served by men such as he.'

No one ventured to contradict Alexander now, though Mamaea felt as any mother feels when her only son decides to risk his life on a whim. The only reason she did not speak out was that she was sure Ulpianus or Callistus would do so.

But Ulpianus had already sought to break the emperor's resolve and been ignored. As for Callistus, something

Alexander had just said must have cut him to the quick, because all at once he no longer looked to be in control of himself, let alone of their situation. This left Alexander free to walk out from the midst of his companions towards the door which Ulpianus had so carefully closed behind them. When he took hold of the handle and turned it with quiet authority, those who cared for him could do nothing but follow him out of their refuge and back into Mamaea's bedroom, which might already have become as dangerous a place as an arena full of lions.

As yet, however, there was no evidence of any incursion, though the baying pack must surely have invaded the palace precincts by now. Indeed there was no sign of anyone at all; mercifully Theoclia had not yet put in an appearance, and left to their own devices Mamaea's handmaids had fled. So Alexander kept on walking, out of the bedroom and on through the apartment into the passageway outside. It was clear from the direction he was heading that he meant to meet the mutineers in the aula regia, the great hall where all official audiences with the emperor were supposed to be held.

This vast marble throne-room with its soaring columns and gleaming polished walls, extravagant in its every feature and dimension and designed to intimidate as much as to impress, was a place where Alexander held court as rarely as he could get away with. He much preferred to address the Senate in the Senate House and the Praetorians in their camp, and to entertain any other visitors in the intimacy of his private chambers. The Roman emperor was not a king – so Alexander would remind his grandmother whenever she turned up her nose at the modesty of his lifestyle – and perhaps if more of his predecessors had remembered this, he was fond of pointing out, their reigns and dynasties might have lasted rather longer.

So his decision to go there now was all the more alarming, especially since the aula was the one space on the Palatine where a large body of soldiers would be able to use its numbers to devastating effect. Then again, Mamaea was all too aware that it would be just as easy for half a dozen armed Praetorians to dispose of Alexander and his meagre entourage as it would for half a legion.

When they reached the aula it too was ominously deserted. The guards who should have been on duty were nowhere to be seen. There were no petitioners seeking audience, no senators or freedmen of the imperial household scurrying about their business or standing deep in discussion. There were no slaves sweeping the mosaic floors or polishing the great bronze doors and lamp-stands. Only the silent statues of gods and dead emperors looked on impassively from their pedestals and niches as Mamaea's son, bearing no symbol of authority and clad in nothing more prepossessing than the plain white tunic in which he had eaten breakfast, walked with echoing footfalls towards the dais on which his throne stood unattended in its apse. There he sat down and invited his companions to join him.

Mamaea mounted the dais without hesitation, as did Ulpianus. They took up positions to either side of Alexander, Ulpianus on his right and Mamaea his left. Mamaea could only be thankful that her own mother and daughter were not there to face the danger with them. Clemens, Callistus and their attendant Hercules lingered at the foot of the steps until Alexander beckoned them a second time.

'Don't you know me well enough by now to appreciate that I would rather have my friends round about me than grovelling at my feet?' he chastised them. 'And not only are you my friends, but currently the nearest thing I am likely to come to a bodyguard. Please. Stand beside me, and let us await our distinguished guests together.'

Clemens obeyed with no further qualms; he had worked at the palace most of his life and associated on a regular basis with every emperor from Commodus onwards. Callistus, who appeared to have recovered his customary composure, wasted little time before complying as well – just long enough to ensure with a glance that the third man of the three understood the emperor's invitation to include him too. With another glance Callistus sought Mamaea's leave to stand next to her – how could she refuse? – and a moment later they stood close enough for her to reach for his hand, though she did not. Clemens joined Ulpianus, but Hercules stopped a step or two short of the top of the staircase and stationed himself squarely in front of the emperor's throne as though he expected his sheer bulk to deter all comers in spite of his being one mere man, and quite unarmed. There had still been neither sight nor sound of the mutinous Praetorians. So Callistus motioned to Alexander and said, 'With your permission, my lord, I should like to pray.'

'*Alexander*,' sighed the emperor, not in frustration this time but rather with the briefest hint of the smile he so rarely made use of. Callistus returned it, and all at once Mamaea could have been back at Domna's symposium once again basking in the warm glow of the lamplight, the wine, the erudite discussion and above all the nearness of this man who had unintentionally awakened so much that she'd believed to be dead within her. How was it possible that here and now, all mixed up with her fear for her own life and for that of her son, those feelings were being kindled all over again?

Now it was Callistus who was beckoning his companions closer. He himself had moved to stand behind the throne and had placed one hand on her son's head and the other on the shoulder of Ulpianus, who was almost certainly in greater danger than anyone else present. Ulpianus' eyes had widened in surprise, but being unwilling to displease the emperor – or risk offending a strange and potentially unpredictable God – he made no objection to the liberty Callistus had taken.

Then Callistus began to pray aloud just as he had done for Mamaea once before: not in especially lofty language or using any formal liturgy, but freely, from the heart, as though he were appealing to some influential kinsman who had chanced to arrive on the scene exactly when he was needed the most.

Afterwards Mamaea couldn't even recall what Callistus had said, only that for a few glorious moments she could truly begin to believe that the hosts of heaven were arrayed around the dais armed with fiery swords and glittering shields emblazoned with the symbol of the cross on which the founder of the Christian faith had defeated the powers of darkness.

Then the spell was broken as the sound they had all been dreading became distinctly audible in the distance. Since it was growing steadily louder, the enraged Praetorians must have been told – or guessed correctly – where the quarry they were seeking could be found..

The state entrance to the aula was from a courtyard at the head of a grand processional avenue which led, through a series of triumphal arches, from the public gateway on the Palatine. It was along this avenue that the rioting soldiers must have come. But if Flavianus and Chrestus had succeeded in maintaining a semblance of discipline while their troops surged through the City, the mounting uproar which rang in Mamaea's ears had to mean that they had definitively lost control of them now.

For the noise which penetrated the still closed doors was not that of marching feet or chanting voices calling in unison for Ulpianus' dismissal. Rather it sounded as though a full-scale battle was taking place in the courtyard into which the avenue had disgorged its raging contents. And when at last the doors were forced open and the first of the Praetorians came crashing through, they did not pour in as a body, unopposed. Nor did they make straight for the emperor's throne.

Instead they were engaged in ferocious combat, fighting amongst themselves not in the manner of crack legionaries but with the reckless desperation of noxii at the Games. They had been unable to form up into any kind of order; the courtyard into which they had poured was much wider than the avenue from which they had emerged, and besides, none could have known before the fighting began who would be his friend and who his foe. But it must have dawned upon some of them at least that Ulpianus' removal was not the best thing for Rome – nor even for themselves – after all; or even if it was, risking the life of the young emperor to achieve it was not in anyone's best interests.

So although the vast bulk of the seething mass was attempting to force its way forward over the threshold of the aula, a sizeable minority was striving with equal determination to force it back. Shield crashed against shield, sword on sword; men grunted, howled and yelled, and some were soon screaming in pain, felled by the blades and blows of their former comrades. Already men lay writhing or senseless on the ground with their blood streaming and mingling, while others though wounded, dying or even dead, were kept from falling by the press of grappling bodies all around them.

A single snatched glance at Callistus' face told Mamaea that he believed his prayers might have been answered. Nevertheless the day would not pass without significant bloodshed.

It wasn't as if Mamaea hadn't seen men fighting and dying in front of her before – she had been to the Games more often than she cared to remember – but never at such close quarters, and never without the protection of the high arena wall to keep the contestants apart from the spectators who were there to be entertained without the need to fear that they were about to feature personally in the performance. The echoing acoustic of the aula amplified the screams of the wounded as well as the clangour of weapons. Swords rang against helmets and breastplates and the iron bosses of shields, and cut through the unprotected flesh of neck or arm like knives through curds. Bones crunched and bowels opened as seasoned soldiers stared death in the face in the guise of enemies who had been their own officers or messmates. Scores of men now sprawled dead and dying on the gleaming mosaic floor, their bodies trampled by others' boots, their blood spreading like pools of unwatered wine and running into the cracks between the tesserae whence no amount of scrubbing would scour it.

And the battle was coming closer to the unarmed emperor and his companions by the second. Though many of the combatants were still striving to push the others back with their shields, because they were not operating as a co-ordinated unit they couldn't get them locked together and were reduced to fighting every man for himself like Homeric heroes. And like Homeric heroes they were falling, as those still intent on tearing Ulpianus limb from limb overpowered them. Mamaea saw that Callistus was praying once again, his lips moving and hands held out in front of him as though he believed he possessed some magical power which could keep the hounds at bay more effectively than any legionary's shield of leather, metal and wood. It wasn't working.

Or perhaps it was? Perhaps the battle would have reached the steps of the dais already without Callistus' intervention. Certainly he seemed to be expending considerable spiritual energy. Beads of sweat had broken out on his brow, and his raised arms were visibly shaking. Alexander meanwhile still sat bolt upright on the imperial throne, either fortified by some sort of faith or frozen rigid with fear. Clemens, Ulpianus and the giant whose name Mamaea did not know all looked as though they wished that weapons would somehow materialize in their hands enabling them to enter the fray on their own account.

But even had this wish been granted, there was nothing they could have achieved other than to die as martyrs for Alexander's cause, which they were more than likely to do in any case. Seeing for himself that this was true, Clemens, who Mamaea had always known to be a Christian, began to pray in the same way as Callistus. She was rather more surprised when their muscle-bound Hercules proceeded to follow their example.

Whether or not the Christians' prayers were having any effect, the mutineers were gaining ground. All too soon they must surely force their adversaries hard back against the dais on which their hated supreme commander stood defenceless at his emperor's side. Suddenly Mamaea was consumed by an overwhelming desire to hold her son in her arms just one last time, if both of them were truly about to die.

It wasn't as though this was something she did every day. Since Alexander had come to power, she had seen so little of him that a perfunctory kiss on the cheek from time to time was all the intimacy they ever enjoyed. So with soldiers grappling, groaning and dying all around them, Mamaea dropped to her knees in front of the throne of the Caesars and pulled its occupant against her. Offering no resistance Alexander embraced her with equal fervour, though she could tell from the angle of his chin upon her shoulder that he continued to watch the drama unfolding before him whilst she could see nothing but the blank wall of the apse behind. She could smell nothing, either, except the light aroma of the perfumed oil with which he scented his hair – his sole concession to personal vanity and to his oriental origins – and the sweet underlying scent that was unmistakeably her beloved Alexianus, fruit of her own womb. And all she could hear was the din of sword on shield and the cries of men dying for no good reason at the hands of their old friends, until above the cacophony rose the voice of one man calling for the carnage to cease.

'Soldiers of Rome, in the name of all that is holy, I beg you, lay down your arms! His Excellency Alexander Severus is the best hope Rome has, and he is only a child. Think how great he may become as a man! He and those who advise him are Rome's future; they are *your* future. Flavianus and Chrestus who incited you to mutiny are the men who threaten everything you should be striving to protect! *They* are your enemies, not this boy, or his mother, or the counsellor on whom they both rely, who alone is worthy to command you. Stop! Stop, before it is too late.'

To begin with Mamaea had assumed that the brave orator

must be Ulpianus himself, but long before his speech reached its climax she had realized it was Callistus. Still holding Alexander in her arms, she turned to see that the bishop and his Hercules had both now interposed themselves between the throne and the Praetorians; Hercules had resumed his former position near the top of the steps, but Callistus stood on the step below, his outstretched arms no longer held up in front of him but spread to either side like a great bird's wings, as though he himself had been nailed up for crucifixion like the God-man he worshipped. The faction of the Guard which had already seen sense and still fought to keep the rebels at bay was losing more and more ground, and more men. Then one of the leading mutineers broke through the ragged line, fetching up face to face with Callistus. It was Julius Flavianus.

'Stand aside, whoever you are, unless you want to die too,' he demanded, and when Callistus did not move, Flavianus seized him by the neck and ran him through with his sword.

Callistus fell, but Flavianus got no further because Callistus' unarmed Hercules in a frenzy of rage and despair somehow succeeded in wrestling him to the ground. With a faint little cry but no forethought, Mamaea let go of Alexander and stumbled toward the steps to take hold of Callistus instead. At any moment Flavianus' supporters would engulf them, yet she cared only that Callistus would not die without knowing that she loved him.

Blood pumped from his belly with every heartbeat, but even though his eyes were already glazing she knew that he could see her. He was even trying to say her name, though his first two attempts sounded like another name, similar but different. The third time she was sure she heard him say it, before his gaze seemed to drift past her until he was looking at something or someone very much further away. At the last moment she was startled to hear him gasp as if in astonishment, and to see his face transfigured in what looked like a split second of ecstasy, before he leaned his head into her breast and was gone.

After that she lost all track of what was happening around her. It was as though nothing else existed but herself and the precious burden in her arms. Even Alexander seemed to belong in some other life. But eventually when something made her look up and out again across the sea of slaughter which until now had been rising so inexorably, she saw that the tide had turned, though she could not tell why.

Had Callistus' words hit home, even though among the Praetorians he was entirely without authority? Had the rioters perhaps been humbled by the spectacle of the boy emperor fiercely embracing his mother as they awaited death together? Had Callistus' sacrifice of himself unleashed some spiritual power which his prayers by themselves had been unable to do? Perhaps all three, or something else altogether; Mamaea could not know.

But she did know that the heart had gone out of the mutiny along with the breath from Callistus' body. She also knew that both Alexander and Ulpianus were unharmed, because they were kneeling beside her with their arms around her shoulders. No one was fighting any longer, and every eye she could see was fixed upon her as she knelt in front of the emperor's throne with the dead Callistus in her arms.

HISTORICAL NOTE

The close of the 2nd century C.E. and opening of the 3rd is a relatively obscure period in the history of the Roman Church. The Church historian Eusebius (c.260-340 C.E.), the source on whom we rely for much of our knowledge of early Christianity, mentions its bishop Callistus only very briefly (Eusebius, *Eccl. Hist.* Bk. VI ch. XXI). Even the date of Callistus' birth is unknown, though in all probability it was around the year 170 C.E., making him almost exactly the same age as his rival Hippolytus.

Most of what we do know about Callistus comes from Hippolytus' own writings, supplemented by hints which can be gleaned from another contemporary, Tertullian, who had no more love for Callistus than Hippolytus did. We have to read Hippolytus very cautiously – and between his lines more cautiously still – to avoid concluding that Hippolytus was the true bishop of Rome and Callistus the impostor. It is only the subsequent history of the Church which shows that this was not the case.

From a non-specialist's perspective, this was an obscure period in the history of the Roman empire as a whole until the release of Ridley Scott's Hollywood epic *Gladiator* in the year

2000. This film portrays very vividly the colourful characters of the emperors Marcus Aurelius and his troubled son Commodus; Cassius Dio the Roman historian who was their contemporary would surely have recognized them, and the fraught relationship between the two. However, there is no evidence that Marcus Aurelius tried to restore the Republic to prevent his son from becoming emperor, as he does in the film. Nor did Commodus die in the Flavian amphitheatre (later – and in this novel – called the Colosseum), though he did fight in the arena as a gladiator on a number of occasions, and was ultimately strangled by his wrestling partner when an attempt to poison him failed.

Our chief sources for the secular history of the period are Cassius Dio himself and Herodian of Antioch, both of whom lived through and even witnessed many of the events depicted in this novel. All if its major characters are historical, as is much of its subject matter, and with the death of Callistus in 222/3 C.E. it ends at almost exactly the same point at which Dio's history breaks off.

The role of Marcia in the life and death of Commodus is attested by both Dio and Herodian. It is from Dio we learn that it was Marcia who warned Commodus about the riot which led to Cleander's downfall (*Roman History* Bk. LXXIII ch. XIII). Dio also tells us of Marcia's role in the conspiracy in which Commodus met his end: it was she who poisoned his food (LXXIII ch. XXII) – or according to Herodian, his wine (*History of the Roman Empire* Bk. I ch. XVII). Not even Hippolytus can avoid mentioning Marcia (*Refutation of All Heresies/Philosophumena* XI:XII), implying that she was a Christian and admitting that she and Hyacinthus had rescued Callistus from the mines and that the Christians owed the comparative freedom they enjoyed under Commodus partly to her. We do not know the nature of the relationship between Marcia and Callistus or even if they actually knew each other personally; the same must be said of Callistus' relations with Mamaea.

Nor do we know exactly how or when Callistus died. According to legend, he was martyred during the reign of Alexander Severus during a riot. We do know that there was rioting in Rome on a number of occasions during Alexander's reign, chiefly involving the Praetorian Guard. A great deal of ill-feeling was stirred up when the lawyer Ulpianus was given charge of the Guard over the heads of the previous commanders Flavianus and Chrestus. Ulpianus subsequently had Flavianus and Chrestus executed, but he himself was killed in a later riot in very similar circumstances to the attempt on his life imagined in the last chapter of this novel. If Callistus did somehow become involved in these events, it could readily explain how he came to be martyred during a period for which we have no record of state persecution of Christians in Rome. The (much later) apocryphal *Acts of Callistus* tells us that Callistus' body was then thrown into a well or cistern, from which it was subsequently retrieved for burial by Asterius, a Roman presbyter.

We do know, from Eusebius and elsewhere, that both Alexander Severus and his mother Mamaea were active seekers after spiritual truth and personally interested in the Christian faith. Eusebius tells us in the passage referred to above (*Eccl. Hist.* Bk. VI ch. XXI) that Mamaea eventually sent for Origen to instruct them both in Christian doctrine, and Hippolytus did dedicate a treatise *On the Resurrection* to the 'Mother of the Emperor' or 'The Queen' of which only fragments survive. (In the Syriac version the dedicatee is specifically named as 'Queen Mamaea'.) It is possible that Mamaea and even Alexander himself both became Christians; if so, Constantine was not the first Christian emperor, nor was Helena his mother the first Christian woman to wield quasi-imperial power. And although he was murdered at only twenty six years of age, Alexander Severus has nevertheless gone down in history as one of the most enlightened of all the Roman emperors. (The $4^{th}/5^{th}$ century biographical collection the *Historia Augusta* is particularly complimentary about him.)

Regarding the Church's teaching on the remission of sins committed after baptism, Callistus left a lasting legacy. Though the North African churches influenced by Tertullian continued to bar some sinners from communion permanently, by 250 C.E. no one in Rome whose opinion carried any weight favoured this draconian practice. Another period of intense persecution – and therefore rampant apostasy – under the mid-3rd century emperor Decius threw this issue into the melting pot once again, and there were fresh arguments and intense rivalries over whether the Church should be a 'society of saints' or a 'school for sinners'. A fashion even developed for delaying baptism until one was on one's deathbed, and much has been said and written about 'deadly' and 'venial' sins over the centuries since then. But in the long run mercy was generally to prevail over intimidation where lapses in conduct among Christians were concerned.

Disputes over doctrine and ethics have continued to challenge practising Christians in every age, though one generation's crisis all too often causes the next to wonder what all the fuss was about. Today the Church is plagued by disagreements over the role of women in public ministry, the legitimacy of same sex marriage and the nature of gender identity; no one loses any sleep over whether a man should be allowed to marry his deceased brother's widow. Yet this latter question led to major friction in the 19th century. Perhaps Jesus' parable of the wheat and the tares (Matt. 13:24-30) still holds the key, and Christians of differing persuasions should simply seek to work peaceably alongside all those who confess the name of Christ whatever their precise doctrinal or ethical position, expending their energy on spreading his gospel of love and salvation around the world and leaving the final judgement to God. Certainly there is far more co-operation today amongst Christians of differing denominations and traditions than there has often been in the past. Dissenting sects often disappear or become reabsorbed into the main body of the Church, given time; Hippolytus' sect disappeared very quickly after his death, but not before he had strenuously opposed Callistus' successors Bishops (or Popes) Urban I (Urbanus) (223-230) and Pontian (230-235). Pontian and Hippolytus were both eventually sentenced to penal servitude in Sardinia, but it may be that they were reconciled there before they died, because the next Pope, Fabian (236-250) had both their bodies brought back to Rome for burial at the same time.

Controversy over the nature of the Holy Trinity continued, and it took a number of major Church Councils, and the best minds in Christendom, several centuries to reach a satisfactory consensus. The Council of Nicaea in 325, convened by the first unashamedly Christian emperor, Constantine, produced the Nicene Creed as a summary of 'correct' Christian doctrine, and it is still used as a statement of faith today, substantially in its original form, by Orthodox, Catholic and Protestant Christians.

Remarkably, both Callistus and Hippolytus were eventually canonized by the Roman Catholic Church and continue to be revered as saints. This represents a significant victory for the principle of 'agreeing to differ'. It is also worthy of note that as long ago as the 3rd century C.E. the Christian Church was prepared to elevate an ex-slave and ex-convict to the rank of bishop. As Roman Catholic writer Terry Matz has put it:

'Sad as it is to realize that the only story we have of his (Callistus') life is by an enemy, it is glorious to see in it the fact that the Church is large enough not only to embrace sinners and saints, but to proclaim two people saints who had such wildly opposing views, and to elect a slave and ex-convict to guide the whole Church. There is hope for all of us!' (From *Catholic Online* website: *Saint Callistus I*).

ABOUT THE AUTHOR

Jill Francis Hudson grew up in Bury, Lancashire, and read Classics and Theology at Cambridge University, graduating with a 'starred first'. She then taught for many years in both comprehensive and private schools. She now lives in West Cumbria with her husband Keith; together they run a worship band, canoe, cycle, hike and ski.

Printed in Great Britain
by Amazon